STRANDED!

His captain and navigator both in critical condition, himself held captive by the natives of Islands, Hark knew his only chance to save his crewmates and complete his mission rested on his regaining control of his lander. But if he did not accomplish this soon, the AI aboard his space orbiter would track down and recall the lander, permanently stranding Hark and his comrades on this semi-feudal world.

Step one was to reach the lander, and this Hark had finally managed with the unexpected aid of two men bent on changing the order of life on Islands. But now, aboard his ship once again, Hark stared around in horror. Someone had lasered the control panel, irreparably damaging the programs which enabled Hark to pilot the lander. And suddenly the odds of escaping had drastically changed. For now Hark's only hope was to seek out the last remnants of Islands' own faltering technology—or be trapped forever on this world where men were little more than slaves!

CYNTHIA FELICE
in DAW editions:

DOWNTIME
DOUBLE NOCTURNE

DOUBLE NOCTURNE

Cynthia Felice

DAW BOOKS, INC.
DONALD A. WOLLHEIM, PUBLISHER

1633 Broadway, New York, NY 10019

First DAW Printing, July 1987

1 2 3 4 5 6 7 8 9

PRINTED IN THE U.S.A.

For Mom

CHAPTER 1

"Airspeed! Airspeed! Keep your goddamn airspeed up!"

It was the on-board computer shouting at Hark in his own vernacular. The stubby wings were icing over even though he had dropped altitude and turned on the deicers. But the sleet had turned to heavy rain and he saw only solid gray through the viewplate. If he didn't put the lander into a high-speed turn *right now*, he was going to fly into the mountain and crash. Is that what had happened to Captain Dace and the engineer?

He put more power into the steep, tight turn; the lander responded to the demands for airspeed, but sluggishly. The deicers weren't keeping up with the ice on the wings and the mountain still had to be dead ahead. There was no help for it. He would have to set the lander down and wait until the storm was over to continue the search. He couldn't risk losing the craft or himself, for if he did, no one would be able to return to the orbiter.

"Ready the cold jets for landing," he said, "and help me find a good spot."

"The lower part of the saddle between the two peaks," the computer said instantly, and it highlighted on the screen what he could not see through the viewplates.

Hark swallowed hard. The "peaks," as the computer had called them, were the twin calderas on the southern flank of the Canis Minimus volcano, one of many active volcanos they'd noted during the orbital surveys. That the orbital craft's on-board artificial intellect had described them as "approachable" didn't comfort him very much just now. He wondered if the AI had downloaded any useful information about volcanos into the lander's little computer, or if it had judged the information to be superfluous to the search-and-rescue mission, which should have centered to the north of the volcanos.

"Is that the best place?" Hark asked, feeling stupid even as he asked. The icing was worse, altitude still dropping. It was the *only* place, and the computer knew it. The wind was tossing the craft madly and he was fighting for the straight and level.

"Just don't let the wind blow you off. It's a long way down." It sounded reassuring now, which Hark took to mean its programming was not taking any chances on startling him. "Keep those counterthrusters ready."

But the storm didn't gust the way he expected it to, and he felt the landing pads grip, one . . . two . . . and an eternity later . . . three. The lander was leaning, but it was down safely. Now if it just would stay put. He eased off the power, wondering if he would have enough control if it started to slip. But it didn't move. He waited with his hand on the throttle, feeling the wind shake the lander. When it still didn't move, he started to fold the wings against the fuselage so that it wouldn't get under the wing and start flying on the ground or flip him. He heard crunching sounds through the hull, ice chunking off the wings. He extended and retracted them again, exercising them gently until he knew they had folded safely. Then he finished powering down.

Hark sighed and sat back in the seat, trying to make himself relax. He couldn't. He'd been trained in planetside search and rescue, but in all his years of piloting for the Guild, this was the first time he'd conducted one. The training was effective though. He had initiated all the dialog with the AI in the orbiter, and it would have been the other way around if he had forgotten proper procedure. But finally the lapping orbiter had dropped below the horizon, breaking the EHF communication link and leaving him alone on the planet known as Insula In Caelum. Then the distress signal failed and the storm had turned into a full gale. The AI could not have predicted these events, could not have averted the forced landing, but its voice would have been reassuring.

"How long until local dawn?" he asked suddenly.

"Two hours and twenty-one minutes," the computer said. It had become slightly metallic-voiced again, very indifferent programming.

"What's the outside temperature?"

"Minus ten degrees Cee," it said.

The AI would have been smart enough to realize why Hark had asked the question and would have gone on to tell him what the statistical odds were for Captain Dace's and the engineer's survival if they were exposed to the full fury of the storm. It also would have told him whether it was better to keep his pressure suit plugged in to the lander's energy system or keep the cabin temperature up by powering up the lander at regular intervals. He switched on the computer screen and did some quick calculations. There was plenty of fuel to power up every twenty-two minutes and warm the cabin air and still have enough to finish the mission and return to the orbiter. He would charge the P-suit in case he had to use it to go outside to knock ice off the lander before taking off again. Until then, there was nothing to do but wait.

Wait and listen, first to the sound of sleet slapping against the lander's entire length like sheets, later to ice-stones impacting with a terrible noise, and finally he listened to the silence, interrupted only by the static from the radio. He kept straining to hear the beep of the other lander's distress signal, tried not to think of what could have happened for the signal to fail *after* impact. It was just a malfunction, he told himself for the thousandth time. It *had* worked long enough for him to get a fix on the signal from the orbiter, ready the second lander, and descend into the atmosphere.

He knew where to look and he would go back to do it just as soon as it was light.

The outside temperature dropped another five degrees Cee even though the storm seemed to have stopped completely, and the lander powered up only fifteen minutes after the last time to warm the cabin. He wondered if the downed lander could power up, if Captain Dace's and Engineer Rene's pressure suits were working, if they were alive.

He stared at the frosty nitrogen tank. Only a few of the jelly beans in it were glowing, just the housekeepers, the smarts that watched time, cabin temperature, and battery backup. Fourteen minutes later two yellow jelly beans brightened. Hot air poured out of the heat exchangers into the cabin, the deicer light came on, followed by a series of ready-lights on the control board. Then the two jelly beans turned murky again, and the ready-lights dimmed to amber. Hark opened the food storage locker and took out a dinner pack, ate the contents dutifully. He stowed the trash in an empty overhead and started to count jelly beans. They cycled through their housekeeping routine five times before the black night outside the viewplates began to brighten and he saw the red glow of the rising sun.

"Wake up," Hark said, "and tell me what's going on outside." Half the assorted jelly beans brightened at the sound of his voice.

"It's minus fifteen degrees Cee, humidity is forty percent, barometric pressure adjusted for Insula In Caelum is thirty point one five. The winds are still."

"What about gas analysis?" Hark said reaching over the control board to unfold the wings. "Just the bottom line, please, compared to standard."

"Nitrogen, oxygen, hydrogen, argon, neon, and helium are present in the standard acceptable percentage range. Sulfur dioxide is present at one point two percent. Carbon dioxide is present at one point five percent."

The volcano gasses. The snow was probably loaded with sulfuric acid and sodium chloride. He zipped up the P-suit and put on the helmet, not eager to expose his lungs even to traces of corrosives. The P-suit was the Guild's and could be replaced easily. His lungs could be replaced too, but he didn't want to cough or hurt all the months back to the Homeworlds.

Hark had never had any special desire to see snow or to touch it, but he was surprised at how little there was on the stark landscape. The fierce wind must have swept it away almost as quickly as it fell. He could see the tops of the landing pads, and the ice on the wings was negligible, evaporated by the deicers when he had the power on to warm the cabin. He wouldn't have stepped out if a visual check of the entire craft had not been mandatory after spending a few hours grounded in hostile atmospherics. Likely he would find no substantive damage from the hail, but he didn't know about the corrosive properties of the volcano gasses, even in such small percentages.

Tentatively he brushed a dusting of grainy white snow off the wing, was surprised to find that it had a discernable substance that collapsed at his touch. He hadn't known that snow could be anything but fluffy. The alloy wingskin didn't look corroded, but they had been retracted during the night. He needed to look at the hull. As he climbed onto the wing, he saw movement out the corner of his helmet visor, and turned to look at the reddish glow at the crest of the closest crater. Smoke and vapor rose straight up, but at the rim he saw a human silhouette moving among the heaps of solidified lava.

"Captain Dace? Rene?" The radio signal from his helmet should reach them with no difficulty; the rim looked to be only a thousand meters up a gentle incline. But no one answered and now he couldn't see anything that looked like a person on the rim, not even when he pulled down the binocular over the regular visor. He returned to checking the lander, found himself glancing back at the rim through the binoculars. He didn't see anyone, but the thought that he *might* have seen Captain Dace or the engineer haunted him, even though he knew they should be several klicks north.

If they had gone down unharmed in the jungles on the northern slopes of the volcanos, the EHF signal couldn't penetrate the thick foliage. If their emergency antenna balloon were damaged, they might have started walking up the mountainside looking for just such a clearing as this vast saddle between the two volcano craters from which to broadcast. And if they got this far, he was sure Engineer Rene would have insisted on going to the rim of the smoking crater. That crazy old woman probably *loved* the feel of walking in the grainy snow, savored the crunch beneath her boots.

The effort was making Hark breathless, but adrenalin kept him scrambling briskly over sharp rocks and boulders to the rim. Finally he stood staring down at almost vertical walls illuminated by the red and golden glow of a vast lava lake that lapped at the edge of a terrace fifty meters below. Steam and smoke swirled over the central pit, giant incandescent bubbles and waves shimmered beneath. It was a long time before he could take his eyes away from the lava lake to look along the rim for Captain Dace and Rene. There was no one close by, and he couldn't see the far side of the caldera because of the steam and smoke from the pit. He looked back at the lander; it was pretty hard to see, easy to overlook if you didn't know just where. He decided he needed to walk around the rim on the chance that they were here and had not seen or heard him land.

He started walking again, then stopped. He hadn't thought of looking *in* the caldera for anyone, but as his gaze was drawn again to the incandescence of the lava lake, he saw someone on the terrace below. It made his skin prickle; couldn't those waves of molten lava slosh over the edge of the terrace? How hot had the AI said the lava must be, over a thousand degrees Cee? Not even Rene was *that* crazy.

He pulled down the binoculars again. He could see plainly now that the person on the terrace was standing at the edge of the pit holding a sampling rod out over the lava lake. Further back, near the vertical walls of the caldera, were two more people; it looked as if they were dismantling some instruments. There were ropes dangling from the rim, their method of descent into the caldera. Hark realized he was looking at a party of locals, probably scientists taking some samplings. He hesitated, uncertain whether to approach them. Much farther down the flank of this volcano was a settlement, the source of the clerical broadcast they'd monitored from the orbiter. The mission Hark and his crewmates had come on was specifically with the civil authorities and the mission description phrased so carefully that Captain Dace overruled the AI and refused to attempt radio contact through the clerics. Before dealing with the clerics of this world, especially clerics who had origins like these, the captain had decided to reconnoiter. There was the settlement at Canis Minimus and another much farther east on the bright green flanks of Mons Selenus, which also had a radio source but so thoroughly scrambled that the AI was having difficulty decoding them. Of course after two full laps, Hark knew they would be decoded by now. He considered going back to the lander to listen to the translations, but he knew that the trip down to the lander and another back up to the rim would be stretching his physical endurance to the limits. It seemed unlikely that any information gleaned from broadcasts so far away could be pertinent to what was happening here at the top of Canis Minimus. Even if these were clerics he was seeing down in the caldera, there was no reason to assume they'd be hostile to a rescue mission, even one from the Homeworlds.

The person sampling the lava had walked back from the edge of the lake and pulled off the anti-thermic helmet; it was a woman, long red hair spilling over her shoulders, almost as incandescent-looking as the lava. He could see her face clearly through the binocular visor: deepset eyes, straight nose, her lips full and pursed, as if dissatisfied with something. She was removing what looked like a sampling bottle from the end of the rod, so it was probably only gasses she was sampling, not the lava itself.

If the lady of the lava lake was a scientist, he decided that by definition she could not be associated with the clerics of Insula In Caelum whose origins were rooted in the repudiation of science, technology, and anything else from the Homeworlds they interpreted as unnatural. And she was young so he didn't have to worry about her being an original settler from the convicts transported to this world seventy-five years ago. He wondered if it was safe to take off his helmet; she was even closer to the source of gasses and obviously was not troubled by them. He unsnapped the neck clips and took it off. The sting he felt was probably only the cold, but it frightened him. But before he could get the helmet back on, he felt as if his skull had exploded and he saw familiar stars.

He awoke staring up at the Guild insignia on the belly of the lander, his head throbbing. Two men clad in white coats huddled over him. One was bearded and middle age. The other was young and clean-shaven. They wore identical white fur hats and white leather belts from which hung mace and machete—both exposed—and a brace of sheathed knives. Both were watching Hark intently.

"He's awake, Orrin," the smooth-shaven one said. He was not talking to his immediate companion, who merely glanced at Hark before crossing his arms against the cold.

"Get him up here, Jeremy." The voice was deep, hollow, and came from the cabin in the lander.

The two men pulled Hark to his feet and pushed him to the ladder. He reeled from pain and dizziness.

"Where did you come from?" Hark asked. "Did you hit me?" He started to raise his hand to his head, but the smooth-faced man slapped it away and shoved him up against the ladder.

"Climb," he said roughly. "Orrin wants to talk to you."

Still dazed, Hark climbed up and stepped into the lander. As his eyes adjusted to the dimness in the cabin and the pain in his head evened out to a tolerable ache, he saw a hundred-kilo mass of militancy waiting for him. A fringe of black hair stuck out from under the man's white cap, an iron gray beard had black streaks like fangs under the corners of his lips. His eyes were sharp and black, fixed on Hark.

"I know it flies," he said. "I don't know how; it's aerodynamically unsound, but I know it flies. I've seen one before, and I know . . ."

Hark felt his heart lurch. "You saw Captain Dace's lander? Where?"

"Tell me *how* it flies," the man said, as if he had not heard Hark.

"There's no time for that. I must find the other lander. My captain may be in trouble. You say you saw it. When? Where?"

The man's eyes narrowed and they gleamed like coals. "I do the questioning. You give the answers. If you don't get that straight in the next two seconds, I'll put a few more lumps on your head. Now, tell me how it flies."

Hark hesitated. "No," he said finally. "I am not afraid of you." He tried to look as if it were true by meeting the man's eyes unflinchingly. "Orrin, they called you. I am Hark."

"You are a fool," Orrin said, "but not one from Selene as I originally thought. You don't sound like a Penitent either."

"I am not from Insula In Caelum at all," Hark said indignantly. "Surely you recognized the Guild crests on the lander."

"Is knowing Latin supposed to impress me?" Orrin said, an unmistakable contempt in his voice. He shook his head. "There's always a schism using one of the old crests, Colonial Transport for the slavers, Artificial Intellect, Fusion Workers. Return-transport dings, all of them. I suppose you're carrying a transport token, too."

"Of course not. I *am* transportation." Hark opened his hand palm out so that Orrin could see the Pilot Guild insignia tattooed there. "Your common sense, if you have any, must tell you that a lander of this quality was manufactured in the Homeworlds."

"Homeworlds, is it now?" Orrin said sharply. "Not

Domusus or Sedes? You're not as well versed as you thought."

"I used Latin for your planetname because it has no counterpart in the vernacular where I come from. I'm not some local imitation or an imposter. I'm the genuine article. Pilot Tom Hark, in the service of the AI Guild." He opened his other hand to display the AI Guild's tattoo.

Orrin's gaze shifted sharply from Hark's hands to someplace behind him. Hark glanced back. The smooth-cheeked one called Jeremy was standing in the hatch opening behind him. Wordlessly he took Hark's right hand and pulled it up to look at the Pilot Guild tattoo closely. The grip was viselike, but the man's skin was smooth, his nails manicured. "The artwork looks right, but then I've never seen a genuine Pilot Guild tattoo. I don't know if I would know one from a good forgery just by looking." He glanced up at Orrin. "But a lab test will tell us if that's gallium in there."

Orrin frowned and his shaggy eyebrows almost formed a vee over his eyes. "You're not here with the spirit-chasers down in the caldera? You didn't bring them here in your metal windship?"

"No." Hark forced himself to be patient. "I think they were sampling the gasses, not chasing spirits, but no, I did not bring them here. I made a forced landing during the night because of the storm."

Orrin reached back, released the catch on the pilot's chair, turned it and sat down. He filled it completely. "We heard you. And we saw fire. For a while we thought we were watching the birth of a new parasidic cone. At dawn we saw a strange craft." He opened his hands in a gesture that indicated the lander. "The only thing of interest up here is the caldera. Why else would you have landed here?"

"It was a *forced* landing. Why can't you understand that? I had been conducting a search for a missing lander, a ship just like this one. You said you saw it. Just tell me where and when so I can be on my way. It must be down and the occupants injured, else I would have heard from them. I must help them."

"Damn," said Orrin. The pad on the armrest absorbed a blow from Orrin's fist with a *thunk*. "I thought it was the Selenians finally making their move." Orrin's voice caught in a fashion Hark was certain was uncharacteristic for this fierce-looking man, catching him by surprise. "It was Double Nocturne. I was certain . . ." His voice trailed off as he stared at Hark in angry disbelief. "You really are from the Homeworlds," he said accusingly. "Why in all hell's depths did you have to come during Double Nocturne?"

"Double Nocturne?" Hark repeated. "What does that mean?"

"It means," Jeremy said from behind him, "that he had advised the War Council to expect a Selenian raid during Double Nocturne. We shot down the other lander the night before last."

"*Shot it down?*"

Orrin nodded curtly.

"Your companions were . . . rescued," Jeremy said.

"They are all right?" Hark asked, feeling hope through the shock.

"Not completely. They're in the maternity clinic, under guard."

"Prisoners, then," Hark said, even more alarmed than before. During the most pessimistic surmising, he had not thought they might be inaccessible to him because they were in captivity. "And hurt. Do you know the extent of their injuries?"

Jeremy nodded. "I am the doctor who supervised their evacuation. One is in a coma and badly burned. I don't expect her to live. The other, the younger of the two, will probably survive."

"You don't have stasis holders and regeneration equipment," Hark said flatly. He had to get them back to the orbiter quickly.

"Stasis is . . ." Jeremy started to say, but then he caught himself and shook his head.

"Forbidden?" Hark suggested. "I already guessed that from listening to your broadcasts, then putting what I heard together with who you are. Don't forget that I know down to the last blanket what you started with and who you started with. I wish you had stasis, for the sake of my crewmates, but I'm not surprised that you don't. The only thing that's important now is time. I must take them back to the orbiter quickly."

"You're wrong. If you are who you say you are, what's important is that the art of stasis holding is forbidden," Orrin said. "Even more important is that everything you think you know is seventy-five years out of date. You, Pilot Hark, are a page out of a history book, a page the pious prefer to skip because of the profanity of your wars."

Hark stared at him a moment. "The wars are over," he said softly.

Orrin shook his head. "Not on Islands they're not. And you and your fine ship will make them worse than ever."

"Or end them," Jeremy interjected, and the comment made Orrin suddenly look thoughtful.

"Don't even think it," Hark said. "It's not a battleship, and I'm not a soldier. The Homeworlds are at peace, and Islands should be, too. In fact, if you're not and don't take steps to secure peace, you risk quarantine."

Orrin chuckled. "Do you really believe threats of quarantine will frighten people who have already endured it for generations? And don't forget that some Islanders brought it on themselves. They may not wish to give it up."

"The clerics and their flock of Penitents?" Hark asked. And when Orrin nodded, Hark sighed. "We had some concerns about that when we heard the broadcasts from the settlement at Canis Minimus. But there must be a civil authority, too. The Penitents were not left alone on . . . Islands," Hark said substituting the local vernacular.

"How carefully you phrased that," Orrin said, " 'not left alone.' And interesting that you would differentiate between Penitents and convicts. Were you afraid of offending us?"

Hark smiled weakly. "The irony of the statement repeated in the records, 'all the population on Insula In

Caelum will do penance,' was not lost on us. I do not yet know if convict origins might be a sensitive issue."

"You have no idea," Jeremy said.

"And you're not going to fill him in," Orrin said glaring at Jeremy.

"No, sir," Jeremy said, "but he is going to answer one question for me." And before Orrin could protest, Jeremy pulled a small token fastened to a sturdy chain from under his fur collar. "Do you still honor these?" he asked Hark.

Hark looked closely at the token. It was a prewar transport token issued by a minor sovereign world whose crest he didn't recognize, but the *navis oneria* icon looked genuine enough. "Tests will show if that's gallium in there," Hark said, not bothering to hide his amusement.

"I've already done them. It's gallium," Jeremy said, his voice as eager as his expression was serious.

"Well then," Hark said, somewhat taken aback, "if it's genuine, any on-board AI will accept it as payment for transport to the next port of call. But you should hold on to it. It may be a collector's item. The right person might pay much more than face value."

"On Islands men have paid with their lives to own one of these."

"That's enough, Jeremy," Orrin said.

Jeremy shot Orrin a defiant and somehow triumphant look that Orrin responded to by frowning more deeply. Hark looked for the glint of a chain at the open collar around Orrin's neck, but saw none. "As pilot, I have certain discretionary powers," Hark said cautiously while his mind raced ahead. "If you were to help me secure the release of my crewmates, it would be within my power to take you to my next port of call. With both my crewmates in stasis, there would be a place for each of you, token or none."

"Orrin!" It sounded like a plea the way Jeremy said it.

"You really are a fool," Orrin said to Hark, ignoring Jeremy's outburst. "You have no idea who you're trying to put in your pocket. Is your pocket—and your ship—big enough to hold my Top, as well?"

"She wouldn't . . ."

"Of course she wouldn't," Orrin said to Jeremy with a look that oddly mingled pride and regret.

"Who's this Top?" Hark asked.

"My commander, Dame Adione. You'll meet her in Fox City," Orrin said.

"He'll be suspect. She may not believe him, not even if he's sworn," Jeremy said, sounding worried.

"He won't have to be sworn if we question him . . . properly," Orrin said.

"Am I your prisoner, too?" Hark said, feeling cold and angry.

"The Top will decide that," Orrin said.

"Fox City is the settlement below, I suppose," Hark said. And when Orrin nodded, Hark asked resignedly, "How many in your party? I can squeeze about six or seven in the lander."

Orrin laughed. "Do you think I'm a fool? I'm not going to let you near these controls."

"What the hell do you think I'll do? I *must* get the captain and the engineer back to the orbiter into stasis tanks, and the only way to take them from Fox and off the planet is in this lander."

"I don't believe they would send anyone all the way from the Homeworlds who was stupid," Orrin said sounding disgusted. "We'll leave the lander here under guard. If you don't understand why, ask your AI next time you get a chance. If you get a chance."

"Their lives depend on speed," Hark said.

"They are receiving the best possible attention."

"I'm flying down," Hark said stubbornly.

Orrin frowned. "I have enough men outside to truss you like meat and carry you down. They won't like having to do it though. You'll be more likely to arrive in Fox safely if you do it under your own power."

Hark knew a threat when he heard one, and though they hadn't reached for their knives or whatever the things in the scabbards at their hips were, his head still throbbed from their first greeting. "Someone will pay for this outrage," he said, but he turned to go back down the ladder. Jeremy barred his way.

"Don't make more trouble," Jeremy warned. "You already have more than you know. Just your being here will change Islands forever. There are many people who won't like that." He stepped aside to let Hark pass, but Hark looked into the man's eyes.

"If Captain Dace dies, I will personally teach you the meaning of trouble."

CHAPTER 2

Hark thought he would die before they reached Fox City. Walking down the mountainside meant fighting more gees than he had experienced in years. He thought his legs would break off at the knees and his lungs would burst. Only Jeremy's calling frequent rests in a professional sounding voice that Orrin scowled at but honored and then consuming copious amounts of water prevented him from collapsing altogether.

When they were below snowline, the troopers stopped to take off their white furs, and Jeremy helped Hark remove his P-suit. Before long the air around him was just as steamy as it had been in the suit. There was water everywhere, dripping off greenery, pools next to the trail and puddles in it, and as the sun rose in their eyes, the air became hot. Hark knew he was walking through what must be distinct belts of vegetation in the mountainside, micro-ecological niches controlled by altitude, but his untrained eye couldn't tell what distinguished one green growing thing from another. All of them were quite capable of making painful welts on his bare arms and legs when he didn't watch the man ahead carefully enough to avoid a backlash smack.

Halfway down the mountainside, hidden by a living hedge of green until they were on top of it, was a monorail head. The track was laid on thick wooden ties that glistened so brightly in the morning sunshine Hark thought they were still wet from last night's rain. But it was hard resin he felt when he sat down, and he noticed rust around the spikes that pinned the track to the ties though the tops of the rail was scoured by heavy use.

He'd barely sat down when Orrin's troopers trussed him with chains in an unlighted railcar compartment, and Orrin slammed the door in response to Hark's shouts. Despite his anger at being chained and manhandled, he may have slept in the hot, dark car. Or he may have underestimated the capacity for speed of the little engine he'd seen. Whatever the reason, the journey didn't seem to take long. When the car stopped, his captors opened the door promptly. The light made him wince, but the air that swirled in did not bring him much relief. If anything, it was hotter than when he'd been thrown in the car.

"I'm taking you to the maternity," Orrin said, unlocking the chains. "It's in the middle of our highborns' neighborhood. I can't walk you through the jewel cutters' quarter brandishing a laser, nor with you in chains, so you must go peaceably. Your friends are in the maternity, so you'll want to cooperate."

"Are they chained to their beds?" Hark said, rubbing his wrists. And before Orrin could answer, he added sharply, "I protest being treated like this."

"Your being a Homeworlder—if you're a Homeworlder—doesn't absolve you of being a spy or criminal of some other kind until proven otherwise. Now I can tell the Top to meet us at the garrison clinic just as easily as the maternity clinic, and your being in chains wouldn't offend anyone we would meet going that direction." His eyes were hard, the half-dozen troopers at the door of the railcar looked wary.

"I do want to see my crewmates," Hark said, still feeling bitter. He tried to stand up. His limbs were like lead and they ached, and he might not have made it to his feet without Orrin's help. Orrin steadied him as he walked to the door where troopers' hands helped him onto a wooden platform.

Along the platform was a marketplace of open shops separated by living walls of potted plants climbing trellises. Gaily dressed women carrying wicker baskets picked through heaps of fruits and vegetables Hark didn't recognize.

"You'll walk easy, then?" Orrin said, his hand on the hilt of his laser, a reminder Hark couldn't mistake the alternative.

"Of course," Hark said indignantly. "You already know I'm unarmed. I'll do no harm." But it seemed they were taking no chances. Jeremy and Orrin walked on either side, the rest of the troopers formed a ring around him. It was difficult for Hark to see past them into the marketplace as they walked through. Despite his aches and his concern for his crewmates and even his own circumstances, he couldn't help being fascinated by the marketplace. There was an astounding profusion of blossoms, usually so dense that the trellises were all but hidden. His nose, so used to the sterile atmosphere in the orbiter, was delighted by spicy perfumes. The wares he saw displayed looked finely crafted, and the fruits—even though alien to him—plump, juicy, and very tempting. It took a few minutes for Hark to realize that all the shoppers he saw picking over the goods were women. "Where are all the men?" he finally asked.

"Prisoners don't ask the questions," Orrin said.

"Surely that's a misunderstanding your Top will clear up quickly enough," Hark said, and immediately felt uneasy when Orrin merely shrugged. Hark frowned. "You're odd captors. You never even asked the obvious questions, like why we came in the first place, or maybe who won the war.''

"Time enough for that," Orrin said, and added, "Can't you walk any faster?"

He tried to, but he had little energy left.

"I can't admit him for that bump on his head," Jeremy said to Orrin as soon as they were past the marketplace. They had turned onto a wide boardwalk that ran between two rows of wooden buildings. The buildings looked old, but all were entwined with flowers growing up from well-tended beds or streaming down from pots on the roofs. Jeremy was sweating, looking uneasily at the tall building at the end of the boardwalk. "It just isn't serious enough. No concussion, no . . ."

"I heard you," Orrin said. He sounded grim. "There must be something you can do."

"I can break his knees," Jeremy said sourly.

Hark stopped abruptly. "Do what? What the hell is going on?" he demanded. Orrin reached back and dragged him along; the troopers pressed closer and he felt fingers pushing him in the middle of his back.

"Let's take him to my mother," Jeremy said. They were under a canopy of flowers that shaded the door to the building. "She'll be in the infirmary. *She* could admit him."

"You would put her on the spot again, but not yourself?" Orrin sounded disgusted.

"All right," Jeremy said. "Interrogation then. You can admit him yourself for that."

Hark steeled himself against the fingers in his back and stopped again. "Why am I going to a maternity clinic for interrogation? What are you going to do?"

"It's painless," Orrin said tightening his grip on Hark's arm. But Hark pulled away violently.

"Drugs?" he asked, feeling panic well up in him. "I'm allergic to . . ." Orrin's troopers took him in hand and he tried to get loose. He fought, but was no match for the strong hands on him. "Listen to me, I'm allergic to a lot of things." The troopers hurried him along, half carrying him through the door. "Don't use any drugs on me! No!"

Hark was terrified. The troopers dragged him inside and trussed him so thoroughly that he couldn't even shout any more. He feared he would choke on the gag if he tried, but was certain he would die if he didn't. He cursed Orrin over and over. He had to make them understand about the drugs, but he couldn't even talk! It was too barbaric to believe.

The troopers clamped his arms and legs into leather restraints and were lacing up another across his chest to clamp him to the table when Orrin and Jeremy came in. Hark shouted and screamed, the noise muffled behind the gag but loud just the same.

A door, not the one they had dragged him through, but another that must lead to the depths of the building, opened and a gray-haired woman wearing a yellow tunic sashed with scarlet stepped through. Hark tried to call to her, but the sounds he made only made her frown.

"What's going on here, you men?" she demanded.

"Nothing," Jeremy said sullenly.

But Orrin stepped forward and said, "It's an interrogation, Dame Barenia."

"You're making too much noise," she said sharply.

"The prisoner is resisting, but if he doesn't quiet down, Jeremy will give him something right away," Orrin said, looking at Jeremy meaningfully.

Hark sucked in a deep breath through his nostrils, but he stopped trying to shout. Jeremy had opened a cabinet that was full of vials and taken one down.

The woman hesitated, then, leaving the door ajar, she went to Jeremy and took the vial from his hands and looked at it. Wordlessly she handed it back to him and went back to the door. "See that you don't leave a mess," she said, and closed the door behind her.

Hark stared at the vial in Jeremy's hand, almost not noticing Jeremy's frown. What did *he* have to be angry about? It was Hark he was going to pump full of poison.

The troopers had finished lacing the straps over his chest

and thighs. Orrin glanced at the job, then told them to leave. When the outer door closed, Orrin put his hand on Hark's shoulder. His touch was firm, but not rough. He pulled up Hark's sleeve and looked at the universal medical code tattooed on his biceps.

"Jeremy?"

Jeremy was staring at the tattoo. "Some of it . . . blood type and tissue type. The script is easy enough, but I don't understand these," he said rubbing his thumb over the icons at the top of the tattoo as if that would clarify them.

Hark tried to pull loose again, but it was useless. They couldn't interpret the icons under his allergy list, and they were going to fill him with drugs that would probably kill him.

"Do you understand these icons, Hark?" Orrin asked him. There were sweat beads on his forehead, and he looked pale under his suntan.

Hark continued to stare at him, feeling even more aghast as he realized that Orrin was either frightened himself or feeling some uncertainties about what they were doing. But finally Hark nodded. He would have agreed to anything to get the gag out of his mouth.

"All right then. I'm going to ungag you, but before I do, I want to explain that we're going ahead with this no matter what. If you make any noise and cause that doctor to come back in here, Jeremy is going to do what he has must to shut you up. The choice is yours. Either you help him select the right medication, or you take your chances. Understood?"

Hark nodded. He felt as if the strap across his chest were constricting his heartbeats; he knew the leather laces on his wrists were cutting into his flesh, but it didn't hurt and he thought they might be giving a bit. He kept pulling even as Orrin pulled the tape off his mouth and took out the gag.

"I can decode them, but I would need the AI to do a proper evaluation," Hark said, feeling tears starting to run down his cheeks. The straps were not giving enough to get loose.

"Tell me what it says under the allergies," Jeremy said, his voice very calm. "Leave the evaluation to me."

"Sulpha, carbocain, sodium aymnatol, hessereid and its derivatives," Hark said.

"Well I know what sulpha and carbocain are, and neither of them apply in this case." He *smiled* at Hark.

Enraged, Hark spat at him. "Goddamn you," Hark whispered. "Don't you put anything in me. Hessereids cause respiratory arrest. You're supposed to save lives, not take them."

Jeremy had calmly taken a tuft of something white from a dispenser and wiped the spittle off his cheek. "I'm going to use something that predates the . . . colony. It's not in the list that you named, and not named in anything I can read either. It's called sodium pentothal. Has any doctor ever warned you against using it?"

"It might now be called hessereid or sodium amnytol," Hark said bitterly. "You may have lost the vernacular."

"You better hope that we have not," Orrin said, "but I wouldn't worry too much. Jeremy's specialty is hearts. I saw him start one once after a man was struck by lightning."

"You're forcing me to participate in my own death sentence," Hark said angrily.

"You're not going to die," Jeremy said sticking a needle into Hark's arm and making him wince.

"Use the . . ." Had he told him about the intravenous valve? Needles were barbaric, too, but so was his dream about Captain Dace. God, but she was a wonderful woman, and her breasts really were as firm as they had looked. Why did she keep asking him to show her his tattoos? "Let me show you something else," he whispered to her.

"Soon," she said, her voice distant but promising. "First tell me more about the orbiter. How many landers does it carry?"

He cried inside.

"Why won't you tell me?" she said.

"Because you're angry with me again," Hark said miserably. "You talk about the ship when you're angry with me. Please don't be angry. I love you, and it hurts so much when I know you're angry."

"I won't be angry if you tell me about the orbiter."

"No angries?" he said, feeling confused.

"Would I be holding you so close if I were angry?"

"You're holding me?" Hark asked, the thought dazzling him with joy.

"Of course I'm holding you. Now tell me about the orbiter, about the landers, about the AI."

Reassured, Hark told.

CHAPTER 3

Hark awoke in time to see the sun set through a window, and after a few minutes, when the room was dark, he realized there was yet another sun and that he was not alone. He squinted and sat up. There was a bruise on his forearm where Jeremy had stuck him with the needle, and his head ached worse than it had before, and his muscles were more sore than he ever remembered them being in his life. A chemlamp burned where he thought the sun had been.

"You fought it a lot," he heard Orrin say, "but never once came close to dying."

"Where am I?"

"Still in the maternity, in a recovery room."

"How long have I been here?"

"Two days."

"Two!" He swung his feet over the edge of the bed. he felt himself swooning and sat still. "Damn you. Is my lander all right?"

"It's fine," Orrin said.

"Are my crewmates still alive? There are two people counting on me for their lives and you screw around with drugs. Did you find out what you wanted to know? Was I lying or telling the truth? Are you satisfied enough to let me return to my ship?"

"Calm down, man, and I'll explain to you," Orrin said. He stood with his hands on his hips, muscles bulging under a forest green tunic that was sweatstained at the chest and armpits, the deepset eyes almost pinioning him.

"Explain," Hark said flatly. He couldn't have moved yet anyway. His head was still light and the room felt as if someone left the heat on too long.

Orrin tapped on the door and Jeremy stepped in from the outside. He was garbed like Orrin in a green tunic; even the sweatstains were similar. The same array of weapons was hanging from his waist that he wore when they captured Hark.

"You still don't look like a doctor," Hark said to Jeremy, and felt some satisfaction when Jeremy frowned.

"He's on guard duty. What he does in his own time is his business."

"Soldier first, doctor second?" Hark said, wondering at the truth of it when Jeremy remained so tight-lipped.

Orrin sat on the edge of the bed. "My commander, Dame Adione, is satisfied that you are telling the truth. The gallium in your Guild tattoos helped, but it was after the abbesses looked at your ship that she was convinced."

"Why clerics?" Hark asked.

"The abbesses study the old books. They have some knowledge of the unnatural sciences so that they can be on guard against them. There's at least one who told her it was possible that it could go into the very thin atmosphere. But as for space travel, they're all convinced it couldn't even make it to the moons, let alone another planet."

Unnatural sciences. He let it pass for now. "They're right," he said carefully. "Only the orbiter can do that. Did they look for that?"

"Dame Adione is looking tonight. If she sees it through her telescope, I think she'll arrange a guardian for you. Then you'll be permitted an audience with some of the jurists, perhaps even Queen Aethelmere herself. Dame Adione's been known to get her to forget about her crowns and jewels long enough to declare a warrant. If you do see any of them, even Dame Adione who is a fair and honest woman, you must understand that many will not believe you are from the Homeworlds, no matter what the evidence . . . or at least they won't admit it in public. Officially, Islands put aside the Homeworlds long ago, declared it fallen. You must win them one by one, privately. If you can't, your mission is lost."

"You know our mission?"

Orrin exchanged glances with Jeremy.

"We know you came to replace the AI, but there is no AI to replace, so we're uncertain what you'll do now. You didn't seem to know yourself."

"The captain hadn't made up her mind. It's not easy to decide where to put the replacement equipment when the original equipment and the whole damn settlement it's supposed to be in is utterly gone," Hark said.

"Hound Volcano—Canis Majus, you called it—blew up twenty-five years ago."

"We figured that out," Hark said glumly. "But it's of no matter now. That mission was scrapped the minute Captain Dace and Rene crashed. My mission is to get them back to the orbiter. Is Rene still alive?"

Jeremy nodded. "I'm sorry, though. She won't live much longer. Most of her skin is completely burned away. She is not suffering though."

"Burn victims don't die back home," Hark said.

"They do on Islands. You won't make it in time to save her, Hark. You must resign yourself to that and let us do what we can to help you save the other . . . and Islands."

"Save Islands? You mean the AI?" He shook his head. "There's not enough time to train you to use it, and if Rene dies, there is no trainer."

"Your orbiter has an AI. Its use is required in your work. You could do the training."

"Not as well as Rene. And I repeat, there's no time. I must get them back. There won't be an AI delivery this trip."

"You sound as if you expect to leave. That's a foolish assumption." Hark looked at Orrin sharply. "We know more about you and your mission than you do about us."

Probably true. Hark tried to think of what he had said while under the drugs. The memories had a dreamlike quality and seemed useless in the face of reality. "I might be able to pay you for your help," he said. There were some valuables in their lockers on the orbiter, some technology he might turn over quickly though he knew much of it was too advanced to be of any immediate value to a backward colony world.

"We can't make such a bargain."

"I didn't think you could," Hark said. "I meant with your court."

"If Dame Adione arranges a guardian, make your request of her."

"What's this guardian thing? It sounds like something for children."

"Yes, for children, and anyone else who needs a benefactress to represent him where he is not permitted on his own."

"They are barristers, right?"

"Not necessarily. The only requirement is that they be Fyxens. If your guardian believes there's some benefit to the bargain, she might agree to speak to the jurists for you. If she's powerful enough, she may do something on her own, without consulting the jurists. But it won't go quickly. It never does."

"But it must. There are . . ."

"Lives at stake, I know." Orrin sighed. "I'll take you to see your Captain Dace just as soon as I'm certain you understand how precarious your position is and that your success depends on my goodwill. You also need to understand I fully support your mission; my future depends on it."

"Your future?" Hark said, sitting back on the bed. The heat in the little room was oppressive even though he was practically naked. He wiped his forehead with a corner of the bedclothes, waited for Orrin to explain.

"There will be changes on Islands if we re-establish communications with the Homeworlds. Islands will progress again as a result of that contact. There will be alternatives available for men, something more than the camps or the troops. You, a man, are in command of a ship that crossed the stars. Your womenkind trust you."

Hark stared at him, not certain he understood. "I wasn't in command," he said slowly.

"I know. But that you were not has nothing to do with your sex . . . right?"

"That's right," Hark said, leaning forward. He was intrigued and beginning to feel uncomfortable. A guardian who wasn't necessarily a barrister, but who was a woman. No women among the troopers he had seen. Where *had* all the men in the marketplace been?

"And the ship, the one orbiting and the very valuable lander we captured, they were your responsibility, were they not?"

Hark nodded.

"Men on Islands are not considered dependable enough to be held accountable for anything of value. In the camps, chain gangs use pitchforks and shovels, never the heavy machinery. In the lumber camps they chop and saw, or put the chains around bundles of timber, but they may not learn to handle the envelopes or fly the windships that carry the timber out. Men in the troops carry knives and clubs, not lasers, and we do not command heavy artillery."

"You do. You ordered the lander destroyed," Hark said pointedly. And Orrin was carrying a laser in his holster, of that Hark was certain. He looked more carefully. The grips were old-fashioned and utilitarian-looking, cheap but durable by Homeworlds' standards. Lasers were not popular anymore, but they had been seventy-five years ago. Did Islands have facilities with sufficient precision to continue making lasers? Or was the laser at Orrin's side original ship's issue?

"I'm an exception: The only man who was not in the original contingent of marines that came to guard the convicts to rise to officers' rank. I am trusted . . . was trusted. I'm not sure now how I stand. My judgment in shooting down the lander was poor. Some will say it was a despicable act. Others will say it was a fortuitous blunder because we now possess your fine lander. But either way, it's an error on my part, and I'll pay for it. I may go before Queen's Court . . ."

"The lander is *mine*," Hark said.

Orrin shook his head. "There's no doubt it's valuable; Dame Adione recognized that immediately and so did the abbesses. You, a man, have no property rights on Islands. At best you will be appointed a liberal guardian who would let you use the lander as you want. But before it ever gets that far in our courts, a far more important question must be settled. If your mission stops now, will others come to finish it?"

"Of course they will," Hark said. "We didn't sneak to Islands."

Orrin smiled. "But you did not declare the full depth of your mission to the Board of Trade either, did you? Or is full replacement of an AI really so routine that it can be called *scheduled maintenance*?"

Hark felt himself turning red. What else had he told them while under the influence of the drug? Not *why* they had come to replace the AI. That would have gotten their attention, and they had not focused on the real *why*. "The mission is an embarrassing one for the AI Guild, but not to the extent that they would abandon us if we did not return on schedule."

"Perhaps, but holding you and your lander would add some time to the delay. Some might guess it would add a lifetime delay, which is almost as good as forever for their purposes."

"They would be wrong," Hark said. "Interstellar travel changed radically after the war. It takes a few months to get home, not years."

"Perhaps so, but such speed defies natural laws. I doubt they'll believe it. However, if they do, it favors the other side of the already existing argument, which is to let you continue your mission, aid you, secure favors from the AI Guild in return for our kindness."

"Kindness!" Hark laughed bitterly.

"Yes, there is the worry of how your people will interpret our shooting down the lander," Orrin said gravely. "Mine will fear reprisal from the Guild. There are many who will believe it's best to obliterate all signs of your mission, to claim ignorance and start fresh with the next envoys."

"We're not envoys," Hark said. "We knew you were cut off, but we had no idea we would be in a first-contact situation. If we had, we would have brought professional envoys capable of dealing with the situation. I'm a pilot in the private employ of the AI Guild."

"Under the circumstances, you are an envoy."

Hark nodded reluctantly. "But I'm not being treated as one."

"No, and I can't guarantee that will change. A great deal depends on Dame Adione, and if you convince her, then it depends on the jurists, and then upon a court decision. I will help you every step along the way, but you must trust me."

Hark frowned. "Trust you? Because you *tell* me you have a lot to lose if I lose?" He shook his head. "You ask a great deal from the man you hit over the head, imprisoned, drugged . . ."

"If it will help, Jeremy can administer the drug to me and you can ask the questions."

That caught Hark by surprise. It could have been a lie, but if so Orrin was a very practiced liar, for Hark saw only sincerity in his eyes. Hark shook his head, half in disbelief and half in refusal.

"You are a man, and therefore suspect. In case you haven't already surmised, men are thought to be brutal and untrustworthy on Islands, unable to rise above what they call masculine pride. Pride that's different without the adjective. We fight to show our bravery, we show our physical strength by working in the camps and we fuck to prove our virility. That's reputed to be the extent of our thoughts. To a large degree they are right, because it's all they see. They won't see much more in you, except the additional threat from the stars."

"They? The women? *All* the women on Islands? Orrin, they are people, too. How can you expect me to believe that?"

"They are as conditioned to their roles as we are to ours, and as you are to yours. You better try to keep that foremost in your mind. Your apparent competence and trustworthiness won't sit well with the women of Queen's Court or with the abbesses, and there are not enough men who think like Jeremy and me to help you convince them otherwise."

"I will convince them," Hark said.

Orrin shrugged. "I'll take you to see your captain. You think about what I've told you. We'll talk again later." He looked up at Jeremy. "Give him something to wear."

Jeremy opened a closet and tossed a lightweight tunic to Hark. "Where are my shirt and shoes?" he asked, pulling on the tunic. It hung loosely.

"They're in the labs. The cloth of your shirt and the leather of your shoes are unknown. The things in the pockets of the outerwear . . ."

Hark nodded. He had been carrying a variety of handy gadgets in the P-suit, everything from tools to entertainments were supplied by the manufacturer of the suit. He wondered what they would think of the entertainments if they figured out how to work them.

When he was dressed, Orrin led the way through a long narrow hallway. It was cooler, Hark realized, because there were windows of a sort: frames filled with tubes that were placed high in the walls to catch the breeze. The way wasn't well lighted, but the polished wood floors were uncluttered, doors along the way made of a white wood, thus contrasting with the honey-colored wood of the floor and walls and easy to see. A few women walked past them, and Hark noticed that all turned to watch them, as if curious about their presence but obviously not alarmed.

Hark was at a loss for how to assess his circumstances. Nothing was as it should be, and the more he learned, the worse it became. He had no edge, no special unearned respect as Captain Dace had predicted they would because he came from the Homeworlds. Orrin had said they might not even believe him . . . just because he was a man? Hark wondered, or because they chose not to believe?

"This way," Orrin said, opening one of the white doors.

Beyond was a recognizable hospital room with a special bed and frame for traction. Captain Dace lay there, much too still, one leg held up, her neck and head trapped in supports, but at least it was undeniably her. Hark felt a rush of relief. He went to the bedside. Her eyes were closed, her breathing labored and noisy.

"Captain Dace?" he said softly. Her eyelids twitched but she did not open them. Hark touched her cheek. She was hot with fever. He turned to Jeremy and Orrin, who watched him from the door. "What are they doing for her?" Hark asked.

"I don't know the full extent. Her being a woman . . . she's not my patient," Jeremy said. He stepped to the foot of the bed and touched Captain Dace's foot, testing for reflexes Hark thought. Jeremy shook his head. "I think she's paralyzed. Her neck was broken . . . her leg, too. She was caught under the wreckage, exposed for the night. Sounds like pneumonia, too. It's a wonder she's alive, but she wasn't burned the way her companion was."

"Get someone who can tell me the extent of her injuries *and* what they're doing for her," Hark said fiercely.

"I don't think . . ." Jeremy began, but Hark cut him off.

"Be a good man and don't think," Hark said. "Just do as you're told."

Jeremy sucked in his breath, but when Orrin nodded, he

slipped out of the room. Hark stared at Captain Dace while he waited. Orrin remained silent.

Jeremy returned with the gray-haired woman Hark had seen when he first entered the clinic. "This is Doctor Barenia, head of the trauma section," Jeremy said.

Hark started to reach out to shake her hand, then realized he did not know if that was the proper greeting, was sure it was not when she did not respond at all to his abortive gesture. "Hello," he said. Her face became stony, her brow raised as if to indicate impatience. "Please tell me what your diagnosis is and what you have done for Captain Dace," he said, trying to keep his voice smooth.

"Captain is it?" she said, suddenly interested. She looked over at the bed and nodded with satisfaction, then looked back at Hark. "Don't be concerned. We are doing our best for her."

"She's dying," Hark said bluntly.

"I'm sorry," she said. "We're doing all we can."

"It's not enough. Now please tell me what the extent of her injuries are."

Doctor Barenia frowned. "I have other patients to tend. I fail to see how wasting my time explaining treatment to you can help your captain."

"Madam, I am losing patience," Hark said, pointedly ignoring the look of warning Orrin was giving him. "You have examined my captain to the full extent of your knowledge, now do not waste any more time. Tell me what I need to know."

Hark could see that she was shocked, but not into silence. Her eyes narrowed and she turned on Orrin. "Take him out," she said. "He's hysterical."

Hark prepared himself to resist if Orrin tried to obey, but a commanding voice came from the doorway.

"Tell him what he wishes to know."

Everyone turned, and upon sight of the two women in the doorway, Orrin and Jeremy fell to their knees and bowed their heads. Hark had never seen the women, but he guessed their identities immediately. The taller woman, fair-haired and very lovely, was a feminine version of Jeremy, his mother or elder sister. The other was older, what beauty she may have once possessed quite faded and overshadowed by her frown. But she wore a crown so exquisite it caught his eye, lapis and diamonds filigreed with gold. Her gown was caught up by diamonds and more lapis, every finger ringed with fabulous stones. He was looking at the queen, he was sure. From behind them stepped a third woman he had not seen at first. She wore greens, a uniform not unlike Orrin's and Jeremy's and she wore lasers on each hip.

"You need training," she said, a hint of amusement in her voice, and when he heard her speak, he realized it was she who had spoken earlier, not the queen as he thought. "You are required to kneel in the queen's presence. Unless, of course, you really are hysterical."

"I'm not hysterical, and it's you who need training. Interworld protocol does not require me to kneel," Hark said.

"Do you think he really believes I care about interworld protocol?" the queen said. Her voice was gravelly, the tone conveyed amazement.

"Yes. I was present during most of the questioning. I'm convinced that he is who he says he is, even without looking through the telescope for the orbiter."

The queen shook her head doubtfully. Then she gestured to the two men on their knees, and they stood up. Hark thought that both Orrin and Jeremy looked dreadfully uncomfortable. The queen gestured again, and Orrin stepped forward, put a hand on Hark's shoulder and pushed him to his knees. As soon as Orrin let go, Hark stood up. Orrin pushed him down again, forcefully this time so that his knees hit the floor hard. Orrin stepped on the calves of his legs so that he could not get up again. Hark glared at the queen, and her frown deepened.

"Show me your hands," she said, addressing Hark directly for the first time.

He felt foolish on his knees and considered refusing her request until he felt Orrin's heel grind painfully into his calf.

He opened his hands to show the Guild tattoos to the queen. She blanched visibly. Jeremy's relative stepped forward and lifted the sleeve of his tunic to reveal the cadusus and icons tattooed there.

"I've seen enough of these to believe it's real." She looked at Jeremy. "Gallium tests?" she asked him.

"Positive, Mother," he replied promptly.

"He really is a Homeworlder," the queen said.

The queen continued to pale, Hark thought. Then suddenly she turned as if to leave. "Wait!" Hark said, but she fled from the room. Jeremy's relative gave the young physician a pained look and rushed out after the queen. When they were gone, Orrin pulled Hark to his feet.

"And you want me to take him to court?" the woman in green said to Orrin.

"Dame Adione, we've had no time to teach him any manners, but he's smart enough and he'll learn quickly . . . won't you, Hark?"

"I come complete with manners," Hark said icily to Orrin. He turned to Dame Adione and stuck out his hand. "I am Pilot Tom Hark of the AI Guild."

She took his hand and shook it, but also shook her head. "You are too bold for Queen Aethelmere, but I like you. If you can acquire a modicum of humility in the next few hours, enough to get you through the court buildings without your causing a riot, I guess we'll give it a try."

"Thank you, Dame Adione. I will personally guarantee his good behavior," Orrin said.

She nodded and stepped back, then looked at Doctor Barenia, who still looked angry and unpleasant. "Tell him what he wants to know."

"We don't discuss . . ."

"Oh, Barenia, you don't put any more stock in that voodoo than I do. Tell the man."

The doctor turned to Hark, her face was bitter and filled with resentment. "The vertebra is broken in the second region; the femur is broken, too. We could cope with that, but she has pneumonia, complicated by the shock of her other injuries. She's not responding to medication."

"Internal injuries?" Hark asked.

"We removed a ruptured spleen surgically. She was a poor risk, but it was essential or she would have bled to death."

Hark nodded. "Captain Dace has a low tolerance for antibiotics because she has a high level of antigens. She's asthmatic."

"I saw no such symptoms."

"Of course not," Hark said. "The condition is controlled by medication, but it's there. On her shoulder you'll find a tattoo containing her allergy list."

Reluctantly the doctor looked at Captain Dace's shoulder and saw the tattoo. She shrugged. "Forest sorcerer's twaddleize."

"Universal medical code," Hark said. "Your grandparents had them, too, if you care to research the fact. If I translate the code, the information would assist you in her treatment," Hark said.

"Possibly," the doctor said, noncommittal.

"Also, in her P-suit pocket you'll find a medic kit. It has several doses of antibiotics that are known to agree with her. One is a blend of many that we use when we're not certain of the ailment's cause."

"Dame Adione, I cannot permit him to prescribe for a patient. It could do more harm than good."

Dame Adione looked at Captain Dace and shrugged. "She's dying anyway, isn't she?"

"But there's hope while she lives. What if he's trying to poison her?"

"Bah! Don't you remember what he said under the drugs? Do it, Barenia. Alive that woman is more valuable than anyone on Islands."

"You are entirely too trusting of men," the doctor warned. "Far too liberal in your views."

"And you are too narrow-minded to recognize when they are right," Dame Adione said.

"Better that than not to know when they're wrong," the doctor said looking from her to Orrin.

"Council will decide that," Dame Adione said. "I have decided this."

Hark could see that they had some private war to fight, and he decided to try intervening before Captain Dace became the battleground. "Madam doctor," he began. "I am grateful for the concern you have for your patient, my captain. Surely you can verify the medication's value with laboratory analysis. I do not presume to prescribe; that was done by physicians. I merely follow their instructions of when to administer the medicine."

"Your sudden humbleness does not move me," she said angrily.

"It impresses me," Dame Adione said with a laugh. "He does learn quickly. Barenia, do as he says or I'll bring him the things he wants and let him do it himself."

The doctor stamped out of the room.

Dame Adione seemed amused, but precisely why, Hark was uncertain. "I'll get out of here before she gets back. Maybe she'll calm down then. She doesn't like it when I pull rank." She shrugged, started for the door, then stopped. "Orrin, why are there no guards at the door?"

"Neither prisoner is capable of leaving on her own," Orrin said. "I decided guarding them was unnecessary."

She looked at Hark and pondered a moment, finally nodded. "Orrin, as soon as you're done, bring him to court, but for god's sake, tell him what to do first."

"Tonight? I thought tomorrow."

"No. I want to get his custody resolved. Aethelmere's not interested, so I shouldn't have any trouble getting it for myself." She looked closely at Hark. "I thought your blond curls would dazzle her. She likes fair-haired men." Smiling easily, she turned to Orrin. "You can plan on leaving him with me for the night . . . if he behaves," she said. "And if he doesn't, you had better put those guards back on the prisoners' doors." Orrin frowned and Dame Adione's smile broadened. "What's the matter, Orrin? After all these years, do you think I've lost my appetite?" She shook her head. "Not for Sweetchucks here."

"Sweet *what*?" Hark said, but she was leaving and didn't stop to answer.

"This is bad, Hark," Orrin said. "We need more time to talk. There are many in court who will be against you."

"What did she mean, *Sweetchucks*?" Hark asked.

"What the hell do you think she meant, man? You can't be that naive." Orrin was frowning and looking angry again.

Doctor Barenia entered the room again and Orrin raised his brows, and Hark took it for a signal for silence. Just as well. He didn't like where the conversation was going.

The doctor accepted Hark's translations of both the tattoo and a vial of medicine in huffy silence, seemed genuinely intrigued by the valve tucked away under a flap of skin under Captain Dace's arm. She seemed less unhappy about the whole event when it was finished, but she still ended with a parting shot. "My laboratory tests will determine if you've been telling the truth. Do you know the penalty for murder by poison in Fox?" she asked.

"No, and I'm certain I won't find out as a result of this," Hark said, gesturing to the unused vials. "It's a big comfort to me to know my captain is in the hands of a cautious and courageous physician," he added.

He realized he could not flatter her into friendship or trust, but it couldn't hurt to be honest. The woman was prudent in her hesitation, and that, in Hark's opinion, marked her as a good physician. No doubt her reactions would have been different if Captain Dace were a man.

CHAPTER 4

The sun had almost set behind the twin calderas above the city when they stepped out of the maternity. Nightbirds roosting on the building rooftops were starting to call, and as if on signal, Orrin heard Jeremy's stomach growl. The spaceman, Orrin realized, must be very hungry, too. Time was short; in a few hours court would open and by then Hark must be prepared to face the jurists. He had wanted to eat early at the garrison so they could be close to the lander, just in case he needed to bribe Hark for good behavior with a side trip to see that it was safe. It had been quite a feat moving it. But the garrison kitchen would offer no hope of privacy at this hour. Orrin turned down the street of shops, heading for a public kitchen.

Shopkeepers were closing their doors. Most lived above or behind their shops. The last of the shoppers were headed home. The street was not very crowded, but there were enough people so that the soft clinking of glass and coral spangles, five and ten deep on the ankles and wrists of the women, caught Hark's attention right and left. Hark seemed less agitated now that he had seen his captain, but he wore a thoughtful frown as he watched yet another shopper go by.

"What's on your mind?" Orrin asked him.

"The men of Fox," Hark said. "Where are they?"

"Workers rarely come into the city. Most of the planta-tions are too far now. The dandies won't come out until after dark. We should see some in this district. They stay near court or their highborns' homes."

Hark shook his head, frowned more deeply. "What about your marines? Don't they get leave to come into the city?"

"Troopers," Orrin said. "We've nothing to do with the original marines. The old marines finished their tours of duty and were replaced with the Queen's Troops. But yes, off-duty troopers come to the city, but their entertainments definitely can't be found in the highborns' district. We won't see any around here." Orrin stepped off the boardwalk and crossed the tanbark street. On the other side was the kitchen, a house on stilts above the shuttered market-stalls. They climbed the circular stairway to a balcony with tables and chairs.

"Let's stay outside. It will be hot otherwise," Jeremy said.

"It's hot out here, too," Hark said, but he selected a table by the railing and sat down.

The balcony was just wide enough for the table and chairs. The kitchen was behind a halfwall of split sedge lath covered with clay. Clean gauze stretched from the top of the halfwall to the ceiling kept insects and birds out of the kitchen, but let the pungent aromas out. Orrin watched Hark look inside. The beldame who owned the kitchen was standing over a brazier stove. She wore a tight fitting short-sleeved bodice and a seamless skirt wrapped hipster fashion. Her feet were bare on the rush mats. Around her, scoured pots and pans lay on freshly papered shelves that were hung with flowers and spices. Apparently satisfied, Hark leaned forward to look past Jeremy at the city. The balcony placed them about three meters above the street and marketstalls giving him view over the long purple and green shadows of the cityslopes, a view, Orrin noticed, that engrossed Hark's attention more completely than the kitchen.

"What are you looking for?"

"The radio tower," Hark said.

Orrin pointed toward the trees behind Hark. "In those trees is a park, the garrison citypost, and the abbey. Above the abbey is the radio tower. It's in the upper branches of the emergent tree, the highest point in the city."

"Those trees are huge," Hark said, turning fully around to see them better.

"Most of them are eighty to one hundred meters tall, all that we have left of the rain forests that used to cover this side of the volcano. The First Migration from Hound cleared them for crops by cutting and burning. Anything else you want to know?"

"Yes," Hark said turning and putting his elbows on the table. "Why so helpful all of a sudden?"

"I was serious when I said I wanted to help you. I want you to leave Islands safely, to have a fair knowledge of what's going on here, and to tell them about us on the Homeworlds."

"What? That you've lost your AI and forgotten inter-world protocol?"

"No!" Orrin said sharply. "That a quarter of the population is wrongfully oppressed."

"Oh, yeah? Who?"

Orrin stared at him, wondering if the man was still foggy from the drugs. Hadn't he been listening in the maternity? But Hark's eyes looked clear and bright, meeting his own with an expectant gaze.

"What have you had to eat today?"

Startled, Orrin looked up at the beldame who owned the kitchen. He hadn't noticed her approach. She'd slipped on outdoorwear, a thick silk shawl and shoes, which she would carefully remove when she returned to the kitchen. She was looking at the notepad in her hand, waiting. "Jeremy and I breakfasted at the garrison," Orrin said.

"Guess I know what that means," she said with a disapproving shake of her head. "Too much nasugar and not enough roughage." She jotted something down on her pad. "And what of your new recruit here?" She gestured to Hark.

"I'm very hungry," he said before Orrin could answer, "but I suppose I should eat lightly." He looked at Jeremy for confirmation, but Jeremy just smiled, realizing as Orrin was beginning to realize that Hark didn't know what answer she expected from him.

"What have you had today?" the beldame asked.

"Nothing," Hark said. "What do you have to offer?"

"Truly nothing?" the beldame said, looking at Orrin now for confirmation. Orrin nodded. "Shouldn't miss your meals like that, young fellow. It's not good for you and it's a big bother for me to balance it all out in just one meal."

"Special orders," Orrin said quickly. "It couldn't be avoided."

"Well, in that case . . . ." She consulted some notes on a pad and nodded. "You two . . . ." she indicated Orrin and Jeremy, "may have some spirits to whet your appetites. I'll bring you—" she nodded at Hark "—a bit of something that will perk you up. You look a bit pale."

"Yes, ma'am," Hark said with a bemused smile. He had caught on, Orrin decided.

The beldame nodded with satisfaction and turned away. She stopped to unveil the chemlamps at the top of the staircase to light the way for two shopkeepers who were starting up, then went back inside to her kitchen.

"Not what I'm accustomed to," Hark said, still smiling. "Tell me if I've got it right. Patrons tell her what they have consumed thus far and she decides what else they need?"

"Correct," Orrin said. "How else would it be?"

"Decide for yourself what you need and want. Eat for pleasure. It's a popular pastime on many worlds."

"It is here, too, if you go to the right kitchen. This is one of the right ones." The two shopkeepers had seated themselves on the other side of the balcony. A serving boy, whom Orrin recognized as the beldame's grandson, immediately came out of the kitchen with two clay cups of frosted plum spirits and placed them on the table before the women.

"You're right, though, about deciding for yourself.

Selecting balanced foods isn't so difficult," Orrin said. "The kitchen nutritionists are a holdover from convict times when there was so much malnutrition because of the nasugar."

The boy brought three cups to them, too. Ice chips were clinking in two of the cups that contained plum spirits. The third contained steaming broth but with a hint of something alcoholic in it, which he placed in front of Hark with an apologetic smile.

"It wasn't just the nasugar," Jeremy said when the boy was gone. "Toxins are a big problem if the foods aren't properly processed. The abbey still requires nutritionists to be certified," Jeremy said.

"If toxins exist, it sounds like a reasonable requirement to me. Why do you sound so disapproving?" Hark asked Jeremy. He had raised the cup to his lips and sipped carefully.

"Because they won't certify me, a doctor who has been trained to treat toxemia. In order to diagnose such cases properly I probably know more about processing food and nutritional requirements than that old woman in the kitchen who's been doing it all her life."

"I'll bet you do," Hark said dryly. "Most doctors are experts on their own Homeworld's foods. Most people are competent to select their own meals on their Homeworlds, too." Hark put the cup down. "So tell me why she heated this soup so damn much that I can't drink it?"

"So you won't take too much too fast," Jeremy said, almost smiling.

Grimacing, Hark reached for Jeremy's cup. Orrin was fast to stop his hand. "Don't," he said hoping that the women at the other end of the balcony had not seen. "Moves like that just confirm their superstitions."

"What superstitions?"

"That a man can't even eat properly on his own. Sip the broth. It will cool down soon."

Hark picked up his own up and lifted it, but paused thoughtfully. "Do you mean that a woman who hadn't eaten in two days would have been given something cool to drink?''

"Probably the same broth she gave you," Jeremy said. "It has a mild stimulant in it, some sugar, and the booze makes it more appetizing.''

"The beldame would have politely reminded a woman to ingest slowly, but she would have assumed a woman could be trusted to do it. You're a man. You're suspect on every count, including your eating habits," Orrin said.

"I'll be damned," Hark said.

"Lower your voice if you're going to use that word," Orrin said, but he wasn't too worried. The beldame had turned on the radio in the kitchen loud enough so that her patrons could hear if they wished.

"How much . . .''

". . . much too much for a span of ordinary . . .''

"Did it pay?"

"Avryl the spice seller to the jewel workers' district has given birth at last to the daughter she carried.''

"Did you feel Hells Gates rumble today? It spilled all the shelves . . .''

"Was it worth . . .''

It was impossible to tell which were the words of the radio and which of the two shopkeepers, who were talking loudly above it; all the voices were feminine. The boy brought tea and little cakes to the women, crisp vegetables to the men. Hark's were steamed again, but there were a few cool ones on his plate, too. Jeremy started eating.

"I want you to know about Islands before you leave, to know all about the men," Orrin said. "It's why I want to help you.''

"I don't mean to be dense," Hark said, "but you said a quarter of the population is oppressed. Half the men on Islands?"

"*All* the men on Islands," Orrin said.

"I don't much like puzzles," Hark said. "But if you insist . . . the female-to-male ratio on Islands is three to one?"

"Yes. You said you knew our origins. If you know anything about the Penitent faith at all, what else could you think?" Orrin said studying him.

"Half of each is normal, no matter what faith they profess," Hark said. "Is there something about being a Penitent that prevents conception of males?"

"No," Orrins said.

"Yes," said Jeremy.

Orrin sighed and shook his head, but he saw that Hark was listening intently now.

"I know the first settlers, the clerics and the Penitents, were all women. But the convicts who were sentenced to transportation to Islands were predominantly male convicts. It should have evened out immediately." Hark sat back. "They weren't celibate or anything I don't know about, were they?"

"No, but Penitents practice artificial insemination as a sacrament," Orrin said, trying to explain. He wasn't very good at explanations when it came to matters of faith, for he had very little of it himself.

"They use consecrated seed," Jeremy said, his open contempt bordering on blasphemy. But he knew to keep his voice low. "That's a religious euphemism for sperm that's been treated so that the male-producing wigglers are killed off." He shrugged and shook his head, an expression of suppressed rage gradually being replaced by thoughtfulness. "You said you knew the original settlers' supplies down to the last blanket. Do you know how large a supply of frozen sperm they brought?"

Hark frowned. "I didn't make note."

"Apparently infinite," Jeremy said, looking sour again. "Do the records you consulted describe the fanaticism of the original clerics and Penitents? Didn't they tell you their offspring would continue to do penance? All female offspring? Couldn't they tell what would become of the male convicts when the clerics and Penitents renounced them out of hand?"

"There were female convicts, too," Hark said, sounding a bit defensive. He resumed eating.

"A few," Jeremy admitted, "almost all of whom took advantage." He smiled sheepishly at Hark. "My great-grandmother took this transport token in exchange for . . . favors. Penitents don't give favors, you see, so she was very much in demand. She accumulated so much wealth that she could afford to accompany the First Migration right here to Fox. She also could afford to pay the clerics for her daughters' education, and their daughters', too. Of course, she had to do penance, but that was what she was here for anyhow. And doing penance like a *real* Penitent never kept her from selling favors." Jeremy shrugged. "I'm the first male in the family, apparently an accident with the holy lights or . . ." Again he shrugged. "Queen Aethelmere's mother was a whore, too."

"The AI should have done a better job of integrating the communities," Hark said apologetically. "It doesn't sound like it was very effective, not even for a little while."

"All I know is that more females than males are born, and it's considered holy," Jeremy said.

"How long was that AI operating? When did the volcano blow up?"

"About twenty-five years ago," Orrin said. "I was just a boy, but I'll never forget. Fox City was covered with white ash like snow. The sun didn't rise for days. It took months to haul it all away."

"Then the AI operated for at least two generations before it was destroyed. It must have stopped learning quite early." Hark started eating the vegetables on his plate. "Did anyone survive the blast?"

Orrin shook his head. "We are the survivors, I suppose. And the folk of New Penance and the clerics of Selene."

"Selene must be the settlement we spotted on Mons Selenus, but what of this New Penance? We didn't see a third settlement. They're not too hard to detect from up there," Hark said, gesturing toward the darkening sky.

"By reputation they're especially pious about the Penance," Orrin said. "But I would have to call them primitive. They live in caves, and in trees, too, I've heard. Good loggers, and the Foxen always hire their plankers to build our rails. They're determined to do penance exactly as the Penance Princess herself. Her granddaughter, Queen Mala, is said to uphold the tradition." He shrugged. Being fair was extremely important to him, though he held so little respect for Penitents, new, reformed, progressive, or traditional. "They have a tough militia, despite their scorn of science and technology."

"And the primitive lifestyle has to do with the penance that required them to live in balance with nature?"

"And if they did, it would end the wars," Orrin said beginning to feel the way he always felt when he talked about matters of faith—uneasy. "But it didn't end the wars, not here on Islands," he said uncomfortably. "And the Fyxen consider themselves Penitents, too, and we have considerable science and technology."

Jeremy snorted in contempt. "Only what the clerics permit. And you may want to call yourself a Fyxen Penitent, Orrin, but I know what kind of penance my grandmother did!"

"My grandmother was a marine," Orrin said stiffly. "But that's not the point."

"Your grandfather was sentenced to transportation to Islands for murder," Jeremy said, refusing to help clarify Orrin's spiritual dilemma, "which makes you a ticket-of-leave man who had just enough luck to stay out of the camps." Jeremy smiled at Orrin apologetically. "You've taught me to be a realist in so many ways; it astounds me that you can even attempt to rationalize what they do."

Orrin smoothed his beard with a quick brush of his hand and shrugged indifferently. In his way, Jeremy was checking to see if he had offended Orrin by speaking so bluntly. Jeremy should know by now that Orrin would never fault him for holding unpopular opinions, as long as he did so quietly. And quiet he had been.

Jeremy, apparently satisfied by Orrin's shrug, turned back

to Hark. "Your AI integrated the communities by support-
ing the Penitents and making every man on Islands ashamed
of his heritage."

Hark looked at him thoughtfully. "It succeeded in
breaking down the religious barriers enough to give you
some technology."

"And a matriarchal monarchy founded on whoredom,"
Jeremy added, "thus a new bitch when the Queen of
Bitches died."

"Is that word allowed?" Hark asked sincerely. "Back on
Homeworlds, unless it's being applied to a female canine,
it's an insult."

"It's always an insult on Islands. We have no dogs.
Livestock didn't survive the famines. But we have a
plentiful supply of bitches. And we have *The Bitch*, who
lives in the minds of all male minds but Orrin's. Now, tell
me what you mean about the AI not learning. You said that
as if it explained everything."

"It probably does," Hark said. He was speaking between
bites, obviously upset by Jeremy's vehemence, but too
hungry to stop. "The AI's brain was defective, which is
why we came to replace it."

"Was the Guild in the habit of supplying defective AIs?"
Orrin asked, wondering if the accusations of depravity in
the Homeworlds were justified. Poor craftsmanship deserved to be dealt with severely. Perhaps his images of what
the Homeworlds were like were nothing more than wishful
thinking. Perhaps he was meddling where he should not.

"Not knowingly," Hark said. "The Guild constantly
checks reliability, but sometimes the problem doesn't show
up for years. The AIs have infinite lifespans when properly
maintained; humankind does not, so it's hard to do life tests
on AIs. But, hard doesn't mean impossible. They load them
up . . ." He paused to take more food. "Never mind.
What's important is that by the time we detected it, the
Homeworlds were at war. The planet your AI was shipped
to was quarantined. After the war was over and the AI Guild
learned there was a problem with that AI, a self-destruct

command was issued from orbit. Because of the quarantine, nothing more could be done. They had no idea that the AI had been shipped to Islands with the convicts long before the self-destruct command was activated."

"How did they find out?" Orrin asked.

Hark had finished the vegetables and now drank down the last of the broth in his cup. He sat back, smiling. "I didn't tell you everything after all."

"Drugs aren't foolproof," Jeremy said. "But don't stop now. We want you to return safely to the Homeworlds as quickly as possible. Soon enough to do us both some good."

Hark shook his head. "Put my captain and the engineer on the lander and let me go. I'll tell them what I've seen. The next mission will be better prepared."

Orrin shook his head. "I can't do that. I would spend the whole time waiting in prison, if I weren't hanged. Jeremy too. We'll help you, Hark, but only to the extent that we don't hurt ourselves."

"Not heroes, eh?"

Orrin shrugged. "Tell me what was wrong with the AI," he said. How could a sick machine explain everything so thoroughly that Hark didn't even remember what he had started talking about?

"The left side of that particular batch of AI brains was subject to overload damage, which wiped out the ability to form verbal memories. Image memory still worked. It made the AI unable to form new memories. Once it stopped working, it had to get by with old data, which was precious little about Islands and a great deal about the Penitents religious practices. It would have supported them, of course; AIs are conditioned to have religious sensitivity."

"But what of the convicts? Wasn't it . . . sensitive to them, too?" Orrin asked.

"It should have been," Hark said. "Or maybe it never learned to distinguish between Penitents and convicts. After all, in one sense, they're the same."

"Everyone on Islands does penance," Orrin said quietly.

He saw the beldame herself coming out of the kitchen. She stopped to slip on her shawl and stepped out balancing five platters. Two she served to the shopkeepers, and she chatted with them a moment. Finally she turned and walked across the balcony. A curious and probably hungry scurry paced along the railing next to her. Orrin shooed it away with a flick of his hand when it sniffed at their table. It scurried back down toward the shopkeepers.

"I'll collect my fee now," the beldame said as she placed the platters before them. "I'll be too busy in a few minutes."

Four more patrons had topped the stairs, and others were on the bottom steps. The streets were more crowded than when they first arrived, highborns and groundskeepers walking home. Orrin reached into his uniform pocket and pulled out a handful of silver and brass coins. The beldame selected the ones she wanted from his open palm; she charged fairly, Orrin thought, considering the extra trouble she went to for Hark.

"The official announcement is just a few days off, isn't it, Jeremy?" she said as she tied the coins in the corner of her shawl.

Jeremy nodded and Orrin could see that his teeth were clenched. The beldame was speaking of Jeremy's wedding announcement, an event the young doctor-trooper dreaded. Orrin wasn't sure why; the bride's family background matched Jeremy's and she was suitably accomplished in medicine. Orrin guessed, however, that like many men, Jeremy's orientation was not toward heterosexual marriage, and that his stay in the troops had not changed his preference.

"Most women prefer their own kitchens," the beldame said without malice, "but don't forget to visit after the wedding."

"Thank you," Jeremy said stiffly.

"You're getting married?" Hark said as the beldame walked off to greet the new patrons. "Congratulations."

"It's not my idea," Jeremy said. "It's my mother's. I

wanted to finish my studies." He shrugged, feigning indifference. "Orrin convinced me that running away to Selene to do it would be foolish. My only hope is to help you."

"I see," Hark said.

"Eat," Orrin said. "We have a lot of information to pass on before we meet Dame Adione in court and very little time."

"The *Top*," Hark said scathingly.

"Watch your tone when you speak to highborns," Orrin told him. "Some take offense easily, and for god's sake no retorts. You can be thrown out of court for being rude."

"But just men get thrown out, right?" He had started on the meat and rootstock on his plate, still eating hungrily.

"In theory, it's both. In practice, it's mostly men," Orrin said. He could tell Hark was unhappy, and he couldn't blame him. "Is there nothing like this on your Homeworlds? Is it really that alien to you?"

"I defer to my captain a lot, but sometimes I tell her she's dead wrong and I don't have to worry that she won't check it out just because I'm a man. And if she's rude, I usually know it's probably nothing to do with me and she'll apologize after a while. If she doesn't, I confront her. She may not concede, but at least she knows how I feel about it."

"Ah, yes, your Captain Dace. Deanna Dace," Orrin said. "Is she your lover?"

Hark looked stunned. "God, no. She's my boss."

"One precludes the other on your world?"

"Well, no. Not necessarily. But it isn't the case in this instance."

"You talked about her as if you were on intimate terms, used very endearing expressions about her breasts. But I also got the impression that your love is unrequited. There are some people who might suggest you harbor bitterness."

"Like your Doctor Barenia? Is that why she was worried about my poisoning Captain Dace?" When Orrin nodded,

Hark laughed with irony. "Men must have a very strange way of showing their love on Islands if poisoning the women of their dreams is very common."

"It does happen. Love is serious business in court. And if your heart is hers . . . well, it could be an obstacle. They might think she's the only one you would be loyal to."

"I am loyal to her, but not like you think. She rates me, and that affects monetary compensation. As a military man, you must understand ratings."

Orrin nodded. "Then you do love her."

"For money," Hark said. There was an edge to his tone that Orrin found cutting.

"Money that you couldn't get without her."

"Orrin, it's not the same thing as love. Don't hold me responsible for subconscious thoughts. I'm not a drug expert, but I do know you can probe more deeply with them than you can a rational mind. Holding that against me is unfair."

"Do you deny that you love her?"

"She's my captain. When speaking to her or of her I would never presume to address her as anything except Captain Dace, no matter what terms I may have used under drugs. Even privately I wouldn't address her differently. If she had wished anything different, she would have given me a sign. She never has, and that's that. I respect her as an officer and as a woman."

"But she is a woman, and that's . . . satisfying to our highborn dames. They will see between you and your captain a relationship they're very familiar with, not the mutual profession and personal respect you're trying to describe," Orrin said pulling the wing off the roasted peacock on his plate. It was drenched in ant honey, very sticky but tasty.

"I've served under male captains, too. It's no different with them." Hark looked exasperated and dismayed. "I'm a pilot. They pay me very well for my skills. It would be insane for them *not* to listen to me. How can I relate to people who have no respect for me?"

"Try," Orrin said. He could feel himself getting angry, angry at Hark because his words made a lot more sense than Orrin's did, angry with himself because he had to say them. "You're intelligent and you think fast. Just think of every one of them as you do Captain Dace, and maybe you'll stay out of trouble. Give lots of respect, wait for a sign."

Hark nodded, but Orrin wasn't certain he was convinced. They ate quietly for a while; the tables next to them were filled now with clinicians in yellow sashes. The boy brought bowls of tea and a tub of fresh fruit for dessert or pockets. The voice on the radio gossiped on.

". . . on the price of rice."

"Was it worth it?"

"The bridge over the arcwright's stream is fixed."

"Another windship was lost . . ."

"The urge was strong and she bore a perfect little daughter!"

"Thank goodness I'm postprocreational!"

"Salt shipment at the depot."

"We shall spin and weave our own."

Orrin pushed back his plate. He'd had his fill. The scurry was back, looking at the untended plate with big black eyes. Orrin took a tidbit and dropped it under the table. The scurry was down from the railing after it in a flash of gray.

"You met the queen," Orrin began again. "You saw how she is. She's typical of most of the jurists . . . wasting time sleeping, dressing, arranging their hair. Different garments for morning and evening so they go through the entire ritual of dressing at least twice a day. They spend time with their dandies or women friends, listen to music or the gossip on the radio. There's very little time left for business."

"Makes me wonder how it runs," Hark said following Orrin's example of pushing back the plate, even to the extent of saving out a tidbit for the lurking scurry. "And it does run," he said emphatically. "It's primitive, but it works."

"If you don't mind stagnation, it works," Jeremy said also pushing back his plate. He drank down his tea and pushed back his chair. "Take a plum with you. They freshen the breath."

"I've had plums on many worlds," Hark said eyeing the bowl of fruit. "They never taste like the ones I ate as a boy." But he took one after Jeremy and Orrin took another. Then they arose and made their way across the crowded balcony to the stairs.

Nightbirds were getting bold as scurries, starting to alight on the railing. In the distance, fireflies flickered in the trees and Orrin could hear the clomping of beasts over the sedge bridges as the entertainers led them toward the court district.

"You must understand," he said urgently to Hark just as soon as they were down in the street, "that you need Dame Adione. She's as eager as we are to bring about changes, and better placed to help you."

"Why?" Hark asked. "What does she have to gain?"

"There's been a complacency since the truce, an influx of wealth since the clerics permitted the rail. She wants the wealth used to prepare defenses against the Selenians for when they break the truce."

"Selene? Isn't that where you wanted to go?" Hark asked Jeremy.

Jeremy nodded. "They're almost wholly clerics, too, which must seem odd after what we've told you. But it's a religious war. The progressive clerics against the conservative. It seems to have to do with your interpretation of what living in balance with nature means. Selenians believe science *is* natural. The truce is a bit shaky right now, though that isn't what keeps me from going."

Orrin frowned at him. The only thing that kept Jeremy safe from himself was Orrin's vow that if he ran again, Orrin would bring him back again. There were no solutions to problems in running away from them. He thought he had Jeremy convinced, but ever since he had showed Hark the transport token, Orrin had begun to have doubts.

"But it wasn't the Selenians who broke the truce," Hark said. "You did, by her order, I suppose."

"It was an honest mistake, one she regrets now as much as I do," Orrin said, feeling pained once again. "She's powerful, but the abbey is more powerful. She merely wanted to open their eyes to the possible danger."

"And ended up with me instead. So now she hopes contact with the Homeworlds will . . . what? Reduce the threat from the Selenians? Or stir up more trouble?"

"I'm not sure," Orrin said frankly, "but she is extremely interested in you, to the point of wanting your guardianship for herself. I consider that a good sign."

"I don't trust your Dame Adione," Hark said. He was walking quickly in the right direction. The meal must have energized him.

"You can trust her," Orrin said. "I've known her half my life."

"I don't trust anyone who calls me Sweetchucks," Hark said.

"She likes you," Orrin said, trying to ignore the pain and anger of admitting it. He looked at Hark. Even in the dim light he was pale, but he was muscular and strong-looking like a trooper, not dandy-slim. And that, Orrin knew, attracted her. Orrin was even more muscular and stronger, but she'd never called him anything but Orrin or First. He couldn't help the twinge of jealousy. Was it the beard? *The beauty of a man lies under his beard,* he had often heard women of the court say. Hair was a superfluity, and the dandies removed it even from their private parts. But Orrin had always thought of his beard as his glory of manhood, more recently with the gray touches, his visible sign of wisdom and experience.

"I don't trust her," Hark said again, "but I do trust you. God knows I have to trust someone. I'll do my best."

"Good," Orrin said. "Just remember to kneel before the queen and . . ."

"No way. It's not my custom to kneel before anyone," Hark said. That irritating tone of voice again.

"Then we try to keep you away from the queen, or if necessary, I make you kneel until she gives you special dispensation. And you address everyone as dame or madam, except clerics who are called mother."

"I'll address them politely," Hark said. "That is my custom."

"And you'll be gracious to your guardian, whoever it is."

Hark shook his head, but Orrin sensed it was in disgust, not refusal.

"Just hope it is Adione. She's bold enough to back you and influential enough to carry it off despite objections. Next to Aethelmere herself, she's the best."

"This guardian shit is completely unacceptable. What do they think they're going to do, assign guardians to every male engineer that comes from the Homeworlds? The AI Guild would never stand for it."

"They would send women once they're apprised of the situation, wouldn't they?" Jeremy asked.

"I don't know," Hark said. "They can be perverse at times. It might depend on the kind of report I make."

"Well, maybe you can convince her of that." But Orrin wasn't certain even Adione was that broad-minded.

CHAPTER 5

Hark counted five good-sized moons. He could see only the brightest stars in the northern sky, and it troubled him to remember that the orbiter would be traveling west to east where it would be difficult to see through the wash of moonlight. The AI would be worried at Hark's lack of contact, but it would be another day before the AI started a search-and-rescue mission for him. Hark might be stranded if he weren't in the lander when the AI located it. He hadn't told Orrin yet of the danger, wasn't sure that Orrin wouldn't try to tie the lander down, or do something equally risky.

"Do you want to check your lander?" Orrin said suddenly, and Hark wondered if he had been thinking out loud.

"Of course I do." He looked up the terraced mountain slope. Even at this distance the red glow from the lava lake was visible in the clouds that were building at the summit.

"Not there," Orrin said. "We brought it down." He gestured to the stand of gigantic trees cutting a black silhouette against the starry sky. "It's in the park."

"Brought it down?" Hark knew they had no pilot, and the lander was too big and the terrain too rough to carry it to the railhead. "How?"

"With a logging windship."

Hark started running toward the trees. It was one thing to drop a load of timber from a balloon, quite another to set a lander down in one piece. Maybe he was already stranded on Islands.

It was dark under the trees and Hark had to slow down. Boles of the massive trees cast shadows that ran up dark shaggy trunks, which cast more shadows until there was not a sliver of moonlight. He felt Orrin's hand on his shoulder restraining him. "Move easy now," he said. "My troops are guarding it, and any sudden moves could alarm them."

Hark slowed to a walk, but pushed on determinedly, certain he would soon find a clearing. But the canopy of leaves overhead persisted, and finally Hark didn't know which way to go. Jeremy, walking steadily, came up behind them and brushed on past. Hark followed close behind.

There was no real clearing around the lander, just a cave in the foliage. He could see it now, dimly lighted by a few chemical lights placed on the landing pads, surrounded by the huge trees. "How the hell did you get it in here?"

"Dropped it in the clearing outside the park and put it on a wagon," Orrin said, and with that Hark realized he'd been walking in a rut left by one of the wheels. No wonder Jeremy had no trouble finding his way in the dark.

"I'll have to move it out from under these trees. The leaves are too thick overhead. They'll stop the signal from getting through."

Orrin's fingers closed over Hark's biceps. "What signal?"

Hark hesitated. "My radio's," he said. "I should advise the on-board AI of the circumstances down here. I should have checked in two days ago. I'll do it verbally. You could even make the call for me if you fear I'll say something I shouldn't."

"Are you sure there's no one else up there in that orbiter, no one but the AI?"

"You should already know that," Hark said. "Surely you didn't forget to ask when I couldn't help but tell the truth."

Orrin nodded slowly. "Radios I understand. You may talk to the orbiter and confine your conversation to what you have described. But if that lander moves or even sounds like it *might* move, I'll cut you down, my friend. That's a promise."

Hark shook off Orrin's grip, knew that unless he had chosen to let him go, he could not have moved. "I'll have to raise the balloon antenna above those leaves," Hark said. "A little windship," he added to satisfy the perplexed look on Orrin's face. "It's as small as a child's toy."

Orrin rocked back on his heels and looked up into the darkness. "What kind of radio do you use that its signal won't go through leaves?"

"Extremely high frequency," Hark said. "We can pack more data in it. Usually it's two AIs conversing; anything less would slow them down."

Orrin nodded, as if to indicate he understood. But then he shook his head. "There's not time tonight."

"It doesn't take long," Hark said. "I can have that antenna up in less than ten minutes. Less than five if I hurry."

"Not tonight," Orrin said firmly. Then he smiled sheepishly. "It's not quick and clean like I thought it would be. A few words . . . quick and clean. Launching a windship . . ." He shrugged and repeated, "Not tonight. This will have to be a quick trip. I just wanted you to see that your lander was close by and that it's safe. You'll be able to move Captain Dace quickly if it goes well for you in court."

"You never mention poor Rene," Hark said.

"If she's alive tomorrow, I'll be surprised. If they let you move that lander in a week's time, I'll also be surprised."

Hark said nothing; he knew Orrin expected no comment. He was speaking frankly again, and even as Hark tried to think in terms of not being able to leave Islands for a week or more, tried to accept that Rene *must* die before he could do anything to save her, his stomach churned in denial. But what could he do? Knock Orrin over the head when they got to the lander and take off? He looked, couldn't even see the forest canopy he knew was overhead, the canopy that was so thick not even the light of *five* moons penetrated. And if he did somehow get past Orrin, which he doubted was possible, how would leaving help Rene or Captain Dace? They were inside the maternity clinic, not somewhere he could just set down and help them aboard.

Disgusted, down-hearted, Hark stepped out of the underbrush to look at the lander. He saw no visible damage on the hull, the pads' tensors seemed unstressed. Even the leaf litter underneath seemed relatively undisturbed. The ruts ended, the lander sat there as neatly as if he had set it down himself. Mollified, he started around toward the hatch, but Orrin caught his arm.

"Something's wrong," Orrin whispered.

A trooper, the one Hark had first seen with Jeremy when he awakened under the lander, was moving stealthily out from under the belly of the lander. A tiny chemlamp strapped to his arm provided enough light to illuminate a worried face. He hurried over to Orrin.

"There's been trouble, big trouble," the trooper said in a rushed whisper. "Queen Aethelmere came to look at the ship. Of course we let her in." His eyes were wide with fear until Orrin nodded and agreed.

"Of course you would let her in," Orrin said, still whispering.

Hark kneeled to look under the lander. There were several people on the other side by the hatch.

"She looked around for a while, poking here and there like the clerics had," the trooper said while Orrin nodded patiently, "but then she pulled out a laser and started burning!"

"Oh, gods," Hark said, leaping up, but Orrin had him firmly by the collar.

"We couldn't stop her. I mean, what could we do to the queen?" the trooper asked miserably. "She just stood there burning it until the clerics arrived. I never thought I'd be glad to see sorry sisters, but I was tonight. They stopped her. Dame Cirila had brought them." The trooper looked at Jeremy now. "Your mother went right in there with the sorries, grabbed the burner right out of the queen's hand."

"Is she all right?"

"Is my ship all right?" Hark asked.

To Jeremy, the trooper nodded. To Hark, he shook his head. "There's sorry sisters inside yet, and a couple of nature boys outside with me."

"Does Dame Adione know?" Orrin asked, sounding worried.

The trooper nodded. "She's been here and gone, looking for you. Shall I call her for you? She's carrying a talkie."

"Let Jeremy do that." Orrin let go of Hark's collar and stepped around the lander to the hatch with Hark on his heels. There was light inside, but not the cabin lights.

Two more of Orrin's troopers, dressed in jungle-green fatigues and wearing the little lights on their arms, stood at the base of the ladder. They were flanked by two musclebound men wearing white, gauzy blouses and trousers. One of the white-clad men stepped forward to bar the ladder when Hark reached out to take hold of a rung. "No one goes inside," the man said.

A woman appeared in the hatch. She wore a drape of black net wrapped so that it covered all but her face, even her head was wrapped, the folds and knots so thick that she looked top heavy. She had a big chemlamp in her hand. "It's Dame Adione's First, isn't it?" she said to Orrin. "Is that the spaceman with you?"

"Yes, Mother," Orrin said.

"Leave your laser and come inside, both of you," she said briskly.

Hark needed no urging. While Orrin handed over his laser to one of his men, Hark scrambled up the ladder. The woman stepped back to the control panel while Hark looked wildly around. He saw the scorch marks immediately and could still smell burned insulation. But spacecraft interiors weren't easy to burn, and he knew this was only cosmetic damage. But he couldn't see the command console because three clerics stood there barring his way.

"What are you doing there?" Hark demanded worriedly. For a moment the three women stared at him, then one stepped aside so he could see. "God da- . . ." he started to say when he saw the canister, but Orrin clamped his hand over his mouth.

"Don't swear," he whispered. He took his hand away slowly. "These women are abbesses—Mother Phastia, Mother Honore, and Sister Carlin."

The one introduced as Sister Carlin wore black like the other two, but over her head she wore a simple shawl, not the unwieldy-looking thick wraps of cloth. "I am Pilot Hark," he said quickly, "and sorry if I offended you, but . . ." He couldn't keep his eyes from the canister. It was scorched and half-melted, the jelly beans in a slag on the bottom. "She had to have stood there for five full minutes or more to do that."

"The nitrogen has completely evaporated," Sister Carlin said. "Will the lander work without them?"

Hark shook his head. "They were the smarts. All this tub of tin has now is an empty brain."

"Perhaps you have spares somewhere?"

"No," he said impatiently. "No spares. I can't fly without the jelly beans, the programs."

Sister Carlin nodded. "I surmised as much. But take a look at the rest of the damage. Nothing else seems serious."

"Doesn't matter," Hark said. "I really can't fly without the jelly beans."

The two older clerics exchanged glances. "The other ship," Mother Phastia said. "The one that was shot down the other night. It was identical, was it not?"

Startled, Hark looked at her. "Yes, in every detail. And yes, they just might have survived the crash." Excited, he looked at Orrin, who shrugged apologetically.

"There's wreckage strewn along half a klick in that valley. I didn't see anything like your jelly bean tank, but then, I wasn't looking for it either."

Mother Phastia smiled. To Orrin she said, "I believe your Top is looking for you to tell you we'll want you on the expedition tomorrow morning."

"To search the crash site?" Orrin asked.

"Yes. Him, too." Mother Phastia nodded at Hark.

His going was the only thing that made sense, but Hark didn't say that out loud. He started running his fingers over the scorches on the bulkhead, making sure none were deep. "Why would she do this?" he said, still outraged.

"It must be apparent to you that our queen does not welcome reestablishing contact with the Homeworlds," Mother Phastia said.

"But why?" Hark said. "It was you clerics we thought would be resistant, not the convicts' descendants. And here you are organizing an expedition to help recover the jelly bean jar."

"Clerics are often misjudged," Mother Phastia said. "Now, if there's nothing else."

"Oh, but there is," Hark said. "I want your assurance that if we do find the jelly bean jar intact that I'll be permitted to take my crewmates back to the orbiter immediately." He brushed off Orrin's restraining hand.

"There isn't much point in discussing that until we find what you need to make the ship fly," Mother Phastia said.

"I like clear understandings," Hark said meeting her eyes. "If you're expecting something in return for assisting me . . . perhaps transport?"

"Nothing like that," Sister Carlin interjected in a shocked tone. "We would never leave Islands."

She might have gone on, but Mother Phastia silenced her with an icy smile. "If we ask anything of you, you can be certain it will not be too much."

"There are lives at stake," Hark said, not trusting her. "My crewmates need attention that I can give them only in the orbiter."

"Then you'll want to be well rested on the morrow," she said easily. "I'm told you don't walk very well. You should be as fit as possible for your friends' sakes."

Hark stared a second. He didn't think anything could melt that icy demeanor. "Yes, ma'am. And I should be better shod than I was on my last walk," he said finally. "I have clothing in my locker. I'll just take them now." He knew they were watching him as he opened the overhead, amazed, he was sure. They probably had examined the ship thoroughly in the last two days, but had overlooked the overheads. He pulled out a bulky planet pack that would have suitable boots and other things he would need. "I'll feel more fit in my own clothes," he said to the staring clerics, "not to mention, more comfortable."

"First," Mother Phastia said sharply to Orrin. "Check the contents of that pack."

"Yes, ma'am."

"Now," she said.

"Of course," Orrin said taking the pack from Hark. Hark watched him fumble with the closure, finally getting it to open. He pulled out a shipsuit, lightweight shirt and pants quite suitable for tropical heat, a dress blue uniform, also lightweight, and boots. Orrin reached down to the bottom and pulled out a pair of underwear, glanced with embarrassment at the clerics, and shoved them back in. "More of the same," he mumbled.

Mother Phastia nodded. "Good night."

"Good night," Orrin said. He handed the pack back to Hark, who shouldered it.

"I'm very pleased to have met you," he said to the clerics. Then he ducked out the hatch behind Orrin.

Jeremy was waiting for them. "Dame Adione's at the garrison. I told her we were on our way."

Orrin had retrieved his laser from the trooper and was already walking briskly down the wagon ruts. "Does Top know the clerics are still in there?" He jerked his thumb back at the lander.

"Yes," Jeremy said. "My mother is at the garrison, too."

"Really?" Orrin said, sounding surprised. "What a bitch this has to be. I wonder what's going on? Sorry sisters in the park with the lander, doctors in the garrison with the Top." He shook his head. "Not to mention our spaceman here smuggling stuff out of his ship under the witches' noses. What is that stuff?"

Orrin was referring to the things besides underwear that never came out of the pack. "An extra medical pack and some instruments that are handy to have when you're planetside. I wanted the medical pack. It has stimulants I can use safely tomorrow. I assume we're walking again."

"You assume right," Orrin said. "Jeremy, take that pack and check the contents. Make sure he's telling the truth."

"It's the truth," Hark said. "There's nothing important in it. Probably not even anything you haven't already seen if you looked at the contents of my P-suit pockets." Jeremy gestured for the pack, and Hark handed it over.

"Why should you tell the truth now?" Orrin asked. "You sure weren't back there when you said you couldn't fly without the jelly beans."

"I don't know what you mean?"

Orrin looked at him suspiciously. "I don't believe you."

"Why not?"

"You're upset, but you don't look like a man who has just been sentenced to spending his life on Islands," Orrin said.

He was shrewd, Hark had to admit. "It isn't hopeless," Hark told him reluctantly. "I don't have spares, but the AI can download new programs into the memory if I could make contact. As long as the lander stays powered up, the programs are as good as if they were in the jelly bean jar. But I must send up the antenna through the leaves."

"You wanted to do that before you knew about the programs," Orrin said, still suspicious.

Hark nodded. "Because if I don't do something soon, that AI up there is going to figure I'm in trouble. It's going to start a search pattern, and when it finds this lander half-dead it's going to call it back, right through the trees. It might break out safely, too, depending on how heavy the branches are. But the AI won't know where I am, so it will take the lander back to the orbiter. As soon as it's sure there's no dead bodies inside, it's going to go home. *Then* I am stuck."

But Orrin was still frowning. "You said it can't fly and

that you can't make contact with the orbiter from here, at least not without the antenna. If you can't contact the orbiter, the orbiter cannot contact you. It will never find the lander."

"Yes it will. It will start by listening for the distress signal. If it doesn't hear it, it will do a narrow sweep looking for it optically and with other sensors. It will take it a while, but eventually it will deduce this lump of metal as being the right size and shape to be the lander. It will download on EHF and get no response, so it will try VHF and UHF. It will keep looking, going through the whole search program again, downloading and calling every lander-shaped hunk of metal in a three-hundred-klick-wide path around the whole equator of this planet. Eventually it will find the right one, and it will take the lander back."

"How long before it finds the lander?"

Hark thought about it. "It could be weeks, maybe months. A lot depends on the pattern it uses and how many hits it gets."

"That's enough time," Orrin said.

"For me, but what about Captain Dace? Her neck is going to keep healing. If I don't get her into stasis soon, she'll be paralyzed permanently."

"You can reverse paralysis?" Jeremy asked, immediately interested.

"Preventing it's easier, and that means getting her help quickly. If we wait, she probably will remain paralyzed."

"And you'll never forgive yourself, will you?" Orrin asked.

"Could you?"

Orrin didn't answer. "If they don't want you to fly that toy windship, you won't. If they don't want you to fly the lander, you won't. Behave accordingly, if you want help."

Hark shook his head in disgust. Orrin was talking about Dame Adione again. Could he do *that* for Captain Dace? She would never ask it of him, he was certain. But he didn't have to tell her.

CHAPTER 6

The garrison was next to the park, separated only by an infantile hedgerow. It was full of gaps that would take a hedger's careful attention to set right, but the hedgers had been set to tending hedges around yet another new plantation. The plantations were relocated so frequently the living fences never quite matured, the hedgers couldn't ever quite get caught up. Dame Adione had sent all the garrison's hedgers to help, a gesture sure to please Queen Aethelmere. They passed through a dead gate of woven sedge stalks, raised by two muscle troopers at the command of the duty guard when she recognized Orrin and Jeremy.

"You're to report . . ."

"I know," Orrin said briskly returning her salute. He walked quickly across the compound toward Dame Adione's command post. There was mulch under his boots, spread over the low spots to control mud during the rains and still fresh enough to know by the smell of benzoin that the woodchips had come from a benjamin tree. The aroma was strongest as they passed the gunnery where they'd covered the rail after the last rotation.

"Jeez," he heard Hark say. "Is that the thing you used to shoot down the lander?" He'd stopped to stare at the blue-metal barrel gleaming in the glow of chemlamps. "It's nothing but a big bullet pusher on a rail. How did you manage to hit the lander?"

"It's more maneuverable than it . . ."

"Jeremy!" Orrin said sharply. The big guns were kept camouflaged by day, the drapes removed only when runners rolled them into the garrison for preventive maintenance. Even constant attention barely kept them from rusting in the humid climate. The hedgerows might be neglected, but the guns were not. Dame Adione saw to that.

Jeremy shrugged and gave Hark a halfhearted push to get him walking again. The spaceman frowned and resisted, stood there kicking aside some of the woodchips. Jeremy pushed him again before Hark could get a good look at the rail. Head down, Hark walked the rest of the way up the path to the steps of the command post.

Orrin knocked on the door, stepped in and aside to let in Hark and Jeremy, then he closed the door. Dames Adione and Cirila were seated in the only chairs, worn ones that exposed wood through the lacquer enamel. There were half-empty goblets on the blistered desk along with two of Dame Adione's precious lasers. Dame Adione returned salutes without taking her eyes from Dame Cirila.

"I want you and ten of your musele troopers ready to move out on an expedition in fifteen minutes," Dame Adione said. She was still staring at Dame Cirila, but she was talking to Orrin.

"I told you I can't get anyone on such short notice," Dame Cirila said angrily. "We have patients to tend. If I call a doctor from the maternity at this hour, I'd be short-handed."

"Send someone down in the morning with the clerics," Dame Adione said evenly. "I'm just going to take some muscle troopers to set up a base camp."

"The very ones who brought those women out of the valley, the ones who know the terrain and just where to look for the brain jewels. Adione, I see through your plan and so will everyone else, including the clerics."

"I can't imagine anyone objecting to my arranging comforts for our reverend clerics, nor of my sparing them the trouble of scouting the area," Dame Adione said, her tone one of not totally unconscious arrogance.

"And if you find the brain jewels?" Dame Cirila asked.

Dame Adione shrugged. "If you're not careful, *you* may never find out." She sat back and lifted one leg to hang langorously over the arm of the chair, daring Dame Cirila to challenge her further.

Disgusted, Dame Cirila stood up and for the first time acknowledged her son with a nod.

"Good evening, Mother," Jeremy said politely. He was carrying Hark's pack under his arm, but neither woman noticed.

Dame Cirila put her hands on her hips, a thoughtful look on her face. Slowly she turned back to Dame Adione. "Take Jeremy with you."

Dame Adione shrugged indifferently, but said, "Aren't his nuptual celebrations supposed to start?" She looked at Jeremy. "When do we muster you out?"

"In two days," Jeremy said.

"We're not likely to get back in time," Dame Adione said shaking her head.

"I wouldn't mind," Jeremy said, unable to restrain the eagerness in his voice. Dame Cirila frowned. "I mean," he said more contritely, "if you could rearrange things, Mother. Norra would understand, wouldn't she? I mean, her being a doctor, the maternity is important to her, too."

Dame Cirila hesitated. "I'd want your assurance you'd let Jeremy act for the doctors."

Dame Adione chuckled inexplicably, but merely nodded when Dame Cirila frowned. "It's settled then," Dame Adione said. "Jeremy will represent Fyxen doctors on the expedition. Won't Barenia be delighted?" She hooted and winked at Orrin, and Orrin realized he'd be expected to keep Jeremy too busy being a trooper for him to be his mother's son. He wondered why

"What interest do doctors have in brain jewels?" Hark asked, and both women looked at him in surprise. He should not have spoken uninvited, and innocently continued talking. "I understand the clerics' interest; they're the custodians of science and technology. Has the doctors' interest anything to do with my crewmates?"

Dame Cirila didn't answer Hark. Instead she looked at Dame Adione. "It should be an interesting expedition, Adione. I just may have to find time to join you."

"Your duty is clearly here," Dame Adione said coldly. "If you don't keep Aethelmere confined, she may do more damage. This time you may not find the sorries willing to help."

"All right," Dame Cirila said with a sigh. She looked at Hark so wryly that Jeremy turned away in embarrassment. Hark was trying to keep calm, pretending disinterest as she picked up her silk shawl. She tied it over her hips in the style started by convict women years ago. It was becoming to women with full hips like Dame Cirila. As soon as she knew Hark had noticed, she smiled mischievously, whipped it off and draped it over her shoulders. Hark turned red behind his ears. Dame Cirila started for the door, and Jeremy and Hark stepped aside. "Be careful," she said to her son, and touched him gently on the cheek.

Jeremy nodded and dutifully said, "Good night, Mother," and then stood straight as possible without looking at Dame Adione, who usually had something sarcastic to say to Jeremy whenever his mother was out of earshot.

But tonight Dame Adione was too preoccupied for retorts. She looked at her watch and then at Orrin. "You have only ten minutes left to get ready."

"Yes, ma'am," he said. "Am I to assume Hark comes along?"

She was unwinding herself from the chair, casually, yet so controlled and graceful. "Correct," she said. "If I leave him here those sorries will get him into the abbey somehow, and if they get him, they just might get the AI."

"The AI?" Hark said looking startled. "I can't deliver the AI. Conditions are not what we expected. I'm not permitted . . . You see, I'm the pilot. Only Captain Dace

could decide about where to place the AI, and she hadn't
made a decision.''

Hark's announcement caused Dame Adione's face to
darken, but she just shook her head. "We'll talk later," she
said. And to Orrin, "Move out. I have to get ready, too."
She reached for the lasers on her desk and shoved them into
a green daypack. "Pack yours, too," she told him.

"The wilderness laws," Orrin said. "The clerics will be
right there with us. If they see . . ."

"Dammit man, listen up. I said pack it, not wear it. And
be careful about where you open your pack or we'll both
end up doing penance."

"Yes, ma'am," he said, and signalled Jeremy and Hark
to step out the door. He hesitated before following, hoping
Dame Adione would relent as she often did and give him a
moment more to conspire, or at least to provide more
information so he would be better prepared to serve her. But
there was no signal forthcoming tonight.

Orrin had to suggest taking a break from the fast pace
Dame Adione set on the trail and explain why because she
hadn't noticed Hark, who was breathing badly and falling
behind.

"Dammit," she said. She drove the tip of her machete
into the ground, a gesture of angry frustration.

"We could leave Jeremy and one of the others to follow
along at whatever pace he can manage," Orrin said.

"No!" she said sharply. "Have you forgotten those
Selenians you left up at Hells Gates, unaccounted for?
Wouldn't they just love to get their hands on him. And
there's always the risk of rounders. I don't want to take any
chances with him. Jeremy, do something for him . . .
sugar, water, anything. Just get him moving."

Jeremy stepped past them to tend to the spaceman, and
Orrin hoped he could tell by Dame Adione's tone to use
some of the means in Hark's own pack, which seemed to
have worked sufficiently well for the first hours. The other

troopers drifted off into the bushes to relieve themselves, leaving Orrin alone with Dame Adione for a moment.

"We'll carry him if we must," Dame Adione said quietly.

We, Orrin knew, meant his muscle troopers. She would not literally share the burden one step of the way. "We'll do what we must," he said, hoping it wouldn't be necessary. The night heat was oppressive and the promise of rain they'd seen earlier gathering at Hells Gates hadn't materialized. Indeed, the sky had cleared and moonbeams occasionally shone all the way through the understory as the foliage thinned on the downward journey. It would get hotter as they continued down the mountainside.

"Did he say anything about the AI after I left the maternity?" she asked him. He could see her eyes clearly, but her face was in soft shadow. Intelligent eyes, sharp, and lovely.

"A little about the one that blew up with Hound. Nothing about his AI," Orrin replied carefully.

"It isn't his," she said. "You heard what he said about their having come to replace *ours*. It belongs to us already."

"I don't think he disputes that," Orrin said quietly, but her sounding so possessive about the AI made him wonder about her interest. She hadn't shown any when they were questioning Hark under the drugs. Or had she carefully hidden her interest because Dames Cirila and Barenia were there, too?

"What did he talk about?" she asked, an edge still in her voice.

"Mostly he listened and I talked," Orrin said. "The plan was to coach him enough to take him to court so he wouldn't disgrace himself."

Dame Adione sighed. "Had I but known what was going on in her mind," she said, and Orrin knew she was referring to Queen Aethelmere's attack on Hark's lander.

"Did she want to keep them from delivering the AI?"

"I never even told her about the AI. She doesn't want contact with the Homeworlds." Dame Adione stepped further away from the troopers who were returning from the underbrush, gestured for Orrin to come with her. "Cirila thinks it's a panic reaction," she whispered, her face so close he could feel her breath on his ear. "But I think the old girl knew exactly what she was doing. She's afraid the Homeworlds won't recognize her regency or any Fyxen claim. The territorial grants were all for Hound. The only regency the Homeworlds would be able to trace to their records is Mala's of New Penance. Aethelmere figured if she stopped this pilot from leaving Islands, any danger would at least be delayed."

"You don't seem too concerned," Orrin said.

"What interest could the Homeworlds have in an old penal colony? What do we have they don't already? You have only to look at the lander to know they've more than even the history books tell." She shook her head. "We'll be one line in some record book somewhere, *Insula In Caelum, silvan in plenum.*"

"You don't think they'll be interested in our trees?"

She shook her head.

"Nor what became of the Penitents?"

She shrugged. "They sent convicts to spite the Penitents. Does that seem like a caring Homeworld to you? This is a fluke, this spaceman's visit. He said so. No one but the AI Guild knows or cares that he's here." She looked up. Jeremy was helping Hark to his feet. She went over and pulled her machete from the ground, then gestured for Orrin to lead the way.

He stepped off down trail, ever down and hotter with each step, though dawn was hours away. He hacked foliage to clear the path for those behind, but not as much as he expected with three days' growth since he'd passed this way with the crash victims. He couldn't help thinking Dame Adione was being naive not to worry about the Homeworlds' possible interference on Islands. He wouldn't disagree with her to her face, but he thought she was wrong. At least, he hoped she was.

CHAPTER 7

Jeremy had pieced enough together back at the garrison to know that his mother and Dame Adione had made some kind of agreement over the AI, and he also knew that something had already gone wrong. Queen Aethelmere hadn't been interested in Hark as fresh amusement in court, nor as personal entertainment, as anyone would ordinarily expect. Instead she had seen him as a threat and for the first time in her reign taken matters into her own hands without consulting his mother, Dame Adione, nor Mother Phastia, the protectors of her court, one at a time, according to Queen Aethelmere's current needs. Now he had heard enough of what Dame Adione had whispered to Orrin to be certain of their interest in the AI. He understood his mother's interest; the doctors of Fox were constantly at odds with the clerics over being forced to research and develop treatments and techniques that were well documented by the Hound AI. Only rarely, when it suited the clerics for bizarre purposes of their own, did they permit lay scientists access to the printouts brought from Hound so long ago. An AI of the doctors' own would make the clerics' books unnecessary, and would probably save countless lives over the years. But just how Dame Adione would benefit by the AI was less clear, though he felt certain she did have a plan.

Jeremy walked behind Hark in the middle of the line of troopers. The spaceman was walking well again, breathing more easily now. Jeremy would have liked to know what was in the patch Hark had stuck behind his ear. A stimulant, yes, but it didn't have the distressing side effects of nervousness and agitation Jeremy was used to seeing. He no longer dreamed of going to Selene to finish his studies; he wanted to go to the Homeworlds. As long as Hark was alive and if they could make the lander fly and *if* Orrin would help, it might be possible.

Orrin, he knew, didn't want to go anywhere, except, perhaps, to Dame Adione's bed, if she would have him on his terms. Impossible, Jeremy knew, but Orrin, for all his intelligence, was blind where Dame Adione was concerned. He kept hoping. Jeremy could tell that Orrin was eager to see Hark succeed, that without any prompting from Jeremy he had seen the spaceman as some sort of path to Adione's heart. That was enough to convince Orrin to help Hark; the Homeworlder was the kind of man Orrin strived to be in so far as he could on Islands. But that help would stop short of betraying Adione in any way. But if Adione wanted the AI and if Hark truly wouldn't deliver it up to her, Hark and Orrin were already at odds. It was too bad, too. If Orrin were on Hark's side, the chances of success were good. Orrin was bottom man to the lace Top, Dame Adione, because he was unequalled as a strategist. Jeremy wished now he had paid more attention to all the things Orrin had tried to teach him since he had come to the troops. There were too many ifs for him to believe events would go as he wished on their own, and he knew better than to believe he could direct them.

"How much farther?" Hark asked.

"At least until dawn," Jeremy said.

"How long is it until then?"

"A few more hours. Will you make it?"

Hark shook his head. "The second dose isn't as effective."

"There's still one more patch," Jeremy said.

"Two's the limit."

Jeremy didn't believe him. If their positions were

reversed, he would be saving the last patch for some extraordinary emergency that might get him home, would not waste it on Dame Adione's forced march.

Jeremy could tell when the stimulants had completely worn off. Hark could barely pick up his feet and perspiration soaked the greens he was wearing so that they were plastered to his body. Wordlessly Jeremy moved up next to Hark on the trail and put his shoulder under Hark's arm to help him along. It took a while longer for Dame Adione to notice that they were falling behind, but she finally called a halt, and glared at Jeremy while he gave Hark some sugared water. The refreshment didn't do much good. Before they were fifteen minutes along the trail, Hark collapsed.

"Carry him," Dame Adione said flatly.

The troopers scowled silently. They were overloaded with extra gear needed for the clerics, and that was enough to make them resentful. Now they had to redistribute the contents of two of the packs so that two of them could carry Hark. Orrin pointed to Haron and Calib, the first two men in line, and they slung their packs down and started to open them.

"Just one," Dame Adione said. "I'll take the other."

She handed Orrin her daypack and shouldered the big one. Jeremy could tell by the twitch at the corner of Orrin's mouth that he was pleased by her action, and Jeremy couldn't suppress the rage that made him feel. She had carried only a daypack for seven or eight hours, and with no more than an hour left until dawn, her own common sense had to tell her they would make better time if she carried one of the big packs. Sometimes Jeremy thought Orrin was a complete fool. Dame Adione wouldn't have bothered if she weren't in a hurry to get her hands on the brain-jewels before the clerics.

Dawn broke as they squeezed through slabs of upthrust lava rocks at the head of the valley where the lander had crashed. Even in the dim first light the klick-long path of the lander was easy to discern. The tops of the tallest trees just below them were shorn off. Further down the valley a scorched line bisected the thick shubbery, ending just short of the placid-looking soda lake. There were three huge pieces of wreckage wedged into the shrubs by the lake, but Jeremy knew there were smaller bits of wreckage strewn along the entire path.

Hark stood down from the chair of arms and stared at the valley, his face pale and tense. Jeremy handed him a canteen.

"What do you think?" Orrin asked. "Did the brain jewels survive?"

Hark shook his head slightly, wiped his mouth with the back of his hand. "I don't know. Captain Dace and .Engineer Rene survived. Maybe the jelly beans did, too." He handed the canteen back to Jeremy. "It looks like she lost the flaps in those trees, then careened on her side, probably rolled and bounced. It wouldn't have broken up that much otherwise." The sun was a trifle higher than it was only moments ago, the valley just a bit brighter. Hark squinted and stared. "Are those people down there?" he asked.

For another moment the seemingly colorless haze offered so little contrast and the scene was so still that only the largest features of the landscape were evident. Jeremy focused on dark shadows near the lake, moving shadows that might have been browsing animals or human forms bent over or maybe on all fours. One by one the bent shadows straightened. The headgear of the highest ranking clerics was too large to be mistaken for anything but what they were.

Furiously, Dame Adione threw down the big pack. "Damn those bitches. They had no intention of waiting until morning. They must have left the minute we got done talking."

"Not quite," Orrin said, pointing to the edge of the soda lake. There was a windship basket there, its envelope already stowed.

"Dammit, dammit!" she said, shaking her head. "They've been here for hours. They must have seen us leave."

Orrin nodded, but Jeremy wondered if perhaps his mother hadn't made yet another arrangement to get the AI. But no. Not that she wouldn't double-cross Dame Adione; she had sold her own son for a lot less than an AI. But the sorry sisters would no more share the AI with Fox's doctors than they would share the written works of the old one.

"There's only five of them," Orrin said.

"I can count," she said sharply.

"I meant that we wouldn't have much trouble keeping track of only five. There are twelve of us. If they do find the brain jewels, we'll know about it."

"If they haven't already found them and hidden them," she said.

"They can't fly it without me, too," Hark said. "Let me talk to them."

"We don't even know if they have them yet," Orrin said. "Let's go down and greet them as quickly as possible. We don't want to give them any more time than they've already had. When we get next to the lake, I want Jeremy to pitch a tent and get Hark inside. No visitors. He's sick if anyone asks. Understood?"

He was looking directly at Jeremy and Jeremy nodded. One glance at Hark told him that it wouldn't be far from the truth, at least, not until after Hark got some decent rest.

"And the rest of you don't even think of sleep until tonight. You trade off watching those sorries and hunting for the brain jewels," Orrin said. The men received his orders stoically. They had not reached the limits of their endurance yet; they knew it, and they knew Orrin knew it. "All right, then. Let's go on down."

Dame Adione picked up the pack again and led the way.

Under a pair of stunted trees that offered a bit of shade, Jeremy pitched the tents. He raised the oilcloth sides on one and fastened down the insect netting, but even so it was hot. Hark lay inside most of the day like a dead man, and Jeremy dozed fitfully outside, preferring to endure the insects and catch occasional relief from the heat from the breezes. He could do nothing but watch the searchers while he ostensibly kept a sharp eye on Hark, who needed no watching.

By late afternoon, when the sun's heat was at its worst, the clerics had to abandon the search. Their black robes were soaking up so much heat that two had fainted and had to be carried into the shade by troopers. The clerics did not ask Jeremy's help in reviving them. Dame Adione wisely called her troopers in, and they slept for a few hours through the worst of the heat, as did Dame Adione. When she woke up, the troopers woke up, and silently returned to the search. The clerics did not, and that seemed to please Dame Adione.

Later, she sat with Orrin in front of the tent going over the detail maps of the valley. The location of each bit of wreckage was carefully marked by a number.

"Good work," she said to Orrin, and he nodded, pleased. She consulted the lists of paper under the map, then shook her head. "If you could only spell no one would know this was done by a man." The comment obviously didn't sit well with Orrin, but Dame Adione didn't notice. She turned to peer into the tent at Hark's sleeping form, then said to Jeremy, "When is he going to wake up?"

"He probably won't until morning," Jeremy told her. "He's not used to the exercise or the heat."

"He's not unconscious, is he?"

"No, ma'am. We can wake him if you wish."

She shook her head and went back to looking at the papers. "Morning is soon enough. They haven't found anything that resembles brain jewels."

The troopers were done eating the camp stew Jeremy had cooked and were sitting by the little fire, not for its heat but because the smoke kept the worst of the night insects away. Hark woke up and Jeremy accompanied him into the bushes so he could relieve himself. Hark probably would have gone back into the tent to sleep, but as long as he was awake and there was a bit of stew left, Jeremy made him sit down to eat. He did so in silence. The troopers were too tired to chat very much, and the sight of Dame Adione at the clerics' campfire only fifty meters away seemed to have a sobering effect on them.

Dame Adione returned to the troopers' camp when Hark was halfway through his meal. She stood with her hands on her hips, a smug expression on her face. "They didn't find it before we got here," she said quietly.

"How can you be certain?" Orrin asked, immediately interested.

"Mother Phastia was far too interested in what *we* found this afternoon after they gave up. I just went over your whole list with her, and we took a torch and looked at the pieces," she said, starting to put the sheaf of papers into her vest. But she took them out again and handed them over to Orrin. "Here. As long as he's up, see if he can figure out where some of this stuff comes from," she said gesturing at Hark. "If there's anything that broke loose from the control panels, I want to know about it. We look where we found those pieces at first light."

Orrin took the papers and nodded.

Dame Adione looked at Hark. "How do you feel?" she asked.

"Tired," he said.

She shrugged absently and looked around at the other men, carefully, Jeremy thought, avoiding himself and Orrin. "How about the rest of you?"

Jeremy was positive they were all tired, but three of them seemed to perk right up, Haron among them. They knew as well as he did what was about to happen. Her gaze fell on Haron, a tall brown-haired man who had been in the troops less than a year. His teeth were clean and straight, his features even and his skin unscarred. "Haron," she said, "dig out a flagon of plum wine from the packs and bring it to my tent." She returned to her tent as Haron got up.

Hark, Jeremy, and Orrin had a perfect view of Dame Adione's tent from where they were sitting. The chemlight silhouetted her on the oilcloth walls and Haron as well when he went in with the flagon. Dame Adione's shadow drank deeply from the flagon, and then handed the flagon over to

Haron's shadow. Her hands stayed on his shoulders for a moment, and then Haron's tunic fell off. While Haron drank, she slipped out of her own clothes, the shadows projected so crisply that they could see her erect nipples and the bush of hair at her crotch.

Hark and Orrin were staring, but each was transfixed in a different way. Hark had stopped eating, fork poised halfway between the tin plate and his mouth, mouth agape. Orrin's mouth was clamped shut, his eyes slits of horror though he had seen this many times before.

Dame Adione had the flagon now, and while she drank Haron kissed her along a line from her neck to her belly until he was on his knees before her.

"My gods," Hark said, recovering slightly. He put the fork down in his plate. "Don't they know the light is on?"

"She knows," Jeremy said, and he signaled Hark to look at Orrin. He was still staring, his jaw trembling, his body tense as a predator ready to spring. Hark looked back at Jeremy, obviously troubled, but Jeremy could only shrug. He didn't know if Dame Adione provided these spectacles specifically to spite Orrin for so many years of refusals, or if she merely enjoyed exhibiting herself. The effect on Orrin was the same either way; he was horrified by what he saw, but could no more tear himself away from watching than he could stop breathing. Jeremy always looked on in disgust and felt angry at what she did to Orrin.

The shadow of Haron's face was one with Dame Adione's thighs, but now they could see his arm groping for the chemlamp. He found it at last, and the tent darkened.

Orrin rolled the sheaf of papers in his hand and shoved them in his tunic. Wordlessly he got up and walked away from the camp, disappearing in the night.

"The poor bastard," Hark said softly.

"You don't know the half of it," Jeremy said sadly, looking into the night after Orrin. He shook his head and looked back to find Hark staring at him.

"Don't be so sure," Hark said. "It's written all over your face."

"I don't know what you mean," Jeremy said, suddenly frightened that Hark really did understand.

"Sure you do. He doesn't know, does he?"

"I still don't get your meaning," Jeremy said. He reached over and tossed a few twigs into the fire. They smoldered a moment before catching.

"Okay, have it your way," Hark said. He put the unfinished plate of food on the ground by Jeremy's feet. "I'm going to get some more sleep. Good night."

"Good night."

CHAPTER 8

Hark awoke feeling restless and uncomfortable. The ground beneath him was so hard that just lying there made bruises on his stiff, sore muscles. He'd had more exercise since landing on Islands than during the last ten years combined. An exaggeration, perhaps, but that's how it felt. The air was so hot inside the tent that he had soaked the bottom with sweat, which added to his misery. Though it was still dark, he decided to get up and go outside, and that's when he discovered he was chained at the ankle to Jeremy.

Furious, he shook the young physician. "Get this damn thing off of me," he said, at the first flicker of response.

Jeremy sat up rubbing his eyes. "Don't get so excited. It's just a precaution."

"Take it off!"

"Hey! Be quiet, will you?" someone shouted from one of the other tents.

"Do me a favor, will you, Calib?" Jeremy said lowering his voice to a stage whisper. "Wake Orrin up and have him bring me the key. The spaceman's got to piss."

"What's the matter, sissy? Doesn't he want you to watch?"

"Calib, leave the punk alone and get him the damn key, will you?" someone else said. "Some of us are still trying to sleep."

"Not anymore, you're not. I can see light in the east, so rise and shine, troops." It was Orrin's voice, followed by a dozen groans.

Jeremy shrugged and smiled. "He'll come in a second with the key."

"He better hurry," Hark said. The fury he felt at finding the chain had not subsided.

"Don't take it personally," Jeremy said.

"How else am I supposed to take finding myself chained like a damned animal?"

"Symbolically," Jeremy said. "Now we're chain·gang partners. Friends? Think, man, of the historical significance. Convicts. Chained ankle cuffs."

"They use brain buzzers back where I come from," Hark said scowling.

"Be thankful the Penitents were successful in having them removed and banned, or you might have a real reason to be angry."

Orrin lifted the net flap and slipped into the tent. "Well, now that you two woke the whole camp, see what you can do about feeding us," he said lightly. He took a key out of his pocket and unsnapped the cuff on Hark's foot. Hark jerked his foot away. Orrin looked surprised. "What's your problem?"

"I don't like being chained," he said angrily.

"You're not supposed to like it," Orrin said. "You're just supposed to get used to it. And you'd better do so quickly. It's probably how you'll spend the day."

"You just try to put one of those things on me again," Hark said clenching his fists to threaten Orrin. Suddenly Orrin leaped across the tent pinning Hark's fists up against his throat. Hark felt the cuff snap shut again against his ankle, then Orrin let him up again and backed out of the tent, easily ducking a wild swing.

"You shouldn't have threatened him," Jeremy said with a sigh. "Now we really will be chain gang partners." Hark whirled on Jeremy, but Jeremy was too fast. He grabbed Hark's fists and held them. "Easy, friend. I don't like it any more than you do. If it's a fight you want all day, just remember I'm faster and stronger, and you're going to be bottom man every time."

Hark struggled against Jeremy's grip for a moment, realized it was useless. He relaxed and Jeremy let go. "Tell me, doctor, how long does it take to get back into shape after years of inactivity?" Hark said.

"For someone like you," Jeremy said looking at him critically, "I should think you could do it in six weeks. Do you have six weeks?" Hark sat glumly thinking of Captain Dace and Rene. "I thought not. Well then, let's stick with realities, shall we? First we learn to walk like friends, arm in arm until you get the rhythm."

It was the most humiliating experience Hark had known. He had never felt such a lack of control, for it was somehow worse than he imagined to have to learn how to live with the chain so it didn't hurt him. When his frustration overtook him, any resistance hurt Jeremy. It seemed to him that "sorry" or "damn" accounted for every other word he spoke. He was sullen and uncooperative when Orrin tried to go over the list of wreckage bits, but fear and worry overcame his anger for a while. Finally he actually looked at the wreckage. The searchers had placed everything in a pile, and Hark and Jeremy worked most of the day laying things out in a spatial order that vaguely resembled the lander. A shard of metal from the fuselage, a knob from the hatch, tumblers, shattered ceramic, plastic, but no jelly beans. Whole seats and parachutes, which made him surmise his crewmates had ejected when they hit the trees and risked that the chutes wouldn't have time to open rather than stay in the lander. Captain Dace's chute didn't open, but Rene's did. Apparently the wind caught it and carried her into the soda lake.

"That's how she got burned," Jeremy told him. "We found her by the edge of the lake and your captain up by the trees."

"How hot is it?"

"Less than one degree Cee below boiling. Water birds and lizards get fooled all the time. There are always bodies along the shore. She must not have been too far from shore or she would never have gotten out at all."

Hark stared at the placid lake, surface shimmering with a deceptively inviting look. Only the white coating of dried minerals on the rocks by the shore gave any hint of the danger. Even if Rene had seen it, she wouldn't have had enough control to fight the wind of a storm.

"You're called Hark, aren't you?"

Hark whirled to find Mother Phastia standing with a bit of wire in her hands. She must have been working on her hands and knees behind the shrubs only a few meters away, unnoticed.

"Yes, my name is Hark," He said. "Tom Hark." He took the wire from her and tossed it into the pile of unidentifiable and inconsequential items.

"Hark is an uncommon name," she said.

"It's my family name. It met the Pilot Guild's requirement for a unique name. I preferred it to choosing one from a list of unused names."

"Something trivial like a unique identity is possible only if there is something as efficient as an AI to keep track of names for you." She smiled that icy smile of hers. "Is yours a family of faith?"

"You mean religious faith?" Of course she did. "Some of us are."

"You?" she pressed.

Hark shrugged, afraid to answer because he couldn't understand why she wanted to know. He was sure he'd been right not to be frank when he realized Jeremy moved to the end of the chain and put considerable pressure against it.

Mother Phastia noticed the taut chain and glared at Jeremy. "Perhaps like Jeremy you believe that persecution of science is a perversion of religion," she said. "He has been in need of purification for years, haven't you, Jeremy?" She looked back at Hark. "The purification will take place in just a few days so that a good Penitent woman can marry him."

Jeremy scowled, but said nothing.

"If he were Penitent, too, the purification would be unnecessary. Let it be a warning to you, Pilot Hark, to keep your feet on the right path." With that, she turned and walked away.

"What was that all about?" Hark asked.

"It was a threat."

"Of what? Purification? I'm not getting married."

"A married man must be purified because his seed isn't consecrated. But unmarried men undergo purification, too, as a sacrament."

"Not castration," Hark said, alarmed.

Jeremy shook his head. "Not that drastic, though it often might just as well be. It's a simple surgical procedure that prevents conception."

"You're going to undergo this procedure that might just as well be castration and you're not worried?" Hark said, staring at him in amazement.

Jeremy smiled easily. "It doesn't affect a man's capabilities for sex. Unfortunately, a lot of men don't really understand that and even though there's no reason for it, they become impotent. I'm a doctor and I know better. I won't have any difficulty."

Momentarily Hark was stunned. "It's barbaric," he finally said. "There are perfectly good contraceptive means."

"None of which are as effective," Jeremy said. He looked at Hark seriously. "You've never had to worry about that, have you?"

Hark shook his head.

"She knew that contemplating purification would frighten you."

"Why should I contemplate purification? It's you who's getting married."

"Purification is a decision your guardian makes for you. Clerics often recommend it to guardians. Or consider, too, that she might be your guardian herself. In that case, you'd want to be especially cooperative."

Hark stared, shocked at the prospect. It was a long time before he could concentrate on sorting wreckage.

It was almost night and two of the clerics wordlessly carried a full wing flap to the pile of unsorted wreckage. They didn't even look at Hark, as they had earlier in the day when they found something less recognizable. They just put the flap down on the pile and started back to their camp. They looked exhausted.

"We might as well go, too," Jeremy said. "We can start the stew."

"Yes," Hark said. He felt disheartened by the wreckage, was almost sure they would never find the jelly bean jar intact. Yet the altimeter was on the ground designated for the control board. The face wasn't cracked and it registered, accurately, Jeremy told him, one hundred and two meters above sea-level when he corrected for local.

"It will have a balloon antenna, too, won't it?" Jeremy asked. Hark just stared at him. "Well, if they do find that, I wouldn't tell them what it is, if I were you. Or is it already here?" He had picked idly at some of the unsorted pieces.

"It's completely crushed, useless," Hark finally said.

"Still, don't tell them," Jeremy said, his voice low and conspiratorial. "I don't think Orrin has mentioned it to Dame Adione yet." He had smiled disarmingly at Hark. "And for some reason he hasn't yet figured out that another radio might work just as well. Probably because you said it was extremely high frequency, which I don't believe we have. But it may eventually occur to him that something might be jury-rigged. Is there another lander you can call down if you can talk to the orbiter?

Hark slowly shook his head. "I have to download the one back in Fox from the orbiter to get off this planet. Is there a movable dish antenna in Fox?" He already knew there was a radio tower.

"I don't believe it moves, and anyway, it's on abbey grounds where men aren't permitted without escort. You wouldn't get near it without being caught by their nature boys. If anyone has one, it's the Selenians."

"Great," Hark had said. "That's just great. I can't even move a meter away from you." With a vengeance, he had returned to picking through the wreckage, but not before knocking Jeremy off his feet again and having to say, miserably, sincerely, "Damn sorry."

Back in camp he fed twigs and dry grass to the fire while Jeremy put food from the packs into the boiling pot. The aroma of the stew was pleasant and reminded him of how hungry he was. But Jeremy didn't pronounce it ready until the sun had set completely and the last of the troopers straggled in from the far reaches of the valley. Then he ladled the stew onto their plates, as well as some for Hark and himself. As she had the previous night, Dame Adione ate with the clerics at their fire.

The troopers were more talkative tonight, asked Hark his opinion about their chances of finding the jelly bean canister intact. He answered them as truthfully as he had himself earlier in the day, told them that it was unlikely, yet, with the altimeter as proof, it was still possible.

"If a windship had fallen from that high, there'd be nothing left to find," the one called Haron said. "Are you really from the Homeworlds?"

"Yes."

"They weren't all destroyed in the wars?"

"Not all the Homeworlds. Many took a long time to recover."

"Yours?"

Hark shook his head. "Mine wasn't so bad."

"Ours?"

"Islands is ours now, fool!" an older man, Calif, said.

The troopers fell to a complete silence when Dame Adione returned to the campfire. "A bonus to the man who finds the brain jewels tomorrow," she said. She looked troubled. "And Orrin, I want the watch doubled tonight."

"What's wrong?" Orrin asked, sitting up straight to look at her.

She shrugged. "One of the clerics claims she saw someone watching her. It may only have been the reflection from a piece of wreckage."

"I'll see to it," Orrin said.

Nodding, she looked at Hark. "Orrin, are those chains necessary?"

Hark swallowed the last morsel of food from his plate and sat stiffly, wanting to answer for Orrin but not daring to for fear he would anger the man again.

"Take them off," she added before Orrin reply.

The big man took the key out of his pocket and tossed it to Jeremy. Jeremy unlocked the ankle cuffs, gave Hark a friendly slap on his calf, reward for keeping quiet this time, Hark believed.

Dame Adione was leaning against a rock, staring up at cloud-covered Hells Gates. "Looks like it's already raining up in Fox. Hope we get some here. I don't think it's rained down here since the night of the crash."

"You mean the night of the attack?" Hark said.

"Yes," she said easily. She had pulled out her binoculars and was looking at the rising moons. "Here," she said, passing them to Hark. "Take a look at the one on the right."

Hark took the heavy binoculars and looked up at the moon. The light-gathering was sufficiently strong to make him wince. He focused on the limb of the moon and saw a mountain of billowing smoke, an erupting volcano. He took his eyes away from the binoculars and sought out the moon. He could tell it from the others now, easily distinguished by a dark smudge trailing from the limb to the center. "That could happen here," Hark said quietly, and he looked up at the clouds that hid the summit of Fox Volcano's Hells Gates.

She took the binoculars back from him. "That's an explosion, like Hound. We only get lava flows."

"That must cause a great deal of destruction, too," Hark said.

"It does," she said standing up. "But nothing can prevent them, not even . . ." Her voice trailed off, and then she said to Hark, "See if you can find something besides plum wine in those packs and bring it to me."

She turned and went into her tent, expecting him to follow, of that Hark was sure. He looked at Orrin, who was staring at the tent, his jaw set. "I'm not going in there," Hark said remembering what he had seen the night before.

But Jeremy shoved him, causing a sharp pain under his ribs. "Have the good grace to refuse her in private," he whispered. "You don't want her abandoning you to Mother Phastia."

Grimacing, Hark followed Dame Adione into the tent, tried not to scowl when she smiled at him and said, "You've forgotten the wine."

"No," he said. "I don't need it for talking."

She shrugged and sat down on a huge round cushion. She crossed her legs and reached for the half-empty flagon of plum wine. She poured two glasses, balancing them carefully until the flagon was empty. Then she offered one to Hark.

Hark stared at her a moment, then took the wine and sat down next to her.

"How big is it?" she asked.

"What?" he said, startled.

"The AI," she replied. "How big is it?"

He moved his hands to show its size, an arm's length, width, and height.

"Good," she said, "then we can conceal it easily."

"Conceal it from whom?" And when she just smiled prettily at him, Hark took her to mean that she intended to keep the AI for herself. The possibility disturbed him greatly, and he frowned. "Even if my lander is made flightworthy again, I can't deliver it to you. You're not the rightful owner."

"The owners are dead," she said. "The Hound civil authority, right? It's dead. I will see that you get your shipmates in exchange for the AI."

"You'll permit us to leave?" he asked. This was the first good news he had heard since he'd landed on Islands.

She nodded and sipped the wine. "After you have delivered the AI, and if," she said thoughtfully, "you still want to leave."

Even though he knew turning an AI over to an individual meant violating Homeworlds' laws, Hark thought about it for a moment. Not only would he have to answer for it, but the Guild would too, first to the Board of Trade and then to the Homeworlds Council. Wars had been fought over AIs because of the power they could provide. Briefly though, very briefly, he wondered if he might be able to convince the Guild that it was the only way he could save Rene and Captain Dace. Surely they wouldn't fault him for that. But had he really tried to do anything different? No. And they would hold him accountable for having failed to try and throw him to the Council in hopes of keeping their license. Hark had no doubt that he would be convicted for a crime of power.

"I can't give you the AI. There's no clear-cut traceability from the Hound civil authority to the government in Fox, let alone to you. My crewmates are injured. In light of these events my job clearly is to take my captain and the engineer home, and then to report. Your AI will be replaced in good time by another mission, one equipped to determine who the rightful owners are. In proper hands, the AI can make life better for everyone on Islands . . . lava flow predictions, for instance."

She shrugged, unimpressed. "That's not the way it works, Hark. You cannot leave without my help. You can't even live until dawn, unless I wish it."

"I don't want to die," Hark said, wondering if a death threat was enough to convince the Guild he was helpless to do anything but agree to give her what she asked.

"Then give me the AI," she said.

"If you kill me, you have no hope of ever getting it. Rene is dying. My captain is paralyzed and cannot operate the lander. They'll send a well-equipped investigative team if no one returns," he said, then added, "perhaps even a military rescue force." But the threat didn't seem to alarm her and he shook his head. "The best thing you can do for Islands is to help me on my way. Make it possible for me to report your cooperation and assistance."

"You can train me to use the AI," she said, still refusing really to hear him. She put her hand on his thigh.

"I'm not a qualified trainer, just a pilot."

"A bit duty-bound," she said sounding slightly amused. "But I like that in a man, and in time I'm confident you'll realize your duty has changed."

"I don't think so," Hark said coldly. He had hoped when he followed her into the tent both of them could leave pride intact, but his patience was almost at its limit.

"I can be persuasive," she said, her voice far too easy and casual for the gravity of the situation. "I promise you won't regret it."

Was it her tone or the words that irritated him so much? The combination, he decided, because he recognized it as one he had tried himself on Captain Dace. Captain Dace had hesitated ever so slightly, then coolly and calmly asked him for the flight plan and proceeded to go over it with him in excruciating detail. Hark found no opportunity to pursue his original intent without looking foolish, and that was that. He would remain in control if, like Captain Dace had, he kept to business. "My duty on Islands is to take my captain and the engineer off the planet before it's too late."

Dame Adione laughed at him. "I can see I must be blunt," she said squeezing his leg. "I like you. I think you like me. I know you will enjoy what I have to offer."

"Are you trying to bribe me?" he asked.

She shrugged. "I'm promising you a good life," she said.

"With you, here on Islands."

"Now you understand," she said. "You wouldn't be just a pilot if you cooperate with me."

"I only understand I must take my crewmates away from Islands," Hark said, realizing he shouldn't have allowed himself to be distracted from his resolve to stick to business, not even for a moment.

"Islands has never had a husband-king before," she said. She kept smiling, no, it was something of a leer, and Hark found it disquieting no matter how much he tried to ignore it. He realized he could not handle this situation as Captain Dace had done; there was no way to make this woman feel foolish by refusing to be led into the conversation she desired; she had no special respect for him at risk. "Husband-king," he said flatly. "And you, I assume, would be wife-queen."

"Queen," she said. "There is no such title as wife-queen. But yes, I would be queen of Fox, then with the AI of all Islands."

"And guardian to your husband-king," he said without trying to conceal his disgust, "some double bond I can't begin to understand. Tell me, Dame Adione, would this be a marriage in name only? A legal hold over your AI operator and trainer? Or is your bed a part of the bargain?"

"You look virile enough to satisfy me," she said moving her hand up his thigh to his crotch. "I wouldn't mind giving you an opportunity to prove yourself."

Hark felt a perverse satisfaction that his body hadn't so much as twitched reflexively. He took a long drink of the wine. She was beautiful and thoroughly feminine, but her touch was sleazy. He took her hand in his and with the other, firmly put the glass in it. "It would look very bad in my report," he said.

"What report?" She grinned impishly as she poured the wine from his glass into hers. "You'll never make one, never want to make one." She set the empty glass down and reached over to touch him again.

"Bad for me if I did it voluntarily," he said pushing her away and standing up. "Bad for Islands if you force me. Madam, please understand, I *will* do my duty."

"I told you, I admire that in a man," she said in a tone

that Hark found maddening. "And I have time to convince you your duties are different than you now perceive them."

Hark shook his head. "You haven't a chance of that," he said, and immediately regretted his words. Her sudden look of fury startled him. Even though it passed almost as quickly as it came, he had seen it and it frightened him.

"Out," she said sullenly, belatedly, too, for he was halfway through the flap. Hark wished he had left her feeling confident. Somehow he knew she would have been less dangerous that way.

CHAPTER 9

Hark came out of Adione's tent looking grim. He stamped past the glowing embers of the fire straight out into the brush behind the camp, bringing Orrin to his feet in immediate pursuit. But before Orrin caught up, the spaceman stopped, stood head down with hands thrust in his pockets, as if realizing how his action looked to Orrin. Orrin slowed down but kept his hand on the hilt of his knife.

"Let's go back," he said to Hark.

The man nodded glumly, but he didn't move.

Orrin waited a moment. Then, unable to resist, he asked, "What happened?"

Hark turned his back to the camp to stare up at the moons. "She offered me the crown in exchange for the AI," he said.

"What?" Orrin said, certain he'd misunderstood.

"I could be her husband-king if I brought the AI to her and taught her to use it."

For a moment Orrin was too stunned to speak. He had never even considered that she might take a husband. "You misunderstood," he said weakly.

"Could she pull it off, Orrin?" he asked, as if he had not heard Orrin. "If I had agreed to help her, could she parlay the AI into a crown?"

"You're lying," Orrin said. "She would never marry, and she wouldn't commit treason." He gave Hark a rough shove to get him moving back to the campfire, and he followed closely, feeling angry, frightened, and sick.

Her tent was empty. Orrin looked at Jeremy expectantly and the young trooper begrudgingly gestured toward the pile of wreckage. Dame Adione stood with her arms folded over her chest, bathed in moonlight. Orrin walked slowly, keenly aware of the *crunch* of dry vegetation under his boots. Though her back was turned, she would know someone was approaching. Did she know his step as well as he knew hers?

She turned around. "What do you want?" she said.

Inconclusive. She hadn't spoken until she turned. "To help, if I can," he said.

She started to shake her head, but grew suddenly thoughtful. "Perhaps you can," she said. "Find out what his weakness is."

"I don't know what you mean."

"A lever of some sort to get his cooperation once we find the brain jewels."

"Considering his treatment, he's been most coopera-tive," Orrin said hesitantly. In her eyes, Hark was being treated well, for he'd not been jailed as a common invader of Fyxen territory would be.

"I'll put him in the garrison prison if I must to keep him out of Phastia's hands, but I don't think doing it would soften him any." She shook her head. "What does he want? What key do I use? Every man has a price, but it can't always be paid in gold. What's his?"

"I don't think he can be bought any more than I can," Orrin said.

Dame Adione frowned. "I find your defense of him annoying. I said he has a price. Every man does, even you."

"You think that I might say yes to your bed if you offered matrimony?" Orrin asked. It was a risky question, but one he felt compelled to ask.

"He told you," she said flatly.

"I didn't believe him until now," Orrin said simply. Dame Adione was ambitious, and he knew she meant to use Hark to her advantage. But he'd failed to predict that she might be tempted to usurp the throne. She was contemplating treason, and the knowledge chilled Orrin.

"And you're jealous," she said with a regretful sigh.

In all the years that he had known her, this was the first time she had alluded to knowing how Orrin felt about her. It made him acutely uncomfortable.

"Well," she said, "don't worry. He didn't accept. You can still have hope."

He loved her and longed for her, that was true, and he knew now she had known all along. She had accepted his stubborn refusals to sleep with her, and thus had been permitted to keep his pride, as well. It cost her little enough. But he was deeply troubled to realize she knew all these years and misunderstood his reasons for refusing her. He'd never considered matrimony, not Fyxen matrimony. That was not love and respect between equals. He realized the hope she offered him was empty.

"How will you use the AI?" he finally asked. And in response he got a look so strange he felt his heart leap with the hope that Hark had misunderstood after all.

"It can do almost anything, Orrin," she said eyes glittering. "Political strategy, battle plans. I will be queen of Islands."

"And me?" he asked, hope destroyed forever.

"You've been bottom man since I took Top in the troops, and I've always been satisfied with your work. I see no reason to change that. It would be quite a step up," she said.

But they'd never call him Top. He'd just be bottom man to a queen, and without the sexual rewards usually implied by the position. But he was too heartsick to protest. He just nodded.

"Talk to him, Orrin. See if you can learn his price," she said. "We have much to gain."

"Yes," he said, but was thinking that everything he had hoped for was lost. She never had any intention of helping Hark return to the Homeworlds. In her way, she was worse than Aethelmere. That left the clerics and doctors of Fox to provide assistance to Hark, and both prospects, he knew, were poor. He had to get Hark away from Fox safely before it was too late to do anything, and he couldn't arouse suspicions before he accomplished that. But he wasn't much good at pretending and she was looking at him oddly.

"You don't sound enthusiastic," she said.

"Sorry," he said. "I was just thinking that if he talked so freely to me that he might talk freely to Jeremy or the other troops. I think I should go back and restore his chains. Perhaps chain him to myself."

"All right," she said. "And keep the guard up all night. I think I'm beginning to agree with the clerics. We're being watched."

He looked around, trying to see what she had seen or heard.

"Have them keep special watch on the lake," she said. "Mother Phastia thinks it was an animal going to drink, but I saw something else at the water's edge."

The lake was a silvery pool, a slight hint of vapors hanging above it as the night air cooled. He saw no movement, but didn't doubt for a moment that Dame Adione had. She had sharp eyes. "I'll see to it," he said, and added, "Good night."

"He'll never make it alone," Jeremy said as soon as he heard Orrin's plan. "Seventy klicks of Black Desert patrolled by your own troops . . . not to mention how many klicks of walking through New Penance forest before he gets to the other desert, which he also has to cross." Jeremy shook his head. They were standing behind stunted brush a few meters from the camp, talking in whispers.

"I hadn't planned for him to make the journey alone," Orrin said.

"I don't like the idea of leaving Captain Dace and Rene," Hark said. "And what if they find the jelly beans tomorrow?"

"Without you, they're useless. They're not stupid enough to try flying it without a pilot."

"Captain Dace . . ."

"Yes, they'll be keenly interested in her, but it will be a long time before she can even begin to help them."

"You're going to take him yourself?" Jeremy said, sounding as if he were about to become belligerent.

"No, you are," Orrin said, heading off the younger man's anger.

Jeremy looked at him suspiciously. "You always said if I ran again, you'd drag me back."

"I know what I said," Orrin said irritably. "You want the wedding? Or do you want to try Selene? There's no telling what kind of welcome either of you'll get."

"I don't want the wedding," Jeremy said, but he wasn't smiling. "You've given up, haven't you? Why now? You always said running solved nothing. Why are you helping me to run now?"

"Not you so much as him," Orrin said gruffly.

"Ah," Jeremy said knowingly. "You've figured the bitch out. What did she do?"

Orrin saw Hark poke Jeremy with his elbow. He was surprised either of them felt they had some insight into the situation, but he didn't dwell on that now. "We've much to plan and this has already taken a hell of a long time for a piss," Orrin said roughly.

"I need to take a crap," Jeremy said, unbuckling his pants and squatting. "You come with us," he added quietly.

"I need to stay behind to look after the lander," Orrin said, "so it will still be in one piece when he's ready to fly."

"I can't leave them behind," Hark said again.

"Just for a while," Orrin said. "I'll have them ready for evacuation next Double Nocturne."

"Where?" Hark asked simply.

"By the river clearing," he said quickly, realizing he'd failed to give the man a rather essential piece of information. "You just pull that lander out of there before Double Nocturne and I give you my word they'll be ready."

"You can trust him," Jeremy said. "If he says he'll do it, he will."

"Yes, but . . ." Hark looked anguished, no doubt torn between escaping himself and deserting his friends. Finally he nodded. "All right. But if you're not at the clearing when I come, I'm going to the clinic," he said. "I'll do whatever I must to get them out."

"I'll have them at the clearing," Orrin said more firmly than he felt.

"Don't think I'll give up on them once I've got the lander, Orrin. I won't."

"I believe you," Orrin said wishing Hark weren't so determined. In truth he had no idea of how he would keep his promise. Jeremy had to know it, too. Orrin looked at him, feeling a terrible twinge of guilt when he saw the younger man gazing at him with such trust and admiration. "Are you sure you want to do it this way?" he asked him.

"I've always wanted to do it this way," Jeremy replied. "I just hoped when you finally agreed with me you would come, too."

"I can't, Jeremy."

"I know," he said simply.

Jeremy was standing up and buckling his pants. Orrin put a hand on his shoulder. "I don't deserve . . ."

"There's something you should know," Jeremy said.

"What's that?"

"I won't be stopping at Selene. I'm going with Hark to the Homeworlds." He took out the transport token.

"You won't need to use that," Hark said. "The ride is free—in exchange for your help."

Jeremy looked at him, then took the chain from his neck and handed the transport token to Orrin.

"No. I can't . . ."

Jeremy jerked away. "When do you want us to leave?"

"An hour after second watch," Orrin said. "Hark will be chained to me for the night. Watch for us to go out into the bushes. When you're certain no one's noticed Hark and I didn't come back, come after us. I'll have the watch taken care of by then."

CHAPTER 10

Hark lay stiffly, ready to move since he heard the watch change. Orrin wouldn't let him speak, not even in a whisper, and the time dragged on forever. Once again he was uncomfortably hot, the ground too hard, and chained at the ankle, though this time it was to Orrin. Just when he was positive two hours had passed, not the single one specified, and that Orrin must have fallen asleep or had a change of heart about the escape, Orrin sat up and silently unlocked the ankle cuffs. He handed Hark his pack and reached into his own for his laser, which he buckled around his waist. Finally he gestured for Hark to follow him out the tentflap.

The camp was silent, lighted only by one small moon. The others had already set, and the last one, Hark could see, would set soon, too. Hark carried his pack under his arm so it wouldn't be too noticeable. They walked quietly into the brush behind the camp, completely unnoticed, except by the watch in the rocks above.

"Don't look at them," Orrin growled at him. "You're supposed to be taking a leak."

Hark nodded and did what he was supposed to be doing. Orrin, he noticed, had taken his laser out of his holster with his right hand. He was carrying the cuffs and chain in his left. He stood silently, waiting for Hark to finish.

"Stay right behind me," Orrin said, and he started walking up toward the rocks.

"First?" he heard one of the guards say softly when they were close to the rocks.

"Yes, it's me," Orrin said walking steadily.

One guard was standing machete in hand facing Orrin, the other a few meters away with his back turned, looking out over the valley. The closer man never had time to become alarmed. The other turned with a terrified look on his face when a bit of brush caught fire and he heard his fellow guard groan. But the laser beam caught him in the throat, too, and he crumpled quickly, silently.

Hark watched Orrin bend over to drag the closest guard behind the rocks, momentarily stupefied. He hadn't realized Orrin intended to kill the men until it was done. He had hit each in the throat, not as swift a kill as a laser belly shot, but quieter. Indeed, Hark was certain he heard the second man still sucking air from the hole in his throat; the sound and the smell of burned flesh made him ill.

"Take their weapons," Orrin said, gesturing for Hark to follow him as he dragged the second man behind the rocks.

Hark did as he was bade, realizing as he buckled the belt of sheathed weapons around his own waist, how much more serious his circumstances had become in these last few minutes. He would be not just an escapee, but one suspected of murder.

"How are you going to remain above suspicion?" Hark asked, looking at Orrin long and hard.

"Worried about me, Hark? Or about your friends?"

"It's one and the same, now, isn't it?" Hark asked coldly.

"Yes, and I'm glad you understand. Don't get caught, and I won't either." He looked back the way they had come. "That had better be Jeremy," he said, lifting the laser.

It was. He took one horrified look at the bodies and fixed the same look on Orrin.

"This time's for keeps," Orrin said simply. "There was no way to let them live and hope to live myself." He holstered the laser, unbuckled it, and handed it to Jeremy. "You must use it on me," Orrin said calmly, "so that they won't be suspicious when I don't give the alarm."

"I can't," Jeremy said. "It would kill you."

"An ear," Hark said, instantly understanding Orrin's plan. "Better than just tying him up and gagging him." But Jeremy was still aghast, so Hark took the laser from him. "Get some rope out of your pack," he said. Jeremy hesitated a second, then unshouldered his pack. The instant he looked away to open it, Orrin nodded and gritted his teeth. Hark took aim and burned Orrin's left ear away. The man groaned softly and sank to his knees in pain. Jeremy dropped down beside Orrin to look at the wound. "Stop thinking like a doctor," Hark said holstering the laser and handing it to Jeremy. He reached for the abandoned pack. "Start thinking like a fugitive. We still have to get away."

"He's right," Orrin said through what must be great pain. "Hurry with the ropes." The big man was gasping to prevent himself from crying out.

Hark found a stash of food inside Jeremy's pack, the rope underneath. He tossed the rope to Jeremy. "Tie him tight," Hark ordered. "Anything less and they'll know it's a sham."

When it was done, they shouldered the packs and walked swiftly away from the rocks. The last moon had not set, but it was hidden by a thin band of clouds on the horizon. The valley was dark.

Jeremy stayed close to the large rocks until they had

worked their way sufficiently far up the valley to take shelter in the trees. They were thin enough to walk between, thick enough to keep them from being seen from the camp below. Once again Hark was being pressed to move quickly, but this time he was having very little difficulty. Adrenalin, he realized, must be flowing copiously. Odd, though, for he felt calm at being in such desperate straits. He knew he would not, could not, have killed the two men as Orrin had done, even to save Captain Dace and Rene. Yet how quickly he had accepted the deed once it was done. He felt his heart accelerate alarmingly. *No thinking*, he said to himself. *Not yet*.

Passing through the narrow sentinel rocks at the head of the valley obviously alarmed Jeremy. He looked up, as if climbing over them might be better, but they overhung sharply. At last he drew Orrin's laser and started through. Hark followed close behind. Safe on the other side, Jeremy holstered the laser and leaned up against the rocks.

"From here we run through the clearing to the trees," Jeremy said, pointing. "There's no sign that they've found Orrin yet, but we're going to run anyhow. It's almost half a klick of exposure and the damn moon isn't quite down yet. You need to use that last patch?" Jeremy asked.

Hark shook his head. "Not yet."

"Good. I'll lead off. Don't follow too close until we get into the trees," Jeremy said.

Hark watched Jeremy run, a swift, crouched gait he was sure he couldn't duplicate, then he took off after him. Even without the crouch to hamper him, the distance between them increased. Something made a sharp noise ahead, an inhuman sound that could not have been Jeremy, and then there was a rhythmic clattering and a monstrous shadow bearing down on Hark. He froze, instantly understanding that it was an animal of some sort that Jeremy had disturbed, but he wasn't certain of whether to run or dodge. Before he could decide, another beast took shape just meters in front of the charging one's path. It shrieked, and the charging creature veered, and Hark started running again, sharply to the right to avoid the second beast. But even as he ran, he realized it was not a beast that had shrieked, and he looked at the place where he'd seen it. He was just close enough to make out her face in the faint moonlight and to realize the shadow that quickly cloaked the vision was her long mane of red hair. The lady of the lava lake dived behind some low rocks. Or was it really her? The beast that had started the commotion was just a dim shadow against the lighter grasses and in the other direction Jeremy was about to reach the trees. Hark didn't pause. He continued running for the trees.

"What was it?" Hark asked when he reached Jeremy.

"A goliath goat," Jeremy said. He was breathing heavily from the run. "How'd you know to shout?"

"I didn't," Hark said.

"Better keep a hold of those panic instincts," Jeremy said with a worried frown. "The noise did us no harm this time, but another reaction like that could get us killed."

"It wasn't me," Hark insisted.

"Have it your way," Jeremy said, sounding disgusted. "But just remember what I said, and stay close."

Hark watched him step off into the trees. He could make Jeremy believe him, he was sure, but what good it would do other than to convince Jeremy that he hadn't shouted in panic he didn't know. Even if it was the lady he'd seen in the caldera, and even if she were a Selenian, they might not find her. If they did, she might not be pleased about it. They were, as far as she knew, Fyxen troopers, and she was obviously a spy, or at least spying. Common sense told him to follow Jeremy, all the way to Selene, and not to try any shortcuts that might prove dangerous. He shifted the pack and started after Jeremy.

"Why the hell," Hark said after following Jeremy uphill for so long that the adrenalin was used up, "are we going uphill again?"

"There's a little camp up this way, isolated. We'll need

some desert garb before we continue. I can trade a few knives for what we need."

"We should go back down, stow away on a railcar to cross the desert. We can be in Fox in just a few hours. It shouldn't be too difficult."

"It isn't, but that's exactly what they'll expect us to do. They'll be watching the rail closely. We won't be anywhere near it. We're going to walk across."

"How long will that take?" Hark asked.

"In your condition, probably more than a week."

Hark reached out to grab Jeremy, as much to get his attention as to take a moment's rest. He shook his head when Jeremy stopped and put his hands on his hips while he took a few deep breaths. "Time . . ."

". . . will mean nothing if they catch us," Jeremy said seriously. "Listen to me Hark. I've run before, always on the rail, and Orrin has always caught me before I finished the crossing."

"He won't tell."

"Not willingly, he won't. I know that. But if Dame Adione has the slightest suspicion, she'll use drugs on him. He'll tell her what he knows, and that will merely reveal my methods of getting on railcars and staying there undetected. He doesn't realize I know about the sulphur bellies' route. There are enough wells for them to make it across the Black Desert in groups of five to ten. That's more than enough for the two of us."

"Sulphur bellies?"

"Big migrating browsers. They cross the Black Desert all the time."

"And what if we meet these big browsers?"

"We stay out of their way," Jeremy said. "Or use up every charge in the laser taking them down. You can't scare them the way you did the goliath goat."

"You really think we have a better chance walking? Even with me being so slow?"

Jeremy clasped Hark's arm in his hand, reassuringly. "We'll make it," he said.

By dawn they were well into the humid microclime of the rain forests of the upper slopes, following animal trails that Hark could barely detect. And just when he believed he was beginning to recognize broken greenery and disturbed leaf litter as trails and he stepped out from one of the little dells of sunlight they'd wandered through to follow it, Jeremy jerked him back.

"Fleckeri," he said pointing to where Hark wanted to walk. Hark stared into the shadowy track, saw nothing but some gelatinous-looking greenery. "Fleckeri," Jeremy said again, tossing a stick. The greenery convulsed around the stick and jerked it high into the air, like a length of rubber contracting from above. Only then did Hark realize that what he thought were plants growing up were really almost transparent tentacles hanging down. "It will spit that out in a minute, but it would have enjoyed a taste of you."

"It's an animal?" Hark said, amazed.

Jeremy nodded. "It has a knack for perching over trails," he said, "and then just letting its fingers hang down to wait for something to walk into them. This one's lost a few fingers, and I can see the bell up there on the branch. It's not a big one. We probably could have gotten you loose even without some alcohol to dehydrate the tentacles. The big ones have tentacles as long as ten meters, and sixteen fingers to a bell. If you tangle with a big one, you're a dead man."

The stick dropped to the ground, and the tentacle followed, shivering for a moment before blending once again with the surroundings.

"It doesn't look very substantial," Hark said, touching the knife hilt on his belt for reassurance.

"It doesn't strangle you to death," Jeremy said. "It anchors the victim with backward-curving spines, then absorbs the fluids. The spines are poisonous so that after a while the victim stops struggling and the fleckeri can enjoy its meal. If you get loose quickly enough, you get away with localized swelling and muscle spasms."

"Okay," Hark said. "You lead. I won't even be tempted to take a turn again."

"Good," Jeremy said, stepping off into the jungle opposite the fleckeri. "The rain forest doesn't know fair from unfair, and I'll consider you my chain gang friend as long as you have sense enough to do what I tell you to do. And until I explicitly tell you otherwise, it's *stay behind*."

"With pleasure," Hark said sincerely.

Within the hour, Jeremy holed them up under the spreading roots of a live tree whose nursetree had long since decayed away, leaving a hollow big enough for the two of them to stretch out. They ate dried food from Jeremy's pack in silence, and then Jeremy spread an oilcloth poncho from his pack.

"If I'm gone when you wake up, don't worry. I plan to slip into that stringer camp at mealtime to get some desert garb for the desert crossing. I might not get back until after dark."

"How will you be able to find me again?"

"Don't worry. I can."

"And if you never come back?"

"I'll be back," Jeremy said firmly as he lay down.

Hark wondered if he should offer the infrared scope in his pack to Jeremy, or even the ground guide, then decided against it. Jeremy had been moving around in this jungle since he was a child, and apparently already possessed whatever knowledge was necessary to do it successfully. He'd also been a trooper for some years, and knew how to do it stealthily, too. If he didn't come back, Hark would need every trick he had in his pack to do half as well.

He stretched out next to Jeremy on the oilcloth. The moist, acrid smell of the decaying leaf litter all around mingled with the pungent smell of the poncho. He heard insects buzzing, but they didn't disturb him, and nor did the pleasant, damp warmth of the living cave. In moments he fell asleep.

CHAPTER 11

They took Orrin to the treatment room where only days ago Jeremy had administered the truth drugs to Hark. And like the last time, Dame Barenia had come in to complain about the noise. This time, however, Dame Barenia didn't leave. She recognized the seriousness of Orrin's wound in a glance, and stayed to treat him. Her ministrations were so painful he just closed his eyes and clenched every muscle to keep from crying out. He hadn't noticed that Dame Cirila came in, too, not until Dame Barenia started bandaging the wound. Then he opened his eyes and found Jeremy's mother staring at him in wide-eyed horror. Her being a physician, too, he knew her intense aversion was not for his wound but for the story Dame Adione was telling of how it had been inflicted.

Dame Adione had come back with him to seek medical help, and some of the sorry sisters had followed them. No doubt they'd been disappointed to learn their destination was the maternity. Adione had been convinced that Hark and Jeremy had escaped together, but even Orrin's wound and two dead men had not thoroughly convinced Mother Phastia that everything was as it appeared. Two dead men! How cold he felt at the thought, as if he, too, were dead.

"And I suppose," Dame Barenia was saying to Dames Adione and Cirila, "that you'll want me to deliver all the bad news to Aethelmere." Her tone was pained, resigned, but she'd spoken as much in sympathy. Dame Cirila was plainly shaken by the news of her son's crimes.

"I doubt that you'll have to," Dame Adione replied. "One of those sorries headed straight for the abbey; I give her another minute before it's on the radio." She sounded pained and resigned, too, but Orrin was sure that was only because there was nothing she could do to prevent the announcement. Queen Aethelmere's love for the radio was well known; the abbey broadcasted its choicest tidbits on a schedule created for the queen's convenience. She would be awake now after her late afternoon nap and, as the gossips had it, begin primping for nightcourt, a ritual reputed to take her an hour or more because it was so involved. She listened to the radio while attendants offered an array of dress and jewels. Kind folk praised her for her dedicated use of time, for doing two things at once. But the kind folk would rationalize *anything*, including the queen's insatiable need to be amused and distracted. Orrin knew he was not alone in his contempt for Fox's regent. But he felt very much alone in his determination that she must not be succeeded by Dame Adione.

"Increase the volume," Dame Barenia said, and Orrin realized that there was a radio on the table and that it had been playing softly all the time.

It was Dame Cirila who stepped over and pushed the lever. Her hand was trembling.

"No cakes for a penny; only lard . . ."

They listened to the wares list for a while, the women seemingly preoccupied with the bandaging procedure. Orrin sat stiffly, relieved to feel the bandage going on but unable to relax. He'd been the subject of Dame Adione's narrative, yet not once did she ask him to relate any part of the tale, nor did the other two women ask him to clarify some detail. It was for the best, he knew. They were conditioned to believe her and Dame Cirila had good reason not to want to believe. But he felt angry at knowing they would not ask him to speak. He couldn't help but think of the number of times he'd seen this very kind of anger in Jeremy's face and that he'd ordered him to keep silent. Truth be known now, he'd felt the anger himself but always chose to deny it. How hard it was to do that again. *Just one more time,* he told himself.

"Murder! It's murder!" the voice from the radio said. "An unconsecrated man has murdered two others. Conceived in violence, never purified, what else could we expect? Jeremy, who walked among you as if he were a child of a consecrated impregnation, Jeremy, who resisted purification, has taken two lives and wrought injury on a third. Woebegone is Dame Cirila for having nurtured a viper as her own. Woe, Woe, Woe."

Dame Cirila's face paled, and Dame Barenia's hands faltered so that the bandage dropped onto the floor. Dame Adione scooped up the bandage, tossed it into the trash. She was grim, but virtually unaffected by Dame Cirila's pain. She was, he was certain, far too involved with her schemes, too busy calculating how this turn of events might be used to advantage.

"No salt at the station . . ."

Dame Adione reached over and lowered the volume. "No mention of the spaceman," she said sounding pleased. "I thought my losing him was what they couldn't wait to tell!"

"They don't talk about the spaceman's vessel in the park, either. It upsets Aethelmere," Dame Barenia said. "Nothing that Cirila or I say calms her; we've instituted a program of sedatives to restore her rest through the heat of the day." Dame Barenia shook her head. Orrin wasn't sure what she disapproved of: Queen Aethelmere being upset, the treatment, or the lander being in the park. Likely, all, he decided.

"Will she allow you to continue attending her, Cirila?" Dame Adione asked.

For a moment Dame Cirila looked at her blankly. "Who?" Then she shrugged and said, "I don't know. I was thinking about my son. What will happen to Jeremy?"

Finally Dame Adione seemed uncomfortable in Dame

Cirila's presence. She put her hands in the pockets of her tunic and leaned against the wall. "I'll have to turn him over to the abbey's court when we catch him."

"And they'll crucify him," Dame Cirila said hollowly. She looked at Orrin. "When he ran away before, you always found him."

"Yes, ma'am. But then he was not running from murder. He's also older now, more skilled in moving through the wilderness."

"We'll find him again," Dame Adione said confidently. "Probably before the day is done."

"You—maybe," Dame Cirila said to her. "But not him. Orrin will have to stay in the maternity. This burn will need treatment daily."

Orrin noticed that Dame Barenia deliberately held back some comment. Dame Adione noticed, too, and frowned. "He doesn't look so bad," she said. He was completely bandaged now, the wound hidden.

Dame Cirila stiffened and looked straight into Dame Adione's eyes. "I said he's staying."

"Look, I'm sorry about the boy. But keeping Orrin here isn't going to help."

Dame Cirila kept her gaze on Dame Adione. "You must realize, Adione, that they could just as easily have put you to shame. He was, after all, one of your troopers run amok."

"I didn't relax discipline with him," Dame Adione said harshly. "And I didn't bear him."

Dame Cirila did not flinch, but it wasn't hard to see that she was angry.

"Look, I'm going to find him anyway."

"Then you won't miss Orrin," Dame Cirila said.

"Let me remind you that you have a stake in finding the spaceman, too. Or do you want Homeworlds technology doled out by the abbey? You know that's what will happen, don't you, if the sorry sisters find him first?"

"I know that this man is too ill to leave. I know that a

spaceman out in the wilderness isn't worth the effort to find, not when I have two more tractable Homeworlders right here in the maternity.''

That caught Dame Adione by surprise, and whatever argument she was about to give remained unspoken. Her tone changed. Dame Cirila was offering her alternatives she hadn't considered before. ''Then the Homeworlders are not dying?''

''The captain will live,'' Dame Cirila replied. ''Barenia got the pneumonia under control.''

Dame Adione looked at the doctor. ''The spaceman's drugs worked?''

Dame Barenia nodded.

For a moment Dame Adione stood silently. Finally she turned to Orrin. ''Perhaps it's just as well that you stay in the maternity, Orrin. I had wanted you to organize the search for the spaceman and Jeremy from the garrison while I returned to the crash site to keep watch over what the sorry sisters are doing there. But if you were with the Homeworlds captain, that would serve me well, too.''

''As you wish,'' he said. Truly, he couldn't have done a good job on the search. But he was keenly aware she was giving him a new responsibility. He'd not be left for long to his own devices on how to carry it out for her. But she trusted him enough to begin on his own. He had to steel himself from cursing at her arrogance. Only yesterday he'd fawned in her trust in him. Today it disgusted him to remember. Suddenly he was exhausted, both emotionally and physically and wanted only to rest.

Orrin had dozed for a while, but the groans from the burned engineer awakened him. Dame Barenia came in and dosed her with sedatives, and she fell asleep again. The Homeworlds captain slept soundly through it all. She was covered with a gauze sheet, barely opaque enough to hide the dark of her nipples, damply molded to her thighs and the dark there, too. Oddly, it was her face that made Orrin

understand Hark's attraction to her. Even in sleep it was one
of a woman of strength: sharp cheekbones, prominent jaw,
mouth too wide to be voluptuous. Yet the overall effect of
such strong features was of finding himself wishing to hear
her speak, as if she could never say anything dull or cruel.

While Orrin waited for Captain Dace to awaken, he sat
by the window watching the rain wash over the boardwalks
below. Most Fyxen waited indoors for the rains to pass, but
there was one woman in the alley below whom the rain
didn't deter. She stood almost hidden in the shadow of an
eave on the building across the valley where blossoms
cascaded from a pot, and for a moment Orrin even thought
she'd just taken shelter from the rain right there. But then
the woman looked up at the maternity and saw Orrin staring
at her, and she spun on her heel and ducked around the
corner of the building. There was just enough light for Orrin
to notice her red hair.

It might not be her, the wench from Selene. Only
yesterday Orrin would have called out the entire garrison to
comb Fox if he'd seen what he just saw now. But today he
didn't want anyone wondering why the maternity would
interest the witch from Selene so much she would stand in
the rain to stare up at the windows in hopes of a telltale
glimpse. He was certain he already knew who she hoped to
see. It would be best if Adione did not.

CHAPTER 12

Jeremy knew he had made the right decision when they reached the Black Desert floor before the five moons had set and there was still no sign of their being followed. There probably was an intensive search going on between the valley and Fox, and precautionary ones along the rails. Unless Orrin had been found out, there was no reason for Dame Adione to believe Hark would try to go to Selene by any means. More likely she would double the guards around the lander and perhaps the maternity. She'd feel confident her precautions were adequate.

Mother Phastia, on the other hand, might worry that Hark had taken her veiled threat more seriously than she wanted, that she'd frightened Hark right out of her reach. Jeremy hoped she would lose a few knots in her hat as penance. The size of it was supposed to be symbolic of her performance of prayer, and surely she would know she'd performed poorly for this to happen.

Meanwhile, Jeremy and Hark could walk in the relative safety of night and the complete impartiality of the Black Desert. He'd already found the sulphur bellies' trail, plain as planking even in the feeble light of the little moon. The only worry he had was from the skies, for they would use windships to scout the near desert reaches. The breezes tonight were out of the south, not good for following the rail as they would wish, but coincidentally perfect for sweeping along the barrens at the foot of Mount Fox and right across the sulphur bellies' trail. But the windships would be easier for Hark and Jeremy to see before they were spotted by the occupants; they were draped in the drab nawick wool desert garb Jeremy had acquired from the stringer camp, which allowed them to blend in with the rough lava.

"At least we're not going up or down anymore," Hark said. "But damn, I feel as if my feet are burning."

"In the daytime, if you were careless about where you placed a bare hand, you would get burned," Jeremy said. "It's that hot."

"It's hard to believe it can get any hotter than it already is." And with that, Hark paused to drink from his canteen, which he held in his hand even while walking. Since there was no danger on this leg of the trip that they wouldn't reach the first waterhole before dawn, Jeremy encouraged him to drink whenever he felt the need. "We gonna stop soon, Jeremy?" Hark drank again and capped the canteen.

"Yes, soon," Jeremy said. He believed that Hark liked to think the long break for day was not far off, that the man was working his fatigued muscles on the just-one-more-step theory. The pace was pathetically slow, but he didn't stop unless Jeremy did.

Jeremy stepped around another heap of sulphur belly dung, the third pile he'd seen, all dry and desiccated. That was another worry that seemed to be turning out well; they were unlikely to catch up with the sulphur bellies that had dropped them.

"Is that stuff what I think it is?" Hark asked, stepping around the dung heap as carefully as Jeremy.

"If your nose is working at all, you've probably figured it out correctly."

"Just how big are these creatures?" Hark asked.

"As you've probably guessed by the size of the dung, they're big. As big as . . ." He tried to think of something to which Hark could compare. "Well, *almost* as big as your lander."

"Whew. I guess we're not likely to step on one's tail, like you did the goliath goat."

He hadn't stepped on the goliath goat's tail, and sulphur bellies didn't have any, but he sensed that anatomy was not what Hark was really interested in. "No," he said. "We won't get surprised by one. We'll see them coming a long way off, and we'll get well out of the way."

"And they won't come after us?"

"Not if we stay off the trail. They're very protective about their trail. Rarely stray more than a few meters from it. You'll see that in places it's more like a tunnel, it's been worn down so deep. In the rain forests there are lots of intersections. Browsing quads, they're called, but they even stay close to the trail to eat. That's why they're migratory. They have to keep on the move to get enough. I've heard that the New Penitents have had to elevate their rails over the trails, the beasts are that stubborn about staying on them. We'll have a chance to see if that's true."

"Does that mean you do plan to use the rail once we get across the Black Desert?"

"I haven't decided yet. It may be worth chancing once we're out of Fyxen domaine, but let's wait to see."

Again Hark paused to drink.

He'd run out of water and started using Jeremy's only a half-hour before they reached the first well. There was a trough made by sulphur bellies' passings down into the depression in the rocks where the water collected from a steadily dribbling spring. The pool was shallow and warm despite the subterranean source, but it was cooler than what Jeremy knew they would encounter later on. They filled their canteens, bathed, ate, and bathed again just as the first sunlight touched the Black Desert. Jeremy showed Hark how to wet the desert nawick and wrap himself, and to fill his boots with water, too, before stepping back in to them. Then they creeped off to the side of the pool, well away from the trough, and lay under a slag of lava that would protect them from the sunlight until past noon. Then they would have to find another spot, but that was all right. There was a plentiful selection of grotesque lava ropes coiled and heaped in every direction, some of which were sure to be casting useful shadows when they wanted them. This day wouldn't be too bad with the pool nearby to rewet the nawick.

By noon they had rewet the nawicks a dozen times to provide some relief from the heat of the red-black rocks, but even that permitted only snatches of sleep. Water dropped on exposed rock vaporized and their hands and faces were becoming sunburned just in the time it took to go from the rock shelter to the pool and back. Jeremy applied ointments to minimize the burns.

The other pools and springs along the sulphur bellies' trail were not as pleasant as the first, some too hot even to bathe in except just before dawn. They felt considerable satisfaction, however, in noting each day that Mount Fox was growing smaller behind them, but the Teton peaks stayed stubbornly small. It was, Jeremy knew, because they were much taller and wider, but at last on the sixth day the massif became more apparent. On the eighth they passed the day in a wooded oasis among both charred and living trunks. They had walked to it in daylight, protected from the morning sun by shadow from the massif. The spring was a cool one and they were almost reluctant to leave it when night finally fell. They wet down their nawicks at the last possible moment to minimize evaporation of their bodies' moisture, at least for a while, then started on what Jeremy believed was the very last leg of their journey.

Hark seemed to sense that success was at hand, for he was more bouyant than he had been for days.

"How long would it have taken you to make this crossing if you'd been alone?" he asked.

"Probably only half the time. We're not even making ten klicks a day . . . a night, I mean."

"Well, I'm glad it's over. I think the heat has finally snapped something in my mind. I keep thinking I hear running water."

Jeremy smiled. "You are hearing running water, Hark. There's a river up ahead. We're even closer than I'd realized."

"A river in the middle of this miserable desert?"

"No longer the middle. All the volcanos have rivers that carry runoff from the high slopes to the sea. This one runs through the Blackland barrens around half the massif's circumference."

It was a shallow river, easily forded, but murky. They didn't care; it was the coolest water yet and they lingered longer than was necessary by eating a meal earlier than usual. A few nightbucks wandered down, oblivious to them until Hark saw them and pointed, then they bounded away, setting up a great splashing until they cleared the river. Insects swarmed noisily along the trail, then were gone and they walked in what seemed a cone of silence. Occasionally they saw light-colored sedimentary rocks poking up through the lava, ghostly in the moonlight. It was while walking over one of these that Jeremy slipped, failed to recover, and pitched over a sharp ledge to land only a few meters below on another outcropping. He knew without looking that his leg was broken.

"Jeremy, are you all right?" Hark asked worriedly from above.

"No, dammit. I'm not." He sat up and started to disentangle the nawick from around his legs, but doubled over in agony.

"Don't move," Hark said. "I'll be right down."

Hark seemed to know his first aid fairly well, needed only occasional direction from Jeremy. There was nothing in their packs to use as splints, so he immobilized the broken leg by padding and bracing it with clothing out of their packs, then taping it to his good leg.

"That will do until I can make a decent splint," Hark said, finally sitting back. "You want a painkiller?"

Jeremy nodded. He'd refused one earlier because he didn't realize Hark would prove so competent. The straightening and bracing had been excruciatingly painful, and now he felt worn out and tense.

Hark fetched out the vials from Jeremy's own pack, and Jeremy selected one. "Why did this have to happen now?"

he said to Hark putting the pill on his tongue. Hark shrugged and handed him the canteen.

"It could have been worse. It could have been your thigh. I don't think a thigh would stay in place with just a splint. But I think that lower leg will . . . don't you?"

Jeremy sighed. He didn't want to think about moving, but he knew he must. "You'll have to find something for the splints, straight saplings or slim branches. And bigger ones for crutches."

Hark nodded. "There were a few trees back by the river," he said.

Jeremy shook his head. "I think it will be closer for you to go on. The savannah can't be far now, and there will be some trees there. Just keep heading up. The higher you go, the more moisture, the more growing things."

"Right." Hark stood up, looking around.

"The sooner you go, the sooner you get back."

"Yes, I know. But you'll catch the afternoon sun here. I'll look around for a better place."

He was gone for almost half an hour, and Jeremy was asleep by the time he came back. The painkiller was working well.

"There's not much better shelter than right here," Hark said, looking resigned. "I'm going to rig some shade with my nawick."

"You'll need it," Jeremy protested. "It's almost dawn already."

"My dress uniform covers almost as much, and the color won't matter so much around here. We haven't seen anything but a few logging windships, and you said those belonged to New Penance. No signs of Fyxen. Small risk."

Boundary-wise, they were already in New Penance territory. More practically speaking, it was no one's land. He wouldn't feel safe from the Fyxen until they were deep in the New Penitents' rain forests where the territorial claim was strong. That would have been tomorrow night, no further away then the night after that, but for this broken leg. Now it was Jeremy who was going to slow the pace.

Jeremy watched Hark rig the shelter. He draped the jungle green oilcloth over the rock and Jeremy, fixing it top and bottom with big rocks. On top, he put his own nawick so that it could not be seen easily. Then he carefully arranged Jeremy's pack and supplies so that they were in easy reach.

"You'll need to take the machete and the laser," Jeremy said.

"The machete, yes. The laser, no. You're more vulnerable than I am."

"And you're more likely than me to run into trouble."

"No," Hark said again. He was pulling off the short trooper fatigues he'd been wearing under the nawick all through the desert, putting on a close-cut light blue uniform. "You're right next to the sulphur bellies' trail here. If any of them come along . . ."

"I'm a dead man anyway if they spot me. I couldn't get more than one down with a fully charged laser. Ours is down a few blasts already. But it will be very effective if you meet any stragglers. New Penance taboos about lasers in the wilderness are even stronger than Fyxen prohibitions. They'll probably run at the sight of it."

"What or who are stragglers?"

"Forest dwellers, ticket-of-leave men who were emancipated back in convict times. They have patronesses in the cities, but in the wilderness on their own they're reputed to be extremely unfriendly. I don't know much about them except hearsay. We don't have many on Mount Fox any longer. They're supposed to be especially mean to Fyxen because they were driven off Mount Fox to the Teton Range when our forests were cut down to make room for the plantations."

Hark was dressed now and, at last, he reached for the laser and strapped it on. He looked at Jeremy as if to say, *anything else?* Jeremy shook his head, reached up to meet Hark's hand with his own. The clasping was firm, unshakable. "Don't spare those pain pills," he said as his parting advice. "I have plenty of my brand, too."

And Jeremy knew he'd probably dig into Hark's supply before this was over. Hobbling on crutches deep into New Penance territory to flag down a railcar was going to be a long and painful journey. But all he said was, "Be careful," and then Hark was gone. Jeremy's bivouac was facing the wrong way to watch him walk away. There was nothing to do now but endure the pain as best he could and sleep whenever possible.

Hark had been gone for a day, a night, and part of another day when Jeremy heard the dragon hiss. He thought it was another nightmare; he'd had more than his share while taking the painkillers. It took him a few minutes to realize he was wide awake and that this was no dream. The hiss was the sound of a windship furnace releasing hot air into the envelope, low enough and close enough to hear plainly. He listened, trying to hear voices. He didn't dare look out, prayed they hadn't seen his shelter. *Not now*, he thought in anguish. *Not after having come so far without so much as seeing a Fyxen windship.*

Not one. But they had seen a few loggers, and those were not piloted by Fyxen. Perhaps he was becoming alarmed for nothing. Loggers on their way home would just fly right over. Even if they'd seen him and landed, they were more likely to provide aid than do harm to an unfortunate traveler. Well, they weren't flying over, that was for sure. The hissing was getting louder, lower and closer. They were landing. He could just reach the edge of the oilcloth with his fingertips, and when he moved it a trifle he realized that the nawick covering had fallen. Now he was certain he had been spotted, but if it was a logging windship, maybe it was just as well. They could wait for Hark and carry them both to their lumbercamp in the windship. They'd have proper first aid there, and probably could arrange transportation to Selene. Yes, maybe it was a good thing the nawick had fallen. Carefully, he sat up and scooted himself closer to the oilcloth, then sat gritting his teeth from the pain in his leg. He was due for another pill, but time enough for that. He looked out the flap.

* * *

Hark saw the windship coming out of the south as he was leaving the savannah on his way back to Jeremy. He had fitted the splint materials in his pack, but the sturdy branches he'd cut for crutches he balanced on his shoulder and steadied with his hand. It meant stopping and opening his pack frequently to take out the groundguide and the field glasses to check the windship's progress. It was apparent it would reach Jeremy long before he did, and now he could tell it was losing altitude rapidly, deliberately. Hark stared through the glasses. The balloon was black, the logging windships they'd seen were all red. A different company of loggers? Or was that a Fyxen craft? He started to put away the field glasses so he could hurry on when he realized he would lose his vantage if he did. Impatiently, he sat in the low dry grass at the edge of the savannah and watched the windship maneuver.

There was no doubt in his mind that they had a perfect fix on Jeremy. They were angling in to the very spot he'd so carefully noted on the groundguide, the gentle morning breeze cooperating perfectly. Two of the crew leaped out and disappeared behind the sedimentary rock outcroppings, leaving several others behind to handle the sagging envelope of hot air. They had it landed and completely under control in just minutes, and it even looked to him as if they were preparing to stow the envelope. That meant, he thought, that it probably was a Fyxen windship, and that it was stopping there at least until the breeze reversed itself. A logger would have been delighted with the direction of the wind. Now he waited only until he was certain they were down to stay. When he saw them pack the flaccid envelope, he put away the field glasses and groundguide, hefted the crutch-saplings and hurried on. They might have found Jeremy, but there was still time to rescue him and a laser to do it with.

The downhill put awful pressure on his knees, but he paid no heed. He hurried on for the better part of an hour before he reached another vantage point from where he might be able to see what was going on. He took out the field glasses again, knowing where to look even without the ground-guide.

The sedimentary rocks were empty, no basket, no balloon, no people. Frantically he searched with the glasses, found them walking single file bearing a stretcher, the collapsed basket, and the flaccid balloon among them. All were wearing the jungle green fatigues of Fyxen troopers, and they were walking south toward the rail. Fear crept over him. He knew they would reach the rail before he could, even if he turned and went on a diagonal to cut down the angle. If there were a railcar waiting, and if they left immediately . . .

He jammed the glasses back in the pack, dropped the crutch logs and started running. He could stop them at the rail just as easily as at the rock, if only the railcar wasn't there to meet them. Did they carry radios? *Talkies* he remembered. Even if it were capable of summoning a railcar from Fox, it would take hours for it to get across the Black Desert.

He had to cross a gorge a little tributary river had carved out of foamy lava. Even though it was shallow, it cost him time, time he wasn't sure he had. He passed two possible vantages before the groundguide told him he was close enough that he had better check to see what was going on. He scrambled to the top of an outcropping rock and looked out over the desert.

The rail gleamed like a ribbon of silver on the red-black lava rock, laced with planking. He could see it clearly for klicks in both directions with his naked eyes, nothing but the rail to see, no people, no stretcher, no railcar. He took out the field glasses. If the Fyxen troopers were out there, they might see the glint of the setting sun off the glasses, but he was already pretty sure they were gone. He looked, but saw nothing anywhere along the track.

During the night, while the five moons were still up, Hark climbed back up to the vantage point and scanned the track again and again. A railcar came out of the east, bound for Fox. He watched it until it was a speck. In the morning, another came out of the desert, bound for New Penance and perhaps Selene. Normal traffic, he realized. Jeremy was probably already back in Fox. Even so, he wasn't completely satisfied that all was lost until he went down the rail and walked alongside for a few klicks. He found a wad of discarded adhesive tape and Jeremy's empty vial of pills. It was enough to confirm what he'd already known since last night. Jeremy had been captured.

Dispirited, Hark pocketed the vial and looked up the eastern stretch of track. New Penance lay somewhere alongside in the high forest reaches of the massif where rainclouds were already beginning to gather. Beyond, completely cut off from view was Mount Selene, the city of Selene, and with luck, a radio with a movable dish antenna. He started walking.

CHAPTER 13

The going was slow through the lichen-covered heath. The slope was so steep that even the big browsers that favored the good pasture of the open forest were not around, only scurries and birds, and those were mostly heard, not seen. But the spongy ground that sustained the fine grasses and herbs were just right for losing the impression of Sellia's bootprints. And she knew from experience that the time she was taking to hide her passing was less than she would lose in a fight with the jungle rounders that were trailing her.

Sellia hurried through beds of moss and liverwort, ducked to avoid disturbing the lichen drooping from the gnarled heather trees. The sun had passed its zenith and sometimes she could see far down slope to the rain forest where mists had formed and were already creeping up the mountainside. Sellia couldn't help thinking of the food in her pack and feeling tempted to stop behind a fringed curtain of lichen to eat. She'd stashed her speeder just after sunrise, certain she was being watched and surely would be ambushed if she stayed on the rail. She went deep into the forest leaving logger ribbons on heath trees, which she hoped would outrage the rounders. They were sure to take the time to collect the ribbons for their complicated coup collections. She'd placed them high with an airgun to cost them as much time as possible.

Eventually she circled back toward the rail, leap-frogging a section to bring her close to another speeder stash klicks away from where she'd left the first. It had taken a great deal of time and a rest stop was past due. But jungle rounders had surprised many a careless traveler at just such a moment. Best, she decided, to be certain they were still following the ghost spore she had left them. If they had guessed her strategy, they would have to use the rail to cross the ravine to get to the next speeder stash. When they did, they would be easy to see. She unshouldered her pack, shoved it under some rocks, then dropped down slope and pushed through a stand of young sedge that stood between her and the rail-run.

Sellia crawled the last ten meters on her belly through a clump of dead, rotting stems, grateful that she'd chosen heavy breeches and tunic of skins for the journey and that she had packed the lightweight wovens. The skins resisted the oozing dampness of the dead spiky leaves and insulated her breasts from hard stones underneath. She took a moment to be certain all her blond hair was tucked under the brown and green cap, then crawled the last meters that gave her full view of the rail-run and the trestle.

The trestlework latticed the fifty-meter-wide swath

cleared through heath and sedge forests, curved around the hip of the massif and climbed over a ravine to heath from where she'd come. Over the single rail suspended between the trestles, fat domed cars hissed on endless schedules between the Islands in the Clouds, trestlework lifting them over browsing quads so that the more stubborn species could not interfere with schedules. But they were not impervious to the savage jungle rounders' cunning. Regular patrols by the abbey's militias deterred the more persistent rounders from annoying the passengers, but they were not much help to travelers in exposed speeders or on foot.

There were no cars passing now, though she had heard two since leaving the rail-run earlier. But on the curve of the trestle she could see the first of the rounders silhouetted above the horizon, creeping around the bend. As soon as they had a clear view of the klicks of track and did not see her on it nor in the rail car, Sellia hoped they would retreat.

While Sellia watched, the rounders—three of them visible now—left the smooth walkway of the rail before completing the curve to climb down the ladder affixed to the top of the trestle and, not having access to the controls that would extend the ladder to the ground, slid down their own rope, pulled it down after them, and melted into the shadows of the trestlework. Looking down the rail-run to the east, Sellia saw why the rounders had hidden.

A man, dressed in light city-dandy colors and carrying a bright red pack, strolled along the rail between trestles as if he were in Fox Gardens. Sellia was surprised. He hadn't been on the trestlework when she first looked, which meant he must have climbed up just since she focused her attention on the rounders. She couldn't imagine why a dandy would be walking the rail through the wilderness, nor how—if there were reason for his mistress or mother to let him—he had gotten so far from Fox. The poor daredevil was walking straight toward the rounders. Even if that were a laser she saw on his hip, the cunning of the rounders was more effective than abbey weapons in the wilderness.

Just as she decided the dandy was doomed, the man

stopped his jaunty gait midstep. He turned and fled back to the trestle behind him, scrambled down the ladder, and jumped to the ground. Something had alerted him, perhaps a moving shadow or a careless noise. Then Sellia heard the distant hiss of a railcar, still faint but audible now. The daredevil must have felt the vibrations in his feet and had taken to the ground, not to avoid the rounders, but to avoid being run over by a railcar.

The rounders mistook the dandy's flight as a sighting of themselves and the three were running under the trestles to catch him, just blurs of brown on the mottled green of the rail-run. Finally the dandy saw them and turned in a dead run for the illusive safety of the sedge forest.

The rounders turned swiftly to cut down the angle of the dandy's retreat, and in so turning they were bearing straight down on Sellia. There was no longer the luxury of lying quietly in the sedge and deciding whether to permit the dandy to be the sacrificial lamb for her own safety or to help him. In seconds the rounders would step right on her. She drew her blade from its sheath, and she sprang for the fleetest rounder's jugular vein.

A railcar whistle whooped a warning as the engineer briefly saw the rounders still in the swath of city-state domain, then it hissed on down around the curve. Sellia paid no attention to its passing. By the time the patrol came, the swath of land would be empty again, or perhaps there would be a few bodies for the patrol to dispose of, but they wouldn't be in time to help her.

The thrust of Sellia's blade had been slightly off the mark, for the fleet rounder had time to let out a howl and struggle with Sellia's grip before she collapsed to finish bleeding out her life. The warning noise gave the other two time to draw their knives before Sellia could dispatch one more and fight the third on equal terms. Now she faced two rounders, one tall and raw-boned, the other tall and sinewy, both with bosoms heaving, their expressions mixed with surprise and rage.

"Double bag," the raw-boned one said with a snarl,

meaning, Sellia was certain, that the dandy would be easy
meat once they took Sellia.

The two separated and the sinewy one sprang. Sellia
dodged easily and had her blade waiting for the raw-boned
one's thrust. A glint of steel passed her shoulder, deflected
from lethal contact by Sellia's arm as she turned and buried
her blade in the rounder's exposed belly. She swung around
again to face the sinewy rounder again, but her foe halted at
the deadly sound of a laser's sizzle. The sharp, acrid smell
of smoldering sedge rose as the beam struck the trunk of a
sapling at her side. Wide-eyed, the rounder backed away as
the dandy stepped into the sedge brandishing a laser.

"Go," he said huskily. "I won't miss the next time."

The rounder continued backing away, keeping her eye on
the dandy until she was certain his laser beam would be
obscured by sedge. Then she turned and ran into the depths
of the forest, her flight marked by the rattle of colliding
sedge stems.

Sellia watched the retreating rounder to be certain the
woman would not stop to let fly with an arrow. The forest
was too thick for it to make a certain kill and most rounders
would not willingly pit their bows against a laser, but some
rounders were not smart. From the clattering sounds, this
one was intent only on escape. Satisfied, Sellia turned to
face the dandy, who had holstered his laser, apparently
assuming Sellia would not harm him. He was tall, fair hair
in a stunning bush that his travels had left in a tangle of
appealing curls around his sunburned face. His light blue
clothing was of the finest weave and only slightly dirtied.

"You should have shot her while you had the chance,"
Sellia said. "She's just going to bring the rest of her chain
gang after us."

The dandy flushed, whether from embarrassment at
making such a foolish error or from fear Sellia wasn't
certain. "Maybe they'll take stock of their losses and leave
be," he finally said. His speech, Sellia decided, was
slightly odd. Not a Fyxen accent, and not Selenian either.

"Perhaps, but we won't count on it. We'll put as much

distance between us and them as we can until sunset. If they don't catch us by then, we can lose them in the dark."

"We'll stay together then?" the dandy said uncertainly.

Sellia didn't answer him. She went over to the raw-boned rounder's body and struggled to pull off the dun-colored tunic. When it came free from the corpse, she tossed it to the dandy. "Your dapper costume isn't well suited to anonymity in the forest. Wear that."

The dandy stared for a second, then turned his back to her and stripped off his fine shirt. His back was not as sunburned as his face, his calves scarcely pink; he'd not worn his pretty blues to cross the Black Desert, but whatever he had worn was gone now. The little pack wasn't big enough to hold desert garb. Sellia saw that his biceps were not well toned. She grabbed his arm to turn him around so she could see his pectorals and even more important to see if there were scars that would indicate he'd been surgically trimmed to please his mistress. He jerked his arm from her grip and held the brown and bloodied tunic over his left pectoral and shoulder. His eyes were wide and defiant, but she had seen what she needed to see. He was young and strong, genuinely young. This man's body could be pushed beyond its seeming limits if need be. She gestured for him to put on the tunic. He turned his back to her again and slipped it over his head.

"The pack," he said, as he shoved the shirt under the flap.

His realizing that the red pack, as bright as a dandy-deer's comb, was as incongruous as his light-colored clothing pleased Sellia. Whatever idiocy caused him to enter the wilderness unescorted at least was not the result of complete stupidity. "We'll take care of that at the first mudhole," Sellia said. "It's canvas and will hold a good deal of stain."

The dandy shook his head.

"Lad, it's mud or your life," Sellia said sternly. "Mud washes off and you'll get used to the flavor if some soaks through to your food."

"But my . . . never mind. You're right, Dame . . . ?"

"Sellia," she said in response to the Fyxen address. She frowned. He still did not sound like a Fyxen. "Quickly now. Follow me and don't drop back."

"I'm called Hark," he said as Sellia stepped off into the thick sedge. It was a strange name, too, but she said nothing.

Sellia retrieved her pack, practically without breaking stride, slinging it on her back as she walked. At the first sinkhole, she thoroughly doused the dandy's red pack in green slime and mud while he grimly watched.

The dandy matched her pace well for the first klicks, then slowly he winded. She gave him credit for his dogged persistence, for he didn't complain and stepped up quickly every time she turned around to frown. She dropped deeper into the sedge forest as the afternoon wore on. The mists had risen, the forest quieting as even the birds began to settle. But they scolded noisily at the passing humans, and sometimes Sellia heard them scolding behind her when they shouldn't, an almost certain sign that they were being followed.

When Sellia heard a stream babbling somewhere ahead, she instantly headed for the sound. She pulled out her machete and hacked a path through the undergrowth, then walked upstream through tea-colored water. The dandy slipped on rocks and splashed needlessly as the glacier-fed creek lapped up over their boot tops. The icy water stung their legs, but Sellia stayed in the stream long past the time the pain would normally urge her out. The water would destroy all trace of their passing and the natural sounds would compensate for the dandy's clumsiness.

They walked upstream, against the water's tug until the last of daylight dimmed, leaving them in clinging mist and increasing cold. They walked in the dark and the cold, out of the sedge forest again and into the heath. When they reached a jumble of dark moss-covered boulders, Hark finally begged a halt.

"If we stop here, Dame Sellia, we will have the rocks to

seclude us from view." Sellia turned. He was exhaling great frosty breaths and leaning heavily on the rocks.

He shook his head, sweaty curls gleaming with bits of ice forming at the tips. "I will continue if you think that's best . . . somehow," he gasped. "But we should stop soon so I can tend your wound. It's deep from the size of the bloodstain on your tunic, and at least should be cleaned."

Sellia smiled at his concern and nodded in agreement. Hark instantly flung down his pack behind the rocks and followed it with his exhausted body. She left him there a moment to seek a vantage of the stream's course from the tallest rock. She could hear scurry-cries over the noises of the rippling water, and she caught a glimpse of a copycat slinking off into the heath. Had it been only the cat following them all this time? It was a reasonable assumption. Copycats were scavengers that habitually followed bolder predators until they abandoned their kill. She wondered if the rounders had retrieved their dead before the cat got over the curious circumstance of its provider not just providing but being the meal. Likely they had, or the copycat wouldn't be lurking hopefully around here. Stupid beast would have to go hungry, the price it paid for not knowing the difference between predatory humans and fleeing ones.

She dropped down to the lower rocks and discovered that Hark had selected a place with a very thick bed of moss. She unshouldered her pack and sat down next to him, not as tired as he, but happy nonetheless for the chance to rest.

"If you'll show me the wound," he said opening his pack, "I'll see what I can do."

Sellia nodded, stripped off the leather tunic and rolled up the sleeve of her blouse to expose the wound. It was deep, she observed, and ached now that she thought of it. She had hardly been aware of it during the fast-paced flight up the mountainside.

Hark took a small, strange-looking case out of the pack, but when he opened it the contents were familiar: sterile gauze, disinfectant in a distinctly Fyxen bottle, scissors, scalpel, pill packs, and smaller cases. Hark poured disinfectant onto the gauze and began swabbing the wound. Sellia winced as he scrubbed deeply, opening the wound, which immediately began to bleed profusely.

"It's not *that* dirty," she said when he continued scrubbing.

"How do you know where that woman last plunged her knife?" he said. "Perhaps into the body of a diseased animal." He continued scrubbing, seemingly forever while Sellia clamped her teeth tightly together to keep from crying out. Finally he stopped. "It should be stitched, if we can take the time. If we let it go much longer, I won't be able to close it and you'll have a brutal scar."

"Time we have, now," Sellia said with a sigh. "Needles we don't."

"I have something just as good," Hark said opening one of the smaller cases. It contained a spool of green surgeon's thread and a caliperlike instrument made of blue metal. He threaded the instrument with a length of suture then dropped the whole arrangement into a bottle.

"What's that?" she said, gesturing to the bottle.

"Sterile solution . . . oh, you mean the instrument. It's a stitcher."

"I never heard of a sewing machine for flesh," she said.

"It's new," he replied.

"Are you sure you know how to use it?"

"Quite sure," he said. He hesitated a moment, then added, "I'm a doctor."

Sellia looked at him suspiciously, but he was staring into the bottle and didn't notice. Doctors of New Penance used suture and needles, not sewing machines, but of course their hands were slender and dexterous. She wondered if the stitcher had been developed especially for thick male fingers. She had met a male doctor once before. He had been a muscle fag and was not a good doctor. Rumor had it he spent more time lifting weights than scalpels. Of course, a sissy wouldn't need to be devoted to body-building, but they had other distracting proclivities. Hark certainly was unduly modest, and he possessed the mandatory gorgeous hair. His untoned muscles suggested he might be some camp muscle's protected punk. But he didn't have the moves of a sissy; indeed she sensed a hetero male air about him. "Probably the stink," she muttered wrinkling her nose.

"What?" he said looking up. "Oh, yes. The blood in your leather tunic . . . gives off quite a smell, doesn't it? I imagine both our clothes are mixed with sweat, too."

She watched Hark take the stitcher from the bottle and swab the wound again to clear it of persistent blood. He placed the caliperlike tips of the stitcher so they straddled the wound. "This will hurt," he said meeting her eyes with a sympathetic gaze. Then he smiled. "Curiosity becomes you, Dame Sellia," he said, almost sounding pleased, then he turned his attention back to her wound.

Sellia winced as the instrument pierced the already painful and tender flesh, felt the thread pass through behind it. "I've known troopers to desert to find a new life for themselves among strugglers or rounders, though it rarely meets their expectations. Sometimes I've seen ticket-of-leave men, especially Fyxen men, grow tired of the camps and they'll walk all the way across the Black Desert to the New Penance wilderness. But a man who's a dandy, and a doctor as well, is the last man I would have expected to find out here . . . unless he is facing secondary punishment or double penance." Sellia watched his face. Did his eyes narrow perceptibly? Or was he merely striving to see where next to plunge the needle.

"And you, Dame Sellia. Is it not just as unlikely to find a highborn woman of the courts in the wilderness?"

Sellia frowned as he glanced up. "We were talking about you, Hark. What drove you into the wilderness?" she asked sharply. "Malpractice? Murder?"

His needle thrust again. "No crime, at least, no major crime. I simply walked out on my mother's wedding plans for me."

"Then you are from Fox," Sellia said, her original

opinion of how he'd acquired his sunburn now confirmed. Only the harlots of Fox didn't believe the unrecorded oath of a goodman was good enough, and insisted on public ceremony, duly witnessed and recorded by the clerics. "She planned to marry you off to some ugly, ancient but rich lace Top, and you rebelled."

"I rebelled, yes, but the woman was young, beautiful."

"Ah, but you loved a ticket-of-leaver, perhaps a shop-keeper's daughter."

"No. My heart is my own. I simply do not choose to marry."

"Why not?" she said, truly amazed. "Most men I know want to be goodmen, and I doubt that's much different from being a husband when you get down to the basics. Few would choose the wilderness instead of the camps, let alone the security of living in a woman's household."

"I'm in the wilderness only as a passerby. I'm on my way to Selene, because they revere science there and would welcome my skills. I can complete my training. That's denied me now in Fox. Ceremony or no, my mother signed the papers, and my future wife would not permit me to continue my studies."

"So you decided to walk to Selene? In blue shorts and a short-sleeved shirt and with a bright red pack, you were going to walk through a hundred klicks of wilderness?" Sellia laughed at his foolishness until he adjusted the stitcher and jabbed her arm again.

"Sorry," he said. "I couldn't very well ride the rail. My mother or fiancée would have found me easily and I would have been brought back. But I confess, I had no idea that I might come to harm walking the rail. We . . . I was told it's heavily patrolled, and I did dodge several of those when I crossed the Black Desert. But I thought the strugglers feared and respected the city-states' domain of the rail-run. Besides, I have my laser. I thought it would deter savages who had nothing more than bows and arrows."

"You've been badly misinformed. First of all, most strugglers do respect the city-states' domain, but only because they're territorial and the patrols know where to find them when they misbehave. The trestlework and machine-powered cars are an affront to the devout and a threat to their hunting ground boundaries. Between sweeps of the patrols, the rails are tribal domain. That you got as far as you did is miraculous. They have their own way of practicing penance, usually ending with absolution by the clan leader instead of a cleric's. The clan leader imposes satisfaction, and can extract it forcefully if the Penitent doesn't submit. Submitting to slavery is usually considered satisfaction for sins like poaching and trespassing. In their eyes you are a trespasser, not a passerby. But strugglers are not your big problem: jungle rounders are. Rounders are chain gangs of varying number that prey on anyone that crosses their path, strugglers, travelers, loggers, rail-plankers, anyone they find. They've managed to escape secondary punishment, so they know they're gallows-fodder if caught. They've been around so long many are born into rounder clans and caught up in crime before they're out of diapers. They're desperate and have nothing to lose. Rounders are always on the move, hard even for crack patrols to catch. They cross the Black Desert at will in stolen speeders, windships, sometimes on foot. We were just lucky the ones we met had only bows and arrows; rounders don't do penance for using more sophisticated weapons. And as for your having a laser, they would have forced you to use up your twelve charges. And when your charges were gone, I don't think you would have fared well; rounders have little use for dandies. If you were lucky you would find yourself gathering firewood for them. More likely you'd be meat on the spit."

"They would eat me?" Hark stopped sewing to see if she was serious.

"It's been known to happen."

Hark shook his head. "Then I consider myself fortunate to have run into you," he said and tied another knot.

"How do you know you are safe with me?" she said

pointedly. "Anyone who doesn't know the difference between a struggler and a rounder is something of a fool. How do you know I'm not a rounder?"

"No," he said with no sign of alarm. "I may be ignorant of your wilderness, but I'd recognize, as they say, Top lace . . . though I can't imagine your reason for being in the wilderness any more than you could guess mine. You should be an officer accompanied by many troopers, or else a trader with private guards and bearers. You should not be alone, unless, of course, you are a spy. Then you would not be riding the rail either, but seeking to enter the city-state stealthily, probably not even using a groundgate."

Sellia smiled good-humoredly at his accusation, decided to ignore it, certain he would not pursue it any further if she offered him no encouragement. "If you've just come from Fox, then you must have heard about the marine from the Homeworlds."

"The spaceman? Oh, yes, I have. He was very popular in the highest court circles. I . . . my mother, being a court doctor, even attended him once."

"Then it's true?" Sellia said in surprise.

"Quite true. Except that he's not a marine; he's a civil officer of some sort. They doubted him at first, but the abbey astronomers have confirmed that Islands has a tiny new moon orbiting the equator. And of course the abbesses examined his landing ship. They disagree . . . some say there is no propulsion engine on it and that it's an elaborate hoax. Others say the system is there but simply beyond our understanding because it's so advanced."

"What of this moon, Hark? Why has he put a moon in orbit around Islands?"

"He says it's his mothership and that it will orbit until he returns."

"Ah, I see. That makes sense in terms of the Penance Princess's arrival, and even the despised exiles'." Hark gave her a puzzled look. "Convicts' arrival?" she said, wondering if that were the correct Fyxen expression. When he still looked puzzled, she shook her head. "Never mind. You men never have had a head for history lessons."

"I have an excellent sense for history," he said, "given the opportunity to hear it. Explain what you mean."

His tone startled Sellia; so impudent. "You wouldn't understand."

"I would like an opportunity to try," he said, and after the slightest hesitation, he added, "Please?"

"The ship for planetfall is probably very sturdy to fly through the atmosphere. The starship would be comparatively fragile and bulky, unable to land on a planet, so history tells us in regard to our own arrival on Islands."

He nodded. "It seems that such information should have been in your science lessons, not history."

"I told you that you wouldn't understand," she said. "Does he say when he will leave?"

"It seems he cannot. He requires some supplies, something or another to . . . repair a malfunction on the planetfall ship or the mothership, I can't remember which."

"Then he's still in Fox?"

"No. He was bound for New Penance by rail to seek his supplies there."

"Fox Court let a marine from the Homeworlds leave? The first contact in seventy-five years, and the Fyxen willingly let him leave? I cannot believe they would let him go."

Hark shrugged. "They have his planetfall ship. He must return to Fox or be marooned on the Islands forever."

"Forever? That seems an exaggeration. Since they're not all dead back there on the Homeworlds and this man found us, others will follow."

"Apparently not soon enough for him. The amount of time it would take for a rescue mission must seem like forever to him."

Sellia thought about that for a moment. A round trip to the closest Homeworlds was two years, but if those worlds were closed or destroyed during the wars—a likelihood since there'd been no word from them for seventy-five years—the trip might be a longer one now, perhaps even long enough to be called 'forever.' She nodded thoughtfully and wondered at his coming at all if his ship were not reliable. But then, nothing from the Homeworlds was reliable. Certainly the marines assigned to guard the original Penitents and convicts had not expected the assignment to last their entire lifetimes.

"So Fox, for all their penance-go-wanting attitude, does not have what he needs. I'm not surprised. Fyxen application of technology has always been sloppy. But I'm surprised he didn't choose Selene over New Penance."

Again Hark shrugged.

"But they wouldn't let him go to New Penance. Not after New Penance Court's decision to supply material for Selene's railcut to the delta when Fox's own railcut to the coast at Coral hasn't yet returned the investment. The Fyxen haven't cooperated with New Penance on anything since that happened."

"I believe he knew that the political situation was volatile, and I think he somehow blackmailed or otherwise coerced the court to provide passage to New Penance."

"But he did go to New Penance. You're certain of that?"

"Yes."

"Then I shall return to New Penance."

"You were seeking the spaceman?"

From her interest, she supposed it was obvious, but she shrugged just to keep him in doubt.

"Don't move like that," he said firmly putting his hand on her shoulder. He took one last stitch and the wound was closed. "You weren't seeking him, but now that you know he's gone to New Penance, that's where you're going, too?"

She didn't risk another shrug until Hark tied the last knot and cut the suture. She was surprised to see that he was still waiting for an answer; most men wouldn't dare. Annoyed, she didn't give him one. "And what about you, Hark? I can't leave you to walk through the wilderness."

"Your concern is touching, Dame Sellia, but despite

what you think of me, let me remind you that it was I who saved *you* from the rounder's knife."

Sellia almost doubled over from laughter. Hark was so serious. "You were brave, Hark, but also reckless and lucky. A wise man would have taken advantage of my plight and saved his own skin."

"I did take advantage. You are now beholden to me for saving your life, not to mention saving you a nasty scar and perhaps an infection, too. To repay your debts, I would like your escort as far as New Penance."

Again Sellia was astonished by his boldness. "Do you think I believe you planned to gain my protection by that little demonstration with the laser back at the trestle? Any muscle would have done it . . . even more, come to think of it. That was pure male impulse, not thoughtful considera- tion."

"Whatever it was, you must admit it worked out well for both of us. You are alive and your conscience will not permit you to desert me. New Penance is the halfway mark to Selene, my final destination." He began replacing his instruments in their cases, seemingly confident.

"Don't be so certain of what my conscience will permit," Sellia warned gravely. "I can make better time without towing a horny dandy along."

Hark's lips thinned. "I resent . . ." He tied down the flap of his pack with quick, sharp pulls, but he didn't finish whatever he intended to say. "You have nothing to fear from me," he said instead.

"I didn't think I did," she said.

"I will try not to slow you down."

"But you will anyway." Yet Sellia considered. He was different from most men, somehow naturally bold, as if he didn't realize he was always on the verge of being rude. She liked his spirit; rounders would break it if they caught him, and that would be a shame. "All right. We'll start at dawn," she finally said.

"As you wish," he said, sounding as if he had forced the politeness. "I have food in my pack. Would you like some?" The offer was equally forced, but Sellia accepted out of respect for his control.

They chewed shriveled hunks of cheese from Hark's pack, dried fruit from Sellia's, and drank long droughts of icy stream water. Sellia's mood improved with refreshment, and she thought Hark's did, too. She put her leather tunic back on as the night grew cold. Her toughened condition and the meal were sufficient to keep her warm. Hark was less fortunate. He shivered until she signaled for him to sit closer so she could share her tunic with him. His hands were like ice when she took them between hers to warm.

"Tell me about the spaceman," she said in a soft voice that would not carry far into the forest. "Have you seen him yourself? What does he look like? Is he . . . different?"

"You mean, has he six fingers or two heads?" Hark's voice was soft, too.

"Yes. Even someone from the Homeworlds might not be human. We don't know which worlds are called Homeworlds anymore. I remember history lessons that described other races."

"Really?" Hark said. He sounded amused. "I must have missed those, too."

"You would have thought it was a biology lesson anyhow," she said dryly.

Hark laughed, then said, "He's a man; one head, ten fingers. But he's different from the men of Fox. He has presence that even the noblewomen of Fox Court recognized to be one of authority and confidence. When he spoke, they listened. When he moved, they watched. He was intelligent, and I think some were afraid of him. Others . . . I don't know. I guess you would say they found him desirable."

Sellia looked sharply at Hark. "Are you trying to amaze me with male fantasies?"

Hark sighed. "No. It's the truth. Think about it for a moment. On Islands, females are the preferred sex . . ."

"With good reason, you would know, if you had studied your history lessons," Sellia interjected.

"But they know this man comes from the Homeworlds, that he's an egalitarian who knows nothing about being a man on Islands," Hark said. "They gave no allowance for that. They assumed he would behave like . . . like . . . men. When he didn't, they either wanted to kill him or own him."

"Why wouldn't he be like other men?" Sellia asked. "He could be compared to our grandfathers—at least, older women could make that comparison."

She felt him shake his head against her shoulder in agitation. "No; there were never any egalitarian grandfathers on Islands. Grandfathers are convicts or just a name on a tube of frozen sperm."

"What about the marines?" Sellia said. "They came to Islands in equal numbers of men and women, and they propagated without favoring female deliveries."

"I know," Hark said, "but I assume they were too few ever to have much influence. They don't seem to make a difference today. But the spaceman, he *is* different."

Hark was right. The original contingent of marines had not made a significant contribution to the overall population. And oddly, their descendants tended to be hedgers or plankers, still concerned with camp perimeters and transportation. Modern troopers were more often of convict descent. The real power was in the cities, and there it was women who counted, penitents or convicts who deliberately used consecrated sperm. "It's hard to imagine what this man will be like, this man you say has no equal on Islands. I can't wait to meet him," she said, barely suppressing a laugh.

"I'm not sure if you're really eager or if you're mocking me."

"I don't know myself," she said good-humoredly. "I probably won't know until I meet him."

"But you're not afraid."

"Of the man? No, of course not." But maybe, she said to herself, just a little afraid of what might happen to all

Islands, if he was not a hoax. "His ship . . . you said the clerics said it couldn't fly?"

"Some said that, not all," Hark corrected.

"They must think it's a hoax, or they wouldn't have let him go. Not to New Penance."

"Think what you wish," Hark said. "I'm going to sleep."

His words were clipped, a bit sharp. Sellia sighed. Probably got his feelings hurt, as if she'd consider going back to New Penance if she didn't really believe him, Hark just didn't strike her as a liar. Or was it because she admired his pluck in walking so long and so far without complaining and his refusing to give up his pride when he so obviously needed her help? All of that, and more, she admitted to herself. He had courage to do what he was doing, and it wasn't all in his nutsack. She was well pleased with herself for keeping him with her.

CHAPTER 14

Jeremy lay in the dark sweating. He could see the shadow of his guard in the strip of light under the door, and dimly, though this was not an outside room, he could hear rain drumming and runoff rushing through the gutters. The rains usually fell at night, so probably it was nighttime. Probably the first night after his capture, and probably the last he would spend in the maternity. He'd rarely seen Dame

Adione so angry as when his mother refused to administer truth drugs.

"Don't do this, Cirila," Dame Adione had said to his mother. She spoke low, practically under her breath like a hissing snake.

"Do what?" his mother said irritably. "You've brought in an injured man and asked me to administer truth drugs to him. In my opinion . . ."

"I asked for Barenia," Dame Adione said, "because you're too involved."

"Barenia isn't available. I'm in charge, and in my opinion he's in no condition to be questioned. He's suffering from exposure and the broken bone could go septic if we don't treat him soon. He might die under drugged questioning."

"I don't care," Dame Adione said. "He's going to hang for murder and treason anyhow."

"He's entitled to a hearing and to be in reasonably good health when it happens. I won't permit questioning him in this condition," his mother said firmly. She deliberately avoided looking at Dame Adione because, Jeremy noticed, her eyes were brimming with tears.

"Cirila, I must find out where the spaceman is. You know how important that is. Jeremy was practically in New Penance when they caught him, and the spaceman wasn't with him."

His mother shook her head firmly. "I'll send word to the abbey for an immediate judgment if need be. I know I'm within my rights."

Threatening to bring in the abbey had brought a snarl to Dame Adione's lips. No doubt she had hoped to get information from Jeremy before the abbey even heard he'd been apprehended. "Cirila, I'm going to get that spaceman. I'll go right into New Penance's caves if I have to. I've sent out spies; Hark will be noticed somewhere, and word will come to me. I will get him."

"There, you've said it yourself. You don't need Jeremy." She was hovering over him, trembling hands probing everywhere except at the break, trying to look like a doctor, but feeling to Jeremy very much like his mother.

"Jeremy will recover," Dame Adione said. "You can't protect him forever. When he's mine again, I'll remember this moment."

His mother grew pale, but by the time she turned to say something, the Top had stormed out of the treatment room. Alone, his mother had wept, and Jeremy had wept, but for very different reasons.

He knew Adione was right, that his mother couldn't protect him for very long. She had set his leg, cast it, and ordered that he be taken to a recovery room. There was a guard outside his door, though with his leg so sore he didn't feel much like attempting escape.

He heard voices outside the door, male voices, low and whispering. Then the door opened, and Orrin stepped in. Jeremy's heart beat wildly. The only person he feared more than Adione herself was Orrin, especially if Orrin were determined Adione should not ever have a chance to question Jeremy and find out the truth about who murdered the two troopers.

The door closed. Jeremy couldn't see Orrin.

"Is he safe?" Orrin asked from the foot of his bed. Jeremy hadn't heard Orrin move away from the door.

Jeremy pulled himself up on his elbows to peer into the darkness. Orrin didn't need Jeremy to speak before striking, for he already knew Jeremy was on the bed. He could have buried a knife in him from the door if he'd wanted to. Then he'd never have to worry about what Jeremy would say under drugged questioning.

"Is Hark all right?"

Jeremy jumped in spite of himself, for Orrin had whispered right into his ear.

"He was fine, close enough to the rail to find it and have jumped a car. He could be in Selene even as we speak."

Jeremy held his breath. The blow should come now, swift and silent, final. He wanted it to be over, preferred receiving it to betraying Orrin under drugs.

The light came on; Orrin's big shoulders were at Jeremy's eye level, Orrin's hands out of sight behind Jeremy's head. *He's going to choke me,* Jeremy thought. He fought the instinct to grab Orrin's arms. Then Orrin's hands came into view, holding the lightshield, and the big man sat on the edge of the bed. "He'd have to change cars in New Penance, if he didn't get caught coming in on the first."

Jeremy sighed, laid back down on the bed.

"What's the matter? You look . . ."

"Scared?" And when Orrin nodded, Jeremy sighed again, relishing the feel of air going into his lungs. "I thought you'd come to kill me before she got to me with the drugs."

Orrin looked horrified, shook his head. "It never even occurred to me, lad. It's as much for you as anything else that I'm doing this."

"For me?" Jeremy asked. His poor heart didn't have time to slow down from the fear of death before it began to beat wildly with hope.

"Of course, you," Orrin said, his voice gruff. "You, and your generation. My life's been spoiled with their poison, but for you there is still time."

"My generation . . ." Jeremy said dully.

"Listen to me," Orrin said as he put his hand over Jeremy's wrist. "I have a plan."

"Of course. You would have a plan." It was insane; not Orrin's plan, but the fire Jeremy felt in his body, just because Orrin was touching him. Jeremy raised his other hand and put it over his eyes, as if to shield them from the light. But it was to shield them from Orrin's gaze, for Jeremy couldn't help what was in them now, and if Orrin saw, he would be repulsed. He tried to listen to Orrin's plan; heard enough to realize it was a good one. It would keep him out of Adione's hands and keep him in the clinic long enough to be rescued with Hark's crewmates.

"Do you think you can convince your mother that you want to dedicate your life to the abbey?"

"As a nature boy? No, she'd never believe it. But I think she'd lie to buy time for me."

Orrin nodded and took his hand from Jeremy's arm. "Do we dare to tell her the truth? I could use her help on Double Nocturne. Getting three of you out of here won't be easy."

"If she were convinced that the only alternative were for me to hang for murder, she would help us."

"All right, then," Orrin said. "Your assignment is to convince your mother that it's the only way."

"Hide behind her skirts, as it were," Jeremy couldn't resist saying.

Orrin frowned and nodded. "We're desperate now, lad."

"I've been desperate before," Jeremy said.

Orrin nodded again.

"If Hark doesn't come on Double Nocturne . . ."

"He'll come. I never saw a man more determined. I know he'll come."

"But if he doesn't . . . Better I hang for treason than go through with purification rites. The sorry sisters have more reason than ever for taking their revenge on me—my mother for educating me, Dame Adione for taking me into her troops, you for shooting down the lander. I don't think they'd be satisfied with the simple cuts of purification if they actually got me under the knife. They'd cut off my balls."

"Hark will come," Orrin said again. "I've been talking to his captain. She is convinced he can do it if anyone can."

"But if he doesn't come," Jeremy persisted.

"Don't worry, lad. I won't let them cut off your balls."

Once more Orrin touched him. This time it wasn't the unconscious gesture of camaraderie; this time he deliberately took Jeremy's hand. And again Jeremy felt the fire deep inside. He would rather be dead than not feel it again.

CHAPTER 15

Hark awakened with a start when sleet splattered on his face. For a frightening moment he couldn't remember where he was and thought it was dark and cold because the power had failed. He remembered a woman's face, a woman with red hair, snow all around. Then he saw Dame Sellia crouched in the lee of the rock out of the rain, and realized where he was and that he was shivering because he was covered with sleet. He'd been dreaming of the lady from the lava lake.

"Is it time for me to watch?" he asked her. He pushed his hair back from his forehead and was startled to find it stiff with icicles.

She shook her head. "Go back to sleep."

Hark moved next to Dame Sellia and out of the sleet, tried to close his eyes again, but lightning and thunder constantly startled him, and he was getting wet despite the protection from the rocks. In one of the lightning flashes, he saw Dame Sellia staring at him, frowning.

"Well, if you won't sleep, there's no sense in wasting more time here in camp," she said, reaching for her pack.

"You should sleep a while," he said.

She shook her head. "I've been catnapping. Let's go."

Reluctantly Hark took up his pack and followed her away from the rocks. He was not well rested.

At least she did not go back into the stream, but almost

immediately he was hard-pressed to keep up with her. The sleet was building into a treacherous slush that gave way with every footfall. The way was dark, lighted only by the lightning flashes, and those also illuminated spiky growths and hideous cerecloths of moss hanging from the trees, all fringed with hoarfrost now. Feigning more weariness than was real, Hark dropped back about once an hour to check their direction of travel on his groundguide without Dame Sellia seeing him. While they had followed the contour of the heath forest on the mountainside, he noted that they kept returning to a easterly direction, in which he knew lay New Penance. It relieved him to know Dame Sellia had told the truth about her destination. From his experiences in Fox, he was wary of Islandish women.

Dawn brought light, but not much. They were well into the heath, and the pass was misty and the sleet continued. The way was ever upward, their footprints draining in fast rivulets behind them. Finally the heather gave way to black lichen and brown mosses in the bleak alpine zone. The air was icy, but at least it was not sleeting. For a short way they even walked above the clouds in bright sunshine, and Hark could see snowcapped Fox Volcano standing well-isolated in the distance. Its lower reaches were shrouded in clouds so that it looked like a towering island rising out of the Sea of Black Desert lava.

Sellia turned abruptly down slope, walking with sure steps, as if following a path Hark could not see. The way turned into a true path when they reached the sedge, and Hark felt very nervous when he stepped over what he was certain were piles of steaming dung. Huge piles, like the ones he'd seen in the desert, except that these were faintly luminescent. The path through the sedge was broad, the stalks broken and pushed aside for a meter or two above his head. He found himself listening for footsteps or some sign sulphur bellies were coming, but he heard nothing except when occasionally the storm gusted and the forest moaned. He knew it was nothing more than the wind blowing through hollow stems of dead and brittle sedge, but it was an unsettling noise. He was glad when they reached the clear swath of land and the railrun.

Sellia hurried to the base of a trestle where a strongbox lock had been forced and pulled loose. She looked inside, then stepped back and frowned at Hark.

"They got it," she said, her lips thin and angry.

"Got what? Who?"

"My rail speeder," she said bitterly. Then she sighed. "It wouldn't have done us a whole lot of good in this rain anyway. The battery needed recharging. But it's the second one I've lost, and they're expensive. Damn rounders. I should have known they wouldn't give up that easily."

"I should have guessed you hadn't walked all the way from New Penance," Hark said, wondering now that he had believed she did.

"Well, we'll walk now," she said resolutely. "And it will be a wet miserable walk; it doesn't look like it's going to clear today." She started back across the clearing. "Come on," she said sharply, "or we'll have to spend another night out in the rain."

He followed her back the way they had come, through the cold and dripping mist in the sedge and up through the heath until they were once again above the clouds.

Late in the morning, Dame Sellia stopped and they ate in the meager shelter of a rocky ledge. Hark's backpack was bright red again, the mud washed away by the sleet and rain. Hark was certain Dame Sellia had noticed, but she no longer seemed concerned. Apparently the rounders didn't like the alpine zone any more than Hark did. There was sunlight here, and the snow patches around them seemed transient compared to what he'd glimpsed higher up, but today the altitude and the storm below were keeping the temperature quite cold.

After eating, Dame Sellia led them back into the rain-filled heath and the going was difficult again, filled with slippery boulders and sharp spiny growing things. Near the day's last light, Dame Sellia turned sharply, going down the slope. Hark dropped back to sneak a look at his ground-guide.

"Are you tired, Hark?" she said.

He had not heard her retrace her steps and he barely had time to put the guide back in his pocket. "New Penance is east," he said gesturing. "Why have you turned south?"

"Are you certain your sense of direction isn't blurred?"

"I'm certain. We've changed direction a lot because of the terrain, but always returned to a generally east direction. Suddenly, when the way is clear, you change direction. Why?"

Dame Sellia wiped rivulets of water that ran down her face and looked at Hark suspiciously. "How could you possibly know which way we are going after fifteen hours of serpantining under cloudy skies?"

Hark felt himself blushing. He hadn't meant to make her distrust him by using the groundguide, yet he couldn't help worrying she might try to take it away from him if she saw it. She would know instantly that it was not an ordinary compass.

"It was a lucky guess," he said, finally, and could tell that she did not believe him.

"In the trees below is a cabin where a clan of strugglers live. I know them. They'll shelter us for the night and give us pack beasts to ride tomorrow."

Hark looked down the slope trying to see through the trees, unhappy at the mention of beasts. Dame Sellia apparently misunderstood his dismay.

"They won't eat you," she said with a sudden, good-natured smile.

"It was rounders, I believe, who are the cannibals. Strugglers are associated with slavery."

"You learn quickly. But don't worry about that either. They won't take you from me. They're of the Cloud Clan, allies of New Penance, and Hilma, the matriarch, is a personal friend."

Hark nodded, but followed Dame Sellia uneasily when she turned again to walk down the mountainside. He believed she would keep him safe from the strugglers, but he hoped the beasts she mentioned made smaller dung piles than the ones he was used to seeing.

The struggler dwelling was more of a hillock than a cabin and he had walked across its grassy roof before he realized there was a structure beneath him.

Dame Sellia jumped a grassy bank into what seemed a ditch, then shucked her pack and shoved it through a hole in the embankment and disappeared. Hark followed her example and crawled on his hands and knees through a two-meter-long tunnel that opened into a warm, smelly, sod-covered pit. The diameter was not more than eight meters, mud walls and roof shored with stout old timber. Hark noted the swords, bows, quivers, and spears hanging on the timbers by the entrance tunnel, and clay and metal utensils on the timbers by the mud oven in the far wall. A fire was blazing, and gruel boiling in a cauldron bubbled over, making the flames hiss and flash. Smoke rose up an invisible chimney, more spilled over into the pit and collected along the damp ceiling. Shadows flickered in the gloom as his eyes adjusted, and finally a human figure emerged from what he had thought was a tree trunk shoring up the ceiling.

"Back so soon, Sellia?" the shadow said. "I told you tha' it was nonsense—dreamstuff."

"It seems the dream I was seeking is on his way to New Penance by rail. In fact, he must be there by now, so I'm returning to New Penance to see if he's flesh or fantasy."

"Can a fish walk through the forest?"

"If you put it in a pot of water, Hilma, and carry it."

"As far as my fireplace," the woman grumbled.

Hark heard noise in the tunnel behind him and stepped aside to permit a boy and several women to enter. They barely grunted to Dame Sellia, appraised Hark with side-long glances as they passed him to shed their wet skin ponchos and to warm themselves by the fireplace. They had to have been close by to enter so soon behind him, yet Hark had seen no one. It made him uneasy to realize they'd probably been watching him and Dame Sellia for quite some time. How often had that happened before he met her?

"Dry yourself, Sellia, and make yourself welcome," Hilma said.

"I thought you would never ask," Dame Sellia said happily as she went over to the fireplace. The others made room for her.

"I almost *did* forget to ask. My eyes ha' been on yer pretty-boy over there. Got to do my lookin' before my ol' dangler gets back," Hilma said with a hearty laugh. "What you doin' wi' such a fancy man, Sellia?"

Dame Sellia had taken off her leathers and was tossing them over a pole, and Hark had already begun to follow her example when he realized all eyes were on him. He looked over at the women and, now that his eyes were accustomed to the dimness, he could see the old one clearly. Her gray hair hung in long neat braids against a garment that was nothing more than a swath of cloth crossed over her breast and tied behind her neck. A soft leather girdle fitted close to her hipbone on her left and draped to rest on her thigh on the right. The drab clothing was oddly becoming to her hard-looking muscles and weathered skin. She continued to stare, openly admiring him. The younger women didn't attempt to avert their eyes either. With some embarrassment, and being careful to keep his tattooed arm toward the wall, Hark finished taking off the leathers.

"Them shoulders is three ax-handles wide, Sellia. He cou' carry twice the weight my Bancroft can," Hilma said appreciatively.

Dame Sellia smiled along with the other women, and Hark felt himself turning red. He wanted to turn away, to put the wet tunic back on or reach for the shirt in his pack, but the expression on Dame Sellia's face was changing from amusement to one of alarm.

"Mother, on his hip!" one of the younger women cried.

Hark almost reached for the laser but saw the slight shake of Dame Sellia's head. "A gift for you, Hilma," Dame Sellia said evenly. "You've always welcomed me in your cabin and never asked payment. In gratitude, I brought you a gift.''

Hark stiffened, but started to draw the laser out of the holster. Hilma and the younger women had blades out of their girdles before the laser's muzzle cleared the leather. Alarmed, Hark looked at Dame Sellia. Her eyes flashed an unmistakable message of warning. Carefully, Hark palmed the muzzle of the laser and offered it to Hilma. The old woman beckoned to him with a single finger, and he stepped across the mud floor and handed over the laser. As soon as his hand was empty, he crossed his arms over his chest, hand clasped over his bicep to hide the tattoo. He heard Dame Sellia let out her breath in relief as she turned to continue drying her sodden skin breeches and cloth blouse.

''Thought for a moment you meant to give me the dangler. But this! Now this is somethin','' Hilma said happily. ''How many rounds are left?''

''Eight, Dame Hilma,'' Hark said.

Dame Sellia looked at him and raised her brow quizzically. It was worth losing the laser to see that expression on her face!

Hark stepped away as the younger women came closer to see the shiny weapon.

''Yes, look well my daughters, and remember it well,'' Hilma said. ''It will burn a hole in your breast at a hundred meters . . . if you wou' try to take it from me.''

''Now, Ma,'' one of the women said.

But Hilma shook her head to indicate she didn't want to hear. ''You would be the first to try, Theda.''

''They're forbidden anyway,'' muttered one of the other women.

Hilma snapped on the target-finder, and the pink light flashed across the speaker's throat. ''And you wou' be the second, Rina, so don't go talking religion to me.''

Rina looked at her mother reproachfully and seemed about to say something when the tension was broken with the arrival of a middle-aged man who entered pushing a stack of wood before him through the tunnel.

"Ah, at last. Where ha' you been, Bancroft? Sippin' the mead in the root cellar?" Hilma snapped off the target-finder light and tucked the laser in her girdle.

"I saved out enough for all," the man said good-naturedly, and brought out a jug from under his poncho.

Hilma took the jug from him and poured the contents into a metal pot, which she hung in the fireplace. Bancroft put some fresh wood into the fire, then began fetching cups down from overhead hooks and passing them out to the women. He brought moss-filled cushions out from a hole in the wall, and frowned at Hark when he had made the third trip across the room with a cushion. Hark wondered if the frown meant he was expected to help. He felt oddly uncomfortable, was still bare-chested, wished he could go to the fireplace and dry out thoroughly, but sensed doing so uninvited would earn frowns, too, or worse, more comments about his physique. His embarrassment, real enough, would seem heightened before long with his arms across his chest. But he didn't dare risk letting them see the tattoo. He stood shivering. When Bancroft began to pour warm mead into the women's cups, Hark stole into a shadow and sat down on the packed earth floor. He pulled his shirt out of the pack and put it on, hoped the shadows would subdue the color somewhat and that he would receive no more unwanted attention.

"Did you find the space marine so soon, Sellia?" he heard Theda say to Sellia.

Dame Sellia was unplaiting her braids by the fireplace, combing the damp strands with her fingers. "Not exactly. The dandy says the spaceman's on his way to New Penance by rail."

"If he's gone from Fox, why hasn't Laurel returned?" Theda said with a frown at Hark.

"Who's to say she hasn't?" Dame Sellia said easily, not seeing the frown. "She may have followed him directly to New Penance."

Theda shook her head. "I still have some of the samples

she took from the volcano. She wou' have stopped here to get 'em.''

"An' I tol' you, you got *nothin*'," the old woman said. "Nothin' but a sack of spongey white rocks. I cou' get just the like from a lot closer than Hells Gates. If it's floating rock she wants, I can get 'em all colors from our own volcano. White, black, gray, even red!''

Hark was listening closely, hardly breathing. Had it been Hilma's daughter he had seen in the caldera?

"They mean somethin' to her, Ma," Theda said. "An' she'll be wantin' me to keep 'em safe. For sure them funny ones. Never seen rocks like them before.''

"Wha' could them mean? Rocks is rocks. There's floating ones and sinking ones.''

Dame Sellia blinked. She spoke simply and straightfor-wardly. "The floating ones are buoyant because bubbling gasses were present when they formed. They help Laurel construct a history of chemical fluctuations of the magma,'' she said. "I'm sure Theda's right. Laurel will come for them.''

Hilma shook her head and drank down some of her mead. "If you say so, then she'll come, an' she'll pay what's due us, too.''

"I wouldn't have imposed on our friendship and ask you to take her if I believed she would deal unfairly with you,'' Dame Sellia said.

"But then, why ain't she come yet?'' Theda asked.

Sellia shrugged. "She may still be in Fox waiting for a chance to slip away undetected. She may have gone to New Penance or even to Selene. I could give you a thousand reasons and still not hit the right one. Laurel is the most unpredictable person I know.''

"All them Selenians is dings," Hilma said. "Next thing you know she'll wan' to look down the gullet of the Bitch Herself, an' to that I say, no!''

"A volcano is a volcano, and she'd pay you well if she needed your aid,'' Sellia said.

Hilma shrugged and drank more mead. Theda drank

silently; Hark was not certain she was convinced that all
was well with Laurel of Selene and that she would get what
was owed. Theda looked over at Hark once or twice, as if
she wanted to ask him something, but she said nothing.
Hark hoped the shadows concealed any curiosity that might
show on his own face, for he longed to ask Theda if Laurel
of Selene had red hair and why she might be spying on the
troops and clerics at the soda lake.

The mead put the clan in a gay mood, one even Dame
Sellia seemed taken up in despite the acrid smoke that
obviously was making her eyes as red as Hark's felt. Hilma
and her two daughters, Rina and Theda, had curled up on
the moss-filled cushions across from Dame Sellia, and the
other two women whose names Hark still had not heard sat
behind them on the cushions. He gathered they were
relatives of some sort, but not Hilma's daughters. The boy
who had first entered with the women sat cross-legged at
Dame Sellia's feet, somehow having earned the women's
acceptance at the fireplace.

Bancroft brought in a basket of fresh fruit, which Hark
realized must have been gathered from the rain forest on the
lower slopes of the mountain. The women all cut or peeled
their own selections and ate with their fingers. When no one
offered Hark any fruit, he took the last morsels from his
pack and ate them. He put his empty holster in the pack,
carefully knotted it shut. He was nearly dry and his muscles
ached less now that he was warm. The bit of food made him
sleepy. When Dame Sellia started to sing court songs, he
began to relax and finally to doze, feeling safe in the
shadows.

Dame Sellia's voice was sweet and the tune soothing. He
came awake when the rhythm changed and Bancroft joined
in the singing in bass voice and by clanking chains he'd
taken down from the wall. The chains were oddly melodic.
He saw Dame Sellia urge the boy to sing with them, and
tousle his hair when he finally did. They ate more, then
Dame Sellia, Rina, and Theda threw daggers into the mud
wall, and Dame Sellia lost badly to them. Hilma filled

Sellia's cup with what must have been the last of the mead in the cooking pot, then poured another jugful in. She placed the empty jug upside-down in a rack next to two others that Hark hadn't noticed being there earlier. When Hilma took the full cup to Sellia, the two women exchanged whispers and laughed. They laughed again when Dame Sellia pulled her dagger from the wall and sheathed it. Curious now, Hark watched as Dame Sellia left the other women to the dagger-throwing sport and made her way toward him. She stumbled over Hark's feet, rebalanced her cup of mead and sat down next to him.

"Why aren't you singing?" she said offering him her cup.

Hark sipped some of the scalding mead because he was thirsty, but he shook his head. "I don't know the songs," he said.

"So, hum along." And when he shook his head she frowned. "Don't be so prissy or I'll think you're one of those moralistic bottom men they keep in Fox Court to irritate them." Her speech was thick, her eyes slightly unfocused, but when he shook his head yet again, she leaned over and kissed Hark sloppily on the lips.

"Dame Sellia, you are drunk," he whispered.

"Very," she agreed as she pushed his arms and knees aside to climb into his lap.

"You need some sleep," Hark said.

"That's not what I had in mind," she said opening his shirt with her finger and touching his bare chest.

Hark chuckled. Her touch was gentle, her eyes already half-closed. "You would hate yourself tomorrow."

She mumbled something incomprehensible, snuggled up closer to his chest, and Hark put his arms around her to support her. It had been a long time since Hark had held anyone so close, and he felt his heart begin to pound with pleasure from feeling her breath against his chest. He closed his eyes to shut out the women at the fireplace and for a moment he felt at peace.

A shadow fell on Hark and he looked up to see the boy

standing before him, watching Dame Sellia. The boy blinked slowly, stupefied by alcohol, lifted his cup and drank deeply. He met Hark's eyes, and Hark saw a sick longing there before the boy passed by and lay down on a straw-filled pallet.

Bancroft touched Hark's shoulder and pointed to another straw pallet with a few blankets hanging from the rafters to seclude it from the others. Hark sighed, got his tired feet under him, and carried Dame Sellia over there. She was already snoring deeply in his arms, completely unaware. When he put her down, the brown and green cap fell off and long blond hair spilled wildly about the pallet. Her face was shiny with grease, yet even that could not hide her beauty.

Bancroft tossed him a blanket, only one, and after a quick count of the remaining pallets, Hark knew there was not a separate one for him. He squeezed in next to Dame Sellia, molding himself to her shape, and pulled the blanket up over them. The songs ended, replaced by soft conversation and, finally, by snores. But Hark didn't fall asleep for hours.

CHAPTER 16

The rain poured as heavily as the day before and the pack beasts were dripping wet when Theda dropped the reins into Sellia's hands.

"These two should give you a good ride," Theda said. "They're sturdy."

Sellia looked at them critically. They were bonebacks,

both young and probably half-wild, for both were fitted with spiracle plugs on the first thoracic lateral plates that were controlled by an extra set of reins. But if they'd been taken from the forest wilds, Hilma's clan had been very selective. The animals carried their abdomens high, forming a natural saddle back behind the thorax, and the bay-plated one looked as if she might be gorgeous if her plates were sanded and polished. She turned to give Hark the reins of the larger doe and mounted the bay herself. Hark stood there with the reins in his hands, staring at the beast.

"Come on, Hark. Don't stand there looking as if you've never seen a boneback before," she said.

"But I haven't," he said, swallowing hard.

Theda laughed and, with a wink at Sellia, she took the reins out of Hark's hands and handed them up to Sellia. "Put your foot right here, boy," she said patting the big doe's midleg tibia, "and climb aboard."

Hark looked dubious.

"Grab the front of the first dorsal plate," Sellia said, and when he still seemed mystified, Sellia cursed and got down from the bay. "Here," she said grabbing the big plate behind the doe's head to show him. He started to reach for it with his right hand and she slapped it away and pulled his left up. Then he put his left foot on the tibia and managed to straddle the beast. Sellia lengthened the stirrups for him and thrust his feet into them. Then she remounted the bay and urged her on. The other doe followed, Hark holding to the dorsal plate until the muscle forced his fingers out. Then he grabbed the wing nubs, and the doe flapped the vestigial wings in irritation.

"I'll bring the beasts back on my next trip," Sellia said to Theda.

The huntress nodded and waved, no doubt content in knowing the bonebacks would be returned quite sleek, tack repaired or replaced, and both does pregnant by New Penance's finest bucks.

When they were out of Theda's sight, Sellia brought Hark's doe up next to her. Hark was hunched over in the saddle, one hand flat over the first dorsal, the other grasping decorative fringe on the saddle.

"You look like a sack of ground cherries," she said, and didn't mention he also looked terrified. "Sit straight, put your knees against the mid-laterals."

He tried to respond to her commands just as the beasts started scrambling up a bank, pace upset as they searched for purchase in the slippery young grass. Hark barely stayed in the saddle.

"Here, take your own reins and sit up straight," she said as they struck out across a highland meadow. "No, not like that. The top reins steer. Put them under your fourth finger. The little reins close off air to the thorax; you shouldn't use them unless she gets out of control. You have more leverage if you keep the thin rein under your little finger." She held up her hands to show him the rein arrangement and watched him fumble to duplicate it. "Now," she continued, "get your buttocks underneath you and put your knees back against the mid-laterals."

She nodded with satisfaction as he sucked his butt under him and straightened up. "Put your elbows against your ribs. You're not a bird, and for now put your hands on the pommel. You're asphyxiating the beast with all that jerking on the reins."

He tried, and succeeded somewhat, and Sellia felt better. She noticed him begin to fall into the boneback's side to side rolling rhythm as they walked across the meadow. That was good. If he'd had no aptitude at all, it would have been a very long ride. As it was, she knew he was going to be sore at the end of the day, even if they took it easy.

"I'm glad you had the good sense to turn over that laser," she said. "It could have gotten quite ugly."

"That much I could sense, but I don't understand why."

"There's a great deal of superstition in the wilderness, and many things from the cities are forbidden. But, as you noticed, some are not superstitious. To someone like Hilma, who isn't afraid to do penance if she's caught, it's very valuable."

"What about patrols?" Hark said. "They're armed with lasers while they operate in the wilderness, aren't they?"

Sellia nodded. "Patrols operate under special dispensation. And if they catch anyone in the wilderness who doesn't have similar exemption, they hang the offender. The abbesses are not as kind."

"Then you've not really done Hilma any favor by giving her my laser."

"Probably not, but letting you bring it in her cabin put her at risk with the abbey without any gain. She would have been damned if she hadn't turned me in for doing it, and damned by the New Penance Court if she had. Besides, someone has to catch her with it first."

"It was stupid of you not to warn me to hide it," he said, meeting her eyes calmly.

Sellia bristled. "I didn't know I needed to. I'm not accustomed to traveling with fools."

"Just who are you accustomed to traveling with?" he asked. "What kind of Islandian knows all about laser prohibitions, yet is someone you'd expect to warm your bed even though you were drunk?"

"What difference does being drunk make?"

"Ah-ha!" he said. "That's why you're so surly this morning. You *do* remember last night." And when she started to protest, he cut her off by saying, "A trooper would meet your expectations." Then he shrugged and shook his head. "Too bad real education isn't provided to everyone. It's impossible to know beforehand who will need it and who will not."

Sellia sat silently, feeling oddly disturbed at agreeing with him, even though she did it silently.

For an hour, Sellia did not urge the beasts to anything faster than a walk. Her head ached from the night in the oxygen-starved cabin and alcohol toxins in her bloodstream, and had nothing, she tried to convince herself, to do with Hark's disturbing words. Most men and boys never would need to know the finer points of canonical law, and those who did received the very best of training in such subjects from their officers. She was just eager to get back to New Penance, impatient because Hark was slowing her down. And just what difference could her being drunk have made to him?

"Are we crossing the volcano's divide?" Hark asked her.

"Sit up straight," she snapped, then said, "Yes."

The rain had turned to snow, but it was light and the pass was short and steep. They would be down in the rain again soon where it was warmer. Up here, the beasts were steaming even though not hard-pressed. Hark sat up straight again, and she urged the bay ahead at a singlefooted pace, leaving him to follow as best he could.

Once down in the heath, Sellia snapped two switches from a tree. "The beasts will start slowing down soon, wanting to turn back home," she said handing one over to Hark. His beast shied as it saw the switch. "Take up the slack in those reins," she ordered.

"There's so much to remember at once," he said pulling up on the reins so abruptly the plugs slipped into the spiracles and the doe obediently stopped, not wanting to choke.

"Ease up on those plugs with the reins under your little fingers. Put your butt back under," she said, and calmly raised her switch and whacked his buttocks soundly. "Now you will not forget."

"Don't do that again," he said, his face reddening with anger. Somehow he resisted rubbing the welt left by the whip.

"I'll do it as often as needed," she said. "Do you want to ride into New Penance looking like a bundle of laundry? Or do you want to learn to do it right?"

"I want to learn," he said, "but without the whip."

"I teach with a whip," she said. "If you don't want reminders, remember everything I've told you on your own."

"Is that how you were taught?"

"Yes," she said, and smacked him smartly on his left

knee. "The difference is that my legs were bare. Now keep your knees against the laterals."

"Damn you," he said, but he kept his knees against the plates.

Past noon the bonebacks picked their way around the last of the snow fields on the continental divide and brought them back into rainy heather for a final time. Had it been clear, the noble houses of New Penance's emergents would already be visible, but today the view was obscured by rain, fog, and clouds. As she turned Hilma's bay upslope again, she realized Hark's doe was not clopping along behind. She reined in the bay and turned in the saddle. The other doe was standing with her back legs well upslope, head turned to look wistfully after the bay, but Hark had a firm hold on the plug reins and was peering down into the gray gloom. He looked up at Sellia and turned the doe, hurrying the beast along until he caught up with her.

"New Penance is down there," he said pointing behind him. "Why are you going up again?"

Sellia leaned out to stare at where the valley should be and rainwater splashed from a poncho crease onto the saddle. She frowned and sat back, for she could see nothing but gray, not the bottom of the slope nor the craggy false summit of White Mountain that would bite deeply into the valley view if she could. "How do you know these things?" she asked turning sharply in the saddle to see him better. It was impossible to believe even for a moment that he was a trooper who had taken on the guise of a dandy. He couldn't have faked that faltering gait all day yesterday and he surely would have *learned* to ride the boneback better today if he were. What lay between trooper and dandy? Ticket-of-leave man, she answered herself—or so she had always believed.

"Why are you angry?" he said, trying to pull the doe back. He was looking warily at the whip poised in her free hand, trying to maneuver out of reach. "Is it still because of last night?"

"Last night? Don't be a fool." She turned the whip so that it lay gently against the bay's throat. "But now that you

bring it up, what difference does it make that I was drunk?"
Casually she flicked water off the bay with the whip. When
Hark didn't answer her, she looked sharply at him. He was
grinning so wide she almost hit him.

"You would have been absolved of sharing half the
responsibility," he said softly.

She stared at him. All desire to hurt him died. "You
needn't look so happy about it," she said.

"That's not why I'm smiling," he said. "I didn't answer
the first time you asked because I thought you wouldn't
understand what I meant or care if you did. I was wrong.
That's why I'm glad."

She began to feel uneasy under his frank gaze. She
collected the bay under the reins. "We can't get to New
Penance from here. The observatory is on the peak just a
klick up the trail," she said. "The living quarters for the
astronomers is even closer. We'll use the observatory's
supply rail to go into New Penance."

Hark nodded, and the beasts stepped out again with just a
bit more eagerness. Had they scented the flesh of their kind
in this rainy wind, or perhaps the grain that would be their
reward? And Hark! How had he known that New Penance
lay below? Another lucky guess? Not twice, she told
herself. Not in the rain-shrouded mountains. She looked
over at him; he was still smiling. Why not? she thought as
she realized she couldn't restrain returning his smile. Maybe
we're both lucky.

The monorail car from the observatory was a simple
supply car, a platform covered with hard translucent resin
and a single engineer's seat, which Sellià had taken. Hark
stood behind her looking out the only clear windows at the
solid green canopy overhead and massive boles at eye level.
They had ridden the winding rail from the alpine zone,
through the heath and sedge, and only moments ago entered
New Penance's rain forest valley, the largest valley in the
transition zone between lowland savannahs and highland
sedge forests. It was very dark, for the forest canopy had

nearly closed over the top of the rail, and of course there were still rainclouds in the sky, which made the way even gloomier. But Hark, she noticed with approval, seemed captivated by the luxuriant foliage.

The air scoops sucked in the warm and humid air of the rain forest microclime, sweetly scented with rotting vegetation and occasional wafts of scratchblossom perfume. The sturdy scratchblossom trees of the valley had been leafless but lacy with swollen white buds when she left New Penance. They must have opened and the rain must have been hard enough to bruise the petals and release the scent molecules. She had smelled their perfume only once before in her life, for unlike most of the rain forest vegetation that blossomed and seeded almost annually, the scratchblossoms did so only a few times in a human lifespan. But Sellia had not forgotten the scent. It had a pleasant tang that she almost tasted more in the back of her mouth than she detected through her nose. She opened the railcar window, wondered if Hark realized what a special treat he was experiencing. There were no scratchblossom trees on Fox Volcano's bare slopes.

The rail ran along the steep valley wall, the one along the top of which she and Hark had ridden only a few hours earlier. But the forest understory growth, vines, young canopy species trees, as well as trees indigenous only to the understory, were so thick that they couldn't see the rock walls. The greenery seemed impenetrable.

"I know we must be in New Penance, but I haven't seen a single dwelling," he said.

Sellia smiled. "You're used to Fox where they clear the land and build houses on the ground," she said. "In New Penance, most of our forest homes are in the understory or up in the canopy."

"Why is that?" he said, craning his neck to look up at the canopy.

"It causes the least disruption in the local ecology. That's the penance. We don't just talk about it here. We do it."

"Doing penance sounds noble. Fyxen view it as punishment."

"That doesn't surprise me. But what do they say about New Penance in Fox?" Sellia asked, suddenly curious.

Hark turned to look at her, and he smiled as if he had received a pleasant surprise. Sellia looked back, wondering if they had passed an especially colorful tree, but she saw nothing special. She would have asked what he was smiling at, but then he was answering her question.

"They say you have useful logging operations, but that you're primitive and live in holes in the ground."

Sellia laughed aloud. "It's true. But I would hardly call them holes. We have good mining operations inside the mountain. It's riddled with tunnels and shafts. Many of our people make good use of the exhausted tunnels. They're cooler and dryer than the forest and, if that's the worst you've heard, you'll be surprised at how nice some of them are."

He resumed looking out the window.

"It isn't, is it?"

"Isn't what?" he asked.

"The worst you've heard."

"No. The lack of respect is mutual."

"I guess they can't help that it was convicts who set the style of Fyxen character," she said.

"Arrogance," Hark said.

"Pardon?"

"Arrogance. Self-righteousness—words I've heard to describe the people of New Penance."

"All right, I had that coming. It is rather arrogant to be doing an act of contrition for all mankind. But it's as much common sense as an act of faith. Where on Islands can we go if we don't stay in harmony with nature? To the Black Desert?" She shook her head.

"I don't know," he admitted. "The Islands in the Sky are pretty limited, but they're all there is. You may be right."

"Of course I'm right. It's too bad the Fyxen's origins left

them with such strong resentment of authority and discipline. You disrupt the order of things," she said.

"I don't seem to be able to help it," he said with a sigh.

"I didn't mean you personally."

"I know." Then, after a while he said, "This natural forest is prettier than Fox's marketplace gardens."

"If you like natural, wait until you see the canopy palace. It's not as big as the palace at Fox, but the garden . . ." Sellia chuckled.

"We're going to New Penance Court?"

"Yes, but that's not the same place as New Penance Palace. We'll go to court first. I'm eager to see this spaceman and that's where he'll be. We'll see what's to be done for you after I have seen the queen," she added.

"Thank you, Dame Sellia."

"Uh . . . Lady Sellia, if you please. Dame is peculiar to Fox."

"Forgive me, I did not know. May I ask what your station in court is?"

"I'm the queen's sister, Minister of the Wilderness," she said deliberately turning to see Hark's surprise. She smiled. "Since rounders don't respect it, the title is of no significance in the wilderness."

"No," he said slowly, "I imagine it's not."

The track had circumnavigated a granite buttress that protruded from the valley wall. On sunny days an array of embedded crystal made it gleam. Today it looked gray, and Sellia found herself wishing that Hark could have seen it in sunshine. She slowed the car; openings in the granite became more apparent through the sheet of water on the windshield, frames and latticework that supported the rails finally visible. She braked, and slipped the car into a tunnel of blue granite slabs. Inside the vast hall were many small railcars standing on shiny parking trestles. The area was well lighted. On the far wall, New Penance Court's agenda was blazoned in colored lights. Sellia studied them for a moment.

"Good," she said. "Court is in session. We'll go there directly."

"Our clothes, milady," Hark protested. They were dryer than when they entered the monorail car at the observatory, but no less dirty.

"Don't worry about how you look, Hark. New Penance does not put on airs in court the way they do in Fox. It's not a social gathering. It's our means of communication, and people come in work clothes all the time."

Hark shrugged and followed her when she stepped out of the car onto the stone platform. It was cool and dry, a relief from the muggy forest. She led the way to a corridor tunnelled out of granite and started walking quickly. Hark matched Sellia's long and hasty stride, his boots echoing with hers.

At the end of the corridor, a trooper dressed in a starched tunic stepped aside the instant she saw Sellia, making way for them to enter the court arena. Sellia stepped inside, whispered for Hark to wait at the entrance, and descended the steps to her sister's dais. The stone stairs were covered with soft carpeting.

The court arena was half-empty today, only the seats near the dais were occupied. No one was looking at the viewscreens, which Sellia took to mean that they were broken again. In the center of the arena was the queen's dais, large enough to hold a resin table of immense proportions, empty now but available for clustering with the queen when she chose. The queen would not permit the table to be removed until the new communication system they had purchased from the abbey in Selene operated without failures from Double Nocturne to Double Nocturne. Three moonless nights had already passed, and Double Nocturne was due again soon. The test would have to start again then, and Sellia would have to see it through—again! Damn, how quickly she got caught up in duty. But she vowed to take just another minute to enjoy life.

Her sister, Mala, stood before the transparent throne. She was leaning over to talk to the technicians in the pit. Her hair was piled in thick looping curls on the top of her head, frosted with gemmed combs and silver wires. The silver wires coiled around her neck, and gleamed in ellipses against her dark-robed breasts. She had on a filmy train, too, and her feet were bare but for jewels crusted onto her toenails. Sellia crossed the pit that was filled with pages and technicians and climbed up the few steps to the dais. The queen turned to look. Her blue eyes, dull only a moment before, suddenly sparkled. Mala smiled at Sellia.

Sellia paused a moment to glance back at Hark, smiling just as Mala had smiled, and watched the recognition come over him when he realized the queen's magnificent face, framed with her lovely coiffure and gleaming gems, was identical to Sellia's, framed in wind and rain-damaged straggles of matching color. Sellia wasn't disappointed. Hark's strong jaw dropped briefly, his eyes narrowed to sharpen the vision for further comparison.

Sellia laughed happily. Playing the lifelong joke always delighted her. Childish perhaps, but just as much fun now as it was when she and Mala were children. She kissed her sister's hand, then flopped down at her feet, content to sit on the thick carpet.

"I didn't expect you for another week," Mala said. "Did it go all right?"

"Very well, I would say. But I'm tired."

"So I see," Mala said, and she sat down on the resin throne and looked up to the balcony of the arena where Hark waited, arms folded across his chest.

Sellia hadn't really bothered to follow her sister's gaze. She knew Hark would catch Mala's eye. "A Fyxen dandy who is also a doctor. I snatched him from a band of rounders. He saved me the trip across the Black Desert."

"Aunt Aislinn is waiting for you to greet her," Mala said under her breath.

A stab of fear shot through Sellia. Quickly she turned to look at the front row of seats, waved and smiled at her aunt. Her aunt nodded stiffly in return, barely disturbing her black headgear. Sellia hadn't noticed Aislinn because of her eagerness to see Mala and to play the old game with her. Aislinn would not be quick to forgive or forget the slight. Sellia sighed, feeling dismayed. It wasn't the first time. But the wonder of it was that Sellia still could not help feeling the same way she had felt when she was a little girl and one of the aunts had scolded her.

Mala shrugged almost imperceptibly, as if to tell her not to worry. But she would, and Mala would, just as much as if she'd been the offender. "Why didn't you go to Fox?" Mala finally asked.

Taffy, the dwarf, climbed up on the dais and sat down next to Sellia. Playfully she patted his amber hair as she answered her sister. "The dandy knew everything I was going there to find out. So I came back." Taffy put his head in her lap and she stroked his hair gently.

"How long are you going to keep us in suspense, Sellia? What did the dandy tell you?"

Mala's voice was sharp and Sellia looked up at her in surprise. "That the spaceman was coming here, Mala, by rail. So of course I returned."

Mala glared at her and Sellia pushed the dwarf away to sit up a bit straighter. Frown lines formed on her sister's face and the corners of her mouth turned down. Without wanting to, Sellia knew her own face was mirroring the queen's.

"The spaceman *isn't* here?"

Mala didn't answer aloud, but her deepening frown confirmed what Sellia had just voiced as a fleeting thought.

"Damn," Sellia said, before she could think not to. She turned to look and see if Aislinn had heard her. She had, and Sellia cursed again, silently this time. "The dandy lied!"

CHAPTER 17

Lady Sellia had turned away from the cleric in the front row to stare up at Hark. Even at a distance he could see the anger in her eyes, and he sensed the gazes of the others were on him, too. She beckoned to him with one finger. He unfolded his arms from across his chest and picked his way down to the arena floor, brushing past many highborn women to stand before Sellia.

"You said the spaceman was going to New Penance by rail." Her tone was sharp, her eyes piercing, but her hand, he noted with relief, was nowhere near the hilt of her dagger.

"That's true, but the spaceman's journey was interrupted by wilderness savages, jungle rounders. Luckily, he chanced to meet a woman of New Penance and the rest of his journey was, if not uneventful, at least safe in her company," Hark said. He smiled at Lady Sellia. "Very wet, too, I might add."

For a moment Lady Sellia stared in amazement. Around her the noblewomen were sniggering. "Damn you, you're a liar after all. The women of Fox didn't let him go."

"I'm sure they wouldn't have," Hark said gravely. "It was quite evident they would never let me go to New Penance or Selene whether I was escorted or not. I took matters into my own hands."

Lady Sellia shook her head angrily. "What of the story

about wanting to study with a doctor in Selene?" She stood up and went to her sister. "Mala, I know he's a doctor, not a spaceman. He's lying, though I don't know why. Look at this." She lifted her sleeve to show her sister the stitched knife wound. "He *has* to be a doctor. The stitches he made are as clean and even as the court's own doctor's."

Queen Mala examined her sister's arm, then looked through the crowd at a gray-haired noblewoman in a white-trimmed scarlet robe. The woman stepped forward as if summoned to look at Sellia's arm.

"A very professional job," she said, eyeing Hark warily, "but I would have expected something more sophisticated than stitches from the Homeworlds."

"Not in a portable medical kit," Hark said. "And the aspiring doctor story was a handy disguise. It was a true story, but it was not my own. It belonged to a man named Jeremy, son of Dame Cirila who is a doctor to Fox Court. I escaped with Jeremy during the prenuptial celebrations."

"And where is this Jeremy person?"

"He fell off the trestle, broke his neck and died," he said, hoping the animosity between Fox and New Penance would prevent them from learning he was probably standing trial for murder. He didn't want to explain about the troopers.

Lady Sellia was standing with her hands on her hips, her eyes still slits from anger. "You're either a dandy who lied about the spaceman or a spaceman who lied about the dandy."

And either way Hark knew she was enraged because he had embarrassed her before her sister and the court. He was glad they were here in New Penance Court when she discovered his deception; he had the feeling she would have used the dagger as quickly as she had used her whip if the blood wouldn't have damaged the deep-piled carpeting.

The queen reached up to her sister's shoulder, and Lady Sellia seemed to relax briefly and she sat down at the queen's feet again. "If you are who you say," said the queen to Hark, "you should be able to prove it."

"The obvious proof is my ship, but that is in Fox Park,

heavily guarded by Fyxen troops. You have my word, though. That I freely give."

"Why should we take *your* word, man?" came a baritone voice from the low place occupied by the dwarf.

Hark saw the dwarf peeking out from under the queen's glittering train.

"It doesn't matter to me if she does or not," Hark said. "I was bound for Selene when this noblewoman," he nodded at Lady Sellia, "found me. I'll be on my way, if that pleases the court."

"Selene!" The queen spoke the word like a curse.

Hark nodded. "Selene is reputed to possess the most advanced scientific knowledge of the three city-states, of which I was told, New Penance is the smallest and least exemplary. Something to do with religious restrictions."

"Penance," Lady Sellia said.

"Selene," the queen said again, very thoughtful, very worried.

"Why would the spaceman want to go to Selene?" the dwarf said in what sounded like a deliberately mischievous voice. "Little Jeremy would want to go there if he were a sissy, but the spaceman? He should be smarter than that . . . if he really came all the way from the Home-worlds."

"My ship is disabled. I need help Fyxen could not or would not give. Selene has what I need."

"What does Selene have that we don't have in New Penance?" the queen demanded.

Before Hark could speak, a low whisper yet audible to all and distinctly male in timbre, said from a place very close to the floor, "Hospitality."

The queen's bare foot shot out from under her skirts, aimed at the dwarf's neck, but he dodged and ran without ever having turned to watch for the attack. Her glittering train took seconds to float to the floor.

Hark lowered his head to hide the smile he felt and saw two brown eyes looking up at him from a head that barely topped his hips. Then the dwarf slipped around behind him.

"I do require cooperation to attain my goal," Hark said to the queen seriously. "I have reason to believe I'll be welcome in Selene."

"What reason?" the queen demanded to know.

"Because . . ." He couldn't say he'd dreamed about the lady of lava lake, nor that the two men had died because he'd refused to marry a Fyxen officer. Indeed, he didn't want to say anything about the AI this time. ". . . a scientist of Selene invited me."

"Which one?"

Hark took a deep breath. "Laurel," he said.

"He's lying again. He heard me talking to Hilma about Laurel."

"And did you mention, Lady Sellia," Hark said, his heart beating wildly now, "that Laurel has red hair?"

Sellia and the queen were both staring at him so hard he didn't dare breathe for fear he would gasp, out of control. Finally the queen asked her sister, "Well, did you?"

"No," Sellia said, and Hark started breathing again. "But Laurel's well known. Even a Fyxen might know she has short red hair."

"Long red hair," Hark corrected instantly.

"That's not proof," the queen said. "Not of knowing Laurel, nor of being from the Homeworlds. But if you are from the Homeworlds, you would know who won the war."

"And you would not know the right answer if he said it, sister dear," Sellia said. Hark smiled at her but got a frown in return. "But tell us anyhow, you, who are so good with words. It will be entertaining."

Hark winced, was certain she was contemptuously telling him she'd already discarded everything he'd ever said to her. He was surprised to realize how much that hurt. "The war ended in a truce. There was so much destruction there was no other way for it to end."

"I've heard better from you," Sellia said scornfully.

"Perhaps you didn't understand after all," he said, softly, bitterly.

"I understand," the queen said icily, "that you would have us believe the Homeworlds would send one ship to Islands without escort or backup."

"I am the backup, milady. The first lander was completely destroyed by Fox's big guns."

Hark heard muttering behind him, but nothing comprehensible. He saw that many of the women had given up their seats and were moving into the pit around the dais, the better to hear.

"What guns?" the queen asked coldly.

"I only saw one," Hark answered honestly, glad to be past the lies. "It was in the garrison on a railcar."

"Brilliant place to put a big gun," said the dwarf from behind him. "In the middle of Fox Park's garrison. It makes sighting so convenient . . . through the foliage."

"The gun looked to me as if it were intended for aircraft," Hark said. "And it, or one like it, successfully shot down my sister ship."

"Was your sister ship larger than our logging windships?" the queen asked, leaning forward ever so slightly.

"Not larger," Hark replied. "The lander would have made a much smaller target than a windship envelope. And the lander is far sturdier than what I assume is a fabric envelope."

The queen shook her head slightly. "Metallic. Almost impervious to lasers."

Hark shrugged. "The ship they shot down was far smaller. The skin is tough heat-resistant ceramic. If you're wondering if the guns could shoot down a windship, I assure you they could."

"You spoke of cooperation? What do you need to make your ship operable?"

"Then you accept my word?" he asked.

"For now, yes. We'll see if you tend to prove or disprove yourself from this point on. We'll forgive past . . . embellishments of the truth until such time as you give me reason to believe you are not the spaceman you claim to be."

"Fair enough," Hark said, feeling greatly relieved until he saw Lady Sellia still frowning. He had hoped to have her support. He was disappointed, even though he knew it was better to have the queen's.

"Now, what do you need?" asked the queen.

"What you do not have. I need the use of a movable dish antenna. I also need a transmitter to recover my lander from the Fyxen."

The queen didn't blink or seem surprised by his requests. "And what will you give in exchange?"

"But you do not have . . ."

"Assume, for the sake of this discussion, that we do have a movable dish antenna," the queen said, which caused considerable whispering in the pit. "What would you give us in exchange?"

"Fox has taken my valuables from me, my lander and all it contained."

"And what did it contain? Armament?"

"No armament of any kind. Not even handguns. But the lander itself . . ."

"Even one such ship would provide tremendous advantage."

"If it were operable, it would. But it's useless to them without me as a pilot."

"That's obvious, even to Fyxen."

"You would think so," Hark said, "and yet only one Fyxen seemed to recognize the fact."

"Only one, eh?" said the queen thoughtfully. "We can be certain it wasn't Aethelmere." She looked at Hark, her blue eyes pinning him. "The abbess? Or Dame Adione?"

"The abbess's interest in me seemed limited to my purification status."

"But Dame Adione?"

Hark shrugged. "What she proposed can't be spoken in public, but I will tell you that from my point of view it was both immoral and illegal. I rejected her proposal. I will, however, strike a bargain with you—if you have a movable dish antenna."

"A man has no true loyalties. Whomever fills his belly and warms his bed gains his sword!" said the dwarf from behind Hark.

Hark resisted a temptation to kick the little man himself, but apparently the dwarf didn't know that. He had dived under the queen's train again.

"Explain yourself, man," the queen said looking at him with a kind of dispassionate curiosity, making her look unlike Lady Sellia for the first time. "Why would you offer us what you would not give to the Fyxens?"

The dwarf sat up and draped the train across his shoulders. When he caught Hark looking at him, he stuck out his tongue. Hark found his breathing uneasy again. He knew he must be careful, perhaps more so than in Fox where at least the presence of muscle men and stripling sons were indulged. And, he reminded himself, where I was indulged right along with them with about as much credibility as the dwarf, and with as much purpose, too. Diversion for the noblewomen.

"Man!" Lady Sellia said sharply. "The queen has asked you a question."

Hark frowned. The address from both sisters was spoken in contempt. They were waiting for him to reply, and he was finding it difficult to speak reasonably when he knew they were ready either to discount anything he said or to laugh at him. And, he realized, Lady Sellia had her hand on her knife hilt. Suddenly the dwarf was at his side. He hadn't noticed him leave the queen's dais; her train had not fluttered the way it did before. The dwarf had climbed atop a resin chair, set a three-legged stool on the chair, and carefully climbed on top of that.

"Better say something soon," the dwarf whispered so softly none but Hark could hear. "I can't climb on air."

Was the little fellow an ally after all? Keeping the court amused while Hark composed himself? He saw Lady Sellia's hand tightening on the knife hilt. "My position is untenable before I even start," he said quietly. "I am a man. It's a foregone conclusion I must be a dandy, a ticket-of-leave man, or a trooper. But I'm not. I'm not even sure I know what those labels mean, so I can't even pretend to be one. Yet I sense that's what you expect. How can I communicate with you if I am prejudged?"

"Do *you* prejudge by virtue of your experience in Fox?" Lady Sellia asked, her tone suddenly mellow.

"Perhaps I am equally guilty. But I don't want to repeat the mistake of assuming what I say will be taken at face value simply because I say it. I'm accustomed to respect and was taken by surprise when it wasn't given in Fox."

He noticed only a few noblewomen nodded in appreciation.

"You don't look particularly respectable, milord," the queen said in her cool voice.

Hark flinched at her scorn.

"He would have preferred to change clothes, Mala," Lady Sellia said. "He reminded me we were not suitably attired for court, but I explained what little emphasis we put on clothes in New Penance. Let's hear him out with open minds."

Hark breathed a little easier, comforted by Lady Sellia's words even though the queen's face did not soften.

"They're interchangeable," the dwarf whispered in Hark's ear.

"Let's see if your position is tenable," the queen said.

Hark nodded. There was no alternative anyway. The women would decide. "I will trade a certain hypothesis and a few technical um . . . advances that will enable your scientists to develop a protective forcefield to surround your logging windships. Doing this violates the letter of the laws under which my ship operates but preserves the spirit. Under the circumstances, it's the lesser of two evils, and I take full responsibility for the consequences I'll face when I return to the Homeworlds."

"You forget to whom you speak. We are Penitents, not convicts. There is no lesser evil in worsening an imbalance in nature. Such temptations must be overcome."

"Since imbalance has already occurred, one even graver

than their guns," Hark said carefully, "I feel morally justified in attempting to rebalance the scales by trading the forcefields for your assistance in returning my lander into operating order."

"What imbalance has occurred?" asked Lady Sellia.

"What did you give Fox Court?" said the queen.

"How did you betray New Penance?" wailed the dwarf.

Hark frowned at the little man, who was standing nose to nose with him on the stool. "I *gave* nothing of my own free will. But the Fyxen opened my ship to their clerical scientists. The scientists will guess, they will surmise, and they will make valid assumptions. In time, they will . . ."

"Fly that ship!" the dwarf said in a dismayed voice.

"In time," Hark continued impatiently, "they will understand the principle of rocketry and be able to deliver bombs to New Penance and Selene at will."

"War," screamed the dwarf. "It's war. And a man has brought it to you."

Hark, speaking loudly to the dwarf to be heard over a sudden outbreak of private conversations among the noblewomen, said, "Shut up before I wring your neck."

"Your energy would be better spent on the sorry sister," the dwarf said grinning widely.

The cleric had worked her way through the crowd to the queen's side. She was as tall as Hark, her eyes so blue they were almost as dark as her velvety gown, her headgear preposterously tall and broad. "The Penance Princess herself told that if men were given positions of responsibility, they would blunder in ignorance, or use it violently," she said gravely, "just as they had done in the Homeworlds."

Hark sighed audibly as the noblewomen quieted. "Women were equally responsible with men for the wars on the Homeworlds."

The cleric never looked at Hark, only at the queen. "Penance is your sacred trust."

"Your position *is* untenable," the dwarf whispered loudly in Hark's ear.

"You aren't helping any," Hark said with a frown.

The dwarf grinned and danced on the stool. Hark had to suppress an urge to knock him from his precarious perch.

"How do we know you're telling the truth?" the queen finally said. "Perhaps this talk of guns is just an attempt to force us to help you."

The abbess leaned over to whisper something in the queen's ear, and the queen shook her head.

"Surely you can verify what I've said about the guns."

"Yes, but not quickly." Again the abbess whispered to her, and the queen finally nodded. "She asks to see your left shoulder."

"Gladly," he said, lifting the sleeve to show her the tattoo.

The cleric didn't react, and the queen just shook her head. "It merely indicates how elaborate your preparations were."

"It's genuine. I give you my word," Hark said.

"A man's word," said the dwarf loudly, "is subject to the base instincts that direct his mind."

"I told you before that I can't be put in the categories you tend to associate with my sex," Hark said trying to ignore the dwarf. "I'm accustomed to being treated with honor and dignity, not accustomed to having my word questioned."

"Delusions of grandeur!" cried the dwarf. "He believes himself to be as morally splendid as the women of New Penance."

"Hardly a delusion, Little Traitor," Hark said, summoning as much scathing to his voice as he could. "I am a man of honor, and to that even a lady of this court can attest."

The queen looked at him sharply. "Do you believe you are a man above all other men?"

"I know I'm not subject to the base instincts you reduce men to. If that makes me unique among men of your world, so be it. The Lady Sellia will tell you this is so."

"I will?" Lady Sellia said with a start.

"I assume you would not lie to this court," Hark said, trying to smile pleasantly. "Let me prod your memory."

"Please," she said sarcastically, and she leaned her languorous frame against her sister's knees.

"I believe you mentioned mankind's violent nature," he said to the cleric. The woman nodded, and Hark turned back to the Lady Sellia. "Please recall who spared the life of the rounder we encountered, you or I?"

"Ha! You missed her, not spared her."

"I missed her deliberately. I could have hit a far smaller target at thrice the distance."

"That's easily proved," warned the queen.

"Milady, I can back my claim with a remarkable demonstration, if that is your pleasure."

"A contest! A contest! A very male endeavor," the dwarf said with relish.

Hark ignored the little man and met the queen's gaze with apparent confidence that was in truth quite shaken as he realized he had unintentionally stepped into yet another male category.

"He said a demonstration, Short Stuff," the queen said. "And for now, until the future proves otherwise, I accept the boast as justified."

"They're interchangeable," the dwarf hissed again.

As Hark watched, the little man rolled his eyes from sister to sister. Hark shrugged and continued. "The lady Sellia can further attest to my lack of violent nature and to my honor."

"Remind me of how," Lady Sellia said with a bad-tempered sounding laugh.

"The first night in the wilderness that we spent alone, quite alone, just you and I. I did not, ah . . . ravage you as one of your troopers might."

"You would have had to get past twenty years of excellence in the martial arts if I weren't willing," she retorted.

"Did I try to get past your defenses?"

"No."

"Did I perhaps try to charm you as a dandy might?"

"No."

"Nor even the second night when you were drunk and . . ."

"No," she said quickly.

"Pity," said the queen.

"Sissy!" screamed the dwarf.

"There are a number of women in Fox Court who will testify otherwise," Hark said unpleasantly to the dwarf. "How many here will do the same for you?"

Lady Sellia laughed behind her hand and the queen smiled. The dwarf's eyes bulged with surprise. With hopes that he had silenced the little man for a while, Hark turned back to the queen. "Milady, I didn't come to debate your values. I came to seek your aid, much as Lady Sellia sought the warrior Hilma's hospitality, and was given beasts to ease her journey in exchange for something of value. Something of value will pass between us, too. But nothing will come of my being here if you can't accept me as an equal."

"You ask a great deal," the queen said. "Worse, you have thrust us to the brink of war."

"Milady, if my ship had landed in the grand valley of New Penance instead of Fox territory, where would it be now?"

The queen nodded and frowned, admitting, Hark thought, that the ship would have had a similar fate in New Penance.

"Surely you cannot hold me to blame."

"We are damned either way, assuming he's telling the truth," the queen said wearily. "If we don't help him, we'll have no defense against Fox's guns. If we do help him, assuming we can get him past his technical problems, we will have to risk war to get his ship back." She looked at Hark seriously. "I'm certain it will come without reassembly instructions."

"Those are here," Hark said, tapping his head.

"Supposedly bright as well as nonviolent and unsexed," Lady Sellia said dryly.

"You'll be violating canonical law, a trust we've held sacred for seventy-five years," the cleric said warningly to the queen.

"Milady," he said to the abbess, "I came in peace, and my goodwill was repaid by theft of my ship and virtual imprisonment of my person. They even drugged me against my will to learn what I would have told them without such means. Are Penitents no different than Fyxen?"

"That was justice, not theft or imprisonment," the abbess replied. "A man needs a guardian, especially if he has worldly goods, or he'll waste them wantonly. A man who has no guardian becomes a ward of the court until one is appointed so that his rights are protected from his own base nature. Those are universal laws, which none of the remaining Islands will ever forget."

"What *rights*?" Hark asked heatedly before he could think what might better have been said.

"The right to fight! The right to fuck," cried the dwarf. "What man could ask for more?"

"I ask more," Hark said. The noblewomen were silent, many seemingly thoughtful. Some looked surprised.

Lady Sellia broke the silence by standing to face her sister. "This isn't Fox. We don't use drugs for questioning or punishment, and guardians must answer to the Queen's Court if they abuse their wards or waste his goods. We know the Fyxen are not as conscientious. We have peace of sorts with those decadent women only because Queen Aethelmere is inept and bumbling. Who knows which fraction will overthrow her? Usurpers, like Aethelmere herself. If we move now, take the spaceman's ship from them right away, perhaps we can forestall their development of rocketry."

"Queen Mala, I must protest," said the abbess. "The only true thing Lady Sellia has said is that this is not Fox. Here we do not keep men in our privileged chambers and allow them to distract us from penance. We left that behind us on the Homeworlds. Cast out this male rabble who would incite us to war."

The queen grasped the glassy edges of her throne's armrest. Her fingernails seemed as transparant as the resin they squeezed. She looked nervously at the cleric who was still visibly angry. "Hark, leave us now. We will call you if we have questions," the queen said slowly. Then she looked at the dwarf. "Take him to your apartment, Small Stuff, and see that he's cleaned."

Hark flushed as the dwarf protested. "I can call a trooper to escort him."

"At least tell me if you really have a movable dish antenna," Hark said.

Queen Mala frowned. "Out!"

The dwarf climbed down from the stool to the chair to the floor, looking at the queen with large doleful eyes. Hark was amazed he didn't stumble. The queen stamped her foot impatiently and pointed up to the doors at the top of the arena.

The dwarf turned and walked heavily from the arena, stealing long and sad glances at the queen. When he was finally certain that her complete attention was with the court, he gestured for Hark and ran up the steps. Hark took a step toward the queen, but some of the noblewomen cut him off and the queen did not look up. Hark followed the dwarf.

CHAPTER 18

The dwarf walked with surprising quickness, leading Hark through a short maze of tunnels drilled out of metamorphic rock to a ladder in a shaft. The dwarf started climbing.

"Where are we going?" Hark asked, eyeing the ladder height warily.

"To the shortcut," the dwarf said. "At least, I hope we can still take the shortcut."

"I don't care about the way," Hark said grabbing the dwarf's ankle. "I want to know where we're going."

The dwarf shook Hark's hand off. "Exactly where she told me to take you—my place," he said irritably, and continued climbing. He topped the ladder and stepped out of sight. Hark followed and stepped into a cavern of immense proportions, far bigger than the underground court chamber. He hadn't thought New Penance would be a settlement of much importance because the orbiter hadn't even detected it. The orbiter wasn't equipped to look through solid rock, but even the AI hadn't extrapolated its existence. Hark was beginning to believe that was a big oversight. The caves were extensive, the chambers enormous, and well used by the local population. This one they'd just climbed into was filled with wooden cages and the echoing murmur only a large congregation of people could make.

He hurried around a corner of cages after the dwarf and found himself in a crowd.

But they were not cages. Behind the polished hardwood slats and waxy-looking filigree were rainbows of silk and sacking bolts, stacks of hides, bins of nuts and grain, shelves of pottery and glassware, all open to the scrutiny of shoppers. A caged bird crowed, its cry startling Hark before it was swallowed by the cavern.

Another turn took them into an alley fragrant with perfume, littered with flower petals, crushed by the softly clinking footfalls of a throng of women. The few men Hark saw wore plain green uniforms with a swath of green-on-green-print cloth crossing their left breasts, circling their waists, and ending in a drape from the right hip to the knee. Under the drape he noticed sheathed knives. One by one they stared at Hark with seemingly unblinking eyes. Hark felt if the dwarf were not with him the men would have done more than stare, for he was certain by now they were troopers on patrol and the sight of a full-sized man not clad like themselves was unusual. Hark hadn't liked being summarily dismissed by the queen, but now he gave up thoughts of abandoning the dwarf to strike out on his own.

The dwarf stopped abruptly to peer between slats at a cobbler's display. A pair of blue shoes seemed to have taken his eye. He looked up at Hark. "I like recreational shopping, especially when I have a pocket full of coins." His eyes glittered for a second, then he hurried on, looking back to add, "When the shortcut's open, I'm within just five minutes of all this."

Their route cut through only a corner of the marketplace, and Hark realized that if the levels of caged shops were three high throughout the cavern, the population it served was far larger than the open-air market he'd seen in Fox or the amount of goods far more numerous, or both. The scents drifting on the dry cavern air were intriguing and flashes of color behind the cage bars lured his eyes. But for the disquieting presence of the troopers, he thought he might have liked what the dwarf called recreational shopping.

"Good. It's still open," the dwarf said. He was referring to a tunnel that, unlike the others they'd passed through, had a sturdy sedgepole gate set off to the side. A narrow passage opened into yet another cavern, but this time they were on a ledge high above the cavern floor.

The ledge was lighted with tiny chemlamps, just bright enough to show the way. Below, lighted by spotlights, was a gang of men sweeping piles of yellow luminescence into carts that other men were hauling up to the ledge and dumping into a waiting railcar. Another gang, this one comprised of mostly men but also a few women, were hosing the cavern floor with water that carried luminescent swirls like oil into a trough. A squad of troopers, comprised this time of women as well as men, was overseeing the work. The cavern stank like feces.

The dwarf had half-run along the ledge to a steep staircase carved out of the rock. He held the safety rail all the way down to the cavern floor where duckplanks, knotted together by rope, had been rolled across the cavern floor, around a bend, and through a shaft of natural light to the other side. The dwarf seemed nervous and in a hurry, and Hark, certain the duckplanks were keeping his feet off of sulphur belly droppings, could understand why. There were even sulphur belly trails in the cavern, plainly visible around the perimeter of the cavern, though why the creatures would come into the cave Hark didn't know. Perhaps, he thought as they walked through the natural light coming in through the cave entrance, to get in out of the rain, for he could see that it was raining again. And if that were the case, Hark didn't want to still be in this cavern any more than the dwarf did. He felt relieved when they reached the other side of the cavern and the dwarf hurried up another staircase that led to tunnels that were far too small for a sulphur belly to follow.

Finally the dwarf led him through a narrow tunnel of what looked to Hark like sedimentary rock. Hark had to duck, but once through the carved wooden door at the end, he could stand up straight.

The chamber was a spa of sorts with pools and bubbling fountains, pallets, benches, and mats. Recesses in the natural rock were curtained with handsomely carved lattices, the floor rendered even with chips of corklike material.

"Pick your pleasure, friend," the dwarf said. "Mineral pool, hot spring, shower, both, or swim in all of them if you like. On second thought, take a shower first, or you'll leave a ring on the pools." He wrinkled his nose.

"Friend!" Hark said with a snort. He walked to the closest pool. Briefly he thought of escape; it wouldn't be hard to get away from the dwarf. But the tunnels and caverns were a maze to him, and there were the troopers to consider. He wasn't in their custody, which was better treatment than he'd had in Fox. He decided not to provoke them in any way, at least, not now. Besides, the water was steaming and looked deep. That seemed a good choice for tired muscles and bones aching from the long ride on the boneback.

"Friend, oh, yes. I do mean friend," the dwarf said.

"You were about as friendly as the sorry sister," Hark said pulling off the smelly leather tunic. "The rest are at least curious, but her—and you!" He shook his head in disgust.

"Don't be a fool, *man*," the dwarf said, his face free of the doleful smiles and winsome glee that Hark had assumed were his most natural expressions until this moment. "I didn't say anything they wouldn't have thought of themselves. The difference is that when I say what's going on in their minds, they laugh. They don't ponder."

Hark stopped stripping off his filthy clothes to look more closely at the dwarf. He was small, of course, no longer young and slightly rotund. He was neither handsome nor ugly, but for the first time Hark saw his eyes clearly. They were deepset, three-cornered like an old man's might be, wise.

"That woman is powerful, but not just because she's the abbey's representative in court. You'll have to deal with her before you'll get serious consideration from the queen or Lady Sellia. And if you do, don't trust one above the other. They're interchangeable."

"What the hell does that mean, 'they're interchangeable?'"

"Just that they are." The dwarf smiled at him, sat down at the edge of the pool as Hark lowered himself in. "You can't tell one from the other, can you?"

"One is the queen," Hark said irritably. The water was hot, chest deep, and it swirled gently over his skin.

"Are you sure?"

Hark looked at him. He recognized the smile as a mischievous one, and he thought the dwarf was playing with him again.

"Let me tell you a story about the queen," the dwarf said, the smile fading. "When twins were born, the first from the womb was tattooed on her heel. The attendants say it was unnecessary. Mala was a sweet baby, full of smiles and coos. Sellia was colicky and complaining. Even when they were older and in training, you only had to exchange a few words with one before you knew who you were talking to. Mala was a gentle child, easy-going, serious. Sellia was wild, uncontrollable, aggressive. Some people said Mala would be a fine and compassionate ruler. Others worried that she would be weak and spineless and suggested that the second born would be more suited. You can guess what kind of factions thought which way. But something started happening some time just before puberty. Mala developed a penchant for tantrums. Sellia suddenly began to excel in her academic training, matching her sister's achievements in short years. It was all over by the time they joined the troops. When Mala ascended to her mother's throne, both sisters had identical tattoos.''

"Are you trying to tell me that you don't know which one ascended to the throne?" Hark asked, looking steadily at the dwarf for any hint of a smile.

"I'm telling you we don't know from day to day," he said seriously. "Sellia today, or Mala? Whoever comes from the Canopy Palace wearing the crown and sits on the throne, we call Mala. But we don't know."

"Then the younger sister grew too ambitious?"

"Or did the elder feel she was too weak to rule on her own? A combination? Perhaps. I don't know."

Hark grabbed onto the side of the pool. "They impersonate each other—no, a blend, you say. That's some accomplishment. Neither is ever entirely herself."

"A blend?" The dwarf shrugged. "Or both schizoid?"

Hark kept looking at the little man, uncertain if he were telling the truth. He was grinning again, but Hark couldn't draw any conclusions. "Why?"

The dwarf handed him a bowl of scented soap, and Hark took some in his hands to lather. "Because no one person can deal with two hellcats forever without getting clawed up a bit, not even Queen Mala. Whoever is Lady Sellia gets to leave court to lick her wounds in the wilderness.''

"What are these hellcats?" Hark said.

"You met one today," the dwarf said. "The abbess, Milady Mother Aislinn. She has another living sister, you know, wombsister, not a sister from the abbey, Meave. The third sister died ten years ago; Finella was the queen who gave birth to twin daughters."

"These hellcats are aunts, then, and have kept the powers of the court in the family?" Hark asked, immediately deciding Aislinn's being the abbey's representative in court probably indicated the other had rank as well.

"Almost all the power," the dwarf said taking off his shoes to dip his feet in the pool. "And it's very hard to find fault with it. Even those who don't believe in genetic memory have to admit the hellcats' bloodline exhibits extraordinary abilities. If you listen carefully, you'll hear some complain their abilities aren't so great on their own, but due only to the queen's nepotism, first Finella's, then Mala's."

"Then there are factions in this court, too," Hark said, wondering if he could use that to his advantage.

"Nah, not really. Not anything that ever comes out in the open. The queen and the hellcats have a lot of support. Nepotism or not, it's their bloodline that has kept New Penance completely independent, which isn't easy considering we do strict penance while dealing with Fox and Selene where they don't."

Hark felt an urge to laugh. "For all humanity, even for the Homeworlds, where they barely know you exist."

"I never believed in the Homeworlds," the dwarf said shrugging his big shoulders. "Not until today, I didn't."

"Because of me?" And when the dwarf nodded, Hark asked, "You don't doubt me?"

"No. I believe you, and I meant what I said . . . friend."

He looked sincere, and Hark nodded. "Thank you . . . I don't know your name."

"Taffy," he said, and extended his hand to Hark. He

shook it gladly, found Taffy's grip surprisingly firm for so small a hand.

"I thought this was a forgotten gesture," he said. "When I tried it in Fox, I was refused."

"By a woman, right?" And when Hark nodded, Taffy added, "You probably wouldn't be refused in New Penance, not even by a woman. Here everyone removes his own dirt with his own hand, so I guess no one's suspect or we're all equally suspect."

"Maybe not of having dirty hands," Hark said bitterly, "but I don't think they have much higher regard for men than the Fyxen do."

"You may be right," Taffy said. "I've never met a Fyxen, so I wouldn't know."

"Do they have what I need?" Hark asked Taffy. "The antenna?"

"You think friendship means telling state secrets?" Taffy asked, and shook his head. "I don't know anything about that, so don't ask me."

"I just don't want to waste my time, like I did in Fox. But at least this time I have a better feel for the power base, the aunts and Sellia and Mala. It helps to know who I must convince."

"A man will convince them of nothing," Taffy said, shaking his head.

Hark sighed. "Back to that, eh? I'm all too familiar with the problem, but this time I don't think it's hopeless. Sellia, for instance, at least listened when we were traveling together. And Mala seems to have the same sense of reason, if her listening to me today was any indication."

Hark resumed washing, then noticed Taffy was chuckling. "You caught her by surprise. I don't think she's ever met a man who didn't knuckle under right away—except me, of course."

"And she's fond of you," Hark said.

"Like her packbeasts," Taffy said. "I amuse her. But you could scare her, and if you do, she'll strike out."

"What would you recommend? How would you proceed if you were me?"

"I would hope she would fall in love with me, let me be her goodman. Then there would be a chance of getting what I want."

Hark didn't answer. Taffy was telling him what had worked for him, if the lovely pools were indicative of the queen's rewards for affection and amusement. But Hark didn't want pools. He wanted help. "She'll just have to get scared," he said under his breath.

"What?"

"Nothing," Hark said. "I just wonder which one I'll be dealing with next. Sellia, I hope."

"I told you before, they're interchangeable. Either both of them like you or both of them don't. There's no way to tell them apart. They even have the same number of whorls in their fingerprints."

"But one of them has a rather obvious wound, and it will leave a scar," Hark said feeling some satisfaction.

"How much would you care to wager that before dawn both of them have wounds?"

Hark looked at Taffy, and he nodded.

"Before dawn," he repeated. "Don't think they haven't already faced that problem. Even the scars are identical."

Hark shook his head and laughed out loud. He turned to check that his red backpack was still with his clothes. It was. And inside was the stitcher and the green thread that Mala would find no where else on the planet. He wondered how long it would take them to realize it, and he laughed again.

"What's so funny, my friend?" Taffy asked, looking bewildered.

"I think I'll have a friend in court by morning," Hark said, and laughed again. He shook his head and climbed out of the pool. "Is there a bed I can use? I'm tired, and I think I can sleep soundly now."

CHAPTER 19

Hark permitted himself only a few hours of deep sleep in Taffy's soft bed, but before his wristwatch could pinch him awake, Taffy did.

"You have to wake up, Hark. There's a messenger here for you," he said when Hark looked at him groggily.

"Messenger?" Hark said. He'd been dreaming of the lady of the lava lake again. His watch pinched him soundly as he sat up.

Taffy was holding a chemlamp that lighted the rough-hewn cubbyhole he called his sleeping chamber. Next to him was a pubescent girl wearing a simple tunic over which a seamless skirt was knotted at her hip. She was holding a roll of paper in her hand, staring at Hark curiously.

"Is that for me?" Hark asked her, reaching for the paper.

She snatched her hand away, the look of curiosity replaced by a frown. "Are you Hark, the pilot from the Homeworlds?"

"I am," he said, and reached out again.

"I must see your tattoo," she said shaking her head gravely.

"Which one?" he asked, turning his hands to show his palms. "These?"

She looked closely, obviously not expecting to see tattoos on his hands, but she shook her head again. Hark then pointed to his bare shoulder, and she nodded. But still she

191

kept the scroll out of reach. "The court requires me to read the message to recipients of your sex," she said.

"I know how to read," Hark assured her.

"Nonetheless, I will read it," she said firmly.

Hark sighed. He had thought the combination of youthful curiosity and seriousness charming until now. "Go ahead. Read."

She unrolled the scroll. "You are commanded to appear at the Academy for Advanced Studies of Nature three hours after dawn for the purpose of answering whatever questions the academicians may put to you to prove or disprove the claims you made in the Queen's Court today."

"That's the first sensible move anyone has made on this planet," Hark interjected with a satisfied sigh. He would be dealing with a body of people who, if they bore any resemblance to academicians and scientists of the Homeworlds, would have scant loyalty to tradition or religious authority. At last he would have an open-minded audience.

The girl looked over the top of her scroll at him. "There's more," she said. And when he nodded contritely, she continued. "You have the right to have your guardian accompany you and to have the summons delivered to her. If you do not have a guardian, the court will appoint one.

"Written by Meave, Queen's Privy Pursekeeper, at the command of her majesty, Mala, Third and Only True Queen of Islands on this fifteenth day after Double Nocturne Three in the Seventy-fifth year of the Penance." The messenger rolled the scroll and still would not hand it over.

"Now what do you want?" Hark said gruffly, his joy at having what sounded like an opportunity to speak spoiled by mention of a guardian.

"I need to know who you want me to deliver this to," she said. "I was warned you might say you have no guardian, in which case I shall return it to the court."

"If you won't give it to me, give it to Lady Sellia and tell her I know she'll understand when I reject anyone the court attempts to appoint as my guardian," Hark said firmly.

"As you wish," the girl said, and she turned to leave.

Taffy went with her to light the way. At the sleeping chamber door, the girl stopped and looked back. "You really want me to say that?" she asked.

"Verbatim," he said, and she shrugged and left.

Taffy returned after letting the messenger out. "I don't think it will do any good to reject a court-appointed guardian," he said. "I mean, I don't think you can. They'll do it anyhow."

Hark shrugged. "At least they're going to listen to me," he said.

"Scholars will," Taffy said. "Someone from court will be there, too, I'm sure, but I wouldn't count on Lady Sellia or Queen Mala. They are probably in Family Court right now with their aunts. The decision of what to do with you or about you will be made before dawn."

"What?" Hark felt a stab of fear. "What's this Family Court? One for choosing guardians?"

"Not officially. Family Court is what the royal evening meal is called. The twins and their aunts often stay up half the night arguing when something important is going on. When that happens, they sleep late in the morning and usually miss morning court."

Hark shook his head, glanced at his watch and made a quick calculation. "Still eight hours until dawn. I guess I'll get some more sleep while I have the chance."

"You're not worried?" Taffy said seemingly surprised.

"No," Hark said. "I still think I'm going to have a friend in court tomorrow." He checked to see that his pack was under his pillow. It was, and he lay back down.

Hark lay quietly in Taffy's deep bed of down quilts, his arm thrown over his pack, his eyes almost closed. Ever since the messenger had gone, he'd slept as lightly as if he were the nightwatch on the bridge in deep space when there was nothing to do but wait. And as the dim flash of an instrument light could bring him to complete awareness, so did the strobe of a light over his bed. But he lay silently, knowing now he was no longer alone.

She had to move his arm off the pack, but first she turned

off the light she carried and waited a long, long time before touching him. She grasped him by the wrist and lifted his arm just enough for her to slide the pack out from underneath, then carefully lowered his arm until it was resting on the bed. He sensed rather than heard that she was moving away, and in seconds he heard the soft *snick* of the carved door that led to the outer chamber. He got up and followed her.

She had stopped in the antechamber to peer into the pack, soft light flowing over her from a plenum above, her face in shadow. Hark thought her an unlikely looking thief in her pretty blue dress and slippers, until he saw the laser holstered in soft leather along her thigh. That made him hesitate a second. She looked up, reflexively reaching for the weapon at the same time.

Hark opened the door the rest of the way "You won't find what you're looking for in there," he said, gesturing at the pack.

Lady Sellia's sharp blue eyes were fixed on him. With the laser levelled at his breast, she carefully set his pack on a table and reached into it with her free hand. She pulled out his groundguide. "I found this," she said sounding annoyed. "A compass with an extra face. Does it keep you from getting lost?"

Hark nodded.

"How does it work? And I don't mean the compass."

"It measures motion, speed, direction, and altitude compared to a basepoint. It's set for Fox Park where my lander is so that I can get back to it, but it works quite well in reverse, too, if you know how to use the deductive logic capabilities."

She put the groundguide on the table and reached into the pack again.

"An infrared scope," Hark said before she could take the other instrument out.

"So that you can see in the dark or through the rain?" she asked accusingly.

"Yes."

"I knew you couldn't just be making lucky guesses," she said, the annoyed tone even more noticeable. On the hilt of the laser, her knuckles were turning white. "Why didn't you tell me who you were?"

"I'm sorry for that now," Hark said sincerely. If he hadn't been completely convinced earlier in court, he knew now he'd made a big mistake in deceiving her. She was angry about it. As she kept the laser pointed at his chest, he began to wonder how far she would go to extract revenge. "My experience in Fox with Dame Adione made me afraid to tell another Islandian woman the truth. By the time I realized you might be different, it was too late."

"Then everything you said while we were traveling was lies," she said. She sounded fierce but the look on her face was unmistakably one of disappointment. Hark was amazed to realize the change of expression on her face made his heart beat furiously, and not from fear. He was certain she had been touched by him, if only a little, by the end of their journey together.

"No," Hark said quietly. "There was no reason for me to lie all the time. I lied about my identity, nothing more."

She looked at him searchingly for a moment; then stiffly, she lowered the laser and slipped it into the holster.

"Thank you," he said. Hark stepped over to the table to put the groundguide back into the pack, aware that she was watching him closely, perhaps expectantly. "Well, you've met the spaceman you were so eager to meet. What do you think of me now?"

"That you're a man," she said in an arch tone. "One head, ten fingers. Too ordinary to be of such importance to New Penance, indeed, to all of Islands."

"I know," he said feeling genuinely troubled. He was the key to the Homeworlds on a planet where the Penitent culture was so successful because there was no escape. He was further troubled to hear Sellia say that he was ordinary. "I'm sorry that I don't measure up."

She looked at him quizzically. "Measure up?"

How was it that curiosity always seemed to set her eyes

on fire, and him along with it? He cleared his throat. "I don't meet your expectations of what a spaceman should be like," he said, bringing his hands up and wiggling all ten fingers, diffusing the flames with the silly display.

Abruptly she laughed with him. "I don't know what I expected, but I think I like what I got." All traces of her anger were gone, so quickly that Hark wondered if he'd only imagined they'd ever been there at all. She was touching his cheek with the flat of her hand, so tentative a gesture that Hark kissed her palm reflexively. He squeezed his eyes shut when he realized what he had done. He couldn't help wanting her to know how much he liked her but felt terribly guilty about it, too. There was business to take care of, and he dared not let his personal feelings get in the way. She made a nice noise deep in her throat as she smoothed his hair with her fingers. "You have no idea what a problem you pose, spaceman," she said.

Hark opened his eyes, but refused to look into hers. "You may be surprised to learn how much I understand about your problems, including the personal problem that brought you here tonight."

"I don't know what you mean." She blinked and took her hand away, giving him a quizzical look that he had to steel himself against.

"Don't bother pretending," he said briskly. "You need the stitcher for your sister's wound, or you'll never be truly identical ever again. Taffy told me how truly interchangeable you and Mala really are."

"Palace gossip," she said disdainfully as she crossed her arms over her chest. "All nonsense."

"Sellia, you wouldn't be here if it were nonsense. You didn't come until you realized the stitches and the resulting scar would never be identical unless Mala's wound were sewn in the same fashion. If you were only interested in seeing the groundguide you could have waited until I appeared tomorrow morning at your Academy for questioning. But there's something you don't know. The stitcher isn't difficult to operate, and I don't doubt you could figure out how very quickly, but an inexperienced hand on the controls will leave a pattern as different from the one on your arm as night is from day."

"You're lying."

"I'm not. You can believe or not; the choice is yours, as is the risk. I will give you the stitcher and you can be gone. Or you can take me with you and let me tend the wound as I did yours, and the stitches will be just alike. You'll be free to keep up your impersonations."

"If what Taffy told you is true and if I accepted your offer, having you around would be a great risk to me and Mala. There would always be a chance you might tell someone."

"I thought of that," Hark said, "and I've seen you kill. But I don't believe you'll risk staying cut off from the Homeworlds by killing me. You've too much at stake. New Penance is built right on a bomb and it could go off just like the one that destroyed the settlement at Canis Majus. Twenty-five years since the last volcano exploded. How many more do you really believe you have?"

"Not many," Sellia said resignedly. Then she sat on the desk, let her hands drop into her lap, and looked at him seriously. "In court you held your own quite well. I was angry because you deceived me, but I couldn't help but admire your courage and begin to hear what you were saying. You claimed to be a man of honor and made a great issue of being accepted at your word. Yet now you don't offer your word on my secret. What am I to think?"

"I was afraid that if I did it might seem . . ." Hark felt himself turning red under her expectant gaze. He shook his head and started over. "I feel very strongly about behaving honorably in everything I do, not just what duty compels me to do. It wouldn't feel right to offer my word when there's the slightest chance you might think the offer abused whatever affinity we have." He watched her carefully, at once worried that he'd assumed too much and overstepped, yet that he hadn't been direct enough.

"You don't like blackmail very much, do you?"

Hark lowered his eyes and shook his head.

"But you do like me." It wasn't a question, yet it demanded an answer.

Hark hesitated, not because he didn't know the answer but because he knew it would have been safer for both of them to leave it unsaid. He met her gaze and said, "Yes."

"Well, I can't believe it's because you wanted to protect me from having sloppy stitches in my sister's arm that you lay awake waiting for me to come. Not when you hesitate to give me a promise because I might think poorly of you for doing it." She smiled. "If you didn't care, you'd just say whatever I wanted to hear and not care what I think, and this wouldn't be so complicated. I like that you do care, but it still leaves me with an unanswered question: What do you really want?"

"To leave Islands. I want whatever aid you can give me to make that happen. If you have a dish antenna here in New Penance, I want your help in getting permission to use it. If not, help me to get to Selene," he said. "I won't ask you to break any laws. Just use your influence to help, or guide me in the right direction . . . whatever your conscience permits. I need your help to do my duty."

"And your duty is to leave?" she said.

He nodded.

Sellia sighed. "Duty I understand," she said. "I can't say that I'd like you to do yours right away though."

Hark breathed a little easier. He had not misjudged.

"But I'm still not certain I can trust you with the secret. Your sense of duty might cause you to betray me and Mala. If someone made the right offer . . ." Her voice trailed off as her face screwed up in consternation. "I have a duty, too," she said, "one to my sister."

"I give you my word that I will not reveal the secret life you and Mala share." She seemed startled, and he smiled. "It feels right to do that now."

"Get your stitcher and let's go."

Hark nodded and went back to the sleeping chamber. He dressed in his ship suit, clean again after a dousing in Taffy's pool. He took the medical kit from the cupboard he'd hidden it in. Back in the antechamber, Sellia handed him his pack.

"Bring it along," she said. "I want to take a closer look at those things."

Hark put the medical kit into the pack and shouldered it. "I probably shouldn't leave without telling Taffy," he said looking at the poolroom door.

"He's not here," Sellia said. "I had him called away so that I could get in easily."

"I might have left before you arrived," Hark said, surprised at realizing he'd been alone.

She just smiled and opened the door to the outer tunnels. There were two armed troopers standing there, one man and one woman. "You're dismissed, Top," she said to the woman. "I'll keep him with me." And to Hark, she said, "This way."

From the cool, dry caves, they emerged into the warm and humid microclime of the rain forest. The rain had stopped, leaving the air rich and fresh. Overhead the canopy shut out the moons and the stars. They followed a boardwalk, which was not lighted except at intersections with other boardwalks and at stairwells that wound around the gigantic boles of the trees and disappeared in the dark understory. Hark noticed words carved into the boardwalk at intersections. Pathnames, he finally deduced, and they were following *Cava*, the way to and from the cave. Then Sellia stepped off the boardwalk onto the forest floor. Mats of rotted vegetation were underfoot, but movement was surprisingly easy, not cluttered with foliage. He was sweating by now; the humidity was overwhelming.

Not far into the forest, they stepped onto another boardwalk and followed it for a while. *Emergere*. Their using the Latin was a moderate comfort, familiar, a practice he could identify with the Homeworlds.

Sellia paused at a well-lighted staircase to break off a slip of vine that had started to overgrow the chemlamp at the base. "A nightly ritual," she commented as she started up the stairs.

Hark paused, too, to read the sign. *Emergens Regalis* was carved into the first step. The center of the carving was almost worn smooth, indicating much use. The railing was worn smooth, too. Balusters were all but hidden by blooming vines. Tiny white blossoms caught the pale radiance of the chemlamp like the pattern on a curtain.

They climbed stairs for a long time, through the under-story where water from the recent rain still dripped off the leaf tips, through the canopy where the upper leaves rustling in a faint breeze parted, occasionally revealing lights, the source of which he couldn't see. Overhead the canopy gave way to a wooden platform anchored by cantilevered beams of the bole of the tree. The flower-curtained staircase coiled up through an opening in the platform and they emerged in a house where moonlight flooded in through windows so brightly as to make artificial light almost unnecessary. The bole of the tree ran up through the center of the room and through the wooden ceiling. Scars of sawed-off limbs were sealed with glistening resin. The room smelled strongly of oranges.

Hark realized the house was higher than the forest treetops. He started toward a window to look out at the silvery top of the forest canopy, when he heard Sellia say, "Why did you bring him here?" but quickly realized the voice had come from the stairs leading to an even higher level and not from the window where Sellia was pulling curtains shut. Mala stood at the top of the stairs looking over the railing at him. She wore a blue dress very much like Sellia's, but she also wore a tiara and a necklace, and was lacking the leather holster on her hip.

"I've come to tend your wound," Hark said before Sellia could answer.

Mala raised her eyebrow, said nothing, but looked at her sister expectantly.

Sellia left the curtains facing the mountainside open and turned to Mala. "It's true," she said. "I'll explain in a minute. But first, let me send the doctor away. Where is she?"

"In the pantry with the guards. You had better send them back out, too."

Sellia nodded and hurried through a door behind the staircase. Apparently there was another room beyond.

Mala came down the stairs to where Hark stood. She stared at him contemptuously, making Hark feel self-conscious because his uniform was soaked with sweat and sticking to his chest. "You might as well start," she said coldly. "It's obviously beyond my control at this point. The numbing drug is starting to wear off and the sedative is starting to take hold."

Mala sat down in a handsomely carved straight-backed chair and he pulled another up by her. He moved a little table over to the chairs to put his medical kit on; it felt damp.

"It must have rained a little inside," he commented as he sat down.

"The palace doesn't leak," Mala said. "It's just the humidity. It will be better soon; the rain stopped hours ago. But we won't be able to enjoy the breezes if we can't open the curtains. And we can't do that until you're done sewing up my arm."

"We're too high up to be seen from the ground," he said. He lifted Mala's sleeve to unroll the bandage from her arm.

"But we're not hard to see from the other emergents if anyone's looking," Mala said.

"And they're sure to be looking," Sellia said, coming back in. "They would love to catch us at this, but they haven't in all these years and they won't tonight." She looked over Hark's shoulder at Mala's wound, seemed satisfied and went to pull over another chair.

Mala's wound was as deep and ragged as Sellia's. "Your doctor was very thorough," Hark said.

"The quality of her work is coincidental. It's her ability to keep her tongue in her mouth afterward that's important," Mala said pointedly.

"Your palace intrigue really doesn't interest me," Hark said. "But I can imagine that if you were discovered now, it would consume everyone's attention and that would distract from my mission. I want your full attention. The entire court's attention, if necessary."

"Sellia, why didn't you just bring the stitcher?" Mala asked. "It can't be that complicated."

"Hark says it takes experience to operate correctly," Sellia said.

"And you believed him?"

"Yes," Sellia said simply, and sat down.

"Sellia, would you please come closer and sit so that I can see your stitches? I was sewing in the dark last time; they might not be even, and if they weren't these ought not be either."

"Lady Sellia to you," Mala said sharply.

"Sorry," Hark said. "That slipped." But he noticed Sellia's mischievous grin and decided that she was not offended, even if her sister was.

Sellia moved her chair closer to him so that Hark could see her arm. She rolled up her own sleeve, undid the bandage and then reached for Hark's pack.

Hark tried to concentrate on what he was doing.

"What's this?" Mala asked her sister. Sellia had the infrared scope in her hands.

"From the Homeworlds," Sellia said. "He wasn't especially intuitive about orientation after all. He had this and another gadget to tell him where he was."

"Is that what you thought?" Hark asked her, slightly amused. "That I had some kind of sixth sense or something?"

"People do," Mala snapped. "Sellia, for instance, and me, too."

"Hardly sixth sense," Hark said, determined not to let her get the best of him while he had some measure of advantage because of the stitches. "It's conditioning and training; I saw men of Fox who were just as good."

"What kind of price are we paying for this repair job?" Mala asked Sellia.

"The same as your sister paid for her stitches," Hark said before Sellia could say a word. He stopped the stitcher and looked up to see the queen's worried frown. "Whatever your conscience tells you is fair, especially tomorrow when any decisions are made about helping me get my ship back."

"That will depend a great deal upon yourself, about how truthful you've been up to now and how truthful you are then. Tomorrow you'll be dealing with our academicians, who are better equipped to determine if you're really from the Homeworlds."

"I welcome the opportunity," Hark said, taking the first stitch. "But I admit that I'm still apprehensive. The Fyxen believed me, but still wouldn't give me the kind of help I needed."

"I'm surprised Aethelmere didn't hang you as soon as she realized who you were."

"She did something almost as good," Hark said. "She crippled my lander by lasering the brain jewels."

"You must feel very frustrated," Mala said, suddenly looking genuinely sympathetic.

He paused, waiting for a hint of malice or amusement, and when her expression did not change, he nodded, accepting her sudden change of mood as genuine. "I'm in over my head," he said.

"I doubt that," Sellia said lightly. "Yours is a very good head . . . stretching a bit just now to cope."

"Stretching," Hark said flatly, and laughed ironically. "You have no idea."

"No," Mala said. "We probably don't, and that disturbs me."

The darker mood had returned as suddenly as it had gone. "If you have questions, milady, I'll answer them," Hark said.

"Oh, yes, I have questions. But I'm going to leave them to the professionals to ask tomorrow. I don't want anything about you left in doubt, as it was in court today. Let's just see if you impress the witnesses at the Academy with your full story as well as you've impressed some people in court with your wit.''

"As you wish," he said, though he realized she was speaking as much to Sellia as to him. He had the feeling Mala had known much sooner than he had that Sellia liked him. He also realized she wasn't at all pleased.

He concentrated on stitching. The twins sat silently for a while, letting him work undisturbed. Sellia took out the groundguide and turned the infrared scope over to Mala, who immediately put it up to her eyes and looked through the curtained windows.

"Hold still, please," Hark said.

She yawned and handed the infrared scope back to Sellia and gestured for her to look out the window. "Meave and Aislinn are still awake," she said. "That's not a good sign."

"They're sitting on the balcony," Sellia said, looking through the scope. "They look strange, but you can tell it's two people."

"Just what did your Family Court decide?" Hark said.

"Taffy must have given you quite a long lesson on New Penance's ruling family," Sellia said putting the scope down.

"You're not surprised that I had the patience to listen and learn?" he asked.

She shrugged. "Your reply to Mala's summons arrived while we were eating. You are perceived to be both impudent and arrogant."

"Do you agree with that conclusion?"

She shook her head. "I understood."

"I didn't," Mala said with a yawn. She watched Hark take the last stitch and yawned again. "It's the sedative," she explained.

"You ought not fight it," Hark said sincerely as he tied the final knot. "A bit of rest would help the healing." She looked very pale and her eyelids were drooping.

She tried to stand up, but wobbled and fell back into the chair. In a panic, she grabbed the arms of the chair and tried to get up again. Sellia firmly pushed her back down.

"It's just the sedative," Sellia said, calmly, reassuringly. "She just didn't want you taking off on some midnight escapade like the last time and busting open the stitches."

"That was you," Mala said, fear draining from her as she gave a lopsided laugh. Clearly she was half-asleep.

"She doesn't know that," Sellia said. Her sister nodded. "I'll call the troops in to carry you upstairs."

"I'll do it," Hark said.

Sellia nodded.

Hark got up, packed up the medical kit to put it in the pack, then thought better of it. He took the stitcher and thread-pack out of the kit and handed them to Sellia. "'Hide them," he said, "or better yet, destroy them. I may need to show your academicians the groundguide and the scope. They don't need to see these and start wondering who used them to put Mala's stitches in."

"They will anyway," she said, but she took the stitcher and thread and put them in her pocket.

"I'll say I must have lost them after I stitched your arm," Hark said.

"No. Don't lie to them. Mala will make sure they don't ask you that."

Hark shrugged, then lifted Mala out of her chair. She stirred in his arms, seemed disturbed when she opened her eyes and saw his face, but was too sleepy to protest. He followed Sellia up the circular staircase and into a dim room that was as expansive as the one below. The screened windows all were open, the breeze sweet and fresh. Sellia pulled back a light covering from the far bed, and he lay Mala down.

While Sellia covered Mala with a silky blanket, Hark went to the window to look at the nighttime sky.

The stormclouds were completely gone, the sky brilliant with stars. He glanced at his wristwatch, then back up at the sky where the orbiter should be. It was there, almost moving too slowly to notice, but the albedo was unmistakable to his practiced eye. He felt a rush of relief. Reassured now he looked out over the jungle canopy, black and silver with no hint of green except where the same tantalizing lights that he'd seen when he climbed the stairs were revealed with the swaying of the treetops. He could see three other emergent trees above the canopy, two of them with faintly lighted dwellings nestled atop the branches. He looked back at the lights in the canopy below them; other dwellings, he decided, in the trees above the trapped heat at the forest floor. And here, in the emergent tree where the breeze pushed steadily through the tight screens, it was cool and comfortable. He realized that his shirt was already almost dry and he understood what a privilege these dwellings atop the emergent trees must be to their owners.

"Can you smell the scratchblossoms?" Sellia asked him.

"I smell oranges," he said. "I've smelled them since I came inside."

"That's insecticide," she said. She worked the latch on the screen, and when it parted like shutters she leaned out. Instinctively he put his arms around her and held the windowsill to steady her. "Smell the air out here," she said.

Without the screen to attenuate it, the breeze was a virtual wind. It loosened strands of blond hair from her long braid. Hark smelled something delightfully tangy, but it didn't intrigue him as much as the scent of her hair and the silken feel of it against his cheek. When she leaned back against him, he took his hands off the windowsill and crossed his arms over her chest to hold her even closer.

"I know I should take you back to Taffy's, but this is another first," she said crossing her arms over his.

"What is?" he asked, wishing she hadn't mentioned leaving but knowing that he should.

"Your touching me without my giving leave and without my asking. If this had happened when I first met you, I would have left you to the rounders. Tonight I find it's refreshing. You're refreshing."

"I'm glad you like it. And I'm glad we had a chance to

travel together. I learned something very important about you."

"And what was that?"

"That you were not like the women of Fox, not trapped by a mindset or fear. You have genuine courage. That's what it takes, you know, to question the codes you've lived by all of your life. It takes an adventurous person to experiment like this."

"Some would call it madness," she said, "and they would be right. I must be mad to stand here and talk to a muscle like he was . . . like my sister." She strained to look up at him for a reaction.

For a moment Hark didn't know what to say. He wasn't sure if she was goading him by calling him a muscle, or complimenting him by comparing him to her sister. He decided to let that part pass. He knew all too well that she would fight with him with little provocation, and he didn't feel like fighting with her. "You're not mad," he finally said. "Trusting me is an adventure for you. I think you learn by having adventures."

"You could be wrong, Hark. I might be getting nothing out of this except some tingling in my toes. You haven't convinced me that men can be barristers."

Now he knew, but still refused to take the bait. "I don't care about that right now. I only care that you're talking to me without all those preconceived notions about how I should behave. For the first time since I've landed on Islands, I feel like me again." He squeezed his eyes shut and kissed her ear.

"And this has nothing to do with your wanting me to help you leave?" she asked.

He opened his eyes. "I'd be lying if I said it didn't. You're the first woman on Islands to see that I'm a whole person, free and responsible unto myself, worthy of some respect. You can't help taking that knowledge with you into court."

"I bring my sense of duty there, too," she said, dropping her hands to turn.

He kept her in his arms. "Me too," he said, kissing the tip of her nose. Then he cupped her chin in his hands and kissed her mouth. Her tongue was sweet on his and he suckled it gently. She trembled in his arms and Hark could feel his knees beginning to get weak. He pulled his mouth away from hers. "I'd better go," he said gruffly. His sense of duty was not exactly overwhelming right now, but he couldn't thoroughly shake it either. Sex was risky when two lives might be lost. He didn't believe she was toying with him as she might many men on Islands, but how could he justify taking the risk? Better to leave now while he didn't have to ponder much over what to write in his report about Sellia. Sellia kissed his chin, stood on her tiptoes to kiss his nose. It took all his willpower to hold her away when she started down to his mouth. "Take me to Taffy's," he said, determined not to strangle on the words.

"There's only a few hours left until dawn. You might as well spend them here," she said, sliding back into his arms.

A sharp *no!* he thought, and a firm push. Then he panicked because he could do neither of those things. Wildly, he looked around, as if he might find strength and resolve stashed in the corner. His eyes fell on Mala.

"She's sleeping," Sellia said quite reasonably. "And I'm not drunk this time."

"No, but . . ."

"But what?" she said, looking at him sharply.

Her flash of anger braced him a little, not enough for sharp words and decisive action, but at least enough to reason with her. "Sellia, I can't, You're too highly placed in court for me to risk even the appearance of behaving like an Islandian man," he said trying to sound impersonal. But it was too late for that; he was unable to resist adding, "It wouldn't be true. I mean, if we . . . it would be because we . . ." He shrugged helplessly. "What I'm trying to say is that my sense of duty won't permit me to do what I want to do very much."

"You have the strangest ways of telling me you like me,"

she said with just the faintest trace of a smile on her face. "That is what you said, isn't it?"

He knew he shouldn't admit it again, just as he knew he should just have refused her out of hand and never have let things go this far. But he said, "Yes," because he could no longer only think of being a conscientious pilot—at least not where Sellia was concerned.

To his amazement, instead of taking advantage now that she had to know how completely unwilling he was to resist, she stepped away from him and crossed her arms over her chest. She drummed her fingers along her biceps as she frowned thoughtfully. She had not just matched his attempt of restraint but plainly had taken the lead.

"All right, then. Let me suggest something that will leave you uncompromised but please me very much," she said after a moment. "Stay with me. We did it once before, we can do it again tonight. The simple truth is that I sleep much better when I'm not alone in the bed." She smiled sheepishly. "It's from being a twin. We shared a bed for years, even after we had two beds, we . . ." She paused and took a deep breath. "I never want to sleep alone."

Hark hesitated.

"Please stay, Hark. There's more to my liking you than wanting you."

"I might never know if you meant that if I left," he said, and he wanted to know more than anything he had ever wanted in his life.

She just nodded, then gestured toward the empty bed.

He sat down on the side of it and leaned over to take off his boots. He felt awkward and a bit foolish in such contrived circumstances. But then Sellia lay down on the bed, pausing only to empty her pockets and take off her holster and shoes. She turned her back to him and pulled the blanket up over herself without offering to share. She probably felt just as strange, he decided, and he lay down quietly next to her.

Through the windows he could see three of the moons and many stars rising. Soft nightcalls of wild creatures on the wing drifted through, but mainly Hark was aware of Sellia's breathing. It quickly became regular as a sound sleeper's. She turned over, her cheek coming to rest against his arm. He looked at her, doubting for a moment that she was asleep, but then realized she really was. He relaxed, thinking he could sleep himself for a while. She turned over, backside against his hip. Every turn she made put some part of her in contact with him. Eventually he became convinced that she was entirely aware that she was doing it, just a comforting habit she'd acquired as an infant.

He must have dozed a while, for when he opened his eyes there was only one moon left on the horizon. The breeze had actually become a bit too cool, and the discomfort must have awakened him. Carefully he disentangled one side of the blanket from Sellia and crawled under it with her. She snuggled back against him and he pulled her close, reveling in the warmth. He didn't quite mean to, but when he found his hand so close to her breast he touched it, searching for the nipple through the fabric of the dress. She stirred and he froze, then carefully took his hand away.

Sellia turned over in his arms. Eyes still closed, she fumbled for his hand and brought it up to her lips and kissed his fingertips. Her touch felt good, so unlike anything he had felt in all these weeks except for the time he had held her when they were in Hilma's cabin. More than anything, it was his hunger for the feel of another human being that made him put his arms around her again, for he knew he should not trust Sellia or anyone else on this planet. When she kissed him, he knew he would not stop this time.

Hark liked his lovers on top sometimes, but he found himself wondering if Sellia ever had made love from underneath.

CHAPTER 20

Someone was pulling the curtains closed, not trying to be quiet about it. Scllia opened her eyes in time to see the last one fly across the rod as Mala whirled to face her sister's bed. Sellia was sure she would have been shaken awake if she had not sat up.

"Aislinn's talking heresy, Meave's muttering about her claim to the throne again, and you're *sleeping* with him?" she said to Sellia. Mala was half dressed, her hair wet, as if she'd taken a shower and then discovered Hark in her sister's bed when she went to the closet to find some clothes.

Sellia shrugged and stretched. Hark was still asleep beside her in the bed, crushed and tousled curls on her pillow all that was visible. She looked back at Mala, who was standing with her hands on her hips, frowning. She'd rarely seen her sister angrier. "Meave's always muttering about her claim to the throne," Sellia said trying to soothe her with reason. "She hasn't pressed it in ten years. She isn't going to start now."

"Don't be so certain," Mala said. "It would be just like her to wait ten years, with her patient suffering filling every one of them, and then press something like this to her advantage. Queen Meave the Martyr."

Sellia winced. There was considerable truth to what Mala was saying. They both knew better than to think lightly of either of the aunts, but especially not of Meave. She had never quite accepted her sister's leaving the throne to Mala, a young woman, instead of herself, who was post-reproductive. Thus while Meave publically endorsed the young queen to avoid any scandal, she privately reminded Mala that she *could* have challenged her sister's decrees, and hinted when necessary that she still *might*. But even as Sellia thought about it, she found herself shrugging. "I'd get some extra penance if they found out that I'd slept with an unpurified man, and that's Aislinn's department, not Meave's. Besides which they can't find out because I don't plan to tell them and you won't either. No harm done, and I had a good time."

"Well, I'm very happy for you," Mala said sarcastically, "but you might have waited until *after* the inquiry. It's daylight out there and we can't avoid him being seen when he leaves. It will scare them, especially since they won't know if it's me or you who slept with him."

"What differences does it make? It's happened enough times for us to know the thought of public censure of the queen or even her sister scares them even more." Sellia was becoming genuinely annoyed. She and her sister had always been full partners in a life of subterfuge that made the life of duty they'd inherited tolerable and, she admitted to herself, quite exciting for both of them. She was accustomed to Mala's complete support. Scoldings were supposed to come only from the aunts.

"There are limits, Sellia. They can ignore troopers coming during the night because every lace Top has a bottom man to satisfy what they call youthful fires during service years. But even that requires discretion and they do punish the ones who are not discreet!"

"So I forgot to close the bedroom curtains and you had to do it. I've done as much for you under similar circumstances."

"Curtains be damned. I've never brought in a lover the night before he was supposed to appear at an inquiry. Aunt Meave is a witness in Academe. What if she *asks* him?"

Sellia was silent for a moment. "It would be out of order for her to ask. You'd have to stop her," she said finally.

"Yes, I would. And in so doing raise a lot of suspicion that we don't want."

"She won't ask him," Sellia said after another moment's deliberation. She looked squarely into her sister's eyes, was met with what her own looked like when genuinely alarmed. "Aunt Meave has too much post-procreative pride to break the rules. She'd lose face if her public behavior were anything but exemplary. I know that and you know it, too. So tell me what you're really afraid of."

Mala's lips twitched for a moment. Sellia's sister had had to learn to be direct, and Sellia had had to learn to circumvent issues. Now it was a matter of knowing which method to use, for they each could use them equally well.

"I would not have slept with him last night," Mala said slowly.

"Probably not," Sellia agreed. "But then we've never shared lovers. Why would we start now?"

"I meant that it's the one thing in which we're not interchangeable," Mala said, still speaking slowly as if with great deliberation. "It didn't seem important until now."

"Why is it now?"

Mala shook her head and frowned. "He has a peculiar sense of honor and I find him altogether too strange. Don't you think his wanting to leave after coming all the way from the Homeworlds is strange?"

"You're the one who failed to ask him why he came in the first place. It wasn't me sitting on the throne yesterday. And he offered to tell you last night, but you turned him down." Mala looked about to protest, but Sellia held up her hand for silence. "No. If you're not going to tell me what's really bothering you, you're going to have to hear what I'm thinking right now. As queen, you had the prerogative and *you* made the decision to wait until the inquiry for those questions. Fine, I understand that his answers will have more credibility with the academics asking the questions. As the queen's sister, I'm not bound by your decisions until I step into your shoes." Those were the rules they followed, and while they both knew them by heart, there were times when they bore repeating.

"But there is a difference this time," Mala insisted. "This one knows the truth about us."

"Is that what you're worried about? That he might tell?"

"No," Mala said looking uncomfortable. "I'm worried because he's different, and even more because you're treating him differently."

Finally Sellia understood. Mala saw Hark as a threat to their bond. "He won't tell," Sellia said quietly, "and you're right. I'm treating him differently. I trusted him last night with our secret because . . . well, because I feel differently when I'm with him."

"How different?" Mala said. "Like you don't have a sister?"

"Nothing will ever change the way I feel about you. You are my sister and half my life."

Mala briefly closed her eyes and nodded, looking relieved. She reached out and Sellia took her hand and squeezed it. Mala looked down at Hark, shook her head and frowned. She wasn't convinced, but she would say nothing more about it. "I'll get dressed and wait downstairs," she said letting go of Sellia's fingers.

Mala went into the closet for a moment, came out attired for morning court in a simple shift and sandals and with an amber tiara to wear on her head so that she would not be mistaken for her sister, who would wear none.

When Mala had gone, Sellia heard Hark stir beside her and felt his arms encircle her waist.

"I'm sorry," he said.

"For what?" she asked snuggling down next to him.

He kissed the tip of her nose. "I was so worried about my looking compromised; I didn't stop to think that it might be just as bad for you," he said.

"You heard?"

Hark nodded. "I thought it would be better if I didn't wake up in the middle of it. She sounded angry."

"Her anger doesn't worry me half as much as her fears," Sellia said sadly.

"Will it help if I give her my word about keeping silent?"

"No. That wouldn't be enough. She doesn't understand why she's afraid of you."

"I do," he said. "She's afraid of losing you to me."

Sellia nodded. "I haven't the slightest worry that I will lose her to one of her lovers. She knows that, and doesn't understand why she has the fear and I don't."

"Neither do I," Hark said.

Sellia looked at him curiously.

"In court, you do appear to be interchangeable. She was as direct as you, quick-witted, and even arrogant. If you hadn't been dressed differently and if you hadn't shared experiences with me that she was not privy to, I might have been hard-pressed to know who was who."

"You wouldn't have known if we didn't want you to. Some suspect; none know for sure."

"Not even lovers?"

"Especially not lovers. You're the first."

Hark thought for a moment. "If you don't tell them, what do you do about them when you exchange roles?" He turned to her. "Never mind. That wasn't a fair question. Besides, I think I already know the answer."

"Tell me what you think you know," Sellia said. His unwillingness to speculate aloud intrigued her.

"The boy in Hilma's cabin must have been Mala's lover, no doubt when she was wearing the Sellia guise. It explains the looks I got from him. You treated him like a child and there I was. He figured you just dumped him, and he didn't know what to do about it. You counted on that."

Sellia nodded. "Something like that. Mala's lovers are always boys. It's easy to discourage them."

"It's cruel."

"I don't like sleeping with boys. She chooses them because they're easy to control. She won't take the risk with a man."

"But you do."

"Sometimes. It's not very satisfying though because I can't get close to them like she can to the boys. There comes a time when I must change roles, and that has to be the end."

She felt Hark pulling her closer to him. "This time it won't matter when you change roles," he said. "I'll know you and care about you whoever you are."

Sellia wasn't so certain, but she said nothing. They'd talked enough about duty last night, and for just a little while longer she wanted to enjoy this easy rapport that she'd never experienced before with anyone except her sister.

"Sellia?"

"Yes?"

"Is it possible?"

"Is what possible?"

"That she could lose you to me? Or is that what you mean by duty, that no matter what we feel, you'll choose Mala?"

Sellia could feel the tenseness in his arms as he waited for her to answer, and she realized that he was afraid, too. She felt inexplicably angry. "Sometimes there isn't more than one choice and you have to make do with the one at hand. I can't abandon her," she said adamantly, and was horrified the thought had crossed her mind let alone been spoken aloud.

"You're doing fine, Sellia," Hark whispered. "You know you can't change her, but you can change. You're already changing. Last night was a first for you and for me."

Easy for him to say. Mala was not *his* sister. She drew back in defiance. "I can't forget my duty. Never!"

"I won't either," he said equally firm. "*My* duty, I mean. Not yours." He sat there shaking his head. "Some things go beyond duty, like you and me. But I know even that doesn't release me from what I have to do. I don't imagine it does you either," he said sadly. "I can't help wishing it did. I love you, Sellia."

She was supposed to say the same to him. She knew that and she wanted to, if only because she'd never said it to any man before. If only because it was a time for change from not saying it. If only because it was true. But suddenly she was every bit as afraid of Hark as her sister was. He was intense, uncontrollable, unpredictable. He knew who she was and he loved her, and that made her feel vulnerable. "Oh, damn," she said, shutting her eyes. "I love you." She opened her eyes and took a deep breath. "Now let's go take a shower. There's still the inquiry to worry about."

She got out of bed. The blue dress was on the floor, his clothes next to it. She picked up his things. Surprisingly, they were not wrinkled. When she tried to hand them over, Hark caught her hand and kissed her palm. His eyes sparkled invitingly.

"I need a shower," she said tossing his clothes at him, "and so do you. Come on. Up with you."

He sighed, pushed the blanket back and followed her into the bathroom. He hung his clothes on a rack and stepped into the shower with her. It was a big shower with a comfortable cork bench in the middle for lounging in the water on hot days. Sellia reached for the water chain, but Hark stopped her with a kiss. She held him close for a moment, enjoying the feel of their naked bodies pressing together, his mouth so openly seeking hers. Then, knowing that if she didn't do it now she would keep Mala waiting until after they'd made love again, she pulled the water chain. Better not to fan the flame of Mala's fears, better not to show the lack of control to which she wished she could abandon herself.

Hark groaned. The water from the cistern was cool from being so fresh and with little chance for the sun to heat it during the past few rainy days. Grimacing, he kissed her through a veil of water. Sellia pushed him away, reached into the shower jug, pulled out a fistful of soap petals and started to lather. He tried to follow her example, but his hand was too large to fit into the neck of the jug. She found herself annoyed with the artisan who'd fashioned the jug only for slender female hands. Hark turned it upside down, spilling the soap petals over his shoulders. The jug was half-empty by the time he was lathered, and he rinsed quickly as she started to wash her hair, had ducked out of the shower by the time she was finished. The cool water encouraged her to hurry, too.

He had found the drybox filled with warm towels and was half-dressed by the time she returned to the bedroom. He slipped his shirt over his bare chest, fastened it, then ran his fingers through his hair. His curls were wet and shiny.

"You're quite handsome, you know," she said as she opened the closet door.

"And you, milady, are so exquisitely beautiful that you should not be permitted ever to wear clothes," he said. "But if you must, wear something blue again. Blue becomes you."

But she selected a yellow dress because it had sleeves long enough to cover the wound on her arm and because she and Mala loved yellow dresses, but mainly she selected it because he had asked her to wear blue. He looked hurt after she slipped it over her head.

"Is this the beginning of the end for me, too?"

"I don't know what you mean," she said tying a matching shawl across her hips.

"Two days ago I might have believed that."

She looked up. He was frowning. "Believed what?" she said. "What in Hells Gates are you talking about?"

"About how *hard* you try to be. I know better now. Deep down you're frightened," he said.

She froze. *Frightened?* What had he seen to make him say that?

"Look, Sellia, I'll give you lots of quarter because, well, because of last night and because I know it must be hard for you to let down all the defenses you must have to be both queen and sister. But please, don't shut me out. I love you."

"Love? I don't think . . ." she started to say, but the protest died in her throat when she saw his stricken face. She had forgotten herself. The denial seemed to form of its own volition. "Love is an awful weapon," she said finally. "Men want it because it gives them some modicum of control through the woman."

"It wouldn't work on you; I never thought it would and I never dreamed of trying it. Ease up a little; trust me."

She untied the shawl and tossed it back in the closet, rummaged through the clothes for a moment and then shook her head. "None of the blue ones have long enough sleeves," she said. "Mala's wound is fresher than mine."

Hark picked up the discarded shawl and handed it to her. "You look lovely in yellow," he said before he touched his lips to hers.

CHAPTER 21

Mala was wearing yellow, too, but a paler shade and more simply cut than Sellia's dress. Hark hesitated at the top of the stairs when he saw she was not alone. Sellia brushed on past him.

"It's all right," she said. "It's our Top, Leniane, and two of her muscles."

He recognized the woman who'd been outside Taffy's door the night before. Neither of the troopers looked familiar to him. Both were young men, one barely pubescent. His cheeks were smooth, color high from self-consciousness, for Queen Mala was staring openly at him. The other trooper signaled to him, and they came toward Hark. They waited for him at the bottom of the stairs, flanked him as he followed Sellia.

"Why the guards?" he asked nervously.

The Top was holding the door open for Mala and Sellia.

"Not to worry," Sellia said, turning easily to look at him. "Just stay between them until we get below. You're less likely to be noticed in a group like this."

They moved briskly, the three women in front, Hark and the two troopers following, as if they'd practiced this routine before. Probably they had, Hark thought.

The outside stairs were slick with dew, the air warm and scented with blossoms. On the landing below was a bridge Hark hadn't noticed last night in the dark. It tunnelled through foliage to another bole, and it swayed as they walked on it. At the other end was another set of stairs, and they went down again. Hark caught a waft of something besides flowers, possibly the scent of something cooking.

They were walking single file now, and Sellia stopped to let the others go ahead. "Hungry?" she asked.

Before he could answer, Mala said, "I'd rather not take him into a public kitchen."

They'd come to another landing, a big sturdy one with benches almost overgrown with greenery. "We'll wait here," Sellia said easily. "You bring us something."

Mala didn't seem pleased, but she nodded and started across another bridge. The Top signaled to the younger trooper, who stayed behind, while she and the other went with Mala.

"Do you . . . I mean, does the Queen of New Penance always have a bodyguard with her?" Hark asked.

"Only since we connected up the rail with Fox a few years ago. There have been incidents."

"Someone tried to hurt the queen?"

"No, but Aethelmere's dislike of Queen Mala isn't a secret. It usually turns out to be runaways, not assassins. But our militia prefers caution, so we have bodyguards."

"Last night you didn't."

"I can dismiss mine. Mala can't."

Hark went over to one of the benches, put a foot on it and looked out over the rail. He could almost see the ground. "Do I hear running water?" he asked, looking for a telltale sparkle.

"You do," Sellia said coming up behind him. "Want to take a look? It's a special place."

"Sure."

"How about you?" she said to the young trooper.

He was startled to find Sellia grinning at him. It took him a moment to realize she was waiting for his answer. "I . . . shouldn't we . . ." He looked nervously at the bridge.

". . . wait?" Sellia laughed. "Sure we should. Now do you want to be rude and come with us? Or politely wait?" Even as she spoke, Sellia climbed onto the railing. She grabbed onto something green, and started climbing down.

Hark started after Sellia, hoped she remembered who was trying to follow and hadn't picked something impossible for him to do. The trooper stared, terrified.

"I take it she doesn't do this sort of thing often," Hark said to him.

"I don't know," the trooper said. "This is my first day."

"You coming?" Hark asked, holding out his hand to the trooper. It would make it easier from him to step from the railing onto the branch.

The trooper looked back at the empty bridge, then stepped up onto the railing to take Hark's hand. Sellia was out of sight, but Hark just climbed down a latticework of branches, dropping only the last two meters. Then he followed the sound of the rushing water.

Sellia was standing at the top of a fall of whitewater, waiting. It was an easy scramble up a well worn path over mossy rocks to a little pool in a dell.

"He came," she said, a little unhappy to see the trooper following him.

"If you didn't want him here, you should have ordered him to stay behind," Hark said, annoyed. He would have enjoyed being alone with Sellia in this pretty place, but was certain she'd deliberately challenged the young trooper. She had to know he was new and would be uncertain of what was expected of him when she behaved outrageously.

"Then he'd never learn to think for himself, would he,

Hark?'' she said, hands on hips. "It's what makes you so attractive. This boy," she said, nodding at the trooper who'd come alongside, "is Leniane's brother." She turned to the boy. "At least, I think you're Leniane's brother."

"Yes, ma'am." He looked bewildered.

"What's your name?"

"Forrie, ma'am."

"Well, Forrie, remember this place. It's special to Mala and me, sort of our secret place."

"Yes, ma'am."

"Now why don't you go back to the landing to wait for the others. Mala will probably guess where we are, but just in case, you can show them the way."

"Yes, ma'am." Still puzzled, he turned to retrace his steps. In a moment, his green-on-green uniform was one with the green foliage.

Also puzzled, Hark caught Sellia's hand. "What was that all about?"

"He's going to be the next to know," Sellia said. "About Mala and me."

Hark nodded. "I saw how she looked at him."

"She won't tell him, but this time . . ." Sellia shrugged. "I just don't have the heart not to tell him when the time comes. I'm tired of breaking little boys' hearts."

"And what about big boys'?" Hark asked.

"I guess we'll see, won't we, after the inquiry. Maybe it's me who will be heartbroken. You might go home."

Sellia dropped his hand and sat down. Nodding, Hark sat down next to her. "But who knows, I might come back. Or . . ."

"Ho!" Mala's shout came from below. "I thought we'd find you here."

Forrie had been given bundles to carry and was bringing up the rear of Queen Mala's entourage. He seemed happier now, no doubt because the Top was smiling good-naturedly. They all climbed up to the top of the falls, sat on the rocks with Sellia and Hark.

"Remember why you're here," Leniane said to her

brother as she gave him a hot sandwich. "Eat, but keep a wary eye."

"I will," he said, sincerely.

"You, too," she said to the other trooper.

Older, more experienced, he just nodded.

"And you," she said, giving Hark a sandwich, too. "From what Sellia tells me, if there's trouble, you just stay out of the way. Did you really let a rounder out of your sights?"

"I saw no reason to kill her on top of her other losses."

The Top shrugged and bit into her sandwich. "She wouldn't have needed a reason to kill you," she said through her mouthful of food.

"So I'm told. I have a lot to learn about Islands."

"And we have a lot to learn about the Homeworlds," the Top said.

"*After* the inquiry," Mala said, sounding a bit sharp.

For a moment, everyone was silent. Even the sound of the falling water seemed to be absorbed by thick moss and dense leaves. Then a bird called raucously, and Sellia tapped Mala's arm and pointed to a rock across the pool. A bright yellow bird stood there looking at them. "It's your friend," Sellia said.

Mala broke a bit of her sandwich and tossed it to the bird. It stared at the tidbit for a moment, then gobbled it down in a flash of yellow.

They watched Mala feed the bird while they finished eating.

"Nice bonebacks you brought, Sellia," the Top said.

"You mean the ones from Hilma? Someone brought them down from the observatory?"

Leniane nodded. "Forrie took them up to the pasture right away."

"Which pasture?"

"The one with the big piebald stag. Is there anything else you want done with them?"

Sellia nodded. "Make sure they're polished before we send them back, and real fat. I sure was glad of the ride."

The Top, Sellia, and Mala talked a few minutes more about livestock, which led to crop discussions. Hark leaned back against a rock, watching them. In this peaceful setting, he could almost believe all would be well for himself and his crewmates. And he found himself hoping it could be well for himself and Sellia, too.

"It's time," Mala said finally. Forrie jumped to his feet to give her a hand up. Sellia wouldn't take Hark's hand, but she smiled.

"This way," she said, going around the pool.

Always, it seemed to Hark, he was following someone on Islands. He hoped to change that in the next few hours.

CHAPTER 22

Sellia took one look around the sky parlor and hurried to Aunt Meave's side, knowing she'd be annoyed by the number of people. Sellia had expected half the Queen's Court. But the men! Several dozen, she estimated, already fidgeting in their chairs, poking each other in the ribs.

"Ask Dean Natala if we must put up with this," Meave said as she lifted her cheek for Sellia to kiss.

Natala was a contemporary of Meave's, her hair slate gray, her body well past middle age. She'd heard Meave perfectly well, and said before Sellia could intervene, "Put up with what? The men?" She shrugged. "They'll get bored soon enough and leave. They always do."

"They're behaving like it's a wrestling match," Meave

said. "Shaming the devil is hard work and their joking around in the background is distracting."

"The machine can't be distracted," Natala said coolly. "As witnesses, we need only ask the proper questions, not evaluate the results."

Meave turned away. "*She* would say something like that!" Aunt Meave whispered to Sellia. "She's as good as me in our mothers' ways of detecting lies. But *she* doesn't take her mother's training seriously."

Sellia nodded dutifully. She didn't want to anger Meave in any way, for she would be a witness to Hark's testimony. There was a machine, too, a very good one. But in some people's opinions, it did not replace a good human witness like Meave.

"Look at them," Meave said of the men. "Who's playing with the children while they're here?"

"Aunt Meave, they aren't *all* here," Sellia said. "It's just that word's gotten out about the spaceman. They're just curious about a man who might be from the Homeworlds."

"This is Taffy's doing," Aunt Meave said crossly. "And Mala's fault for letting that runt into court. We never meant for public meetings to be *this* public."

"Public inquiries are Natala's doings, not Mala's," Sellia said honestly, but didn't mention how much she approved of the public inquiries.

"Natala!" Aunt Meave said. "She doesn't even keep an orthodox kitchen. Wears her outdoor clothing and shoes, and trusts her goodman to scour the pots. It's trouble, nothing but trouble. Let them prepare a few simple meals and next thing you know, they're wanting to be nutritionists." She looked critically at Sellia. "Where will it all end?"

Sellia shrugged. She liked Dean Natala, thought her habits were peculiar, but liked her all the same. But she didn't dare defend her now. Meave was vengeful, and she was likely to strike anywhere—at Hark, if she couldn't get Natala.

"Where is this so-called spaceman?" Meave said, looking around.

"Coming right now with Mala," Sellia said, stepping aside for her sister.

People were beginning to notice Mala. The men were scuffling to their feet in their big, heavy shoes. The women were rising too, but silently. Even Meave stood up.

"Dean Natala," Mala said. The old woman looked at her queen, then got to her feet. They exchanged nods, the customary greeting. Then Mala said in her formal voice, "The principal is here. You may begin whenever you're ready."

Everyone in the parlor was on their feet now, waiting for Mala to sit down. Mala would have hurried to do so, rushed through the ritual as she always did, but this time was stopped by Dean Natala.

"Has he brought his guardian?" Dean Natala asked Mala.

"I have no guardian," Hark said stepping around from behind Mala and Sellia. "And with all due respect, I do not wish to have one appointed for me."

His speaking directly gave even Natala a start, but with her usual disregard for tradition, she shifted from talking to Mala to Hark as easily as if it had been to Sellia.

"It's not my requirement, young man, but if you are who you say you are, you should realize that someone familiar with our customs would be an asset to you," she said to him. "The Queen's Court will provide one eventually; it might as well be now."

"No thank you," Hark said firmly.

Natala, Sellia could see, didn't care one way or the other, but she did look at Mala to see if the queen approved. Mala gave her a tight-lipped nod, and Sellia sighed with relief.

Plainly, Meave was displeased. "You sit here," Meave said to Hark, gesturing to the chair in front of her table. It would put him facing the witnesses, his back to the audience. Hark looked at the chair suspiciously.

"This chair . . . What are these wires?"

"That's none of your concern," Meave said.

"A proper guardian would have told you what to expect," Natala interjected, just enough chiding in her voice to let him know she could become impatient. "The chair is connected to various apparatus that will measure your pulse, breathing, blood pressure and galvanic reflexes during the questioning."

Sellia watched Hark's gaze follow the wires to the instruments on the table behind him. "For what purpose are you gathering all this data about my body?"

"Correlated to your answers, it will tell us whether or not you're telling lies."

"Natala, you forget yourself," Meave said with special sweetness. "As witnesses, we're supposed to ask the questions."

Meave's comment brought a chuckle from the audience. Natala just looked steadily at Meave, said quietly, "I have not forgotten our purpose here. It will be better for all of us if he's at ease."

"For your machine!" Meave said icily.

"Are drugs involved?" the Hark was asking, taking no notice of Meave.

"No," Dean Natala said.

"Pain?"

"No."

"In all my travels, I've never heard of such a thing," he said still looking at the instruments. "How does it work?"

Sellia hoped Hark would stop asking questions; even Dean Natala had limits. But even when he looked up and caught her frown, he apparently misunderstood.

"I mean," he said, "how do you do the data correlation?"

"My techniques are not under scrutiny here," Natala said. "You are."

"Yes, milady. I understand that. But if the data is improperly interpreted, everything I say could be biased."

"Hark," Sellia said before Dean Natala could answer

him yet again. "It would be a gesture of good faith if you'll just sit down in the chair."

He looked at her in surprise. Sellia just stared back, tight-lipped and grim.

Finally Hark nodded and went to the chair to sit down. "But not before the queen sits!" Sellia added sharply. He caught himself and remained standing.

Sellia followed Mala to the seats Aunt Aislinn had saved for them, sat down after her sister but before everyone else. Hark's eyes were fixed on them.

Hark waited until everyone was seated, then turning his back to the audience, he took his chair. He sat straight.

"Your name is Hark?" Natala asked him. Natala had rigged an electronic screen so that the audience could see the tracings on the graph at the same time the witnesses did on the one on their table. The screens came to life even before Natala added, "Answer yes or no, please."

"Yes," he said, and Sellia watched the graph spark in the truth zone.

"Are you wearing a blue shirt?"

"Yes."

"Is your hair black?"

"No."

"Please answer the next question falsely," Natala said, giving Hark a slight reassuring smile. "Is your hair curly?"

"No," he said, and the tick-lights all showed up in the false zone.

Sellia relaxed a bit. Control questions were not particularly interesting.

"Did you see a gun in Fox large enough to down a logging windship?"

"Yes." The truth zone again.

"Are you from the Homeworlds?"

"Yes." Truth zone.

"Are you from Fox?"

"No." Truth zone.

"Did you know a doctor named Jeremy?"

"Yes." Truth zone.

"Is my hair brown?"

"No." Truth zone.

"Is Jeremy dead?"

"Yes." False zone, and Sellia leaned forward to take another look. Yes, false zone. She swallowed hard.

"Is your lander disabled?"

"Yes." Truth zone.

"Is my hair gray?"

"Yes."

"Is Jeremy dead?"

"Yes." False zone again.

"Is Laurel's hair red?"

"Yes." Truth zone.

"Did Laurel invite you to Selene?"

"Yes." Another lie, which the machine confirmed. Sellia's pulse was racing with fear. She glanced at Mala. She sat rigidly, looked too stoic.

"Have you told us the truth?"

"Yes." False zone on the machine.

Natala snapped off the screen. "For a while now you will not be limited to yes and no answers," she told Hark. "You may provide in depth responses. Would you start, please, by explaining why the Homeworlds sent you."

"Our mission was very routine. Islands records had been lost during the war, but were recently rediscovered in some AI Guild files lodged in a brain that was being repaired. Those records indicated the Guild had provided an AI to Islands seventy-five years ago, and we came to perform routine service that was long overdue."

"What," Meave said interrupting him, "is an AI?"

"I'm sorry to have used a term you're not familiar with. I was led to believe it was still in use. It's an initialism for Artificial Intelligence," he said. "Perhaps I should explain what that means?"

Meave shook her head. "The very word tells us what we need to know. Artificial intelligence is opposed to natural intelligence."

"If by natural intelligence you mean human intelligence, putting AIs in opposition is . . ."

"Please confine yourself to answer the question," Meave said. "Why did the Homeworlds send you if, indeed, you come from the Homeworlds?"

"Indeed, ma'am, I do," he said, his voice steady. "We came to perform routine service on an AI, but there was no AI here for us to service. It was destroyed when the Hound Volcano exploded, so our mission was in vain."

Sellia listened carefully as Hark described a mission of routine fly-bys ending in disaster. Natala's questions led him through his captivity in Fox, and finally to his journey to New Penance, where he described in some detail the death of the male doctor Jeremy.

"Let's go back to the yes and no answers for a while," Meave suggested to Natala. The dean nodded and leaned back. Meave turned to the man. "Are you a pilot for the AI Guild?"

"Yes." Truth zone.

"Did you come to perform routine service on the Hound AI?"

"Yes." False zone.

"Is Jeremy dead?"

"Yes." False zone.

"Did you and Jeremy leave Fox on a railcar?"

"Yes." False zone.

"Did you leave during Jeremy's nuptial celebrations?"

"Yes." False zone.

"Did Jeremy fall from a trestle?"

"Yes." False zone.

"Do you know Laurel of Selene?"

"Yes." Truth zone.

"Did Laurel invite you to Selene?"

"Yes." False zone.

Sellia was on the edge of her chair. Hark wasn't telling the whole truth, not about why he had come from the Homeworlds nor how he had come from Fox.

Meave gave the interrogation back to Natala; the dean

returned to open-ended questions. Hark was describing his meeting with Laurel when she invited him to Selene. Natala listened carefully, face impassive, giving him no sign that she knew he was lying. Too soon Natala looked at Mala.

"We should recess for a meal. We can resume afterward if you wish."

Mala shook her head. "I think we've heard enough." Cool. Regal. Sellia's heart sank.

"Enough, I hope, to convince you that I'm worthy of your aid," Hark said, half turning in his chair to look at them. Mala's glare obviously alarmed him, and he stood up. "Milady?" he said, hands out in an innocent gesture.

"You lied repeatedly," Mala said. "You lied yesterday and you lied today."

"But the data isn't even correlated," he said looking hesitant.

"That data's correlated instantly," Mala said in disgust.

"But it's so primitive," Hark said. He looked stricken. "It's probably not accurate. You can't possibly put faith in such archaic and crude devices."

"You think because it was not made on the Homeworlds it can't be good?" Sellia said, so angry that she'd gotten to her feet leaving her sister seated. He stared at her helplessly.

Yes! It was plain on his face.

Sellia bit her lip. He'd condemned himself before he had begun. She shook her head sadly, saw his face filling with confusion. She turned away just in time to see Meave exchange a glance with Aislinn. The cleric nodded.

"The abbey would like to petition for guardianship," Aunt Aislinn said. "It's quite obvious he needs firm guidance to a more righteous path. We know how to deal with men who . . ."

"Now just a damn minute," Hark said angrily. His face was white with fear, but it didn't stop him from practically shouting. "I'm a Homeworlds citizen, not an Islandian and you cannot treat me like one."

Leniane and her muscles had come in from the porch at the first sound of a raised voice, and Mala gestured for them to take Hark. He saw them coming and backed away. For a moment Sellia thought he was going to try to run, but there were already a dozen more troopers coming in, and he must have realized he didn't have a chance. He stood stiffly, closing his eyes in repulsion when the troopers grabbed his arms. When they jerked him along, he opened his eyes and sought out Sellia. *Please help me.* There was no mistaking the look. Sadly, she shrugged.

He had straightened his shoulders and was trying to shake the troopers' grips on his arms. The arrogance had not gone out of him. The troopers wouldn't let go.

"My petition," Aislinn repeated.

"Don't give it to her," Sellia said, almost shouting to be heard above the stir. "Give custody to me."

The sky parlor suddenly became hushed again. Mala frowned and put her hands to her temples. "Not now," she said. "Petition me in court."

"As you wish," Aunt Aislinn said. She gave Mala a look of stone.

Sellia started for the back door. Mala fell in next to her.

"You can't be serious," she whispered to Sellia.

"Completely," Sellia said. "It's the only way I'll learn the truth."

"He lied, Sellia. Lies!"

They were out the door now and Sellia stopped on the stairs. "But not all of it."

"Lies in court, lies in the inquiry," Mala hissed.

"Your sister is right," Meave said coming up behind them. "Lies everywhere."

"He was telling the truth when he said he knew Laurel," Sellia said fiercely.

"And lied about her promising to help him in Selene," Mala reminded her coolly.

"Yes, but she does know him. And I intend to find her and find out how."

"Laurel could be anywhere. It could take weeks to find her."

"I'll find her though," Sellia said determinedly.

"This is madness," Mala said. "You can't still believe him."

"Mala, we're not talking about just this man. We're talking about saving the world."

"Are we?" Mala asked her.

"You're condemning it to contamination," Meave said in a righteous whisper. "You're beginning to sound as if you want Homeworlders to come to Islands. More liars. We've spent seventy-five years minimizing what they did to us with that shipload of convicts. You'd open the door to more?" Meave shook her head gravely. "Be grateful that he's been caught in his lies. Stay out of it now and let the abbey protect us from him and his Homeworlds minions."

"Mala?" Sellia said sharply.

For a second an implacable look crossed Mala's face, then she suddenly shoved her hands in the pockets of her dress and turned to stare silently out over the canopy.

Meave moved close to her. "A timely decision on Aislinn's petition would be wise," she said quietly.

"Ye- . . ."

"Mala!" Sellia had shouted, startling Meave.

Mala swallowed hard, then straightened her shoulders. "I don't think there's anything to gain by acting hastily," she said to Meave. "He'll be safe in the pits for now, and that will give me time to think about the future."

"You mean Aislinn's petition," Meave said, pressing for a commitment.

"No!" Sellia said. She hadn't shouted this time, but Meave looked at her as if she'd lost her mind. But Sellia couldn't be stopped. "What do you plan to do with the next visitor from the Homeworlds? Throw him into the pits too? And the next one, and the one after that?" She looked desperately from her sister to her aunt. "How many Homeworlders do you think the pits will hold, Aunt Meave?"

Meave stared at her, looking frightened. Then suddenly she spun on her heel and walked away.

Mala was white. "Everything will change," she said.

"Dear Lady, nothing will ever be the same again. Sellia, you mustn't go."

"I must find Laurel."

"No," said Mala. "I'll go."

CHAPTER 23

Orrin sat quietly between Captain Dace's and Engineer Rene's beds, listening to the radio. The engineer drifted in and out of sleep, for she was heavily sedated. To the amazement of the doctors in the maternity, she continued to live despite the extent of injury. Lingering, they called it, for she was definitely not recovering. Captain Dace, however, was doing better. Her body was besting all infections, her bones were beginning to knit, and her mind was clear, though understandably troubled. She could not move and realized she never would if she stayed on Islands.

"Crushed coral at the station and fresh mussels . . ." the radio crier was saying.

"More food?" Captain Dace asked. "Don't Fyxen grow anything themselves?"

She listened to the radio whenever she was awake, hoped, Orrin was sure, to hear some comforting word about Hark. But the criers never even alluded to the existence of his captured lander let alone the spaceman himself, but that didn't stop Captain Dace's questions. She wanted to know everything about Islands, just as she'd insisted on knowing every detail of her condition.

"The mussels are delicacies," Orrin said, "no toxins to worry about. Crushed coral is decorative stone. They're putting it down in the streets and alleys instead of tanbark to beautify Fox. And yes, we grow some things ourselves, but not much. Much of the land has gone to ruin without the rain forest to replenish it. Fox depends heavily on what comes in on the rail."

"Why do you let the loggers come all the way from New Penance to cut down what's left of the forests?" she asked.

Orrin shrugged. "We have to. We've nothing else they want to trade for food and goods, and we must have those."

"And when the last of the trees is taken?"

"Officially, I don't know. Unofficially, I can see our militia growing more rapidly than any attempts to reclaim the land. When the time comes, Fox will take what it needs."

"Plums the size of your fist and verified low in nasuger by the abbey's kitchen. You'll want to bring a man to carry home a bushelful of these beauties."

"I want a man to carry *me* home," Captain Dace said wistfully. "A crewman named Hark."

"Not to worry," Orrin said with a quick look at the door. Dame Barenia had the habit of slipping in quietly, especially, it seemed to Orrin, when he and Captain Dace were talking of things they shouldn't. The door was firmly shut. "We'd have heard if he'd been caught. This maternity is filled with interested people who don't rely on the radio for all their information."

She lay, as always, quite still, but it was easy to detect when she was thoughtful and not just resting. "Dame Adione hasn't been here today," she said finally.

"The day isn't over yet. It's not even dusk." He tried to sound reassuring, but he felt some alarm in her absence himself. She'd come every morning to talk with Captain Dace, charmed her with her concern, and yesterday began to ask for specific information on how to fly the lander.

"You say you took Hark back to the lander once. Are you sure he didn't ask to go back again, that he didn't ask for ten minutes alone with it?"

Captain Dace had asked him the same question before, phrased a bit differently each time. Orrin had wondered why until Jeremy reminded him the little windship antenna could have been used to download the lander. Then he realized Captain Dace was being cautious with what she told him, probably not completely certain she could trust him. Orrin couldn't blame her. Her circumstances must seem utterly bizarre to her. "You must be wondering why he didn't try to use the windship antenna to call the orbiter, why he chose to treck a hundred klicks to find another."

"Antenna?" she said, as if she'd never heard of such a thing.

"A balloon antenna, Hark called it. An essential piece of information missing from the story I've been telling you. You're suspicious. He was suspicious. I knew the antenna existed, and that he could use it to activate the lander. But he did determine that he couldn't get near the lander alone. Jeremy told him how heavily guarded it was. I can surmise, as you must be doing, that he dismissed the possibility of using the balloon antenna."

"He wouldn't have started walking," she said, suddenly dismissing any pretense that the antenna was insignificant.

"He would—and did—once he determined the only other antenna in Fox was in the abbey, which is also in the park and even less accessible to him than the lander."

"You didn't tell me about that."

"I didn't know it was important." Orrin sighed. "I had a fair amount of time to talk with Hark, the meal, and during the expedition. I haven't repeated every word of our conversation, only what I thought was important."

"Perhaps you should tell me again, this time leaving nothing out."

"That wouldn't be fair to Hark."

"How's that?"

Orrin hesitated. It wasn't *fair*, but it was crucial that this woman trust him and know he was telling the truth about Hark. She could betray him on a whim, could be betraying him already with Dame Adione, or at the least trying to keep her options open with Dame Adione, too. He cleared his throat. "Remember I told you we used drugs on him."

"And learned about the AI. What else?"

"That he was in love with you."

For a moment she said nothing. Then, "What else?"

"He believed you respected him as a pilot and, to use his words, 'that was that.'"

"Good crew, that Pilot Hark," she said, almost smiling. "Dame Adione thinks he's a fool."

"I told you what she offered him."

"Pilot Hark can't be bribed," Captain Dace said matter of factly. "It's just very hard for me to believe he had no option except to walk to Selene."

"I don't want you to think it wasn't thought out, for it was. But I made it a more final decision than he realized he was agreeing to by killing the troopers. I had to commit Jeremy as well as Hark to the success of the venture."

"You couldn't have trusted them unless they feared for their lives?"

"Not Jeremy. I know him well; he always looks for an easy way. It had to be something his mother couldn't help him get out of. If Hark was harboring any secret thoughts of going back to the lander instead of to Selene, Jeremy would have set him straight on how foolish that would be."

Now she frowned. "What kind of man kills two of his own troopers?"

"A desperate one," Orrin said.

"Or one more ruthless than anyone I've ever known," she said.

Orrin shrugged. "I'm committed to the outcome. Maybe it's all the same."

"So is Dame Adione. I can't help being afraid that she'll find the balloon antenna in the lander. And if she flies it, the orbiter will zero in on it, and . . ." Captain Dace paused, and Orrin had the feeling she would have turned her head to look at him if she could. "What, no quick reassurances?"

"She's not stupid," Orrin said. "She may well recognize an antenna if she sees one. But she won't know how it can help her as long as you don't tell her. No one knows about the downloading but us. They think the jelly beans are what's required to make the lander fly.''

"Hark knew better. And I keep wondering why he didn't wait here in Fox for an opportunity to use the antenna he had instead of trekking a hundred klicks to find another.''

"You can't appreciate how well guarded that lander is by judging from your treatment at the maternity. There are sorry sisters inside the thing and bully-sized nature boys outside and a perimeter of my own troops watching them, and foot patrols in the park. You mentioned something about ten minutes. Is that how long he needed to use the antenna?''

"Yes. Ten minutes, if nothing went wrong. If only he had waited. I could have gotten Dame Adione to let him use it.''

"Don't trust her," Orrin said to her. "Don't believe her promise." He couldn't help worrying what went on during Dame Adione's meetings with Captain Dace.

"Prayers to keep Hells Gates closed to spirit-chasers offered tonight in the abbey. Give your coins at the door so that we can renew our patrol of the summit. Be alert against Selenians in your marketplace; don't talk to strangers of internal affairs.''

"That's your patrol, isn't it?''

"Not this time," Orrin said. He wondered what had prompted the announcement. Had someone else seen the wench from Selene?

The white door opened, and Dame Cirila stepped in. She was wearing a bright yellow scarf knotted on her hip and another just like it draped loosely over one shoulder. Her hair was caught up in yet another and fastened with amethysts on either side of her head. Court garb, definitely her finest, and set off with the frown she seemed to have worn since Jeremy was captured.

"He's been found," she said stepping over to the radio and turning down the volume.

"Hark captured?" Captain Dace asked in alarm.

"Not exactly. Just word of him through Adione's spies.

He's in New Penance. Queen Mala has sent her minions here to look for Laurel, the Selenian witch. They're little better than rounders, these creatures of Mala's, but they do seem to know that Hark's in New Penance, and that Laurel's on her way to him.''

"That explains the announcement," Orrin said. "But what's the connection between Laurel and Hark?"

"Laurel has pieces from the crashsite. These rounders or whatever they are watched the lander go down. They were on their way to Hells Gates. I gather she saw Hark's lander up there, and from there had the rounders lead her to the crashsite. Then they split up, the rounders were supposed to go home, but some didn't. Adione caught two of them in the marketplace and has come to some kind of agreement with them. I don't know how Mala got the spaceman, but she did. They described him perfectly. Now that she knows where Hark is, she wants to go after him.''

"Will Queen Aethelmere let her?"

Dame Cirila nodded. "She doesn't know about Laurel, just that Hark's been located. She doesn't want Mala to have him.''

"Are they certain this Laurel person has the jelly beans?" Captain Dace asked. "I mean, the brain jewels.''

"I don't think so. They told her they carried rocks in their packs for Laurel, rocks of many colors, and that they picked up bits of the wreckage, too. Aethelmere didn't make the connection, but I did, and so did Adione.''

"Damn," said Captain Dace. "If I could just get out of this bed.''

"I've just come from Aethelmere; she's given Dame Adione permission to go into New Penance to take him out," Dame Cirila said. "Mother Phastia gave special dispensation for her to use lasers. And I have been asked to let you, Orrin, out of the maternity to help her.''

Dame Cirila was visibly distressed. If Hark were caught, there'd be no saving Jeremy from the abbey. There had already been one hearing on Jeremy's fate and, as his guardian, Dame Cirila apparently had been eloquent in her arguments that the salvation of Jeremy's eternal soul was more important than hanging his body for treason and murder. It was no small embarrassment for her to admit that she had been remiss in providing an upbringing lacking in religious training and proper purification. If they would spare his life, she would give guardianship to the abbey. It hadn't taken Mother Phastia two seconds to realize control over the boy's life also provided some measure of control over the mother's, far more useful than the satisfaction of his death.

"Orrin's leaving?" Captain Dace said.

Dame Cirila shook her head. "I'm here to examine him and determine if he's fit. I don't think Aethelmere will require a second opinion when I tell them he's not."

"You mean you're not going to let me go? But you must. I can determine the outcome of the hunt!"

"That's why you mustn't go," Dame Cirila said, exasperated. "You increase her chances of finding him. If that happens, Hark won't be free to fly the lander and save Jeremy. And perhaps with Adione gone, Captain Dace can teach *you* what you need to know to fly that lander. Then you could take Jeremy away even if they do catch Hark."

For a moment Orrin was speechless. Dame Cirila couldn't possibly believe what she was saying, and yet there was nothing in her manner to indicate that she was anything but serious. Just as she had never considered the consequences of teaching Jeremy to be a doctor, she had not considered anything beyond his rescue. "Where," Orrin said gently, "would I take him? His crimes are infamous now. Do you seriously believe the Selenians don't monitor our broadcasts? Why do you think they prowl around Hells Gates? Just to catch a glimpse of souls down in the caldera?"

Dame Cirila stared at him, bewildered, tortured.

"You must let Orrin go with Dame Adione to New Penance," Captain Dace said bluntly. "Jeremy's only hope is to come with us to the Homeworlds. That can happen only if Hark can get the lander. Let Orrin go."

"I don't know," Dame Cirila said wringing her hands. "If Orrin goes with Dame Adione to New Penance, he can affect the outcome. Here he's as useless as we are. Dame Cirila, let him go!"

For an anguished moment Orrin thought she would refuse, but finally Dame Cirila nodded. Orrin stood up, gestured for Dame Cirila to precede him through the door; he'd need her signed release to show to Dame Adione. She nodded and turned.

"Orrin?"

They both paused to look at Captain Dace.

"Tell Hark . . ."

"Yes?"

"Just tell him that if he doesn't get me off this damned planet, I'll ground him."

CHAPTER 24

The troopers lowered him down a hole in the earth, threw the rope in after him, and Hark sat there with his head in his hands for an hour before he realized he wasn't in a pit. It was a cave. The stench wafting in from the tunnel ahead told him to which cave this little chamber connected. Hark moved out of the draft being sucked up and out the blue hole overhead, put his back to the wall opposite the tunnel and sat down. The smell was not so bad over here.

He picked at the dirt, barely registering that it wasn't really earth at all but some kind of mixture of sawdust and chips of bark. He had told the complete truth in Fox and had been a prisoner, so he lied in New Penance but still was a prisoner. He was no closer to rescuing Captain Dace and Rene than he was the first day he landed on Islands. He began to wonder when the on-board AI would take the orbiter home, for by now he knew it was well into its search for the remaining lander and only a matter of time before it succeeded in finding it. He began to hope it didn't take too long to conclude the search because it would cut down the length of time it would take the Guild to send another ship to Islands. Or would it?

There'd be a thorough examination of the on-board AI's memory, which would of course reveal that there was no longer an AI on Islands to be concerned about. They'd wonder what happened to the replacement team, of course, but he wasn't certain the mystery would be compelling enough for them to deadhead all the way to Islands to solve it. They might just make a routine report to the Worlds Council, pay casualty bonuses to the crew's heirs and be done with it. Even an intensive audit of the Guild's reports wouldn't bring any action; auditors were concerned with making sure the Guild had followed the AI maintenance laws. Even though one had been violated for a while, it was a moot point because there wasn't any AI on Islands anymore. A human relations committee might look to be certain the casualty bonuses were paid on time. Rene and Captain Dace had no close heirs; they'd spent much more time than he had in the uptime circuits and the only relatives they had probably would have forgotten they existed until the casualty bonuses arrived. Hark's family would make inquiries, but it would take years. He shook his head; nothing he could do about any of that and it was depressing to think about.

Also depressing to think about Sellia. What must she think of him after his tender little lecture about trust this morning? He had deceived her during the journey, and though it had made her angry, she'd understood his reasons enough to forgive him. Now he'd done it again, and Hark knew she must feel certain he was completely untrustworthy. He'd let her down, failed Rene and Captain Dace, and wished now that he'd never been born.

Voices from the tunnel brought his head up. He waited quietly, but no one appeared. Overhead he could see the jungle green camouflage uniform of one of the troopers, full view truncated by the thick walls of the hole. He couldn't possibly get through there, rope or no rope; the hole was trimmed and polished to offer no purchase and the diameter was so narrow that he'd have a tougher time getting his shoulders out than the guards had getting them in. The threat of being hit with a big plank had made him figure out in a big hurry how to scrunch up enough to get through.

Idly, Hark coiled the length of rope while watching the tunnel. Murmuring sounds, and was that laughter? He felt no great desire to explore. He had no torch and the smell of sulphur belly dung would be stronger in the tunnel, but there was a way out if the tunnel led to the sulphur bellies' cave; he'd seen the light of day when he'd passed through with Taffy. He'd seen troopers there, too. Still, he knew the little shaft of light from the hole in this chamber would dim with night soon, so if he was going to explore he'd better do it now while he had the bit of light to guide him back. He fastened the rope to his belt and went into the tunnel.

The other end of the tunnel opened into the sulphur bellies' cave, but not to the floor as he expected. He found himself on a natural balcony as high above the cave floor as the path on the other side that he and Taffy had used. A few caged chemlamps marked the edge of the balcony; a quick glance down told him it was a perilous overhang. And down *there* were faintly luminescent undulating *things* whose true shape he could not discern.

"It's the new cock," said a voice from deep in the shadows of the balcony. Hark turned, but could see nothing in the black depths until someone turned on a chemlamp. Three men in ragged clothes huddled around the lamp, staring at him. "If you have food to share, you can come up. The Caveman won't even know you're here until the next shitshift."

"He's gonna find us if you don't turn the damn light off and we're gonna have to move again," one said in a whining voice.

The light went out, and the recesses went black. Hark couldn't see them at all, and he couldn't hear them either. "I don't have any food," he said.

"Too bad, fellow," said a voice different from the first. "You'll have to take your chances out back."

"Out back?" Hark asked. "Do you mean below?"

They laughed. "We see your rope," the first who had spoken said. "If you decide to try it, let us know so we can plug our ears first. They get noisy when they're excited."

"The sulphur bellies?"

"Of course the sulphur bellies, you stone ding."

"Will you please shut up? Caveman could be sitting back there listening and we'll have to move again," said the whiner.

There was silence again, interrupted occasionally by crunching sounds from below. Hark abandoned any thoughts of using the rope right away, but was equally alarmed at this unnamed menace "out back." Not feeling adventurous, he decided to return to the little chamber.

"The screws won't help you," the first said to him, laughing.

"Shut up!"

"Better take a rock."

"If you don't shut up right now I'm leaving!"

The threat silenced the speaker, and Hark considered the tunnel again, but the little chamber was very confining. He stepped away from the lighted edge of the balcony and walked parallel to it in the darkness. Underfoot was dirt and pulverized bark, no rocks. He moved back deeper into the darkness keeping one of the little chemlamps in view so he could find his way back. After a while, he realized the light was practically being swallowed by the darkness; he stopped and dug in the soft dry dirt, hoping to get down to rock. He heard something and stopped, heart pounding nervously. Nothing but the soft echoes of the sulphur belly sounds. He started digging again, and was shocked by bright light painfully flooding into his eyes.

"Look what's fresh from pussy city," someone behind the light said.

Hark's eyes couldn't adjust to the continued onslaught and he raised his hand to protect them.

"Oooh, and something that sparkles on his wrist. No muscle ever gave you anything that shiny. You're some lady's dangler for sure. You must have been a real bad boy for her to send you here." The speaker's voice was mocking, the tone chilling. Now Hark could make out several pairs of boots when he looked through his fingers. "Let's just see what she gave you." One set of boots took a step toward him, and Hark crouched to meet an attack. He was grabbed from behind by the arms, and suddenly the whole scene was illuminated by a circle of chemlights snapped on in unison. There were at least twenty men around him, all wearing leather footware, some tattered but all soft, attesting to how they'd snuck up on him.

A tall man with dark greasy hair and wearing a cruel smile stepped forward and clamped his hand over Hark's wrist and looked at the gold watch. The smile spread to reveal crooked teeth.

"Now this is real nice," he said. "Looks like genuine Homeworlds crafting, and not even dented. She must have liked you a whole lot; dressed you nice, too. Is that what dapper danglers are wearing up there these days?" He was admiring Hark's shirt, oblivious to the Guild crests on the collar or not caring or understanding what they signified. "Mmmmmm. Smells nice, too," he said leaning close to Hark's neck. Hark tried to jerk away and the man laughed. "Pure muscle, eh? I've changed many a man's mind about that. Better to be one of Caveman's own fuck boys than bottom man to everyone." He leered long and hard, which Hark met with a defiant stare. But there was nothing more useful to do with his arms pinned and almost two dozen more waiting to jump him if he could get loose.

"The screws!" someone said in alarm, and the lights

went out plunging them into darkness. A hand clamped over Hark's mouth before he could think to let out a cry.

"Hark! Hark? Hark, it's me, Taffy. Come on out."

In the light of the distant chemlamp at the edge of the balcony, Hark could just make out Taffy's grotesque silhouette and those of a half dozen troopers around him. All the troopers were male, looked exceptionally large though that might have been just by comparison to Taffy, and they were carrying lasers.

"Is that you they're calling?" Caveman whispered.

Hark nodded.

"All right. I'm going to let you go. But if you tell them screws where we are, you're dead meat."

The grips on his arms loosened, and he sensed that Caveman and his friends had melted away rather than wait for Hark to leave. He walked toward the light.

"Hark? Hark, where are you?"

"Here, Taffy," he said when he was close. One of the troopers shined a light in his eyes.

"It's him, all right, " the trooper said. Another bright light scoured the cave behind him. Hark turned around to watch: nothing but recesses and cavewalls. Caveman and his friends had gone as quickly and silently as they'd come.

"Hark, are you all right?" Taffy asked. He was carrying a cloth bundle, looked concerned.

"I'm all right, for now," Hark assured him. He wondered if it would do any good to tell the troopers about Caveman, decided it would not. The six of them looked very alert, their attention more on the recesses of the cave where they could not see than on Hark and Taffy, whom they could see. No doubt it was Caveman or others like him they were on guard against.

"She sent me," Taffy said.

"Sellia?" His heart quickened.

Taffy shook his head, looked around nervously at the guards. "Is there somewhere we can go to talk privately?" he asked Hark.

Hark shrugged.

"Go to the rim, Taffy. We'll wait here," a trooper said.

They weren't far from the rim to begin with, but far enough that if they kept their voices down, the guards wouldn't hear them. They'd be in plain view, though, and Hark never would have believed he'd be grateful for it. He led the way, his arms still tingling from Caveman's crew's tight hold on him.

"She sent you some food and a blanket," Taffy said.

"Then you're not here to get me out?" Hark said, realizing only then that he'd been hoping that's why Taffy had come. When Taffy shook his head, the disappointment he felt was acute. The fear of what awaited him when Taffy and the troopers left stabbed even deeper. But he nodded calmly and took the sack from Taffy. There was something hard inside, too. He looked, found a chemlamp. He left everything in the sack and sat down. "She wouldn't come herself?" *Of course not!* "Is she very angry?"

Taffy shrugged. "You figure it out," he said. "It was a damn fool stunt to pull. What's amazing is that you must have thought you could get away with it."

"Something that primitive . . ." He shook his head. "I figured it was more for show, or maybe a scare tactic. I'm still not convinced it's reliable."

"It's reliable," Taffy said, "and you are in deep trouble."

Hark gave a sardonic laugh. "Tell me about it," he said. "Sulphur bellies down there and a Neanderthal that calls himself Caveman up here."

"Someone always calls himself Caveman; it can't be the original anymore. He'd have to be fifty years old by now."

"What I don't understand is why they don't control the likes of that brute."

"It's lawless down here. The pits are supposed to make you grateful to follow the rules outside, if you get outside again." Taffy glanced nervously at his escort of troopers. Their stance was less rigid, but they were alert. "I've heard it's dangerous to go near the rim, but I guess it's all right while the troopers are here. She says for you to be careful and not to take any chances."

"For how long?" Hark asked, suddenly hopeful. "Is she trying to get me out of here?"

"Hark, I don't know. I can't think of anything she can do for you except make me come here to bring things to you so you won't starve. Beyond that I honestly don't know. I'm not a barrister. Maybe once guardianship is settled . . ." He clamped his lips when Hark shot him a contemptuous glance, but then apparently decided not to keep silent. "If the abbey gets control, they might recommomend purification and . . ."

"If the abbey gets control I'll wring their clerics' necks one by one before I submit to their purification. You can tell them that for me," he said fiercely.

"Not me," Taffy said. "You tell them when the time comes." He sat down next to Hark, crossing his little legs. "Look, I've heard that it's not so bad, that . . ."

"Is that why she sent you? To see if I'd cooperate? You tell Sellia that if she wants a mutilated man she'll have to look elsewhere."

Taffy let out a little whistle. "It makes a little more sense now," he said.

"What does?"

"Her sending me here. I was pretty sure she had been crying when she told me to come to you," Taffy said. "I haven't seen either of them cry since they were kids. She cancelled afternoon court, probably because she didn't want *them* to know she'd been crying. She's never done that before."

"Sellia cancelled court?"

"No, Mala. Sellia went back into the wilderness."

Hark looked at him, puzzled. "I don't think Mala would waste any tears over me. If anything, she might be glad that I was out of the way."

"The Mala who sent me had been crying," Taffy said seriously, and Hark realized they must have changed roles. "If I had to guess I'd say you've made her fall in love with you. There can't be any other explanation for her crying. I know I told you it was the best way, but I didn't know anyone could do it in a single night."

"It wasn't a single night," Hark said slowly, thinking and trying to remember just when. But he couldn't be certain even for himself except to know that he'd been so happy when they sat on the bonebacks in the rain and talked for a moment about sharing. He wouldn't have called it love then if anyone had asked, nor even when he first got into her bed. But by this morning, he knew there was no sense in labeling it anything else, and she'd all but admitted it was the same for her. And he'd repaid her with betrayal. "Tell her I'm sorry," he said. "It's not how it seems. I know she may not understand this, but tell her anyhow that I just didn't believe I could be successful in my duty without lying . . ." He shook his head. It sounded glib, even to him. In the end it boiled down to her trusting him and him betraying the trust.

"Hark, she could have sent troopers down here with the sack. But she sent me. She didn't tell me anything except what I already told you, but that was a message a trooper could have carried . . . unless she was hoping for one back that she wouldn't trust to them. Have you ever considered telling her the truth, whatever it is?"

"Yes," Hark said feeling the irony of knowing the truth had made no difference. But then he sighed because that had been in Fox with Dame Adione, and this was New Penance and the woman was Sellia. "It may make things worse," he said finally. "They may not even offer me purification but, hell, she deserves to know. All right, my friend. I hope you have a couple of hours, because the telling won't go quickly."

Taffy brushed some dust off his shoes. They were the ones he'd admired in the marketplace . . . was that only yesterday? "We'll eat while you talk," Taffy said opening the sack. "If what I hear about this place is true, you're better off to carry your food around in your stomach than in a sack. And this stuff is from the twins' own pantry; none better in all New Penance."

While Taffy ate with full gusto, Hark told him about their mission to Islands and how, when they got here, they had started to carry it out and how it had gone wrong. He left nothing out this time, not the replacement AI and not the killing of the Fyxen troopers, both of which he had thought of as his terrible secrets. When Hark paused toward the end of his story, he noticed that the sounds the sulphur bellies made had ceased and the cave was truly silent. Taffy handed him a slice of pickled meat. Hark accepted it absently, realized he'd been eating tidbits all along and that his hunger was satisfied.

"She should be glad you wouldn't bargain with Dame Adione for the AI," Taffy said seriously. "But what I'm not sure of is who should get it."

"Maybe no one," Hark said. "Captain Dace was going to try to figure out if there was a justifiable link between the Hound civil authority and either Fox or Selene—we didn't know about New Penance—or if we should just leave it in the crate and take it home."

Taffy nodded slowly. "I don't think I'll tell her about the part where you were in love with Captain Dace," he said.

"Don't leave anything out, Taffy, not even that."

"But . . ."

"Tell her *everything*," he insisted. "If she finds out about one detail left out, she'll wonder what else was left out. Don't skip a thing."

Taffy looked dismayed, but he finally agreed. He started rewrapping the leftover food and putting it back in the sack.

"Taffy, we're going to have to leave," one of the troopers called over to him. "The lights are coming on; they'll be starting the roundup soon."

Lights in the lower cavern where the sulphur bellies had been were flickering on. The cave was empty of the beasts but littered with phosphorescent piles of dung.

"Good," Taffy said with a quick look down at the lights. He started to get up. "I can take the shortcut when I . . ." He stopped and looked at Hark. "They'll feed everyone who works on cleaning the cave and give them the use of the hoses for showers, too. But I've heard you can avoid the work by just staying out of sight until after they round up a big enough crew."

Hark looked across the cave to the other side; troopers armed with lasers were filing onto the ledge, others going down the stone steps to the floor below.

"Let's go, Taffy," came a sharp voice from behind. "If you're still by the edge when they put the ladders up you might get burned."

"Gotta go, Hark," Taffy said. He shoved the sack into Hark's hands and half ran to his escorts.

With no concern for Hark being on the ledge, the troopers surrounded Taffy and started walking away. Hark looked back at the big chamber. Some of the troopers had reached the bottom of the cave and were picking their way through the dung heaps to get to the other side. There, Hark supposed, they would raise ladders and climb up while the other troopers on the ledge across the way, who probably were marksmen, prevented any of the prisoners from doing them harm. Hark realized that they'd soon perceive him as a threat. He backed away from the ledge, but didn't want to go into the dark recesses where Caveman and his friends might be waiting. Then he saw the three men who had first greeted him standing just inside the light, waiting he was sure to volunteer for work and dinner. Hark wasn't hungry at all, but he followed their example of standing just inside the light. Shovelling shit had more appeal than having the same beat out of him by Caveman and his friends.

CHAPTER 25

Sellia went back to the guard shack where Laurel was waiting. "The First can't free up enough troopers to escort us into the pits until the hedger is finished," Sellia told her.

"What does she think we'll find down there that we haven't encountered in the wilderness?" Laurel said putting her hand on her knife hilt.

"Have you ever been in the pits?"

"No."

"Neither have I. The First knows who we are and she insists on providing an escort."

"I don't see why," Laurel said. "There's never been an escape, has there?"

"No, but there are attempts."

Laurel stepped up to the window. "They would have to get up through the manhole, single file, then run across the dell to the sunhedge. Admittedly they've got quite a gap there, but the place to stop them is at the manhole. All it would take is one trooper armed with a club." She looked at Sellia.

"It's not escapees she's worried about. I'm the queen's sister, you're highborn Selenian; she wouldn't want to answer to my sister if either of us were harmed."

"Are visitors frequently harmed?" Laurel asked too sweetly.

Sellia sighed. Laurel never stopped asking penetrating

questions, a habit she hated and her sister admired. "There are no visitors except by express orders from the queen. Fortunately for us the First believes I wouldn't make a request the queen would refuse or we'd be waiting for a messenger to run to the palace."

"How often does the queen grant visit requests?"

"As often as she gets them," Sellia said taking off her pack.

Laurel, apparently convinced that she would have to wait, threw down her pack on the bench under the window. "How often do people come to visit your pit inmates?"

"Never that I know of. They're all rounders and criminals, so are their families."

"Chain gangs get visits from family or old guardians."

"Our inmates are rounders, Laurel, not muscle offspring of highborns or even ticket-of-leave boys. We can't deal with them in chain gangs and don't try to tell me you're succeeding in Selene."

"But we are," Laurel said. She was digging in her pack for something, found it, and tucked it in her belt. "We're using good, old-fashioned chain gangs with constant supervision. We've already released one into society. We appointed him a guardian and . . ."

"One?" Sellia laughed. "You Selenians simply don't understand the scope of the problem. We're felling the last of the primary forest on Fox Volcano to supply lumber for the rails to the sea. The Fyxen themselves burn off the secondary forests for their damnable plantations. There's nowhere rounders can hide anymore, so they cross the Black Desert to New Penance. We'd be delighted if they'd continue on to Selene, but one desert crossing apparently is enough for most of them. We don't deal with one or two; we have dozens, and you can't have dozens of incorrigibles in a chain gang without chaos."

"Dozens?" Laurel said uncertainly.

"Too many," Sellia said, for she didn't know the exact number. She was only certain no one in New Penance liked having them in the pits, but no one knew what else to do with so many.

Laurel pulled her feet off the floor, shoved the pack under her head and stretched out on the bench. She lay staring at the thatched roof, apparently at a loss for more penetrating questions to ask, especially since she was at a loss for answers, as well.

The hedger was still clearing away the undergrowth, laying the gap clear, and Sellia started pacing. She walked to the rear of the shack and back to the window and paused. He was cutting back thorn bushes and splitting stems down to the rootstock. It would be a while yet before he had finished weaving runners and split stems around the rods he had yet to drive into the ground, months before the new growth that he would carefully cut back so it would be thick and strong at the base had bound the hedge thoroughly. The rest of the hedge looked perfect to her. The shells of the ancient nursetrees had rotted away a generation ago leaving four living green fences that butted at almost perfect right angles, a fence so thick that only the smallest forest creatures could creep through. Sometimes an overly eager boneback or twotail broke through, attracted by open grazing in the dell. This gap had been made by Hilma's big bay mare, still unused to accepting easier foraging that it would have found further up the ridge.

The trip out had been a good one, restful and jolly just waiting at Hilma's cabin for Laurel to show up. Sellia made one-day forays along the trails Laurel might use on the chance that she'd meet her, but they were more sport and gesture than any real attempts to find the Selenian. Finding anyone in the vast wilderness forest was a matter of luck; they could pass within a quarter klick of each other on the forest floor and never see or hear one another let alone know if someone were in the understory directly overhead. Sellia knew that until Laurel was ready to pick up her specimens at Hilma's she would not find her. To be sure she'd sent Hilma's kinswomen to the likely places: back to Hells Gates and to the Flower Market in Fox to query the stragglers who came in to sell their wares, but mostly she rode or hunted with Hilma and came back to find the mat in the corner stuffed with fresh minty leaves and the boy as horny and eager as the last time.

When Laurel arrived, the interlude ended abruptly. She had stories of her own to tell of flying vessels falling out of the sky and wreckage she'd seen with her own eyes and which was still being picked over by Fyxen clerics. She listened to Sellia's account of the spaceman in New Penance, said it fitted what she already knew. What remained a mystery was how he seemed to know her, for Laurel was certain she'd never seen him. And Laurel had alluded to Hark's not being the only Homeworlder on Islands, which was certainly news to Sellia and if true, would be proof of one more lie Hark had told. She didn't like her sister championing any man, let alone a lying Homeworlder. He wasn't worthy of her.

Sellia paused again. The hedger was gathering up his rake, billhook, and mallet, tucking them under his arm. The First watched him walk to the deadgate, which was raised by two muscle troops so he could leave. The living fence was secure again. She looked over at the guard shack. The First saw Sellia watching her and signaled for her to come ahead. Sellia reached over and shook Laurel. "Let's go," she said.

The stench in the pits was disgusting, and Laurel made a rude comment.

The First, who'd elected to head up the team escorting the queen's sister herself, said, "The sulphur bellies have been inside for days. It's worse than usual, but it can't be helped. The sentries say this is the last bunch. Perhaps you'd like to wait until tomorrow? They'll be forming chain gangs to clean up the droppings; tomorrow it won't smell this bad."

"No," Sellia said. "I want to talk to the spaceman now." They'd come through the little tunnel to the grand balcony, which was kept dimly lighted so as not to disturb the sulphur bellies' rock grazing. Even after all these years, the beasts had not become accustomed to artificial lights. No one knew why.

"How do you find anyone down here?" Laurel asked. Sellia knew what she meant. The lights were not adequate for much more than marking the edge of the balcony, certainly not for reaching to the full depths of the caverns.

"They'll find us," the First assured her. "My bottom man here will call for him. They'll produce him soon enough; they don't like us searching their burrows, and the only way to avoid it is to give us who we want."

The bottom man had a rich baritone voice that carried and echoed sharply. He named the spaceman several times, and threatened search if he didn't come forth in fifteen minutes. They waited, listening to the sulphur bellies chewing the rocks below. The trails were solid with phosphorescent dung, the glowing parasites dropping off the great bellies of the beasts to breed is such large numbers that *these* sulphur bellies' great abdomens almost didn't glow. Only occasionally could Sellia see a rippling glow as the great grinding muscles flexed.

"Hark. We want Hark, and we want him now," the bottom man said at the end of the alloted time. He'd turned on his searchlight and aimed it into the depths of the cave.

"I'm here," said a voice still far away.

They waited. The bottom man probed shadows and blackness with his searing light, the other muscle troopers followed movement with lesser lights. The First kept her hand on her laser.

At last the searchlight caught the shape of a man limping slowly toward them. His feet were bare and dirty, he wore rags that didn't even vaguely resemble the blue uniform Sellia had last seen the spaceman wearing. His hands were up in front of his face to save his eyes from the light. When he was close enough and the bottom man convinced he was carrying no rocks or other weapons, he replaced the powerful flashlight with the gentle light of a chemlamp. The prisoner lowered his hands, stood still, blinking. It was Hark, but she barely recognized him.

"Lovely prison you have here," Laurel said dryly.

Even Sellia was taken aback. Both Hark's eyes were

swollen and discolored, his lip split so recently that blood glistened in a dribble down his chin. He held his hand over his ribs as if they hurt and he leaned unsteadily on his feet. He looked nothing like the arrogant spaceman she had met in court.

"Do you want us to clean that lip up a bit?" the First asked.

Hark needed more than a few drops of disinfectant, but Sellia knew they wouldn't offer more. "Yes," she said.

"Sellia?" he said at the sound of her voice. There was no mistaking his hopeful tone. He was still blinking, trying to focus. "Sellia, is that you?"

He was staring through swollen slits, reaching his filthy hand to her. She stepped back and gestured to the troopers, said icily, "Get busy cleaning him up."

Hark stood quietly while the bottom man swabbed his face with disinfectant, not wincing though Sellia knew it must have stung. When he was done cleaning, the bottom man gave Hark his canteen. The spaceman drank a great deal of the contents before returning it and thanking the bottom man. The troopers withdrew a few meters, leaving Hark with Sellia and Laurel.

"I trust your stitches are healing well?" Hark said looking directly into Sellia's eyes, deliberately defiant to have spoken without leave. Sellia ignored him.

"Do you recognize him?" she asked Laurel.

"I don't know that I would if he were my own brother," Laurel replied. "He's a mess."

"Nonetheless you should recognize me," Hark said. "I recognize you, Laurel."

"Lady Laurel to you," Sellia said sharply.

"It wasn't a slip this time, *Sellia*," he said equally sharply, and with such emphasis on her name that Sellia knew he was aware that she was not *his* Sellia. "Lady, I can see the hate in your eyes, and it scares the hell out of me because you have almost all the advantages. But just remember, I've got one. Don't make me use it."

"I don't think he likes you, Sellia," Laurel said, still studying him carefully.

"The list of reasons why grows with every passing hour down in this hole," Hark said. "She . . . the queen knew exactly what she was doing when she sent me here. It was the next best thing to cutting out my tongue."

Sellia swallowed hard. "I didn't know the beatings were this bad."

"You stupid bitch," he said. "The beatings are not the worst."

Angrily, Sellia raised her hand to slap him, but his defiant glare stayed her hand. Hitting him would only antagonize him, perhaps into telling about the stitches. She lowered her hand calmly. "I don't think we're accomplishing anything here." She started to walk over to the guards, and Laurel, apparently fairly well shocked by his outburst herself, was right behind.

"Wait!" Hark said. "Don't go. Laurel. Lady Laurel, I saw you at Hells Gates taking gas samples in the caldera. It was the morning after the storm. You were wearing an antithermic helmet; I saw you through binoculars. You took off the helmet before you detached the sampling bottle. I think you were angry about something; at least, you were frowning."

Laurel stopped and looked back at him. "The bottle was cracked," she said.

"And I saw you again above the soda lake valley. You saved me from being trampled by a goliath goat," he said. "The dead of night, just one moon . . ."

"That man was dressed like a Fyxen muscle troop," she said.

"I wore their garb," Hark said. "Orrin, the First, thought it more suitable. We had been searching for the jelly beans . . . the brain jewels from the lander that went down the night before the storm."

Laurel was nodding. "I wondered what they were searching for," she said and turned to Sellia with a grin. "They'll never find them."

"Why not?" Hark said, stepping closer to Laurel, looking tense.

"I found them," she said.

"Is the nitrogen canister intact?" he asked eagerly.

"I didn't open it to find out. I knew what it was, and I didn't have any nitrogen to replace it with if I couldn't reseal it. I decided to wait until I got back to Selene."

"If I didn't think you'd be offended, milady, I would kiss you."

"I don't understand why you're so pleased," Laurel said. "The ship was wrecked."

"There's another lander," Sellia said realizing now that these jelly brains had something to do with the repairs he wanted to make.

"Then it was a Homeworlds lander," Laurel said eagerly. "I watched them carry it down to the rail. I *knew* that's what it was, but then the only talk I could pick up in town was about the one that had crashed. I saw that from the rim of the crater before entering the storm; it wasn't difficult to figure out where to look." She looked at Hark. "You really are a Homeworlder."

"Maybe so," Sellia said, "but his reasons for being here are far from clear. He lied in court about having an invitation to Selene from you. There's also the matter of there being other Homeworlders on Islands, not just the one man."

"It's true," Hark said simply. But he didn't elaborate; he turned back to Laurel again. "I didn't use to believe in dreams."

Laurel raised her brows quizzically.

He shook his head, smiled lopsidedly. "Suffice to say that I'm glad the brain jewels are in safe hands. If they're not damaged, they're all I need to return to the Homeworlds."

"Them and a pardon," Laurel said sardonically. "You're in serious trouble for lying in court and in the inquiry. Even worse that you're a Homeworlder. It's difficult to imagine why anyone from the Homeworlds would come here, but since that much seems to be true, your lies trouble me as deeply as they obviously troubled Queen Mala. One very reasonable scenario is that you're a criminal from the Homeworlds, the downed lander your pursuers. That would account for your not telling that they're still alive."

"Both of them?" Hark asked, then added quickly. "I mean, that's not what happened. I'm not a criminal. They're my crewmates and I want very much for both of them to be alive. They were both alive—so I was told—when I left Fox, but the engineer was not expected to live the day." He tried to take a deep breath but it seemed his ribs pained him. "Are they still alive?"

Laurel looked at Sellia, a bewildered look on her face. And Sellia shook her head. "I told you everything I know, Laurel. I don't know why he's changing his story now, except, that he might be trying to fit the new bits of information in to the lies he's already told."

"Or I might, at last, be telling the full truth," Hark said. "Let me list the lies for you. Knowing them might help."

"Better to know why you told them in the first place," Sellia said.

He looked at her squarely. "I have one duty on this planet, and that's to save my crewmates. I did it the best way I knew how under circumstances I still only half understand. I tried telling the truth in Fox, not realizing I'd become a pawn in criminal politics because they could use the lander and the AI on board the orbiter to rule all of Islands. I don't usually make the same mistake twice. When I came to New Penance, I adjusted the story so that I'd be less attractive as a pawn."

"So you lied?"

He nodded.

"But now you expect me to believe you?" Sellia said in amazement. "That now we get the truth, the whole truth, and . . ."

"And nothing but the truth," Hark finished for her with a vigorous nod.

Sellia shook her head, disbelieving.

"Lie number one," he said turning to appeal to Laurel as

soon as Sellia shook her head. "The original mission was to replace the Hound AI, not merely perform maintenance on it. I've a bright new one that's going to stay in my orbiter until my captain tells me what to do with it, *if* she tells me what to do with it. Do you know what an AI is?"

Laurel nodded.

"Good, then I don't have to explain to you why Dame Adione wanted it. Some day when you have a lot of time, you might explain it to your friend here," he said. "Now, lie number two. Jeremy was not dead when I last saw him. He was captured by Fyxen troops on the base of your own New Penance volcano. He had a broken leg, but he was very much alive. Lie number three: we didn't escape from Fox on a railcar, we left from the valley by the soda lake the night you saw us. Did you see Jeremy running in front of me?"

"I saw two men. The first roused the goliath goat and sent it stampeding at me. I'd have left you to save your own skin if mine hadn't been in the way," Laurel told him.

"Back in the camp, two men died when we escaped," Hark added somewhat hesitantly. "I didn't kill them, but I guess I'm the cause of it."

"They buried two men in the morning," Laurel said, nodding, frowning. "Would you tell all of this to the court and before the witnesses for truth?"

"Laurel, he's going to say whatever he thinks you want to hear."

"No," Hark said harshly. "Only the truth from now on. I promised her that, and I give you my word, too. Let me face your witnesses again and that damned machine, too."

"It's not in my power to free you, not even just for that. There's no condition to a sentence in the pits; it's the final resort."

Hark shrugged. "Tell me what to do," he said. "My crewmates are depending on me. Are you going to want to face the next Homeworlders and tell them you prevented me from saving them because I was the wrong sex to be credible in your courts? No second chances for men? And don't try to tell me it wouldn't have been any different if I were a woman. I haven't seen one down here."

"The Homeworlds would have no right to interfere with our faith," Sellia said nervously.

"You're right," he said. "They wouldn't and couldn't if you can justify that it's truly a matter of faith. But I defy anyone to defend this pesthole as anything but what it is: hell on Islands. Produce one convert who's doing your heavenly penance aboveground that ever was in this pit and maybe you'll get someone to believe you. But I don't think there is one. Do you?"

"It's pretty poor tactics on your part to be pursuing this, fellow," Laurel said. "I'm trying to get you your second chance and you're insulting the very soul of the woman who can help."

"Forget it, Laurel," Sellia said. "It's not in my power. Even if I got guardianship, his lies are a matter of record. Aunt Meave would fight me openly on this; it could take years."

Laurel looked at her placidly. "I suggest that you get started," she said. "Let me explain my position. He's definitely from Homeworlds, and in my opinion that's reason enough to keep him someplace safe. I think he's telling you the truth, but I'm quite willing to have that verified by the queen's own witnesses, in an inquiry for truth." She stopped Sellia from protesting about the lies again by holding up her hand. "Even if he turns out to be some sort of criminal, we'd get much more gratitude from the Homeworlds if we turned him over to them intact. The fact is, Sellia, that any Homeworlder is too valuable to us to be left down here. I plan to stay with him until you arrange his removal."

"You can't do that," Sellia said, aghast. Laurel was a friend of Mala's court, and what she was suggesting would strain the relations between New Penance and Selene.

"I can," she said quite calmly. "I will. Get him out!"

"Damn!" She'd not bargained for this, but she could see

by the look on Laurel's face that she was determined to carry through.

"I think I love you," Hark said to Laurel, "but, milady, I don't think even two of us are enough against those thugs. Their treatment of me . . . Thank you for the gesture, but I don't believe a woman would last as long as I have. Their contempt for you is unbelievable."

"It isn't a gesture, Pilot, so be quiet. Let Sellia think."

Sellia bit her lip. She couldn't leave Laurel down here. Did she dare leave the escort with her while she talked to Mala? No; there really wasn't anything Mala could do. It was all tied up in the guardianship, and that . . . She looked at Hark. "If you were to appeal to the abbey to take guardianship and if I removed my claim so that Mala could grant it immediately, we might be able to get you out right away."

"No," Hark said fiercely. "You're talking about purification."

She nodded. "It's the only way they'll have you. Your immortal soul is considered more important than your mortal body; a desire to redeem your soul is the one thing that would carry more weight than the lies. Even Meave would feel safe if the abbey took custody."

"No," he repeated.

"Don't quibble," Laurel said. "It's a good solution."

"How the hell would you know?" he said angrily. "You don't have any!"

But Laurel just looked at Sellia and said once again and very calmly, "It's a good solution. I'll wait here with him until you return."

Now that she had Laurel satisfied, she ignored Hark's continuing protests. The problem wasn't completely solved. The escort would be unwilling to abandon Laurel, even for the little while it would take to find Mala and the aunts and come to an agreement.

Putting her hands behind her back, she walked over to where the First and her bottom man were waiting. "Look, I have a problem. No, I guess *we* have a problem," she said to the First. Instinctively the woman looked at Hark. He had stopped talking and was glancing nervously back into the darkness. "I know it's high-handed of her and I want you to know that it disappoints me, too, but Lady Laurel refuses to leave this man. You see, he's asked for the abbey to take guardianship . . ."

"I have not!"

". . . and in his condition, Lady Laurel is afraid he might not survive long enough for me to get to the abbey and back. I can't convince her that he'll be all right, and I can't let her stay down here alone."

The First officer seemed more than dismayed by the message, but no doubt it was the tone, so abnormally sweet, that got to her. "We can carry her out," the First said without batting an eye.

"You do and I'll go straight to the Selenian Consulate and file a protest," Laurel said promptly.

Sellia whirled on her. "What do you expect me to do? My hands are tied. We'll come back for him just as soon as we can."

"We could take him into the dell," the bottom man suggested timidly. "Technically, it's still the pits."

The First shrugged and nodded. Sellia sighed.

"Please, Lady Laurel, I know you're trying to help, but not like this," Hark was saying. But Laurel was quite satisfied with the solution and was watching Sellia expectantly. She rocked back on her heels. Hark turned to Sellia. "Don't do this to me. She wouldn't want . . ."

Sellia looked at him sharply. Did he think Laurel wouldn't wonder who *she* was? Would he next threaten to tell about the stitches? She turned to the First, whispered: "Do you have a gag?"

The First was completely baffled, but she nodded.

"The man is subject to fits that cause him to say foul things. I've heard enough for one day."

"He may struggle," the First said, also whispering.

"I'm sure he . . ."

Hark had broken and was running into the shadows, the

bottom man hot on his heels and two of the other troopers right after. Hark was slow, and the bottom man tackled him before he got ten steps.

"The whispering did it," Laurel said shaking her head sadly. "He'll thank us one day. It *was* a good solution."

"Yes," Sellia said, "but to the wrong problem. He still has a tongue and I still don't trust him."

"Another inquiry before witnesses will take care of that," Laurel said lightly.

But Sellia was not afraid of his lies now, only of the truth he could tell.

CHAPTER 26

Gagged again, and his arms trussed securely behind his back, the guards dragged Hark through the tunnel to the antechamber with the hole in the ceiling. He'd dreamed of going back out through that hole all the time he'd been in the pits, and never would have believed he wouldn't welcome the event. He'd been abused beyond anything he could have imagined by the inhabitants of the pits, but they'd only damaged his pride, not his manhood as was planned for him now.

Someone let down a rope ladder from above, which Hark refused to climb. It took four of the big muscle troopers paired up on the ladder with the fifth and their lace First managing his kicking feet at the bottom to pass him up through the hole to the lace troops waiting to receive him on top. Daylight blinded him for an instant and he didn't understand what the shouting was all about until he saw one of the muscle troopers he'd been struggling with drop into the dirt at his feet, blood spurting from his jugular vein.

"Move, Spaceman!" the lace trooper ordered. But it wasn't one of New Penance's lace troopers. It was Dame Adione wearing their harvest greenery. She shoved Hark to waiting hands—Orrin's and Theda's, both dressed in blood-soaked harvest greenery.

The sunhedge had been breeched, the compound's defenders still lying where they'd fallen, some bodies plainly trampled under the cleats of milling bonebacks. Half a dozen of the beasts were standing by the guard shack, vestigial wings aflutter, cleats aprance and digging in place, their reins firmly in Rina's grip preventing them from running.

As Orrin and Theda dragged him toward the bonebacks, Hark tried to pull free. Amazingly, he broke Orrin's grasp, but Theda held true. He caught a glimpse of the First bursting out of the manhole behind a muscle trooper who fell almost instantly to Adione's knife. Then Hark felt the muzzle of a warm laser barrel under his chin.

"Move quickly now," Theda said, "before I burn away what's left of your face."

Orrin had grabbed him again, and Hark was shoved up on the back of one of the beasts. With a few quick motions, Theda wrapped leather straps over his thighs, pinning him into the saddle. His hands were still bound behind him, but Orrin reached up and ripped the gag from Hark's mouth. "He'll need to breathe," Orrin said checking Theda's protest. Orrin took the reins of Hark's mount from Rina, leaped to the back of the next animal and started running them past the manhole toward the gap in the sunhedge.

Sellia and Laurel were out of the pits, fighting hand-to-hand against the Fyxen along with the First and one muscle trooper. Most of the Fyxen were finding mounts, no longer fighting, but even so they outnumbered the three women and lone male defenders. Two grabbed Laurel from behind,

and Hark saw Sellia fall to a blow on the head before the
bonebacks cleared the gap and raced along a narrow path
through the forest. And even though it wasn't his Sellia who
had fallen, he cried out, horrified and anguished to see her
face go blank and crumple helplessly.

"Orrin!" he shouted, but Orrin stayed crouched over the
boneback's neck.

"Hi-eee, run!" It was Theda shouting from the boneback
behind, urging the beasts to greater speed. If Hark hadn't
seen Dame Adione in the midst of the fray, he might have
believed Orrin and the struggler woman had somehow
teamed up to rescue him from a fate worse than death. As it
was, his terror increased.

Hark hadn't known the bonebacks could run so fast, so
far, and so long. The spiracle plugs were fully open and he
could feel hot air hissing from the vents close to his legs. To
keep from getting unbalanced, he hunched down and tried
to grip with his knees as his mount careened down the
sloping path after Orrin. He saw little more than the flash of
Orrin's mount's cleats as they threw up clods of mud and
rotten vegetation, but he could hear the thunder of a dozen
or more of the beasts behind him. They ran through dense
forest until they reached a wider path, a sulphur-belly trail
by the looks of the droppings, and here the speed of the
bonebacks increased, something Hark wouldn't have
guessed was possible. He felt as if he were riding a tornado
through the forest, not an animal of flesh and blood.

They ran full out for what seemed like hours to Hark, the
high-speed pace a swinging motion as the bonebacks'
bodies twisted from side to side. The bonebacks were
heaving for breath now, slowing discernably. The queen's
troopers must be after them and he hoped that despite the
long, fast run they would catch up soon. He had a vague and
probably wild plan to escape from everyone as soon as the
next battle started. He was sure it must; this was New
Penace territory, the little band of guerillas leaving a trail
that a child could follow in the dark. And dark it was
becoming.

Hark heard an animal scream somewhere ahead of them, and Orrin abruptly reined in his boneback. The one Hark was riding overran, and for a second he was face to face with Orrin. He could see nothing in the man's rugged face, no fear, no apology, no hatred, nothing to explain how he'd come to be here with Dame Adione.

And Theda and Rina! The two of them were alongside now, their bonebacks bunched up on the trail with Orrin's and Hark's mounts. For a moment they sat silently, looking and listening for what Hark did not know. He couldn't see any further than four meters into the vegetation and the only sound was the labored hissing of the bonebacks sucking in air. Theda put her hand on the grip of the laser in her holster, as if she feared the silence. Hark recognized the laser; it was the one he'd given to Theda's mother. He looked at Orrin, wondered if he had recognized the laser, too. But Orrin's attention was on the silent forest, just like the two women's. Then Rina made a noise from deep down in her throat, very much like the animal sound they'd just heard. There was an answering scream from the black-green shadows just ahead and to their right.

"They're coming, all right, and not from far," Theda said to Orrin. "Tiz time."

Orrin nodded and looked past Hark to signal to those behind. Hark turned around. He saw more muscle troopers, some in harvest-greenery, some in Fyxen fatigues. Bringing up the rear he caught a glimpse of Dame Adione holding the reins of someone else trussed to the saddle. Laurel! Why had they brought Laurel?

Abruptly Orrin urged his mount off the trail into the untrodden underbrush, tugging for Hark's boneback to follow. Hark had to lean over the beast's head to keep from being raked by low-hanging branches. Then in something of a dell cleared by a fallen forest giant, they stopped and Orrin dismounted. Under Theda's watchful eye, her hand once again on the laser grip, he unstrapped the leathers that had held Hark on the boneback.

"What's going on?" Hark asked.

"Quiet!" Theda ordered sharply. The other riders were gathering, dismounting. Dame Adione had turned Laurel's mount over to a muscle trooper; two others were pulling Laurel down, all the way to the ground until she was spread-eagle. Methodically, Dame Adione began searching her and one of the muscle troopers shoved a gag in Laurel's mouth when she tried to protest. Dame Adione finally tore the bulky brown and green sash away, stepped away with it in her hands and teased the knots open. When the sash fell, she was left holding a scorched canister. Even in the dim forest light, Hark knew exactly what it was, and he groaned silently and leaned his head against the boneback.

"Courage, man," he heard Orrin whisper.

He looked up, but Orrin was already moving toward Dame Adione, admiring her prize. She looked at Hark triumphantly. Hark turned away, sick and sad. Now he knew why they had brought Laurel. Somehow Dame Adione had found out that she had the jelly beans, and with Theda having her mother's laser, Hark didn't have any trouble figuring out just how she'd found out. Theda had been holding Laurel's samples, more than just the lava rock he'd known about. It sickened him to think they might have been in Hilma's cabin, and he'd lain there awake listening to the lot of them snore.

"Let's keep it quiet now," Theda whispered. "They're coming."

Their pursuers? Wouldn't they see the broken foliage where they'd turned off the trail? But it only took Hark another few seconds to realize why his captors weren't concerned enough to gag him again so he couldn't give warning. It wasn't pursuing troopers on the trail. It was sulphur bellies; the rumblings of their bellies was almost as loud as their footfalls, and he could feel the earth trembling to the rhythm. Through the foliage he could see them, massive brutes with gullets in front that looked like caverns full of teeth and so big they could crush a boneback in one gulp. They were moving fast, still some stretched out their gullets to close it around plants growing close enough to reach, never missing a stride. Until the last one. It lurched to a stop, then stepped off the trail in the direction of the fallen tree where they were hiding. It stood, sucking air through the massive gullet. The entire party of prisoners and guerillas stood soundlessly. Not even Hark wanted to tempt the beast further with a noise.

Finally the sulphur belly closed the gullet over a bush, ripping it out by the roots and sucking it in. Then it followed the others down the trail.

Dame Adione looked at Hark, seemingly for the first time. "With luck, they'll catch our pursuers at a full gallop, too late for them to turn off the way we did," she said. "You'll be back in Fox before they figure out how we've gotten you there." She held up the canister for him to see, smiling, lips twitching with contempt. "Your captain is conscious now. She was very depressed over hearing that there was a perfectly good lander but that these little gems were missing. She seemed to think she might be able to manage a flight even paralyzed, if only she had these."

"I don't imagine you were stupid enough this time to mention what you wanted in exchange," Hark said with equal loathing.

"Hold your rude tongue," Orrin snarled, "or I'll take your ear off like you did mine." He was wearing another laser and he reached for it, but Hark realized he was being warned not to make assumptions about the circumstances here, not threatened.

"I wasn't aiming for your ear," Hark muttered.

"You did a thorough job on my men," Orrin said, "and you'll live to pay for it . . . if you don't give us any trouble."

So, he was accused of the murders. They must not have used drugs on Jeremy when they questioned him, or Orrin would not have been standing here accusing him. He wondered, though, what had become of Jeremy. He was very frightened for him, but at the moment even more frightened for himself. He didn't like being in Dame

Adione's hands again, and even worse, for her to be in possession of the jelly beans.

"It would seem that during your absence some of the grit has gone out of you," Dame Adione said.

Hark caught himself biting his lip. He stopped, but she just laughed.

"I *don't* need you anymore," she said tucking the canister into her girdle. "The only reason I'm taking you back at all is that someone has got to hang to pay for my dead troopers, and since it can't be Jeremy, it's got to be you. But don't fool yourself into thinking that's too important. Any one of us would be pleased to execute you here and now. If you're much of a bother, we will." She turned away from Hark to face Laurel, who was on her feet now. "The same goes for you, Sister Laurel. The clerics want you for heresy, and the Queen's Court for spying. We have a witness to your treks into Fyxen territory."

Laurel glared at Theda, who merely touched her laser with mysterious pride. Laurel shook her head in disgust.

"All right, then," Adione said, adjusting her girdle for a final time. "Do you think you and Theda can handle it alone?" She looked up at Orrin expectantly.

"You can count on it," he said. "We'll lead them a merry chase and be at the railcar before you."

"If you're not, we'll have to leave without you," she said. "We can't afford to wait."

"I understand," Orrin said.

"But the windships will come for us, won't th'?" Theda said. She sounded a bit nervous.

"Of course they will," Orrin said, but Theda looked as if she didn't even hear him.

"I'd rather Rina came with me," Theda said to Dame Adione. "A sweaty, hairy man is too noisy in th' jungle."

"That's the whole idea," Dame Adione said, "isn't it? To be certain they follow you with the bonebacks instead of us?"

"Aye, but I'd feel better if th' cou'n't smell th' spoor, too. Th' got lace what can smell a man, you know."

"So I've heard, but I've only muscle to send with you, Theda, no lace of my own. And Orrin does know how to signal the windship if you need it."

Theda nodded unhappily, but at last seemed resigned as she stepped away from Dame Adione to hug Rina quickly before gathering up the reins of about half the bonebacks. She started back toward the way they had come, was almost gone from sight in the deep evening shadows when Orrin took up the reins of the rest of the beasts.

"No screw-ups," Dame Adione said harshly to Orrin as he walked past. "You mess this one up and you're done as my bottom man. You understand me?"

He nodded curtly and walked on by, the boneback's trailing, and Hark realized he wasn't going to see him again until they reached a railcar somewhere, no chance to get more information. He looked at Laurel. She was gagged and couldn't speak, but her eyes gave no hope and she shook her head silently. He took that to mean she, too, understood Dame Adione's plan for Orrin and Theda to lead any pursuers astray and she thought it was a good one. Hope for rescue was slim.

As they walked through the forest, the rains began and the way became so black that Hark had to feel his way through the slippery vegetation. He was certain no one would ever find him in this place where he couldn't even find himself.

CHAPTER 27

Sellia felt the throbbing in her head, but her first instinct was to ignore the pain and leap to her feet. Hands held her down, gentle hands, and her sister's voice stopped her from struggling.

"You're all right, Sellia. You're safe now. Be still another moment."

"What happened?" Sellia said. She opened her eyes to see Mala hovering over her anxiously.

"Are you really awake this time?" Mala asked. She was wearing a sashed harvest-print blue, the long end tucked back into the sash and still dripping from her being out in the rain. Her hair was soaked, the tiara crooked. "Don't fade out again. You've got to get up and let me take you home."

"I'm in the infirmary," Sellia said flatly, finally recognizing the antiseptic smells that were gathering behind the closed windows. Rain beat relentlessly there.

"Right. Do you remember what happened?"

Sellia nodded, remembering too late that it would hurt. She groaned. "I saw Theda . . ." She sat up in fright, suddenly remembering everything in her throbbing head. "Laurel! They took Laurel!"

"Took her? Or had she arranged everything?" Mala asked. "They tried to make it look like rounders by bringing all muscle, but our First recognized their Top lace. It was Dame Adione."

"Fyxen in the heart of New Penance?" Sellia said. She felt herself beginning to swoon, and she put her hands against her temples. There was a big lump on the right side of her head, but the dizziness passed. "What gall the bitch has."

"She's desperate," Mala agreed, "and by damn, she got away with it. They got Hark, and they got away clean. Leniane and her troopers just got back. At least, a few survivors did. It's going to be hard to pick up their trail again in this rain."

"Fyxen took down Leniane's troopers?" She looked at her sister, saw worry and anguish in her face.

"No. They got charged by sulphur bellies. Forrie . . ." Mala shook her head. "Look, Sellia, you've got to get up and come home. It's the only way I can go after Hark."

"You don't give up, do you? You won't give *him* up."

"You don't understand the half of it," Mala said. "I know the real reason he came, and . . ." Meave stepped in through the door, and Mala changed her tone blithely. "No, Sellia. You should stay here where the doctors can keep an eye on you. I won't order you to stay, but you know you should."

Aunt Meave came over to the bedside. "Five dead in the first fray, seven more in the second, not to mention the wounded who might still die." Meave looked grave, her great bosom heaving under her rain-wet wrap. "They got what they wanted. They won't come back," Behind her aunt, unseen, Mala was gesturing for Sellia to get up.

Sellia swung her feet over the edge of the bed. "I'll rest at home," she said more steadily than she felt. She would have preferred to put her head back on the pillow and close her eyes again, but she knew quite well that Mala would not ask her to do anything she wouldn't do herself. She had to get up and go home, away from Aunt Meave's all-seeing eyes.

"The Top of your household guards is at the abbey asking dispensation to carry lasers into the wilderness," Meave said. "I don't think you should let her go. It should end right now. Let the Fyxen deal with the Homeworlder. We don't want him or need him, nor," she said with more fear in her eyes than Sellia had ever seen before, "nor do we want what will follow him."

"My Top lost a brother in that fight, and since Sellia can't go herself, I can't think of anyone more determined to send."

"No," Meave said. "I won't have it. The Penitent Queen should not be wasting women's lives over one of those dirty beasts from the Homeworlds."

"Aunt Meave," Mala said, "I know you won't believe this, but New Penance *is* strong enough to withstand Homeworlds' influence whether it comes today or a few years from now. Our faith has been unshaken for three generations despite corruption right here on Islands. The Homeworlders can't be worse than the women of Fox. At least they don't take bribes."

Meave's eyes narrowed. "What makes you say that?"

Mala sighed. "Hark. You said yourself he was telling the truth when he refused Dame Adione's offer."

"That may well be, but we don't know what she offered, do we?"

Mala looked at Sellia imploringly. *But I do know. Get up!* There was no denying her sister, not while there was will. Sellia struggled to her feet and took the rainshawl her twin held out. She wrapped the narrow end around her waist and tied it with her sister's hair ribbon, which appeared in her hand as soon as she needed it. Then she pulled the long end up around her shoulders. She nodded at Mala and they started for the door. Sellia needed her sister's arm to steady her.

"Mala! You're too headstrong to listen to reason, but I'm going to ask you one more time. For decency's sake, let them go. End it right now."

Mala shook her head. "You don't understand. Whether we have him or they have him, it's going to happen. Everyone seems to understand that except you and Aislinn." She stopped a moment and looked back at her aunt. "That's why you're here, isn't it? Aislinn couldn't prevent her robed sisters from granting dispensation, could she?"

Mala gave a funny laugh. "Meave, even the clerics know it's inevitable. Why can't you see that?"

"Nothing's inevitable, not even you're being on the throne," Meave said coldly.

"Meave, if you think you're more fit to rule, say so in court and let's find out if enough agree with you to make it happen. I'm tired of your veiled threats. Make them in the open."

"If it weren't for the rest of the family having to feel the shame, I . . ."

Mala slammed the door in Meave's face. "She doesn't even understand what it's about. When it comes right down to it, she can't even stay on the right subject. She grabs at anything to make me give in, because she can't defend her position and she knows it!"

Sellia stopped. "What if . . ."

"Don't be afraid. That's what they've used all these years to control us. Fear! Fear of losing our pride. Fear of losing their love. They're worse than men, but we were too afraid to realize it. Don't you see how they've been manipulating us?"

"Yes, but what if she *does* make a claim to the throne?"

"She's too afraid to do it, but so what if she does?"

"What if we lose it?" Sellia asked, feeling fear clutch her heart.

"Good. Let her have it. It's certainly not been fun, has it?"

Sellia felt panic washing over her and tears coming to her eyes. "But then I would lose you, Mala. You wouldn't need me anymore."

Mala looked at her sister, tears filling her eyes, too. "Don't you do it, too, Sellia. Please. I couldn't stand that." Then, as if in a panic herself, Mala reached for the door and threw it open and pushed Sellia out into the rain and tried to hurry her along the dark boardwalk. It was swaying in the strong wind, making Sellia quite dizzy. Mala put her arm around her waist and helped her along.

They'd walked only as far as the next anchor-bole when Taffy came out of the sodden shadows. Sellia couldn't even see his face because he was wrapped so thoroughly in a rainshawl, but there was no mistaking his form.

"Taffy's going to take care of you," Mala said. "I've got to go, but I couldn't leave you completely alone with that head wound. Most of the guards will be with me. Before I go, tell me again what you said about Laurel."

"What? I don't remember that I . . . Oh, that she was taken by the Fyxen."

"The trooper who brought them up seemed to believe Laurel had forced you to bring Hark up. That led us to believe that she'd known they'd be waiting, that Laurel betrayed us."

"No," Sellia said slowly, struggling to remember just why she was so certain it was not so. "Theda was using a laser. You . . ." She hesitated and glanced at Taffy. "It was given to her mother, not to her. Hilma's probably dead, and Theda's the traitor."

"But how could they have known Hark would be coming up from the pits?" Mala asked.

"They didn't. He was a bonus. They were waiting for Laurel. She had something they wanted more than they wanted Hark. I guess I should be grateful they didn't catch up with us earlier. If they had, they would have had plenty of time to give me more than a lump on the head."

Mala squeezed her sister to show that she was glad she was all right. "What did Laurel have?"

"Brain jewels. The set from the lander that crashed. Laurel found them."

"Listen to that, Taffy! Laurel found them."

"Yes, but now Dame Adione has them," Taffy said. "And she has Hark."

Taffy's words silenced Mala for a moment and they turned in a rainswept dell into a caged boardwalk; a family of silvanwolves lived nearby. The thick wires kept them off the boardwalks and habit kept Sellia watching the wires for a clawed hand.

"Do you remember seeing a bearded man, Sellia? One not young, graying. He supposed to be quite a big man."

"There was one like that with Theda. Between them, they got the Spaceman."

"You think it was Orrin?" Taffy asked.

"Hoping it was," Mala said. They came out of the caged boardwalk onto the deck with the final bridge to their emergent tree. "Can you make it alone from here, Sellia?"

"Yes, but . . ." She looked warily at Taffy. Mala couldn't leave her as Sellia here with Taffy, then turn up as Sellia somewhere else.

"Taffy has a long story to tell you, one he told to me. I think he knows he's going to be telling it to Mala again, don't you, Taffy."

Taffy sort of shrugged. "I always knew you didn't listen when I talk. I'm used to telling you over and over. I used to think it was because I was a man. Women never listen to what men have to say."

"First, Hark, now Taffy. Who's next?" Sellia said. She felt sad; Mala had shared the secret with two men without even telling her she was going to. She had always believed the two of them would take the secret to their graves.

Mala hugged her, hastily pulled the tiara she was wearing in her hair. Water rolled out of the jeweled flowercups onto Sellia's face as she placed it on her head. "Why don't you decide who to trust next? Think about it, sister dear. Hark could have tried to use it to keep himself out of the pits, but he didn't. Taffy . . ." She looked down and patted his head. "I can't even imagine how you might want to blackmail us. We already spoil you so."

"I'll have a list ready when you get back," he said. "Go on, Sellia. Hark needs your help. God bless!"

"You're sure you're all right?" the Top asked Sellia for a second time.

They were in the staging barn bridling the bonebacks and some twotails because so many of the best bonebacks had been stolen. "I'm fine. Honestly, just a graze. Hardly a mark to show for it. Do you want to see?"

"No, of course not. It's just that the way Meave talked, I thought you were badly hurt."

"How's your mother taking it?" Sellia asked, referring to Forrie's death.

"Mother's a stoic. Even her goodman is holding up."

"And you?"

"Sellia, this mission is going to do wonders for me, but not if I don't stop thinking about Forrie."

"Just don't let your anger blind you," Sellia said. "Hark mustn't be harmed."

"It's the rain that will blind us. What rotten luck."

"A dozen bonebacks ought to leave more than cleatprints for us to find," Sellia said confidently. She led her mount to the front of the barn where most of the troopers were already waiting. As was typical, most were muscles, the officers all lace. The women were young, but the men were of all ages. For a moment, she studied the muscle troopers. The ones no longer young were bearded, a traditional sign of a career trooper who no longer desired any female companionship. She'd known most of them for years, a few even intimately before they'd become hirsute. They were fine soldiers, yet she'd never considered one of them for promotion. Among the smooth faces, she knew the potential for leadership of every lace trooper, and which muscle troopers were good lovers, if not firsthand then by reputation. She found herself wondering if any of them, like this Orrin of Fox, might be a brilliant military leader, if only she would notice.

"What's the matter?" the Top asked, coming up so silently that Sellia was startled.

"Nothing." She took the ready-pack the Top offered and got ready to ride.

They rode through the rain-sodden forest as quickly as they dared, carefully avoiding the sulphur bellies, which cost them some time but which was accomplished safely. Dawn was fast coming, they were still on the sulphur-belly trail, encouraged by fresh-enough boneback droppings.

The rain stopped at first light, and they stopped long enough to pull off their ponchos and to eat from their packs. Their mounts were tired, but no more so than the ones they were trailing. They pushed on hard, fast, but not recklessly. By midmorning, they were rewarded with cleatprints in the sulphur-belly trail.

"This trail will take us to the high country soon," Sellia said to the Top when they'd paused to count the prints in the trail. The full dozen were there. "It doesn't make sense for them to go up there."

"Unless they're going to pick up fresh mounts at Hilma's cabin. How many beasts does she have?"

Sellia wasn't sure. She hadn't seen Hilma's corral when she'd been there with Hark, and she hadn't had time to get a full report of her sister's last trip. She shrugged. "Enough, if Adione's counting on having them. But Hilma's was a good-size clan. Even if Theda betrayed her mother, there's no way to be certain the rest fell in with her. If they didn't . . ." Again she shrugged. She stood up. "All right. Let's go as far as Hilma's cabin. I know a shortcut we can take."

Sellia led the way, running her beast at full swing. The boy, at least, wouldn't be quick to turn, not with her sister being the most recent visitor. Sellia was thinking he might prove useful when suddenly the wet trail a few meters up suddenly steamed and popped: A warning laser burn! She barely had time to pull up before running in to it.

"Just hold them steady now," a man's voice said from somewhere in the understory. "I've got your Top in my target-finder."

The pink light was square on the Top's left breast. She didn't move; nor did Sellia. The beam of light could move more quickly than they, and they knew it.

"That's fine. Now, Top. I want you to walk easy on down the trail just to that little bend up there. I think you'll see something that will interest you."

Leniane glanced at Sellia. There was no choice for now but to obey. She nudged her mount and walked on. Sellia kept searching the understory trying to see exactly where the target-finder beam was coming from. Finally she saw him. A bearded man dressed in harvest greenery sitting on a platform of branches lashed with vines. He had a perfect view of Sellia and the troopers behind her, and the Top as well. There was no way to take him down with her own laser before he could burn the Top.

The Top was coming back. "It's Theda," she said. "She's been burned in the back. She's dead."

"A traitor to New Penance, right?" the man said. "Also my peace offering. I'm coming down now." He holstered his laser and dropped a line over the side of his perch, climbed down.

"Drop your weapon," the Top ordered. She'd unholstered her own laser the moment the man put his hands on the line.

"I'd rather not surrender quite that much," he said. "I think you'll see it my way when you hear what I have to say." He was careful to keep his hands palm out and away from the laser and any secreted weapon. "You are looking for the spaceman and Sister Laurel of Selene, aren't you?" He was talking to the Top; he didn't know who Sellia was. But she was beginning to believe she knew who he was.

"You're Orrin," she said. "Dame Adione's bottom man."

"And how would you know that?" he asked, looking at her.

"Because Hark told me."

"Just what did he tell you?"

"Everything. Even how you killed two of your own men to help him."

Orrin nodded thoughtfully. "If he told you everything, then you know I'm a friend."

"And if you're Orrin, you'll have Jeremy's transport token."

Carefully, he pulled a chain with a token on it from under his shirt.

Sellia nodded slowly. "Put the laser away, Top. I don't think you're going to need it."

"He's a Fyxen," Leniane said, unwilling to obey.

Sellia shook her head. "Maybe once. But he's already gone too far ever to be called Fyxen once the truth is known. He's committed to something else, aren't you, Orrin?"

"Completely, and I need your help. And you need mine."

"Put it away," Sellia said again to the Top, and finally she obeyed.

"And who may I ask are you that you can give orders to the queen's own Top? And don't tell me I'm misreading the insignia. I've been a trooper too long to be mistaken."

"I'm Sellia. Queen Mala's sister," she said, and was surprised by his defiant glare.

CHAPTER 28

Orrin crossed his arms in front of his chest. He hadn't given up his weapons, nor would he kneel before this woman just because she was a princess. He was surprised to find how much that meant to him, was fully aware that only a short time ago he'd forced Hark to conform to the very tradition he was breaking. She was staring at him, her face a puzzled frown. Finally she dismounted, handed the reins of her boneback to the Top and walked over to Orrin.

"I believe you were about to tell us where we'd find Hark," she said quietly. "Does my being Lady Sellia change that for some reason?" She put her hands on her hips, was looking at him expectantly. Sweat had beaded on her forehead and stained the armpits of her simple brown tunic. She was hot and tired and apparently as unwilling to make an issue of his rudeness as he was willing. Orrin relented.

"He'll be on a railcar bound for Fox in a few hours. The car's hidden. If you get there first, you can be waiting inside."

She nodded, comprehending. "Lead the way," she finally said.

"There's more," he said. "I've made a bargain on Hark's behalf he doesn't know about. You must see to it that he keeps it."

"What kind of bargain?" she asked suspiciously.

"You know about his captain and the engineer? That they're in the maternity and Hark won't leave Islands without them?"

"Yes, yes," she said impatiently. "I even know he's in love with his captain." She was frowning, looking down at the dung in the path. And when he didn't answer her quickly enough, her jaw shot up. "Well?"

"I'm just surprised he told you that," Orrin said suddenly worried. He'd assumed that chemicals were not used on prisoners in New Penance because their clerics would not accept monetary payment in exchange for dispensation. He was beginning to worry now that he'd made too many assumptions, taken too much upon himself.

She was staring at him again, her blue eyes as cool as rainwater. "I know everything," she said. "Everything that has damned him on Islands or will in the Homeworlds, and it turns out to be about everything he's done. He's blundered badly since he set foot on Islands, told the truth when he ought to have lied, lied when he ought to have told the truth."

"You think he's a fool," Orrin said, angry with himself for having trusted yet another woman, even for a moment.

"He walked on the rim of a volcano, insulted Aethelmere, infuriated Adione, invited rounders to attack him, made me look silly before my sister's court, was overconfident during his inquiry and anyone so determined to rush to his own destruction must be a fool," she said. Then she raised her brow. "Or he has the heart of a emergent. I don't waste my time with fools, Orrin of Fox, and I don't believe you do either."

She was telling the truth, he was sure of it. "He does need help," Orrin said with a sigh. "I tried to give him an opening to escape during the fray. He wasn't enough of a fighter to recognize the advantage and use it."

"Don't be so certain. He knows his limitations well enough that he might have reasoned he'd only get cut down if he tried. A lesser man would be dead many times over," she said. "Now, tell me about this bargain you've made and how it affects Hark."

"He's determined to take his captain and engineer back to the Homeworlds with him. I've arranged to get them out of the maternity safely during next Double Nocturne in exchange for his also taking another person to the Homeworlds."

"You?"

Orrin stiffened. "No. Dame Cirila's son, Jeremy. He's accused of murder, as is Hark."

Sellia smiled wryly. "You could clear them another way, couldn't you, Orrin?"

He shrugged. "Dame Cirila doesn't know that. She believes she's saving her son from certain death."

"He was wondering how you were going to get them out of the maternity for the rendezvous."

Orrin nodded. "So was I. At first I believed he would give up the notion, realize how futile it was. But as I came to know him, I became more certain that if I failed to have them at the rendezvous, he'd carry out his threat to raid the maternity, and probably get killed in the process."

"Probably fly that lander right through the sights of the big guns," Sellia said.

"Probably," Orrin said. No sense in denying them, but for all his anger and disappointment in Fox and Fyxen, his heart pumped wildly as he realized a military secret was known to the enemy.

"He didn't say how many there were," Sellia said to him.

"He doesn't know," Orrin told her. He held her eyes for a moment, and he thought he saw a flicker of approval there before she sighed and shrugged.

"Well, I suppose you know that I can't commit Hark to take Jeremy back with him."

"You don't have to. He'll take him."

"You can tell him yourself," she said looking back at the Top and her troopers. She gestured for her mount.

He thrust the transport token into her hand. "I have to go back to Fox. Jeremy's in the garrison jail. It's going to be up to me to get them to the rendezvous on Double Nocturne. And there's still another problem," Orrin said.

She took the reins of her mount from the Top and turned back to him. "What's that?"

"Now that the brain jewels have been found, it might be more effective for New Penance to invade Fox so he can take his lander back."

"Might be," she agreed cheerfully. "I'll tell you the date and time if you'll tell me how many big guns we have to take down."

Orrin frowned darkly.

"I thought not," she said. "There are limits, aren't there, Orrin?" And when he wouldn't answer, she said, "Are you going to tell us where that railcar is hidden or show us?"

"I'll fetch my mount and show you the way. You'll never find it otherwise."

CHAPTER 29

Hark was much better off than the lady of the lava lake, for he was permitted to walk ungagged. She'd been suffering from oxygen starvation since the sun came up, at least that was when it had become plain enough for him to see. At one of their brief rest stops, called only when Laurel had fallen and been unable to rise, he'd pretended to collapse next to her and succeeded in getting the gag out of her mouth. Their captors didn't notice until Dame Adione gave the march command again, and the deed had earned him a sharp blow to his head and a grateful glance from Laurel before they shoved the gag back in her mouth. He never got an opportunity to do it again.

When the sun was directly overhead, they were below the rain forest in the sloping savannahs, Laurel and Hark baking like meat on a spit as they made their way to the lava rocks of the Black Desert. He actually recognized the terrain as being near the place he'd last seen Jeremy, and he assumed they were waiting for a railcar to come out of the west to pick them up. But he was wrong. The railcar was already there, on a siding only meters from the main rail, so well hidden Hark didn't realize what it was until they started pulling off the camouflage. Lava rock taller than a man came down as easily as net and foam. He realized now he'd never had a chance of saving Jeremy; they'd had a car waiting.

His guards hoisted him through the door of a railcar not

much bigger than the one Sellia had driven from the observatory down to New Penance. Laurel was thrown unceremoniously on top of him, and suddenly the door slammed shut on the guards' fingers. The engine roared noisily, almost drowning out the shouts coming from outside and inside. Someone stepped on Hark in an effort to get to the windows. He saw harvest-greenery and lasers, and heard a war whoop from the engineer's chair. He got off Laurel and just before a muscle trooper pushed him back to the floor, out of the line of fire, he saw that the railcar was rolling out onto the track, the siding aimed so that it could take off straight for Fox. But, miraculously, as soon as the car was on the main track it started backing up, gaining speed. In a minute, the shouts from outside sounded distant, the muscle troopers at the windows were leaning back and grinning, slapping each other on the back to congratulate themselves. Only then was Hark certain they'd been rescued by Mala's troopers.

"Untie me," Hark said to the nearest man.

The trooper leaned over and slashed the bonds on Hark's wrists. Hark took the knife from him and turned to Laurel. Her lips were blue, her eyes glassy. He cut the sash tied around her face and as he pulled the end of it out of her mouth, he realized she had swallowed some of it. She coughed, turned her head and retched bloody phlegm. He held her forehead, pulling her red hair away as she gasped. The man who'd handed him the knife finally realized her distress, and he took the knife back to cut the bonds from Laurel's wrists while Hark continued to hold her head.

"Water?" Hark asked, and the trooper gave him his canteen. Hark pulled out his shirttail, wet it down, and wiped Laurel's face. Her lips were not so blue now, her eyes less glassy. He helped her take a sip from the canteen, and she began choking. "Can you speak?" he asked her.

"Yes," she said in a squeaky voice.

Hark took her bowed head in his hands and lifted it to keep her airway open while she gasped. "Are you all right?"

She took a few deep, clear sounding breaths and nodded.

Her face still in his hands, he looked at her eyes to see if they were evenly dilated.

"Top! Take this engine," he heard Sellia's voice say. He looked up to see her stepping away from the engineer's chair and a lace trooper slipping into it.

He felt Laurel's hands on his, guiding them away from her face. He glanced back at her once more to assure himself that she was all right, then looked back at Sellia. There was something about her eyes that he didn't recognize, certainly not the joy in seeing him that *his* Sellia's eyes would display. He sank back on his haunches, waited for Laurel to finish with the canteen. She handed it over, and he drank deeply, uncomfortably aware of Sellia staring. Carefully he capped the canteen, then met her eyes. "If you think I'm any more inclined to submit to your barbaric purification rites just because of this, you're mistaken."

"Stop bristling," Laurel said, putting her hand over his. "This car's going to Selene." She turned to look at Sellia. "Isn't it?"

Sellia nodded and sat down in one of the empty seats. She looked forlorn, faintly hostile, very much like the morning when she was Mala. So be it, he thought. I don't like you any more than you like me, but somehow we're in this together and have to make the most of it.

Hark stood up and offered Laurel a hand up. She took it, needed it, was shaky when she was up. The car lurched around a bend in the track, throwing her off balance. He grabbed her and guided her to a seat.

"Are we really going to Selene?" he whispered to her.

She nodded. "It's the only thing that makes any sense. We have the big dish antenna with a good radio for you to use, and I think we're in a hurry, too. Dame Adione has the brain jewels now."

"I wouldn't have trusted anything in that scorched canister," Hark said softly.

"She's going to have to. But with a little bit of luck, we'll get to Selene before she gets to Fox and has a chance to try it. She either has to walk, or wait to hitch a ride from New Penance . . . if she dares."

"I can't believe that I'm really on my way," Hark said, "and riding! I'm not walking." He laughed.

"I can't believe how tired I am," Laurel said, sagging down in the seat. "I've been awake for two days now."

"I have, too," Hark said. "But I'm too happy to sleep right now."

"I'm not," she said, with a yawn. And she leaned her head against his shoulder and closed her eyes.

Hark sat staring out the window. Already they were climbing out of the savannah into the rain forest, effortlessly. He wasn't moving a muscle, not even trying to keep some hopelessly confusing arrangement of boneback reins straight between his fingers. He felt himself grinning and knew how stupid he must look. He was still wearing rags that someone had given him when Caveman took his blues, and he smelled from days of not washing. How could Laurel stand to rest her head on his dirty chest? But when he leaned over, he realized that her pretty red hair, at least, smelled equally foul and was too scraggly at the moment to look good. He sighed comfortably and looked up to see Sellia glaring at him. Grimacing, he leaned against the windowpane and, so as not to disturb Laurel, he put his arm around her. He'd have given a lot to have it be *his* Sellia.

They'd bypassed New Penance and crossed the eastern Black Desert. Hark had napped briefly by then and seen enough to realize it was no different than the western desert he'd crossed with Jeremy: hot, dry, and ugly. He was very grateful that the rush of hot air through the open windows kept drying the sweat that was pouring out of him and everyone else. Selene's volcano was in view, fully lighted by three moons. Laurel slept on, but Hark scanned the skies, looking for the orbiter. He couldn't be sure what time it was, for he no longer had any of his equipment. But it seemed to him that the moons were in about the same position as they were when he and Sellia had seen the orbiter from the windows of her emergent. He graphed the sky mentally, checking each quadrant along the orbital path carefully. The longer he searched and didn't find it, the more his heart started to beat painfully. Surely the orbiter didn't find the lander, call it and leave the solar system in these last few days. Not when he was finally so close to success!

Laurel sat up and blinked. "What shot you full of adrenalin?" she asked. "Or does your heart always beat like that?"

"Sorry," he said. "I'm looking for the orbiter, but I can't find it."

"Probably in the moonlight," she said reasonably. "Where else could it be?"

Hark looked at her, realized she didn't know. He'd told Taffy everything, and presumably *his* Sellia knew of the danger, but Laurel and *this* Sellia hadn't complete information. "It could have left for home," Hark told her. "The on-board AI knows to take it home once it's satisfied it can't do anything for me. I've been out of contact too long."

Instantly concerned, Laurel leaned over him to stare out the window. "If I had my pack . . ." she straightened. "Sellia, do you have any binoculars with you?"

Sellia turned, pulled her pack out from under her seat and handed it to the man behind her to pass on. When the pack reached Laurel, she tore it open and pulled out the binoculars and surrendered them to Hark. "What about the lander?" she said to him. "Will it be all right?"

"If it's operable, and not damaged getting out from under the canopy, it's still going to be gone, too," Hark said bitterly. "The orbiter will try to take it home. Wouldn't matter if it isn't gone. Couldn't fly it without downloading it from the orbiter anyhow. If the orbiter is gone . . ." Suddenly his heart took a massive shot of adrenalin and he lowered the binoculars and grinned at Laurel. "But it's not gone," he said handing the glasses to her. "Seven o'clock off the big moon. You understand seven o'clock?"

"Roger," she said, leaning across him again. She came away with a big grin, too.

"Roger?" Hark asked, puzzled, but smiling because she was smiling and because if he got to a radio tonight, he'd be able to talk to the AI during the next lap.

"Roger . . ." Laurel shrugged. "Maybe that's too far back. Linguistics aren't my specialty."

"Volcanos are. We can help you with that," he said seriously.

"Hark, I'm counting on it. They're all rumbling; the seismic readings are ominous. But which one is going to take the pressure off?"

"I just hope we can get back in time to tell you."

"What about a dump from your AI," she asked. "If it has any orbital survey data we can use . . ."

Hark nodded. "Probably. I'll see what I can do."

Sellia was threading her way down the aisle, and Hark sat up straight.

"The orbiter is passing by, happy and healthy," Laurel said, handing her the binoculars.

She looked at them strangely, then shoved them in the pack. "I know," she said finally. "I saw it an hour ago." She looked past Laurel to Hark. "I met your friend Orrin. He's changed the plans slightly."

"Orrin? He's all right then?"

Sellia nodded. "He's going to have Jeremy at the rendezvous with your captain and the engineer. Dame Cirila is apparently going to deal with getting them out of the maternity in exchange for your taking Jeremy to the Homeworlds with you. I told him that you might not . . ."

Hark waved her off. "I was planning to take Jeremy if he wanted to come anyway. I just hope Orrin doesn't have any trouble."

"I didn't know about your taking anyone off this world with you," Sellia said stiffly.

"We never spoke of it after that first day when he asked me if transport tokens were still honored. He didn't get the chance to bring it up again because . . ." He looked at her. "Why don't you sit down, Sellia? Let me tell you everything I told your sister." He glanced at Laurel. "You both deserve to know everything." *Almost everything.* He could not tell these two that Jeremy was not the only Islandian he hoped to take with him to the Homeworlds.

Sellia sat down, folded her hands in her lap, and Hark

began to tell them the same story he had told Taffy to tell to Mala. And yet, it was not the same. The emphasis Fyxen had placed on his unwilling revelation of affection for Captain Dace seemed unimportant now, although with Laurel having come through so gallantly, he did elaborate on his dreams of her, and she laughed, just as he thought she would. He was glad to amuse his new friend, even at his own expense. Sellia didn't seem to understand the joke. He hoped *his* Sellia had, and he started feeling nervous about her again. This was her twin, after all. What if she'd not been amused? But that couldn't be. Mala, his Sellia, had sent her sister to rescue him. Would she have done that if she didn't fully understand?

"Did you see Mala at all before you left New Penance?" Hark asked Sellia.

She nodded.

"Did she . . ." He caught himself. Laurel was here with them. He couldn't very well ask if she'd sent her love, or some message that would let him know all was well between them. "I trust she's well," he said instead.

"Yes," Sellia said, giving him a blank stare.

Bitch! he thought, flinging himself back against the seat to glare at her. *There's something, but you won't tell me. Damn you!*

She flinched, looked down at her watch. "Less than an hour now," she said. "But maybe I can sleep that long."

Hark watched her get up and walk away. She didn't look back.

The spartan shower at the Selenian radio shack felt like heaven, and this time Hark welcomed clean Islandian clothes. Shorts and tunic, someone's plain brown fatigues that smelled of flowers just like everything else in the rain forest. The windows were open, but the shack was in the understory, too low to catch any breezes. The air was hot and muggy. He was working with a radio engineer named Hedia, a slate gray-haired woman with a startlingly sonorous voice. She'd turned the antenna to track the orbiter on its next pass, which wouldn't be until after dawn.

Laurel came in wearing a fresh green dress, her hair dark and damp from a shower, smelling like the flowery soap. "I checked the scheduled freight runs from New Penance to Fox. It looks like Dame Adione could be arriving in Fox right now, and she's even got one more chance to get there just after dawn," she said. "Unless she's walking, we've missed our chance to surprise the Fyxen completely."

But Hark shook his head. "They're going to be surprised," he said. "Even if they pop the canister in and get something to work, the AI can override anything they try to do. That is, if Hedia and I can make the right connection." He turned back to the engineer. "I'm going to need a good map," he said, "and a landing site somewhere around here, too."

He noticed that Laurel sat down to watch, keenly interested. He gave her a reassuring smile. Everything was going to be just fine. Hedia was fantastic. Laurel smiled back just as Sellia announced that she was going to take her shower now.

"Come on, you sack of beans. Lock on and answer me!" Hark said impatiently. Unless he'd miscalculated the orbit, the AI should have heard him ten minutes ago. "Anything from the spotters?" he asked Laurel. She was sitting before another radio. They had people with field glasses up in the emergent trees looking for the swiftly moving morning star. It would be difficult to see until it was well above the horizon, which it was not . . . yet.

Laurel shook her head.

"Let me check the antenna again," Hedia said, sitting down at the controls. "It gets cranky sometimes." She moved some knobs and looked at Hark apologetically. "Sometimes the wind catches it and I don't get a true reading here because the baseline is off. Try it again."

"Hark to Orbiter. Are you listening up?"

"You damn-well better believe it," the AI boomed in the vernacular. "Where the fuck have you been?"

Hark blanched when Hedia raised her brow. "Keep your end a bit more businesslike, will you AI? I have some friendly Islandians here who might . . . uh, misinterpret vernacular."

"I can use Islandian vernacular, if you prefer. I've acquired quite a lot if it now," the AI said.

"No," Hark said. "If you do that, I may misinterpret. We've got some work to do here, and I don't want any mistakes."

"As you wish," the AI said. Then, "What are you doing in Selene?"

Hedia was duly impressed with the fast fix. "It's a long story," Hark said.

"I have forever," the AI replied.

"I don't," Hark said. "Would you knock off the chatter and let me get down to business?"

"I do have mandatory data to collect," the AI said, deliberately sounding offended.

"Yeah, okay. Let's get through that fast. I'm uninjured, in good health, and presently not under coercion of any sort. Captain Dace and Rene are both injured. They're in Fox, in a clinic, probably under guard. I have a rescue plan. Have I left anything out?"

"The landers' conditions," the AI said dryly. "And I confirm from voice analysis that you're presently not being coerced."

"Lander One took a projectile, broke up over the eastern edge of the Fox Volcano near a soda lake. Pretty big lake . . ."

"Location confirmed by opticals," the AI said. "Would you reconfirm that Lander One was shot down?"

"Affirmative," Hark said. "Lander One was shot down. Lander Two is in that little clump of forest by Fox City. It appears to be undamaged, except for the jelly beans. They're gone."

"Opticals can't get through that foliage, but . . . there she is. Confirmed by metal-mass detection now that I know where to look."

"Just leave her quiet and unchecked for a minute, pal. Lander Two's our first problem."

"Are you going to work in the extent of injuries to Captain Dace and Rene?"

"You just abandon any more secondary data collection right now and stay away from them until I give you leave. Got it?"

"Pursuit of secondary data collection abandoned," the AI said flatly.

"The persistence is built in," Hark explained to the women who had gathered around the microphone and amplifier to listen in. "It won't ask me any more direct questions, but it will still try to gather the data from inference if it can." He turned back to the microphone. "Look, I want to get the lander out from under those trees, but you're going to have a half-klick-long run just above the ground with only a meter or so clearance all around. And your cold-jets are facing the wrong way for optimum. You may also have hostile Islandians on board who will recognize the first signs of life, and may take offensive action. There's even a chance that the canister from Lander One have been put in the pod; they may be faulty. The hostile Islandians may be trying to operate the lander."

The AI whistled. "Anything else?"

"Yes. An outside chance that Captain Dace has been brought on board to talk them through a power-up. She's completely paralyzed, won't be able to . . ." He choked up a bit. "She couldn't even talk when I last saw her, but apparently she can now."

"Okay, I've got the picture. Now let me ask a few questions."

"Shoot," Hark said. Hedia and Laurel drew back, alarmed. Hark rolled his eyes and put his hand over the microphone. "I tell it not to use the vernacular, then I do it. Shoot means . . . go ahead. Ask your questions, in this case. There are no weapons on board. I told you that; it was the truth."

"How much overhead clearance do I have where I'm parked?" the AI was asking. "And am I tied down?"

Hark turned his attention back to the microphone. "You must have two or three meters absolutely clear to where the understory foliage starts. That stuff is usually pretty thin. But above that, the branches could be a meter in diameter. You weren't tied down when I last saw you."

"Then if I have hostiles on board, I can fly on the ground and dump them out the hatch before I close up."

"And if Captain Dace is on board?"

"Then I sense for weapons. If there's nothing that can damage me, I'll close up and bring them to you to deal with. Can you handle that?"

Hark looked at Laurel. She was frowning, but Sellia nodded. "We can handle it," she said.

"What if they threaten Captain Dace?" he said to her.

The AI answered. "I'm two minutes from you. Let her go and race for stasis."

"Unacceptable. She's paralyzed. You've got a long prep to do as is."

"Offer me something better," the AI said.

"Shit!" He leaned back from the microphone to think.

"Hark, she may not even be there," Laurel said. "Dame Adione isn't in a big hurry, remember? She still doesn't know about the orbiter and downloading."

"You have some pretty intelligent friends down there," the AI said. "You better listen to them."

"I want every contingency we can possibly think of planned out ahead," he said, feeling angry over being pushed from both sides. "Less chance of being surprised, less chance of making mistakes."

"I concur, of course," the AI said. "Perhaps I can help draw up a plan for taking the hostile Islandians out safely once the lander gets to you."

"That's better," Hark said. "Sellia? The AI can give you any information you want about the lander. How long it takes the hatch to open, what kind of angles you'll have while that's happening."

She stared at him, frowning deeply. Thoughtful? Or angry? For a moment he thought she was going to refuse any aid, when suddenly she said, "Let me get the Top and confer about how to save your captain."

"Your sister would be proud to know that you've just taken to listening to men," he said.

"AIs," she retorted over her shoulder.

Hark shrugged. "Now, what else? What are we forgetting?"

"Maybe it could be thinking of how to transfer the orbital survey data on volcanos?" Laurel suggested hopefully.

"Confirm that, pal," Hark said quickly, "but put it in background mode. We'll do it when there's time. Now, what else do we need to get that lander away clean?"

"Permission to begin," the AI said. "I can start looking around quietly if you'll just let me."

"You don't move that lander until Sellia has her battle plan drawn up. It's fifteen minutes from there to here!"

"I'll begin by disabling ready-lights and have lots of time to look-see, if you'll just let me. They can't see into the core, and there's no indication that they have anything sensitive enough to know that a signal is incoming."

"All right; take a look-see."

"Ready-lights disabled, and downloading. It will take about three minutes at this frequency."

"Is your signal delay going to bother you?"

"I don't think so. I can always move in closer if I think it necessary."

"No you can't, smartass. We're doing a manual track and could lose signal."

"I understand," the AI said.

The amplifiers fell silent, and Hark couldn't think of anything more to say into the microphone. He wiped the sweat off his brow with the back of his hand. Laurel handed him a handkerchief to use and he mopped his entire face. He was sweating profusely, nerves adding to the morning heat. Sellia came back in, followed by the Top.

"All right," she said. "We have a plan. We figure we can put three or four people through the hatch at once, depending on how wide it is and how fast you can open it. You just don't open it until we give the signal."

"Those better be pretty thin people, Lady Sellia," the AI said. "The hatch is only a meter wide and two meters high. I can have it fully open in three seconds. A person on top can get through the first second, the next two from the upper sides during second number two, and the last person can gain the floor during second three."

"The Top and I are smallest, and we'll take the two

smallest muscles with us and leave the others outside for backup.''

"I could go," Laurel offered.

"I know how my men will respond," Sellia said, declining briskly. "Just where is this landing site? We need to make sure we can get there in time if this ship can really do the distance in fifteen minutes."

Laurel and Hedia spread the maps, and the four women crowded over them.

"Would you care to give me a good narrative on that site so that *I* can find it?" AI said. "Ah, download complete. And I'm looking around. You were right, several people on-board and lots more outside. I don't think any of them is Captain Dace, however. No, she's definitely not on board. Oh-oh. We've got a hole in one of the panels, and it's starting to rattle from the core energy. Something must be a bit out of balance. Hark, are you ready to begin? People are starting to pick their heads up down here."

"You've got control, AI. Keep me informed."

CHAPTER 30

It seemed to Orrin that only Queen Aethelmere was missing from this gathering of the enfeebled protectors of Fox Court in the park, all them slouching and tiresome in their rhetoric, even Dame Adione, with her quick, loud-voiced retorts.

"And what will you do when they attack, Mother Phastia?" she was saying. "Hold them back with prayers?"

The cleric didn't want Dame Adione to replace her clerics with heavily armed troopers.

"What makes you so certain they will attack just because they have the spaceman?" Mother Phastia asked her. "They have had him all this time and haven't come here yet."

"Oh, they'll come, all right," Dame Adione said. She was still wearing harvest-greenery, one sleeve ripped away from the shoulder exposing a red welt on her forearm where she'd been burned by a laser reflection. She untied the knots in her girdle and pulled out the scorched canister, holding it high with her red wealed arm for everyone to see. "They'll come because now they know I have the brain jewels."

The sight of the scorched canister silenced Mother Phastia for a moment, but Orrin knew it was a mistake for Dame Adione to let the cleric know she'd recovered the brain jewels. By now he realized Dame Adione had more style than real power, and it had been that way all along. Orrin might have warned her, and Dame Adione might have heeded his warning and kept the brain jewels hidden away in her girdle, but helping her now as he always helped her in the past wouldn't have suited Orrin's plans. Let them struggle with each other, keep their attention off him until Double Nocturne. He stayed in the background, not at Dame Adione's side as he used to place himself so he could signal her silently.

"You've done well, my daughter," Mother Phastia said wearing her secret smile, "to bring these minions of Homeworlds technology to me."

But Dame Adione's triumphant smile didn't fade quickly as Orrin expected it to. "Of course they are yours," she said handing the canister over. "And to assure your safety while you learn to use them, I and all the forces I command will be right at your side."

Orrin frowned. In his anger with her, he was beginning to underestimate her. She lacked charisma, but not shrewdness. An alliance between the abbey and the military would provide Dame Adione with a great deal of technological information she wouldn't have otherwise, probably speed any learning process she must go through to fly the lander and ultimately to command the AI.

Mother Phastia was clutching the canister to her bosom, jeweled fingers caressing it as if it were a beloved infant. Orrin could well imagine that she was wondering if there were any other way to protect her treasure from the Penitents and Selenians than to accept Dame Adione's offer, and so was he. An alliance between Dame Adione and Mother Phastia was not what he wanted. While most of the women of the court watched her, silent, lest they miss hearing her reply, Orrin realized that Dame Cirila was looking at Orrin, her face a mask of tragedy. Orrin risked a smile and a slight shake of his head. She raised her brow, puzzled.

Dame Adione turned to Orrin abruptly, perhaps as much to hide the fact that she couldn't restrain her triumphant smile as to force the matter at hand to a satisfactory conclusion. "First! Post the guard."

"Yes, ma'am," he said snapping to attention. But before he could issue the order, they heard a rapid palpitating noise come from the inside of the lander. The sound grew to a pulsating clatter as a nervous-looking novitiate appeared in the hatch.

"I don't know what it is," she said directly to Mother Phastia. "I felt a breeze, then . . ."

A thunder clap from behind the novitiate so sudden and loud startled everyone; the novitiate fell out the hatch and for a moment Orrin was sure she'd been shot. Explosive sounds as rapid as drumfire deafened them, and then the hatch of the lander snapped shut. The sounds of explosions repercussed in their ears along with fierce roaring and barking. Instinctively Orrin had drawn his laser and the women of the court were beginning to run for the trees, but Orrin couldn't see any attackers and no one was falling to injury. Even the novitiate was on her feet now, running after her mistress with speed that belied serious injury.

The lander popped a meter into the air like a cork and turned on its axis with a heated roar. Then it darted through the tunnel of green, making a wind in its wake that sucked vines from above and debris from below into a maelstrom of grit. Then the lander was gone from sight and hearing before the debris could settle and the women of the court realized they could stop running. Only Dame Adione and Orrin was left in the little clearing.

Orrin had known what to expect, had realized what was going on as soon as the lander hatch snapped shut. Even so he was shaken, his heart pounding with fear, finding himself reflexively in a defensive stance. But Dame Adione was holstering her laser, lips thin with fury in an ashen face.

"How did he do that?" she said, her voice trembling with anger. She looked at Orrin. "How?" she screamed.

Orrin shrugged. He thought she was going to hit him, just to strike out because her frustration was so great. But Mother Phastia was creeping back out of the trees, staring in horror at the empty place where the lander had been, and Dame Adione seemed to gain control of herself with her first glance of the returning cleric.

The cleric straightened her headgear and marched up to Dame Adione. "Is this a demonstration of your military efficiency?" she said to Dame Adione.

For the first time, Orrin's commander had no sharp retort. She hung her head in red-faced shame.

CHAPTER 31

For the third time in as many hours, Sellia checked the guards posted around the lander. Hark had moved it from the original landing site in a dell only minutes from the radio shack to a rock ledge above Selene where he said he didn't care if she kept her guards posted or not. The lander had sufficient observation equipment to prevent anyone from approaching unobserved. And as long as he was inside, he felt confident he could take off, as necessary to elude an attack, before any damage could be done. It had taken all of Laurel's considerable persuasive powers to prevent him from returning to the orbiter to await Double Nocturne in absolute safety. Sellia almost wished Laurel had not succeeded. The two of them were still in the lander, Laurel taking copious notes on what the AI was telling her about Islands' volcanos, Hark presumably still checking the condition of his lander, which she had observed included his crawling over the stubby wings, running his hands over their smooth surface with as much affection as he had her breasts.

"Is that devotion or dedication?" she had asked him as he got down off the wings. She'd intended no malice, no deliberate affront, but he'd frowned and shook his head.

"I'm so glad to see this machine again not even you can spoil my mood, Sellia," he'd said flicking a bit of dust off the wings before brushing past her to get to the ladder at the hatch.

"I pick you out of the enemy's clutches, escort you safely to Selene, ready my troops to give their lives to save your captain if need be, and get deprecating remarks for my trouble. You Homeworlders have a strange way of showing your gratitude."

"I haven't forgotten who sent me to the pits, nor how eager you were to let them cut my balls off to get me out," he had replied.

"Do what?" she'd asked, genuinely confused.

He paused, hands on the ladder to look at her. "Oh, I know they don't really cut them off, but I'd be willing to bet you were hoping the ritual knife would slip and short of that, hoping mental castration would be just as effective. Are you going to recommend purification for every man she looks at?"

Sellia began to understand. He'd been defiant in the railcar, ranting about purification. She'd ignored him as she was wont to do to anyone who said anything mystifying, for there always a risk of asking a question that her sister would not and thus jeopardizing the impersonation.

"Hark?" It had been Laurel calling from inside the lander. "The AI wants to talk to you."

Hark had finished climbing the ladder and gone inside, leaving Sellia standing, unable to deny his accusations within Laurel's hearing. She'd gone back to checking the perimeter, checking the lander at equally frequent intervals to see if Laurel had left.

At last she saw Laurel start to climb down the ladder only to stop when Hark leaned out of the hatch to speak to her. He had changed clothes, was now wearing blue shorts and shirt that looked very much like the ones he wore when she first saw him. Sellia couldn't hear what Hark said to Laurel, but she noticed it gained him a smile, which he returned so eagerly Sellia felt the same gut-wrenching fear she'd experienced when she saw him holding Laurel so tenderly in the railcar. She stared at the hatch long after Hark had gone back inside the lander, wondering that his obvious affection for Laurel could have such a frightening effect on her.

"I'm going back home to drop off these notes," Laurel was saying, "and then I'm going to roust the best nutritionist in town and have her prepare a feast for that man. He deserves better than the crap he got out of the locker." Laurel was clutching a sheaf of papers tightly under her arm. "Have your troopers eaten?"

Sellia nodded. "From their packs," she added.

"I'll have better brought for them, too," Laurel said. "It's going to be a long three days. The story he told us spared considerable detail. You should hear the full story as I did when he told the AI. Islands does not come off well in the telling."

Sellia had feared for him while he was in the pits and what Laurel recounted was worse than she imagined. But for all the bitter recriminations he'd made no hint of the twins' secret, of that she was sure. Laurel would have been probing now in her direct manner if he had.

"He says he'll let me ask his captain about bringing the

AI here to Selene, *if* the on-board AI says she's in sufficiently stable a condition to answer," Laurel said in conclusion. Then she shook her head. "He seems very protective of her, almost as if he were the captain and she the crew."

"Or maybe he's in love with her," Sellia said flatly.

Laurel considered a moment, then gave a quick, laughing shake of her head. "I hope not," she said lightly. "That would complicate matters." She glanced up at the sky; the sun was setting and shadows were encroaching on the rocky ledge from the jungle. "I'm going to go now. I want to get back by the time the orbiter finishes lapping. Hark's going to have the AI take it behind the big moon so that the Fyxen will think it's completely gone. Once it's there, I won't be able to talk to the AI until Double Nocturne. After that . . ." Laurel shrugged and looked wistfully back at the lander. "Well, I'm going to go do what I started out to do. You want to come with me? Or are you staying here?"

"I'm staying," Sellia said. Laurel gave a quick nod and stepped on by, and Sellia hurried toward the lander.

Lights from the interior of the lander flashed eerily in the crepuscular silence. Tentatively Sellia put her hand on the ladder.

"Leave your laser outside on the ground if you want to come in, Sellia," Hark said from inside.

She climbed up.

"I said to leave your laser outside," he said. The chair he was sitting in seemed to turn under its own power to face her. He was frowning.

"I haven't expended all this time and energy to wreak havoc on you or your lander now," she said coming inside. There were laser burns on the bulkheads, but still it looked fascinatingly slick and alien. No hands had ever fashioned anything that looked like this. "What are all the lights for?" she asked, looking at the array behind him.

"The lander is completely powered up, and will stay that way until I get back to the orbiter. The lights are ready-lights and status indicaters so that I know everything is operating correctly."

"What's operating?" she asked, for there was no sound of machinery working. He'd fixed the troublesome panel that had alerted the Fyxen.

"Opticals, infrared, microphones, recorders. If anything does happen to me, this time the AI will have a pretty good idea of what."

She gave him a puzzled look, which brought him forward in his chair, staring at her so closely she felt uncomfortable. "How would it know?" she said. "It's on the far side of the planet, out of communication. Lapping, you called it."

"It would play back everything, look at who came in, listen to what we said," he told her still leaning forward.

"It's recording our voices?" she asked, and when he nodded she realized she could not say what she had come here to say. "Then I cannot speak freely," she said to him. "Come outside."

At last he relaxed, then he shrugged. "I could do that, but I should warn you that won't solve your problem. The lander has very sensitive ears. We'd have to go a great distance before it could not hear what we said, farther, for instance, than the place where you and Laurel stood talking about my dinner. But at least you finally know everything I related to your sister; maybe you'll ease up a bit and realize I mean you no harm."

"You're certain that Mala knows that now?" Sellia said watching him carefully. It was tricky to know which twin the other was speaking of, herself as Mala or her sister. This was a problem she had never experienced until Hark learned of the impersonations.

"Completely. She wouldn't have sent you to bring Laurel if it were any other way. I was worried for a long while because Taffy never came back. I thought I'd made yet another mistake by telling everything." He smiled confidently and leaned back. "But your sister has a great deal of trust and courage."

"You think I lack those qualities?" she snapped defensively.

"You're brave," he said, "but that's not the same as having courage of the heart."

Sellia felt her cheeks beginning to burn. How could he believe that a woman who would rise up out of a hospital bed without even asking for an explanation was a woman lacking in trust or courage? But he didn't know Mala had done that. Nor did he know how much courage it had taken for her sister to defy the aunts. *He* had never faced losing a twin. "I want to talk to you without those recorders on," she said angrily, "and I want to do it now."

But Hark just shook his head. "Tell it to me, and you tell it to the AI and the Homeworlds, or it will just have to keep. I'm not taking any more chances. I'm too close to accomplishing what I set out to do."

"Damn you," she said, and she turned on her heel to leave.

Outside night had fallen and there was only the light of the first little moon to guide her off the rocky ledge. Sellia walked quickly, completely frustrated by Hark, his recording devices, and her own unwillingness to share what she wanted to share only with Hark with the AI and conceivably the entire populace of the Homeworlds.

CHAPTER 32

Laurel had brought the feast as promised, the likes of which Hark had never seen in his life. And she had changed her clothes, wearing now baggy trousers so she could sit cross-legged comfortably on the floor of the lander. The filmy blouse he guessed was designed to keep insects away from her flesh, certainly not for modesty. Hark ate heavily, but he took no wine.

He slapped another insect off his forearm.

"Here," Laurel said reaching into the pack behind her. "Try rubbing some of this into your skin." She brought out a jar of creamy paste. He recognized the scent as soon as she opened the lid. It smelled like Sellia's bedroom. "We usually rub it into the furniture and that's sufficient to keep the insects away. But I don't see a stick of wood in here, and it won't hurt your skin."

"What do you do when you're walking through the jungle?" he asked. "You don't carry sticks."

Laurel laughed. "Our clothes are washed in another repellent. You could change again and let me take the ones you're wearing to be laundered."

"No," he said, but he did rub some of the cream on his legs and arms. He found it somewhat disturbing to have Laurel here cutting up his food because he'd started to do it wrong, and now looking like she wanted to rub the cream on his arms the way she was hovering. It was so maternalistic, so typical an attitude of these Islandian women toward adult males. And yet he'd come to think of her as a friend, and wouldn't a friend do these things, too?

"I brought more analgesic cream for your face, too," she said. "Does it still hurt?"

Hark shook his head. "Hardly at all," he said. The swelling in his eye was going down rapidly since he took the proper pills that were in the pocket of the spare pressure suit.

"Looks better, too," she said. "The cream must be working. Let me put some more on."

He thought of refusing, knowing it was his own medication and not hers that was working so well. But it couldn't do any harm. Besides, he liked her gentle touch.

"Was it like this in your dreams?" she asked him, pausing to squeeze more of the cream onto her fingertips.

"You tending my wounds?" he said. "No. It was nothing that specific. Just your face and your red hair, and somehow knowing that you were the person I needed to find. I think it had to do with instantly recognizing you as a scientist. My mind just associated a scientist as being one who would have scant respect for tradition, which is what seemed to get me in trouble all the time."

"But why?" she said, sitting back on her haunches while she closed the jar.

"Because scientists are used to seeing the theories of one generation rejected by the next. They tend to be open-minded. I guess I was groping for someone who would behave in a familiar way, and I projected the behavior on you whether you deserved it or not."

"That's not the most flattering reason a man might dream of me," she said. "But I shouldn't quibble. I don't believe anyone has dreamed about me for a long time, not for any reason."

Hark was surprised. "Why, I do believe you're trying to tempt me into dreaming up something better."

"I admit I'd welcome it, but I don't know how to encourage you. I'm afraid my usual tactics would invoke ghosts of Dame Adione, which I'm sure would be fatal with you." She shrugged helplessly, and Hark could see she was glowing from something inside that seemed to him a mixture of friendly amusement, restraint, and plain old passion.

"A direct approach between friends is not the same as my circumstances with Dame Adione. She was my adversary, and it was very frightening to me. I like directness," he said taking her hand in his. "But I don't like risking friendships over misunderstandings that can come from sharing sex."

"What kind of misunderstanding?" she asked putting her other hand on top of his.

"The kind that might result from us not knowing each other long enough and well enough to be certain how the other is going to react when it's done."

Laurel sighed and took her hands away. "I can see we're going to have to talk this through for so long that I'll probably have forgotten what made me think of it in the first place."

"Look, I'm sorry. Friendships are important to me;

you're the first woman friend I've found on Islands. I don't want to lose you and I don't want you to get the wrong impression."

"For someone who professes directness, you're not very," she said. "Talking about misunderstandings without saying what might be misunderstood leaves a lot to my imagination. Wrong impressions doesn't tell me what kind of impression you want to be left with, or is it me you want to be left with one. If so, which one? I'm beginning to think you're trying to prepare me for some anatomical mutation that's been inflicted on Homeworlds men, or maybe an announcement that they've lost their sex drive altogether."

"God, no!" he said reaching over and putting both his hands behind her neck, her mass of thick hair like silk under his fingers. "I'd make love with you in an instant as long as I knew you realized it didn't give you some kind of hold on me, and if I could be certain we'd still be friends afterward."

"It had better be the same for you," she said. "I don't want some jealous Homeworlds woman coming across the stars to call me out for stealing seed." She kissed him lightly on the side of his mouth that was not bruised. Her lips were warm and slightly salty, her tongue sweet.

"Um, Laurel," he said drawing back slightly. "If it's important to you that I don't have any attachments elsewhere, we'd better stop right now."

"Holy Mother, I have never met a man so determined to be honest. Hark, would she care if you took solace with a friend while millions of klicks from home?"

"I don't know," he said honestly. "We never had a chance to talk about it."

"I'm amazed that you didn't insist," she said. "But no matter. What's more important is how you will feel. Will you feel guilty if we have sex?"

"No," he said promptly. "Not as long as . . ."

"Oh, shut up and kiss me," she said with exasperation that Hark was sure was real. He pulled her close and felt her lips opening to his, her breasts pressing through the filmy blouse, nipples already hard.

"Lady Sellia is approaching the lander," the on-board computer said in its flat voice.

"I could close the hatch before she gets here," Hark whispered to Laurel.

"That would be rude," the voice of the AI interjected. "Hark? Sister Laurel? What are you doing?"

"I've forgotten," Laural said, breaking away from Hark with a forlorn sounding sigh.

"I'll remind you later," Hark said giving her a sympathetic pat.

"I beg your pardon?" the AI said.

"We're having dinner, AI," Hark said dryly. "How long have you been up?"

"Just finished lapping," it said. "But tell me why you'd want to close the hatch on Lady Sellia. Does she pose a danger?"

"No, AI. We needed some privacy," he said. The AI said nothing now, the intuitives finally engaging sufficiently to realize that it was imposing in a forbidden realm.

"Lady Sellia on the ladder," it said almost apologetically.

"Come in, Sellia. We're just finishing dinner," Laurel said feigning more brightness than Hark could manage. "Do you want some?"

Sellia shook her head and sat down in the co-pilot's chair. "Top and I were talking about the rescue. If this fellow Orrin can't make good on his promises, what do you plan to do?" she asked Hark with a directness reminiscent of her twin. It was difficult to believe this was not the woman he loved sitting in front of him.

"Park the lander in the street in front of the maternity and take them out myself."

"Didn't you mention guards at the maternity clinic?" the AI interjected.

"Yes, but I'm still going to try," Hark said.

"I thought as much," Sellia said unhappily. "You'd never make it."

"Maybe not, but I'm not leaving Islands if Captain Dace and the engineer don't leave with me. I've been through all the arguments before," Hark said more for the AI's benefit than the women's, "and I know that if it comes to that, none of us may leave. But I couldn't live with my conscience if I didn't try, especially since anything that will be lost is mine to lose. The AI can take the orbiter back to the Home-worlds. It doesn't need me."

"You won't make it into the maternity alone," Sellia said, continuing to speak almost as if she hadn't heard him. "So Top and I have come up with a plan so that you won't be alone."

"Thank you, Lady Sellia," the AI said.

"How many people can this lander hold during flight?"

"Seven or eight," the AI said promptly. "It depends on the amount of mass in the ones you choose."

"That might be enough," she said, looking thoughtful. "Two to hold the lander clear while the other five go inside. It will be tight getting them out with only one weapon to clear the way for the troopers who are carrying the prisoners, but it might work."

"Pretty risky with so few," Laurel said.

"We have surprise on our side," Sellia said.

"I wouldn't even count on that," Hark said. "If Orrin's not at the river with them as planned, it can only mean he's been found out. They apparently never used drugs on Jeremy, or they would have known that Orrin planned my escape and killed his own men to make it succeed. They were quick to use drugs on me; I can only surmise that somehow Dame Cirila prevented that from happening to Jeremy. Orrin doesn't have that kind of protection."

"We really have more to worry about at the rendezvous," the AI said. "They won't know what you'll do if Orrin doesn't meet you because he can't tell them what he doesn't know. But they could plan to trick you in some way at the rendezvous."

"You make a lot of sense, AI," Sellia said thoughtfully.

"Just doing my job," it said with uncharacteristic modesty.

"One thing we'll have to agree on," Sellia said. "Hark stays inside the lander no matter what happens outside. He's least adept in a fight, and the only one who can fly the lander."

"I can fly it," the AI said.

"Not if something gets damaged so that you can't see or hear what's going on. We need Hark inside," she said.

"Yes," the AI agreed. "You need Hark inside. How about it, Hark. Do you concur?"

"I'll stay inside as long as any in our party are outside and still alive. If you all get killed," he said looking at Lady Sellia, "the deal is off."

"You probably won't understand why, but I want you to save yourself no matter what happens to us," Sellia said.

Hark looked at her. A gesture of some sort for her sister's sake? He wondered if she were capable of anything that generous. "I'll keep it in mind," he said.

"Well, AI," Laurel said, "now that that's settled, I'd really like to spend a few more hours talking about volcanos."

"Sorry, Sister Laurel," the AI said. "I'm getting ready to put on a show for the Fyxen. I don't think it would be wise to wait for zenith; they might guess it was a sham. I'll do a few flashy turns so they don't miss finding me, then I'm off for your big moon's darkside, which is close enough to a good trajectory to the Homeworlds to lead the Fyxen to believe Hark's gone for good. And for good measure, I'll broadcast a farewell in Hark's voice. Any parting words you want me to use?"

"I'll be back, is what they fear hearing," Hark suggested.

"It's also what we don't want them to expect," the AI said. "Yet there's some merit in giving voice to subconscious fears. Most will think you mean in a few years. So be it. If you want to watch, Lady Sellia, you'd better go outside. I'm in the east."

Sellia nodded and stood up. She looked expectantly at Laurel.

"Yes, sure," Laurel said, getting up. "I can finish dinner afterward."

As the two women stepped out the hatch, Hark got up and

looked at the control panel. One of the optical displays was trained on the orbiter, just where he'd left it. He also knew the orbiter's maneuvering would have been just as effective at zenith, or even at the other end of the lap almost four hours away. "Thanks, pal," he said.

"Don't mention it. She seems like a nice lady."

Hark smiled absently, sat back down in the chair to wait for Laurel to come back and finish her dinner.

CHAPTER 33

Sellia knew by looking at her watch that the last moon had set, but looking at the sky told her nothing. It was thick with black, angry clouds and lightning flashes.

"We should get on board," Leniane said looking at her watch also. She was wearing Selene's black-green trousers and blouse, chosen especially for the Double Nocturne mission, her face blackened with greasepaint. The four muscle troopers standing behind her were similarly garbed.

Sellia nodded and buckled on her laser holster. It seemed strange not to have to take a pack to journey all the way to Fox, but the lander would have them there in fifteen minutes. She took one last glance around the darkened campsite at the muscle troopers who were staying behind, then she led the way to the lander.

Laurel and Hark were already inside, Hark in his blue shorts and trousers sitting in the pilot's chair, Laurel in black-green like Sellia and her troopers. Both turned to watch them file in. Hark seemed remarkably calm. His face was almost completely healed, only a purple streak remained under his right eye; it might just as easily have been greasepaint.

"Is the hatch clear?" he asked.

"Hatch is clear," the Top told him.

Hark turned back to the control panel, flipped a rocker switch and the hatch snapped shut. "Grab a strap and hang on," he said. "It's going to be a little bumpy going through the clouds."

Hark had screwed six bolts into the ceiling of the lander from which hung leather straps that the six of them were to wrap around their wrists and hang on to during flight. The engines hummed, growing louder, then she felt the pressure of lifting. Her heart thumped wildly; the muscle troopers murmured in amazement.

They were badly buffeted going through the clouds. Sellia hung on with both hands. But quickly enough the little lander stopped pitching and Hark turned around to look at them.

"Everyone all right?" he asked, and hearing no negative replies, he smiled. "Easy going for the next fifteen minutes, just straight and level. But keep one hand on the strap in case we hit some turbulence." Then he turned back to his instrument panel, concentrating on it.

"I see you're on your way," said the voice of the AI.

"Is Fox socked in, too?" Hark asked.

"Fox is cloud covered," the AI replied. "I'm going to tweak your landing site a bit. Last night's rain caused a landslide; we'll be off about four meters."

"Not enough to worry about," Hark said in response to a worried look from Laurel. "We're big. He'll see us."

"If he's there," Laurel said.

"I think he'll be there," Sellia said.

Hark looked up at her, as if to ask how she could be so sure.

Sellia shrugged. "He took us by surprise. He obviously doesn't make many mistakes."

They rode in silence that wasn't broken until the AI announced that they were beginning their descent. "We're going to lose EHF signal in those clouds," the AI said. "I'm going to switch us over to UHF and go dumb on you in case they're listening in."

"Okay everyone, get ready. It's going to get nasty again."

It was worse than before, and Sellia could tell Hark was having trouble keeping the lander on course from the number of times he touched the control panel.

"Infrared's on," he said. "If Orrin's there we should see him soon."

Sellia looked at the scope, but she couldn't see any human forms like she had when Hark had demonstrated it earlier in the day.

"He can probably see our burners now. Let's hope the rain is keeping the guys with the big guns from doing likewise."

"There!" Laurel said, reaching over to punch the scope.

"One, two, three, four, and five. Dame Cirila must still be there."

"Six," Sellia said. "No, eight . . . eleven. There are six more off to the right."

"Damn, you're right, and they're on the move toward the others. Do you think they know he's there? Or could it be a routine patrol."

"They know," Sellia said. As they watched, the group of six converged with the five. There was no question that they were watching a struggle, but it was pitifully brief.

"Now what?" Laurel asked. "If they have lasers, they could damage the lander."

"Not if it's Dame Adione," Hark said. "She wants the lander too badly to damage it. She must have something else in mind. I'm going to park as close as I can, and then we'll find out what."

"No. Put it down off to the right," Sellia said, "and point the hatch away from her. Leniane and the muscles will try to come up through the trees behind them."

Hark maneuvered the lander, still keeping the scope trained on the people in the trees. They were right at the edge; they had not moved.

Sellia felt the lander settle onto the ground. Almost immediately the hatch opened and the wind blew the rain inside. Leniane and the four muscle troopers leaped out into the darkness.

"Laurel, guard that open hatch," Sellia snapped. As Laurel slipped out of the chair, Sellia sat down, her eyes fixed on the scope. "Can't you make this thing hear what they're saying?"

"I'm trying," Hark said. "The rain noise is making it difficult to tune it."

"Look! One of them's coming out," Sellia said.

Hark reached over the control panel. Another scope brightened with life, and then it displayed a perfect image of a man on crutches, holding his hand up against a bright light. "Jeremy," Hark said.

"Hark, can you hear me?" The voice came through one of the voice pickups.

"I can hear you, Jeremy," Hark said into a microphone.

"Hark, it's all gone wrong. You have to give it up. She says she'll kill us if you don't come out. She has Orrin, your captain, and the engineer. She says she'll kill us one at a time until you come out."

"Buy some time," Sellia whispered. "They need a few more minutes to get around behind."

"All right, Jeremy. I'm coming out. Did you hear me, Adione? Don't hurt them."

For a moment, Sellia stared aghast. "Not like that," she said. "You're not stepping out of this lander."

"It's the easiest way to get them some time," Hark whispered back.

"No," she said again, thinking furiously as he started to get up. "Wait." She pushed him back down in his chair. "Give me your clothes and I'll go. She won't be able to tell right away." Even as she spoke Sellia was pulling the black-green tunic over her head. She threw it down. "What are you waiting for?"

Finally he complied, pulling the shirt over his head without unfastening the zipper. Sellia grabbed it and pulled it over her head. She'd dropped her trousers and pulled on Hark's, holding them up by tightening her laser holster a notch. She left Hark sitting in the pilot seat in his underwear, ducked past Laurel and dropped out of the lander.

Sellia ducked underneath the lander to the front where the light was trained on Jeremy ten meters ahead of her. He was leaning on the crutches, rain plastering his hair down across his forehead. She wished she'd thought to tell Hark to turn out the light. She didn't dare walk in it; the clothes would fool them for a while in the dark, but the spotlight would reveal too much. The only thing to do now was to head directly for Dame Adione and her troopers, walking as if Jeremy were of no concern.

Vegetation heavy with rain splattered beneath her feet; she walked heavily, deliberately swinging her arms as a man might.

"I'm sorry, Hark," she could hear Jeremy say. He hobbling toward her; thankfully the spotlight didn't move. "I knew it was going too well to be true. She must have known all along! I think my mother told her. She traded my life for your lander, so she could get to the AI."

Sellia didn't look at him, walked steadily toward the trees.

"Hark, I . . ." He hesitated. Was he close enough now to realize she was not Hark? She chanced a glance; he was scrambling out of the spotlight. His crutches went out from underneath him. Sellia stopped. Hark, she knew, would go over and help him.

"Keep coming straight along," said a woman's voice from the edge of the trees.

Sellia hesitated another second, then turned and went to Jeremy. Hark, she was sure, would have done likewise. She put her shoulder under Jeremy's arm.

"Thank the gods he didn't come out," he said to her. "Who are you?"

"Never mind," she said, helping him to his feet. "Just don't stare, and take your time. We want this walk to last as long as possible."

"There's six of them," Jeremy said. He hobbled clumsily, lost his balance and fell again. "Give me your knife," he said when she started to help him up.

She slipped the knife out of its sheath and reached around behind him to put it in his hand. They went on. Sellia wished she knew if the Top and muscles were in position yet. She could see Dame Adione with her laser in hand standing over the two stretchers, another woman, no doubt Jeremy's mother, and Orrin with his hands bound behind him. There were also a half-dozen lace troopers who looked ready for anything. And if she could recognize them, they must also be able to see her and perhaps be coming to realize that she was not Hark. Sellia kept her eyes fixed on Dame Adione, watching for a sign.

A slight widening of her eyes, so slight that Sellia was not certain it meant anything until Orrin flung himself against Dame Adione. Sellia drew her laser and took down the closest lace trooper while Jeremy lunged for another but fell into a pile of them. Sellia swung around and took a shot at Dame Adione, but the woman rolled clear only to have the laser kicked from her hand by the Top who had just leaped from the bushes behind. The smell of burning flesh and vegetation grew thick as the four muscle troopers burst in, and then there was no way to use their lasers, the risk of hitting their own too great. Orrin was using his legs, Jeremy his knife; it was close and hard but in the end only one of the muscle troopers, Sellia, Orrin, and Jeremy were left standing. The Top was down, her throat slashed, but Dame Adione lay lifeless beneath her. Dame Cirila was nowhere to be seen.

Quickly Sellia checked the other three muscle troopers; one was still alive. "Take him to the lander," she snapped to the remaining muscle trooper. He picked up his fallen comrade, hoisted him over his shoulders and started for the lander. "Orrin, you take one, I'll take the other," she said stepping toward the figures on the stretchers.

"No," Jeremy said. "You've got to use the stretchers, and be careful about it, too."

"Damn," she muttered. "It's one at a time then. Quickly, Orrin." Jeremy was cutting Orrin's bonds.

"You're hurt," Jeremy said to him.

"It will keep," Orrin said, rubbing his wrists vigorously.

"Jeremy, start for the lander."

"I'll stay with the engineer," he said.

"You'll start for the damn lander," Sellia shouted angrily. "We don't have time to carry you, too." And to Orrin, she gestured to pick up an end of the captain's stretcher.

It was too slippery to run, the risk of falling great, but Orrin in the front of the stretcher was surefooted. They reached the lander without mishap, and lifted the stretcher in.

Hark was at the hatch to receive her. "Where's Rene?" he demanded.

"We're going back for her now," Sellia said ducking back under the lander. Orrin was right behind her as she ran back to the trees. They picked up the second stretcher, Orrin again leading the way. Jeremy had almost made it to the lander; and she and Orrin were closing the last of the distance. "We've done it," she shouted triumphantly, but then she felt her legs give away and her back crumple in on itself in the oddest way. There was no pain; the last thing she remembered before blackness took her was the smell of burning flesh.

CHAPTER 34

Hark saw the laser flash take Sellia down and he stopped the power-up, leaped out of the chair to the hatch and out into the rain. Orrin had grabbed Sellia's laser and was burning the place where so many had already fallen. As soon as he saw Hark coming, Orrin leaped to his feet and charged the stand of trees, firing wildly until the laser ran out of charge.

Hark reached the stretcher; Rene had rolled out. Carefully he picked her up. Her eyes were open beneath a swath of bandages.

"Hark," she said.

Laurel came to his side, the muscle trooper with her. "We'll take her. Get back to the lander, Hark."

"Sellia," he said.

Laurel shook her head. "She might as well be dead already. Her spine's burned away, right through to her guts."

Hark turned to Sellia's crumpled form, touched her neck. There was a faint pulse in the carotid artery. Swiftly he gathered her up in his arms. As he stood up, he saw another flash from the trees. "Orrin!"

"Come on, Hark!" Laurel shouted. She and the trooper had Rene's stretcher between them.

With Sellia in his arms, he ran for the lander. It took them a moment to get Rene and Sellia inside; there wasn't sufficient room for four prone people. They'd put the injured muscle trooper in the co-pilot's chair, bunched Captain Dace, Rene, and Sellia so close Hark had to step over all three at once to get to the pilot's chair. He looked at the infrared scope; someone was coming out of the trees. He couldn't be certain, but he thought it was Orrin. He moved the spotlight onto the approaching figure. It was Orrin; he raised one hand in salute.

"What's that," Laurel asked coming up behind Hark and pointing to the infrared scope. There were figures in the forest, many of them.

Hark grabbed the microphone. "Run, Orrin. More coming."

Apparently he didn't have to be told, for he was already running. Hark started to build power so he could move the lander the instant Orrin was on board.

"This time, the bitch is dead," Orrin said, breathlessly coming through the hatch. There was barely room for him to stand.

Hark snapped the hatch shut. "Hang on," he said, full knowing that some of them had nothing to hold. He put full power to the vertical thrusters and shot out of the clearing.

"AI, are you listening?"

"Listening up," it confirmed.

"Ready all stasis chambers," he said.

"All of them?"

"All," he confirmed. "Lady Sellia's dying."

"Hark, she's not crew. I can't . . ."

"Don't argue, AI. I'm taking full responsibility. Jeremy, how are those injured doing back there?"

"Not good," Jeremy said. "Captain Dace is unconscious and Rene needs a painkiller. All this moving around isn't helping a bit. Can't you ease up?"

"What about Sellia?"

"The other woman?" He shook his head. "Dead."

"Mark time, AI."

"Counting," the AI said.

He had five minutes to get Sellia into stasis, five minutes before her brain was irreparably damaged. He had to match orbit perfectly on the first try, or there wouldn't be enough time to do it again—at least, not for Sellia. They were past the buffeting clouds, well into the ionosphere.

"Four and still counting," the AI said.

"Is the bay open?"

"Open and ready. Better start warning your passengers about weightlessness."

"Find something to hold," Hark said, "and don't try to move around. You're going to float, and when that hatch opens I want to be the first one through."

The thrusters cut out, and they were gliding toward the final rendezvous with the orbiter. He could see it in the scope, getting larger.

"Three and still counting," the AI said.

"All right, AI. Counter-thrusters to break and match."

"Come along hard; those grippers are new. We can take one hard catch."

The orbiter filled the screen, the bay door was wide open, the lander grippers filling it.

"Attitude," the AI warned, and Hark quickly compensated to keep the plane of the lander correct for maximum dispersal of energy through the grippers. "Two and thirty and still counting, and—Contact!"

The bounce was the worst he'd ever experienced. It snapped him hard, and threw the passengers against the bulkhead. Someone screamed in pain. Unheeding, Hark unbuckled his restraints, pushed off toward the back of the lander.

"Outer bay door closed," the AI said. "Fixing atmosphere . . ."

Hark unfastened the straps holding Sellia down.

"Hark, she's dead."

"Not for two more minutes, she isn't. Not if I can get her in the tank."

"Opening lander hatch," the AI said.

Hark grapped Sellia around the waist, not paying much attention to her wound. He might do more damage by hurrying so, but he didn't think it would matter much.

Either he got her into the tank in time or he didn't; an extra month or two of recovery didn't seem particularly important.

The AI had the overhead trolley line in gear; Hark grabbed the closest strap and felt himself being pulled through the bay. The hatch to the corridor was open; he let go and flew through, his momentum carrying him halfway down the hall before he could catch another trolley strap. This time he hung on until it came to a stop. He had to turn to get into the sick bay.

All three stasis chambers were open. He shoved Sellia headfirst into the closest one. Inside, the blanket was coming down on her, straightening her body. "Reach in and pull her right arm down," the AI said. Hark stuck his torso into the chamber, pushing himself to the back of the tube until he could feel Sellia's arm. He pulled it down to her side and backed out. The blanket finished clamping her down. "Close the door," the AI said, and Hark complied.

For a moment he hung onto the handle of the stasis chamber, feet dangling in the weightless atmosphere of the orbiter, heart beating wildly.

"Will you reconfirm that you're taking full responsibility for using a stasis chamber for someone who's not crew?" the AI said.

"Confirmed," Hark said, still breathing hard.

"I'll pop the tank if you want to change your mind. I'm obliged to warn you this is a serious infraction."

"I know. Leave her be."

"You're sure?"

"I'm sure."

"As you ordered, Pilot Hark, I'm providing full coverage to stasis tank number three, occupied by non-crew."

It was final now. The AI would have been recording the dialog for the record. Hark's intent would be clear to those back in the Homeworlds who needed to know. He let go of the handle. There was nothing else he could do for Sellia. He started back to the lander.

"I've asked your passengers to stay put," the AI said,

"but one of them claims to be a doctor and he's flailing around. Does he know what he's doing?"

"Yes, AI. That's Jeremy."

"I've asked him not to do anything to Captain Dace or Rene. He's concentrating on the wounded trooper."

Hark floated into the bay again, caught the trolley strap and went back into the lander. Laurel and Orrin and one trooper were along the ceiling, holding tightly to the straps. Jeremy was upside-down by the wounded trooper. "Not easy, is it?" Hark said. "But hang in there. I want to get Captain Dace and Rene into stasis. It will take me a while; there's no reason not to prep them properly."

"Captain Dace is unconscious," Laurel said. "If she wakes up I want to ask her about the AI."

"She's not going to wake up," Jeremy said. "If it weren't for Hark's stasis chamber, I'd have said she was as good as dead. Too much careless movement for her to tolerate. She's going sour."

But she was breathing, and that was all Hark needed to know. He looked at Laurel. "Sorry," he said briskly. "The AI stays on board."

Grimly she nodded.

The orbiter's AI was bringing proper stretchers over on a trolley gripper. He released one and brought it inside to transfer Captain Dace into it. As he pulled himself down to the bulkhead, he saw Rene looking at him.

"How you doing, Rene?" he said gently.

"We knew you'd come," she said weakly. "Stasis?"

"Yeah. The captain first. Then I'll be back for you."

"Don't you put me in there until you tell me what's going on," Rene said. She was talking so softly Hark had to lean over her to hear the words. "I'll have bad dreams."

"We'll have some time while I prep you," Hark said, and he turned back to Captain Dace. He pulled the restraints loose; the white hospital blanket came loose and floated aside. She was nude underneath, her bones plainly visible beneath her skin. There was a time when he would have hated to see her this way for fear she'd be angry when she knew. He clamped her into the stretcher, carefully bracing her head and neck. He took the handle and reached for the trolley strap. "Hey, Jeremy. How's that trooper doing?"

"He's in a lot of pain, but he's going to make it without any heroics. He could really use a painkiller, but I don't have anything to give him."

"Talk to the AI," Hark said, pressing the go button on the trolley strap. "I'll bring something back with me."

Prepping Captain Dace took a long time, Rene's even longer. But every moment saved them recovery time back in the Homeworlds, permitting some mending to be taking place even while they were enroute. Sellia would not be so fortunate. She would have to wait until after they'd grown spare parts for her to begin her recovery. He wondered about the regulations he was breaking—ones that would bring him a reprimand? Or the kind that could ground him? He didn't much care. At least he could offer *his* Sellia hope for her sister's life.

At last Hark brought the others to the sick bay where Jeremy would have things at hand to tend the trooper and the deep cut on Orrin's arm. Hark dressed while Laurel held onto a float strap.

"What am I supposed to tell Mala?" Laurel asked when she began to realize what he'd done with Sellia.

"Nothing," Hark said. "I'm going to tell her."

"I don't think she'll be grateful," Laurel said.

"Her sister will live this way. She'd have died otherwise."

Laurel nodded silently, obviously not convinced that Mala would appreciate the trade. Hark wondered how much she knew about the twins. He already knew the surviving twin would be devastated because now she would wear the crown of New Penance entirely alone. What was worse was realizing she wouldn't even consider coming back to the Homeworlds with him. It had been a wild dreamlike hope that she might leave the throne to her sister and come with him. No chance of that now.

"Your AI says it can make my break knit faster," Jeremy

said. He was finished with Orrin now, putting the instruments back into the autoclave.

Hark nodded. "I'll help you with it as soon as I get back. I'm going to take Laurel and the troopers back to Selene, then I'm going to New Penance. You two think you can manage alone for a while?"

Jeremy stared blankly. "Orrin's staying, too?" he asked.

Hark shrugged. "There's room," he said.

But Orrin shook his head. "I'm too old to start over. I'll go back."

"To what?" Jeremy asked him. "She's dead."

Orrin frowned, as if he'd just realized how bleak his prospects were back on Islands. "What would happen if I went with you?" he finally asked Hark.

Hark shrugged helplessly. "I don't know, Orrin. There's a well-established military back on the Homeworlds, but it's not like you're used to. I'd help all I could . . . There'd be something for you for a while, if only helping to brief the AI Guild about Islands. I just don't know how much you can count on me. I've broken some rules. I don't know my own future, let alone be able to predict yours."

"I'll go back to Islands," Orrin said finally. Jeremy was crestfallen.

"Come to Selene," Laurel said. "I can always use a good trooper." Orrin hesitated. "At least give yourself time to think. You'll be safe in Selene."

Orrin nodded.

"All right, then. Back to the lander. Jeremy, if you need anything, you have only to speak. The AI will help you."

Hark took the injured trooper, who was now so dazed by painkiller that he seemed to be enjoying his surroundings. Laurel and the other trooper followed close behind. They'd already settled into the lander and had to wait a few minutes before Orrin joined them. He swung through the hatch, fairly adept at catching one of the ceiling straps to stop his momentum. Hark closed the hatch.

"Take this," Orrin said reaching out to Hark. He had

Jeremy's transport token twined in his fingers. "Go on, take it. I won't ever use it. I remember your saying it might be valuable. Might come in handy."

Hark hesitated.

"Please," Orrin said. "I don't want any reminders. Take it."

Hark took the token and slipped it into his breast pocket.

Hark brought the lander in next to the railhead by the observatory. A speeder was waiting, the queen standing outside in the light snow with Taffy at her side. She wore lightweight woolens that fell past her knees. The garment was blue, and a tiara of lapis banded her hair. She looked gorgeous in blue.

He breathed deeply, eager to see her, but not to bring her bad news. He opened the hatch, gasped at the rush of icy air. He'd forgotten that it would be cold. No help for it now. He had nothing else to wear. He stepped outside and walked through the snow.

She was clutching a shawl to her chest, her eyes darting to look behind him. "Laurel sent word on the radio that you had news of Sellia. What's happened?" she demanded. "Where is my sister?"

Hark stared at her. She was not glad to see him, not curious about what had happened, only worried. He closed his eyes in denial, prayed that when he opened them *his* twin would be there. He looked again. Blue eyes, wide with fear, stared into his. "Mala," he said flatly.

She looked at him curiously, but it was not the look he cherished. Mala's curiosity was apprehensive, impatient. Mala, and not *his* Sellia wearing the crown.

"Dear, God, how could I not have known?" he said.

"Known what?" she said. "Where is my sister? What have you done to her?"

"Mala, I'm sorry. She was hit by laser fire."

Mala stiffened. "Dead?" she asked, her voice very small.

Hark gestured helplessly. "She's in stasis. Do you know what that is?"

"Not dead!" Mala said eagerly. "She's going to be all right?"

"I hope so," he said. "There's no way to be sure yet."

"When can I see her?" Mala asked.

Hark shook his head and put his hands in his pockets. "It will be years, Mala. I have to take her to the Homeworlds."

"Have to?"

Hark nodded. "It's the only way to save her life."

Mala's eyes narrowed. "I won't permit it," she said angrily. "You have wanted to take her away from me, but I will not permit it."

"If I brought her back now in her present condition, all you could do for her is arrange a funeral."

"You're lying!" Mala said. "You've kidnapped her. You planned this all along."

"I know you won't believe this, Mala, but until I saw you right here on this very spot, I didn't know it was her up in the orbiter. I thought it was you. I was coming to say good-bye to . . ." He shook his head. "I can't deny that I wouldn't have offered to take her back with me. I don't know if she would have come. I hoped she would."

"No," Mala said. "She wouldn't leave Islands. Not with you or any man."

"You may be right. I knew she wouldn't have left if it were you up in the orbiter. I thought I was coming to say good-bye to *her*, but now . . ." He tried to think past the good-byes, tried to grasp the reality. He shook his head sadly. "I don't know how she'll feel about it when she realizes what happened. Had it been you, I would have known you'd want to return, and I was going to tell her that I'd do everything I could to help. But it's *my* Sellia. Dear God, I didn't know."

"Sellia will want to come back," Mala said firmly.

"It will never be the same. You'll have lost years of common knowledge. You'd never be able to impersonate each other again."

"So you think now you have what you wanted in the first place," Mala said. "You think you've won her."

"No," Hark said hanging his head. "We've both lost, Mala. There would have been some hope of my returning if she were here wearing the crown. But taking her with me like this . . . I don't know if she'll be grateful for a life she didn't freely choose."

"Then bring her back now. Let me bury her decently."

Hark shook his head. "Right or wrong I'm going through with it. Don't say anything more, Mala. You can't make me feel any worse than I already feel. I didn't know it was *her*!" he said, and turned away because he could feel tears coming in his eyes. "I thought I could tell you apart, but I couldn't. What kind of love is it when you can't even recognize the woman you love?" He looked at her.

Mala didn't answer. She just stared at him through angry, frightened eyes. And Hark realized there was nothing more to say. Everything he'd stored up to say the last few days he wanted to say to Sellia he couldn't say now.

He turned to go.

"Hark!" It was Taffy. Hark stopped and turned around. The dwarf stepped over to him. "I don't think I'd want to be you when she wakes up."

"I'm not sure I want to be me then either, but I don't have a twin."

"You will be there for her, won't you? No matter what?"

Hark nodded. "I love her."

"She's going to need you, Hark."

"She might appreciate a friend even more. Do you want to come along?" Hark asked. "I have room for one more."

Taffy smiled eagerly, but then he looked back at Mala and shook his head. "She's going to need someone, too," he said.

Hark nodded. More than his Sellia would have needed anyone, Mala would need Taffy. Sadly he shook his head.

"Thanks for the offer though," Taffy said. "Have a good journey."

Hark took the transport token out of his pocket and

pressed it into Taffy's hand. "Maybe someday you'll want to use this." Then without looking back, Hark put his hands into his pockets and walked back to the lander.

On the ladder he paused to look around for a last time. Mala was walking back to the speeder, her shape a shadow in the swirling snow. It could have been Sellia he was watching. But she was in the orbiter suspended for the duration. There was no going back now, no way to give her a choice. And at last he understood what she meant when she told him so angrily, *There isn't always more than one choice. All you can do is make the best of the one at hand.* The gnawing in his stomach seemed to subside a bit. "All right, then, milady," he said. "Let's go make the best of it."